The Missions of
Indian Territory
Book 3

I0564741

COME

to

LOVELY

COUNTY

JONITA MULLINS

ISBN-13: 978-0-9789740-5-3

ISBN-10: 0-9789740-5-0

First Printing November 2016

Published by Jonita Mullins

Printed in the U.S.A.

List of Characters

Union Mission
Epaphras and Rachel Chapman, mission directors
Eliza Cleaver, housemother
Samuel Douglas, bookkeeper
Stephen and Amanda Fuller, farm director and cook
Paul Gillard, farm assistant
Marcus and Clarissa Palmer, doctor and teacher
Abraham and Phoebe Redfield, superintendent and housemother
George and Sarah Requa, mechanic and seamstress
Ella Selden, seamstress
John and Alice Spaulding, schoolmasters
William and Asenath (Asie) Vaille, pastors
Alexander and Martha Woodruff, blacksmith and midwife

Fort Gibson
Colonel Matthew Arbuckle, fort commander
Colonel John and Sallie Nicks, fort sutler and shopkeeper
Lieutenant Charles Summers
Private Bill Waldo

Hopefield Mission
Bird, Osage warrior; Bearpaw and Deer-in-Water, his children
Chief Monepasha, Osage clan leader; Kickingbird and Hunts-the-Bear, his sons
William and Harriett Montgomery, pastors
Will and Susan Requa, mission directors
Star-That-Travels and Teresa, Osage interpreters

Three Forks
Ian and Lilla Bradley, trapper and caterer
Tassie Bradley, clerk
David Brearley, Creek agent
A.P. Chouteau, fur trader
Monday, freedman boat builder

Claremont's Town
Chief Claremont and his son Mad Buffalo, Osage

Lovely County
Richard Bean, salt miner; Jesse Bean, his nephew
John Jolly, Cherokee chief
Mr. Lee, trapper
Spring Frog, Cherokee warrior
Walter and Elizabeth Webber, Cherokee leaders

Harmony Mission
Daniel and Martha Austin, millwright and cook
Mary Austin, housemother

Dwight Mission
Jacob Hitchcock, superintendent
Cephas Washburn, director
Edmund Webber, Cherokee interpreter
Gage and Eleanor Weeks, doctor and teacher

CHAPTER ONE

Union Mission
Lovely's Purchase, Arkansas Territory
September 1824

The morning was cool as Asie Vaille walked along the dirt path cut through the dense river cane. The delicate blonde woman seemed not to notice when a wayward branch of the cane slapped at her shoulder or teased at her long muslin skirt. She walked with a steady purpose, but her eyes were hollow and unseeing. In her arms she carried the listless form of her baby daughter wrapped in a white crocheted blanket.

Two babies had died of the fever yesterday, her husband had told her. Now her dear Charlotte was dying as well. With determination Asie carried her baby to the fast flowing Neosho River rising high in its banks after recent rains.

She lifted her skirts with one hand and carefully stepped onto a sandstone outcropping at the bank. The clear water lapped against the rock with a soft murmuring and birds filled the air with songs from their perches among the cane and the cottonwood trees that lined the river. These soothing and cheerful sounds seemed discordant with the tragic look on Asie's face.

She stood still, looking down at her daughter as if memorizing the flutter of dark lashes against her flushed cheeks, the soft rosebud mouth, the damp curls that framed her face. Then she stared for a long moment at the water flowing by, looking cool and inviting.

"Goodbye, my little one," she whispered. "You were too precious for this terrible world."

She was unaware that her husband was at that moment frantically searching for her and their child. William Vaille, the pastor at Union Mission, had returned to their cabin from the communal dining hall and found it empty. He raced back to the kitchen where most of the women were washing the breakfast dishes.

Rev. Vaille pushed open the door of the log kitchen and ducked to get his tall frame into the room. His eyes darted quickly around the space but didn't see his wife among the women working there.

"Have any of you seen Mrs. Vaille?" he asked. "She is not in our cabin."

The women turned to look at him with concern. He had shared during their devotion time this morning that Asie was in a terrible state of mind due to the suffering of their daughter from the mysterious fever that plagued the mission every summer. They had all promised to pray for her and check on her often since she refused to leave the baby for even a moment.

"I haven't seen her since I checked on Charlotte before lamp lighting yesterday," Martha Woodruff responded. Martha served as the midwife for the mission and had helped to bring Charlotte into the world just a few months earlier.

Since their doctor, Marcus Palmer, was away at Harmony Mission in Missouri to help with a smallpox epidemic, Martha also was overseeing the care of those who were sick with the summer "intermittent" as they called it. A woman in her fifties, with dark hair streaked generously with gray, Martha acted as mother to all the young missionaries serving at this outpost in far western Arkansas Territory.

"We'll help you look for her," volunteered Sarah Requa, the mission's seamstress. "I don't mind running anywhere I need to. We don't want her wandering off by herself."

She dried her sudsy hands from the dishwater and reached for her bonnet draped over the back of a cane-bottomed chair. She was about to tie it over her coffee-colored curls, but a restraining hand from Martha stopped her actions and her usual flow of words.

"You best not be running around, Sarah," she advised. "Not in this heat and not in your condition." Sarah was expecting her first child with her husband George, the mission's mechanic and cobbler. Martha would be helping her with the birth within a few months.

Sarah got a stubborn look on her face, and seemed about to disagree, but finally nodded and replaced her bonnet on the chair.

"Eliza," Martha said, turning to the youngest woman in the kitchen. The beautiful blonde twenty-year-old quickly closed the cupboard where she had been stacking their enamel breakfast plates.

"Yes, ma'am?"

"Why don't you run down to the river. It's always a bit cooler there in the shade. Perhaps Mrs. Vaille thought it might help to get Charlotte out of the stuffy cabin."

"Yes, ma'am," Eliza said again, taking up her own straw hat. She briefly laid a comforting hand on Rev. Vaille's arm before exiting the kitchen.

"I'll check the outhouse," Amanda Fuller, their red-haired cook offered. "Or maybe she wanted some water from the springhouse. I'll go there too."

"Good," Martha agreed. "Alert the men as well. Those who aren't sick are probably working in the mill."

Amanda nodded and also left the kitchen.

"I didn't see her anywhere in the compound," Vaille said. "But perhaps she went to the chapel."

"I can check there," volunteered Alice Spaulding, Eliza's older sister. She had been feeding her daughter Allie some porridge, but quickly wiped the girl's face and passed her to Sarah. She left through the dining hall which faced the chapel and school located on the other side of the mission yard.

Martha put a hand to her mouth suddenly. "You don't think she might have started towards Cantonment Gibson, do you? To see Dr. Baylor there?"

"In her distressed state of mind, she might have," the minister said. "I have no idea what she could be thinking."

Cantonment Gibson was a small fort located twenty-five miles south near the fur trade community called Three Forks. It would take hours for Asie to walk there and would have been a totally impractical undertaking. But they all knew Asie's mind was clouded with fear for her daughter's life.

At that moment Paul Gillard, the Negro farm assistant, stepped into the kitchen with a load of kindling in his arms.

The pastor turned to him quickly. "Paul, you haven't seen my wife anywhere, have you?"

Paul could hear the concern in the man's voice. "No, sir," he said as he dropped the kindling in a basket by the massive kitchen fireplace. "Is she missing?"

"Yes," the minister said. "Would you ride with me down toward the fort? I fear she may have decided to take our daughter to Dr. Baylor."

Paul's brow furrowed. "That would be a powerful far walk."

"I know. But she isn't thinking clearly right now."

Paul nodded his understanding. "I'll saddle two horses. Have 'em at the corral in just a few minutes." Then he too hurried from the kitchen.

Paul was always glad to make a trip to Three Forks because his sweetheart, Tassie Bradley, lived in the neighborhood and worked at the sutler's store just a half-mile from Cantonment Gibson. Any chance to see Tassie was welcomed by the slight nineteen-year-old.

Sarah moved out of the kitchen to settle Allie on a blanket spread on the plank floor. Then she sat at one of the dining tables nearby and reached for a basket that held her mending supplies. Her lips moved in a silent prayer as quick as her darning needles. She might not be able to search for Mrs. Vaille, but she could pray for her while repairing the socks of the children here at the Osage mission.

In the kitchen, Rev. Vaille placed his face in his hands. "What have I done wrong?" he sighed.

"Don't blame yourself, Pastor," Martha consoled. "I've

4

tried to help your wife myself, but she seems unable to pull herself from this malaise."

"She's been depressed since Joseph was born two years ago," the tall minister said. "I thought Charlotte's birth would help, and it might have if she hadn't taken ill."

"You and I both have done all we know to do. We must put your wife and daughter in God's hands."

"It's a far easier thing to say than do," Vaille replied. "I have certainly said it often to my parishioners. Now I feel those words are mocking me and my faith seems very weak indeed."

"But when we are weak," Martha responded, "that is when the Lord is strong."

The pastor looked down at the motherly woman. "Thank you for reminding me of that."

They stood in silence, watching for Paul to emerge from the barn with the saddled mustangs owned by the mission. Their horses had been gifts from the Osage chief, Claremont, whose village was about twenty miles to the east.

As everyone made their search for the missing mother, Eliza hurried down the path to the river. She pushed through the overgrown cane, thinking that the farm director Stephen Fuller would have to bring his machete to cut the cane back again. It grew with amazing quickness in the fertile river bottom land.

The path led to a smooth boulder of sandstone that the missionaries often used as a fishing point. It was also a favorite picnic spot on those rare days when they took a break from their never-ending chores for a little recreation. It was the best way to access the river.

Eliza came around a bend in the path and caught sight of Asenath Vaille standing like a porcelain figurine on the rock. Something warned Eliza not to call out to the woman. Instead she turned and raced back toward the kitchen.

She pushed open the door and hurried inside. "Rev, Vaille," she gasped. "I found her down by the river, at the rock."

"And the baby?" he asked.

"I didn't see her," Eliza said, her eyes widening with fear as she realized she had not seen the infant girl. But the woman's back had been to her.

The minister didn't wait to hear anything more but rushed out the door and down the path to the river, his long legs covering the distance much faster than had petite Eliza.

He reached the sandstone and came to an abrupt stop. His wife was standing in perfect stillness, her face devoid of emotion. In her arms, Charlotte's body hung limp and lifeless.

"Asie," he breathed quietly as he slowly approached her. "I am here."

She turned her head to look at him. "She's gone."

William gathered his wife and child into his arms and though she didn't resist him, neither did Asie respond. She seemed numb with shock and grief.

"Why did she have to go? Why our baby?"

He hesitated for a moment before speaking. "I have always tried to avoid trite platitudes when comforting a parishioner," he began. "I will do no less with you. The truth is I do not know why babies die; why God allows such a thing. It seems the cruelest death of all. Yet hardly a family is spared such sadness. We are not alone in our grief and you must not think that it is your fault."

"My faith wasn't strong enough."

"No," he argued as he gently stroked her silky blonde hair. "Your faith is strong. But Charlotte was not. She could not fight this terrible fever."

"We should never have come to this awful place. There is no fever in Connecticut."

"No fever such as we suffer here," he agreed. "But fever is just as real in New England. You know that. Remember Mrs. Conroy in our church in Fairfield? She lost three children to scarlet fever. You were such a comfort to her."

Asie shuddered and shook her head. "My words come back to mock me now. 'They're happy in heaven now,' I said. She should have slapped me."

William smiled at her sudden vehemence. He lowered his forehead to rest against hers. "Find comfort in your faith, dear," he said softly. "The Lord and I will walk through this valley with you."

At last tears filled her eyes. "But it is a very dark valley. And I am so afraid for all my children." Her words gave way to sobs and she tightened her grip on the baby.

"Our other four children are fine. They are strong and healthy. But I know they are worried about you. Let's go to them now. There is nothing more to be done for Charlotte, but the other children need you."

For a moment Asie resisted as her husband tried to gently guide her back to the mission. But she wiped her eyes with a corner of the white blanket and let him help her up the dirt path toward the mission compound.

They arrived to find that everyone in the mission family was keeping a watchful eye toward the river. The men were gathered at the grist mill where four yoke of oxen were grinding corn from their summer harvest. The women waited at the kitchen door, unwilling to go back to work until they knew their sister Asie was alright.

Rachel Chapman and Phoebe Redfield were working with the children to clean the classrooms for the start of school this week. Though Miss Johnson, the girls' teacher, was away working in Missouri, school was set to begin at the Persimmon Moon.

As the Vailles came into view from the river path, Richard Vaille their thirteen-year old, saw his parents through the open window of the boys' classroom. He spoke to his younger siblings and they all walked toward their parents. Beth, the eleven-year-old girl, carried little Joey.

The children had been made aware of the search for their mother when Alice came to check the classroom which also served as a chapel. Now they hurried to be gathered into their father's arms. The scene brought tears to Eliza's eyes.

Looking over Richard's head, Rev. Vaille caught the eye of Martha who waited at the corral with Paul and he somberly shook his head.

The midwife turned to the young man who stood beside her. "You'll not be going to Three Forks today, Paul."

"No, I guess not." Paul couldn't hide his disappointment.

"Perhaps, tomorrow," Martha encouraged. "Mr. Fuller is expecting a shipment of supplies and I sent an order to Colonel Nicks for more quinine. It should be here by now."

"Tomorrow," Paul sighed, then he added quickly. "It's good that Pastor found his wife." He loosened the reins of the horses from the corral fence.

"After you put up the horses, Paul, tell my husband that he'll need to fashion another little coffin." Mr. Woodruff was the blacksmith at the mission, but sadly he had been called upon often to build a coffin or dig a grave in their little cemetery.

"Yes, ma'am," Paul assented as he turned the horses toward the barn. "Seems like we've been doing too much of that lately."

"Yes, we have," Martha agreed as she reached for the hem of her apron to catch the tears that coursed down her cheeks. She watched as the Vaille family made their way to their cabin where the minister would have the difficult task of comforting his family.

In the little town of Pappinville, Missouri, Clarissa Johnson Palmer poured more water into a wash basin and took up the bar of lye soap sitting on a rough towel beside it. She had lost count of the number of times she had scrubbed her hands after tending to a patient and now they were rough and red.

She smiled ruefully as she dried them. A few weeks ago she would never have wanted to ruin her hands with lye soap. Funny how her priorities had changed since her marriage to Dr. Marcus Palmer. She was no longer a single schoolteacher trying to set an example of proper behavior to her students. She was now a doctor's wife and had been plunged into his world.

For the past two weeks she had worked alongside her husband in a makeshift hospital set up in the community church. Together they fought the smallpox epidemic that had swept through the small town.

Marcus had been called from Union Mission to help the besieged town of Pappinville and the Osage village of Chief Pawhuska located a few miles to the north. Clarissa had joined Marcus on the journey into Missouri along with two other missionaries, William and Harriett Montgomery.

Today they finally felt they had stopped the spread of the smallpox. Despite their best efforts they had lost three children and an elderly man to the disease, but no new cases had developed in the last few days.

Clarissa stood at the little wash stand and watched her husband go through his examination of one of the patients. He folded his lanky frame into a chair beside the bed of a young man who was about fourteen years old. The doctor gently measured the boy's pulse and then laid a practiced hand on his forehead to gauge his temperature. He leaned down to hear something the boy said and Clarissa recalled other occasions when she had studied the back of the doctor's head during a medical exam or surgery.

He seemed to always need a haircut and she made a mental note to try to locate some scissors so she could take care of that chore for him. Not that she minded the dark curls falling across his forehead, but she knew it annoyed him. He had a habit of pushing his fingers through his hair, moving it back off his face, especially when he was overworked or worried. He had been doing it often in the last two weeks.

Marcus stood from the boy's bedside and reminded the young man's mother to keep giving him water to drink. Then he made his way past other beds crowded into the church sanctuary to where Clarissa waited at the wash stand.

"He's turned the corner?"

"Yes, thank God," Marcus replied as he washed his hands. "He should recover, though he'll bear the scars."

Clarissa gave her husband a towel and he dried his hands while he looked at her closely. He was ever on guard against her contracting the dreadful disease.

"You look tired," he said.

9

"So do you."

"Comes with the job," he shrugged. "But you didn't sign up for all this."

"Yes, I did."

They shared a smile, both recalling the moment at Union Mission when Clarissa had practically flung her valise into the wagon and announced that she was coming with him to Missouri.

"I shouldn't have let you come," he said, but his voice was teasing.

"You couldn't have stopped me." Clarissa smiled at the irony of her statement. A few months ago she would not have had the courage to risk her job and her health to follow this man into an epidemic. Love was a tonic that made one brave.

"I didn't want to stop you," he countered, his smiling eyes looking at her mouth. He wanted to kiss her, but now was not the time or place.

Instead he slid a hand down her back and turned her toward the church pews that had been shoved against one wall.

"Why don't you rest a bit," he suggested. "Most of the patients are sleeping; you should too."

Clarissa eyed the long wooden benches. They were not comfortable but she had found she could sleep on them if she was tired enough. She had slept on them often in the last fortnight.

"You rest too," she said giving his arm a squeeze.

"I will. But first I want to check with the pastor to see how supplies are holding out. We may need to lift the quarantine to allow goods in to the mercantile."

You think it is safe?" Clarissa asked, hope in her voice.

"Safe for limited contact, I think," Marcus replied. "Enough for a teamster to bring in a wagon of supplies."

"Good," his wife said, barely stifling a yawn.

"Get some rest."

"I will. Wake me if you need me."

Clarissa walked to the pews and settled on one, using a stack of hymnals for a pillow. She was quickly asleep.

Marcus watched her for a time with a smile on his tired face. Then he went in search of the pastor.

CHAPTER TWO

Union Mission
September 1824

The next day, after morning chores were done, Stephen Fuller saddled two mustangs and a pack mule for the ride to Three Forks. Paul would join him for the half day journey. They would pick up supplies at the Chouteau Trading Post and then cross the river to Cantonment Gibson to see if they had any mail.

A final stop at the Nicks & Rogers Mercantile would give Paul an opportunity to see Tassie. She worked for Sallie Nicks as a store clerk.

Paul seemed anxious to be on their way. The young man would never miss a chance to visit Tassie, but he actually appeared worried as he mounted the spirited mustang named Thunder.

They waved to George and Abraham Redfield, the mission superintendent. These two men were nailing split wood shingles onto the roof of a new cabin for George and Sarah.

Up on the higher ground where the mission's cemetery sat, Alexander Woodruff toiled at digging a new grave for Charlotte Vaille.

There would be no funeral for the baby. Asie had been nearly hysterical when Martha had come to take the child to prepare her for burial. A quiet committal was all Rev. Vaille wanted for his grieving family.

"Sad day," Stephen commented as the two men struck the

trail through the cornfield where dried stalks stood gathered in bundles. They turned south onto the Texas Road, a broad but rough thoroughfare that ran all the way from Missouri into the Mexican territory of Texas.

"It surely is," Paul agreed. "You reckon Mrs. Vaille gonna be alright?"

"I pray she will," Stephen said, pulling his hat further forward over his light brown hair. "Seems like a mother's heart grieves more than anyone's over a child."

Paul could only nod. He had lost his parents when he was fourteen and had drifted aimlessly around Arkansas for a time until taken in as an apprentice at the mission. Now he had a paying job there and he and Tassie were making plans to marry and start a family of their own.

The two men rode steadily in companionable silence for most of the journey to the Chouteau Trading Post at Three Forks.

Chouteau's was the largest of the various trade outfits there and the one often utilized by the mission for ordering supplies. Besides trading furs with the Osages, Colonel Auguste Chouteau also built flatboats to haul furs, hides, honey and pecans to New Orleans. From there his river crew brought back a wide variety of trade goods. Most anything the mission needed, Chouteau could supply.

The trade community was quiet today despite sitting at the juncture of three rivers – the Arkansas, Verdigris and Neosho. There were no keelboats tied at the banks of the Verdigris, the middle river, which was lined on both banks with various trading houses.

"Why don't you go on over to Nicks'," Stephen suggested as they stopped in front of Chouteau's post. "I'll meet you there after I pick up the mail."

Paul grinned at the farmer's suggestion. "Don't mind if I do," he said. He nudged his horse into a trot to cross French Point and then take the ferry across the Neosho to Cantonment Gibson. From there a well-used trail would take him to the Nicks mercantile . . . and Tassie.

Paul arrived at the ferry landing to find a group of young

soldiers also waiting to cross. There were several ferries in the area, but this one was operated by the fort.

The soldiers eyed Paul curiously, possibly wondering if he was one of the slaves owned by Colonel Chouteau and who labored at his boatyard. Paul patted the pocket of his coat where he always kept his free papers. He never traveled anywhere without the documents.

"How'do," he said in a friendly manner. "Name's Paul Gillard. I works up at Union Mission."

The youthful soldiers all nodded at his greeting.

"Hear there's good eating at the mission," one private said.

"Yes, sir," Paul agreed. "Mrs. Fuller is a mighty good cook."

"She could give our mess cook some lessons," another soldier muttered to the laughter of his friends.

Before Paul could reply, the large, flat ferry boat they had been waiting for bumped to the shore. The soldiers scrambled aboard and then Paul eased his horse onto the ferry. The mustang seemed skittish so Paul kept a tight hold on the reins as they crossed the river.

The fort's ferry was free for the infantrymen, but Paul was expected to pay for the service so he flipped a coin to the private who manned the skiff. Then he urged his horse up the sloping bank of the Neosho and turned south through the trees that lined the river.

When he came within sight of Nicks & Rogers, he pulled his horse to a stop and dismounted slowly to keep the animal quiet. After tying the mustang's reins to a tree branch, he walked to the edge of the woods and scanned the grounds of the mercantile which stood a few feet from the home of John and Sallie Nicks.

He caught sight of Tassie sweeping the front porch of the store. He stood quietly admiring the slender fifteen-year-old woman who looked pretty in a blue cotton dress covered with a big, white apron. She wore her hair in thick braids, but she had pulled them together at her back and held the ends with a beaded leather cover like the Osage women wore.

Tassie had her back to him so he cupped his hand to his mouth and made the call of a redbird. It was a signal he had learned from Star-That-Travels, the Osage interpreter for the mission.

Tassie didn't react at first, so he made the sound again, a little louder this time. She paused from her sweeping to listen carefully while her eyes darted around the area. Paul called a third time and Tassie turned toward him, a smile creasing her soft brown face.

She waved in his direction then set the broom against the wall. Putting her head in the open front door, she told Sallie she was going to take a walk down to the river.

When Paul saw her step off the porch, he retreated back toward his horse and Tassie followed him. He was quick to pull her into his arms and give her a kiss when she reached him in the shadows of the tall pecan trees.

Tassie pulled back from him and asked pertly, "Why you want to meet out here in secret? We ain't going to be out here kissing. My mama raised me better than that."

"I know." Paul seemed affronted by her words. "My mama raised me to treat a lady proper."

"Then why are we out here?"

"Cause the last time we talked, you start asking me about runaway slaves," he explained. "That's a conversation you don't want no one else listening to."

"Mrs. Nicks wouldn't care," Tassie stated. Then she seemed to think better of her remark. "Least I don't think she would."

"Mrs. Nicks is a Southern woman. She's real nice and all, but who knows what she thinks about slavery. You can't be taking chances where runaways are concerned. People gets all riled up about such things."

"I guess you're right."

"What made you ask about helping runaways?" Paul's voice and face showed his concern. "I don't want you mixed up in such a thing. It could be dangerous."

"Monday asked me when he brought supplies over to Mrs. Nicks. He'd just got back from New Orleans where he

15

sold Colonel Chouteau's furs. I guess somebody there asked him if the missionaries up here helped runaways."

"Monday's a slave," Paul exclaimed. "He could get himself killed even asking such a thing."

Tassie shook her head. "Not anymore. He sold some of his own furs down river and he bought his freedom. Now he just works for the colonel at the boatyard."

"Monday's free?"

"Uh huh. He showed me his papers. He was real proud of them."

"Still," Paul slowly shook his head. "It would be dangerous for any of us to get involved in helping runaways. Folks get angry about it and freedom papers won't protect you from trouble."

"There ain't no bounty hunters way out here."

"There's a fort full of soldiers less than a mile away," Paul countered pointing toward Cantonment Gibson. "They're the law around here."

"Lots of them soldiers are from up north . . . like the missionaries. They don't hold to slavery."

"Maybe," Paul said. "But neither you nor I know which soldiers is which. So if Monday asks you again, you tell him to talk to me. You leave this to us men. I don't want you involved."

"Women can help too. Mama's told me stories."

"Just tell Monday to talk to me. Promise."

Tassie had a stubborn look on her face to match the stern one on Paul's. But she finally nodded. "I'll tell Monday next time I see him."

"Be careful 'bout talking to anybody 'bout this," Paul warned.

"I know," Tassie rolled her eyes. "Can you come up to the store for some coffee? Mrs. Nicks always keeps a pot on the stove."

"Yeah," Paul agreed. "Mr. Fuller's supposed to meet me there. I hope he hasn't already arrived. He'll wonder where I've been."

Holding hands, the two walked back toward the

mercantile. When they stepped inside, they found Lieutenant Charles Summers and another officer visiting with Sallie Nicks. Sallie turned and greeted Paul with a smile.

"I wondered what was keeping Tassie," she teased. "Now I can see."

"Sorry, ma'am," Tassie said sheepishly.

"I wasn't scolding," Sallie drawled with a wink at Lieutenant Summers. "I know what young love feels like."

The officer's face flushed a little at the woman's words. He personally had long felt an interest in Eliza Cleaver at Union Mission, but she had been cool towards him. Still he did not let that stop his pursuit of her affections.

"Good afternoon, Paul," he now said.

Paul nodded to the man while Tassie poured him a cup of coffee.

"I hope all is well at the mission," Sallie said, directing her question to Paul. "You're not still battling the fever up there, are you?"

"Afraid we are," Paul replied. "Rev. and Mrs. Vaille lost their little girl to it."

"Oh, I'm so sorry to hear that." Sallie tsked.

"There's been a great deal of fever at Gibson, as well," Charles said. "I hope Miss Cleaver hasn't taken ill."

"She had a little bout with it," Paul supplied. "But she's well now."

"Seems like once you get the fever, you have a little bout with it every summer," Tassie observed. She had suffered with it terribly the summer before. It was as regular as the heat of the season, the dropping water levels of the rivers and the rise of mosquitoes.

Before anyone could respond, Stephen Fuller stepped onto the porch and its wooden planks gave a pleasant creak. Removing his hat, he stepped inside the cool interior of the building with its familiar smells of salt, soap and saddlery.

"Welcome, Mr. Fuller," Sallie greeted him.

"Ma'am," he nodded and then shook hands with Summers and the other officer.

He made his way to the counter lined with glass jars of

hard candy. "Did the quinine Mrs. Woodruff ordered come in?"

"Why yes it did." Sallie stepped around a barrel of crackers, careful to keep her skirt from snagging on its rough skin. "I put it back for you. I'll just be a moment."

While she searched among the special orders set aside on a shelf, she asked over her shoulder, "Have you been by the fort? I think John had some mail for you."

"Yes," Stephen replied. "I just came from there." He patted his pocket which bulged with several letters inside. "He also shared all the news from Little Rock."

"John brings us as much news as the *Gazette*," Sallie smiled as she returned with the brown bottle of medicine. "That's one advantage of having a sutler who is also a legislator."

Colonel Nicks represented the area known as Lovely's Purchase in the Arkansas legislature and had just returned from a trip to the territorial capital.

"How much do I owe for the quinine?" Stephen asked.

"It will be a dollar."

The farmer winced slightly at the price. "Will you take Mexican coin? That's how Chouteau gave me change."

"Sure," Sallie agreed. All the trading houses close to the Texas Road accepted the silver coins from south of the Red River.

Stephen laid the *pesos* on the counter and took the bottle Sallie handed him. Slipping it into his other pocket, he turned toward Paul. "We best be heading home," he said, "while we still have daylight."

Paul nodded and after squeezing Tassie's hand in a silent goodbye, he followed Stephen out of the store.

"Where's your horse?"

"Left him in the woods," Paul explained. "Flies ain't as bad back there."

"That's true," Stephen agreed, but with a curious look on his face. "Well, let's get your horse and then get the mule at Chouteau's."

The two men set out on the ride back to the mission and

even the mule seemed to be anxious to return to its stall of hay. They made good time as the sun slipped toward the horizon and the Persimmon Moon came into view.

"School's set to start tomorrow," Stephen noted as they turned off the road toward the mission. "I wonder if all the children will be well enough to attend."

"Guess we'll see in the morning," Paul replied. "Mrs. Chapman seemed anxious about teaching the girls in Miss Johnson's place."

"Yes, and she's worried about the preacher, too. Her husband's been sick longer than anyone."

Paul dismounted to open the corral gate and led Thunder and the pack mule inside. He took Stephen's reins and removed the saddle and tack from the horses while the farm director unloaded the burlap sacks full of supplies from the mule. Then Paul took all three animals into the barn.

Stephen set the sacks into the storage leanto by the kitchen then both men washed up at the big basin. Most of the missionaries were still in the dining hall when the men joined them.

Amanda was quick to jump up and greet her husband. "Let me dish up some supper for you two," she said.

While she quickly scrambled several eggs, warmed slices of ham and placed the coffee pot back among the fireplace coals, Stephen distributed the mail to the mission family. Most everyone had received a letter from their folks back in New England. The regular movement of steamboats on the rivers now meant letters could be exchanged in only weeks instead of months.

Rev. Vaille perused the thin sheets of paper he pulled from an envelope that had been sealed with red wax. He sighed heavily after reading the missive.

"Something of concern, Reverend?" Martha asked the pastor.

"I had hoped Asie's sister Ella would come to Lovely's Purchase," the minister explained. "But she now reports that she will be unable to travel out here. She has formed an attachment with a young man in our church back home."

"That will be a disappointment for your wife," Eliza observed from where she sat nearby.

"Yes, I had hoped Ella might cheer her; help her . . . recover."

"She is ever in our prayers, Brother Vaille," Rachel Chapman assured him.

He looked up from studying his hands, his fear for his wife visible on his face. He seemed to have aged just in the last few days. "Thank you, Mrs. Chapman. For now that is all I know of that will help my wife."

CHAPTER THREE

Fairfield, Connecticut
Early October 1824

Ella Selden tapped her ink pen against the blotter in agitation. She sat at the secretary in her parents' parlor, trying to write a letter to her sister Asenath. She was feeling guilty about refusing her brother-in-law's request to travel out west to the mission. She wanted to help her sister, but she was sure Samuel Douglas was going to ask for her hand just any day now.

"You're going to tear a hole in that blotter," Ella's mother observed from across the room. She sat in a rocker by the lamp stand crocheting a doily.

Ella sighed and set the pen back in the ink well. Checking her fingers for any stains and finding none, she smoothed back her pale blonde hair. Like her older sister, Ella had a fragile beauty with a complexion as clear as a china doll. But her face was marred with a look of frustration.

"I'm trying to write to Asie and apologize for not going out there. But I can't think what to say that doesn't sound selfish."

Mrs. Selden looked over the glasses perched at the end of her nose. "And why is that, dear?"

"Oh, you know very well, Mother." Ella stood and paced the floor. "I can't go out there right now. I don't want to risk losing Samuel. He is hardly the kind of man who would wait on me for a year. And he hardly would want to settle on a mission outpost."

"He doesn't seem to be the kind of man who wants to settle down at all."

"Don't start, Mother," Ella sighed again. "People are all against Samuel because he is British."

"Or perhaps because he seems to owe all of them money," Mrs. Selden said, almost under her breath.

"That's just an ugly rumor," Ella replied. "Samuel assures me it is all a misunderstanding."

"Yes, dear." Mrs. Selden appeared to want to say more, but instead clamped her mouth shut. They had had this conversation before and Ella was unwilling to hear any disparagement of the man she had fallen in love with. She could not see beyond his dark good looks and crisp British accent.

Ella flounced back to the secretary and dropped into its chair. Taking up the pen once again, she began the letter to Asie. All the while, she tried to tamp down the doubts that her mother's words had stirred back to life in her heart.

A few days later in Missouri, most of the smallpox patients cared for by the Palmers had recovered enough to be moved out of the makeshift hospital and back to their own homes. Only two remained and neither was doing well. Marcus feared they would succumb to the illness and there would be two more graves in the little cemetery beside the church.

He sat at the bedside of a boy about ten years old. He suffered from a deep cough and labored breathing. Having done all he knew to do, Marcus could only try to make the boy comfortable as his life slipped away.

The doctor's shoulders slumped and Clarissa could tell he was berating himself for losing another patient. Marcus was hardest on himself in such situations. He felt his failure whenever someone in his care did not recover.

She wished she could go to him and offer comfort, but she sat at the bedside of the other patient. She was trying to help the elderly woman take small sips of water, but Mrs. Foster struggled to swallow.

While she worked, Clarissa kept one eye on her husband. She saw him lay a finger at the boy's throat then shake his head. She could read the words "I'm sorry," as he spoke to the boy's mother who sat across from him. The woman cried softly as Marcus pulled the sheet over the boy's face.

Tear's filled Clarissa's eyes but she tried not to let her grief show lest she discourage her own patient.

But Mrs. Foster knew what was happening across the room. She could see Marcus stand and lay a comforting hand on the young mother's shoulder. He prayed with her quietly.

"It should have been only me going on," the elderly woman murmured.

"Don't say that," Clarissa shook her head.

"I've had a good long life," Mrs. Foster countered. "Outlived nearly every family member. I'm ready to cross over and see them again. You tell your young doctor not to grieve himself over me."

In a few minutes Mrs. Foster too was gone, but a slight smile graced her beautifully wrinkled face.

Marcus helped Clarissa stand and gathered her into his arms. Their work was done here and he for one was eager to go home to Union Mission.

The next day, family and friends gathered at the two gravesites. The boy's mother had asked Marcus to speak at the committal service.

"Bobbie sure liked you, Doc," she said. "I'd be pleased if you say the words over him."

"I'd be honored," Marcus agreed.

So Pastor Long gave the eulogy for Mrs. Foster and then Marcus spoke over Bobbie's grave. The little congregation sang a hymn about heaven and then slowly made their way out of the cemetery.

"You missed your calling, young man," Pastor Long told Marcus as they walked toward the church. "You should have been a preacher."

"I wanted to be," Marcus replied, "when I was young. But my father convinced me to follow in his footsteps and study medicine. I've often wished I had followed my heart though."

"No reason why you can't now. Doctoring and preaching can go together."

Marcus smiled and nodded, but said nothing more in his pensive mood.

Clarissa was surprised to hear of her husband's early interest in the ministry. She was still learning about this man after just a few weeks of marriage and she supposed there would be many more discoveries to make as they shared their new life. She slipped her hand into his and they walked together to the pastor's home.

It was time to pack their few things and travel to Harmony Mission. They were eager to learn how William and Harriett had fared at Pawhuska's village and hoped that the crisis was sufficiently passed so they all might return to Arkansas Territory.

Marcus and Clarissa spent two days at Harmony being fed and fussed over by the women at the mission. Clarissa slept for twelve hours the first day, but it was exactly the respite she needed.

"Are you feeling rested now?" young Mary Austin asked her when she brought some tea for the schoolteacher late one afternoon in the mission dining hall.

"Yes, thank you, Mary." Clarissa watched the fourteen-year-old girl deftly pour the tea and offer it to her.

"You've certainly grown into a fine young woman," she observed. "And your hair is such a pretty auburn now."

"Yes, not that awful red," Mary agreed, wrinkling her nose to show what she thought of the color. She now wore her long braids caught together at the back of her neck and held with a wide bow.

Mary sat in a chair opposite Clarissa and the teacher could tell the girl wanted to ask something but was hesitant.

"I hope everyone was well at Union Mission when you left," she finally said.

"Yes all were well then," Clarissa said as she sipped her

hot tea. "I hope that we'll find everyone well when we return."

"Even Brother Requa?" Mary asked in a casual tone.

Clarissa remembered that Mary had once expressed a desire to marry George Requa even though he was ten years older than she. It was a surprise to learn that the girl still had an interest in their fun-loving mechanic. But George was happily married now. She would have to break the news to Mary.

"Yes, Brother Requa was well," she began, "as was his new wife, Sarah."

"He's married?"

"Yes, dear, I'm afraid he is."

Clarissa was surprised to see tears form in the girl's green eyes. She had no idea Mary had felt so deeply about George.

"But I was sure he was God's choice for me," Mary said in a forlorn voice.

"Oh, Mary," Clarissa reached across the table to take the girl's hand. "You are still quite young to be thinking so seriously about a man and marriage."

"But there is no one else for me," Mary sighed.

"Don't say that," Clarissa responded. "You have plenty of time for courtship and marriage. Aren't you going back east for more schooling?"

"There's no money for finishing school. I've taken Mrs. Montgomery's place here as a housemother."

It saddened Clarissa to realize Mary would have no opportunity to further her education. She had already taken on adult responsibilities and there probably were few prospects for marriage at this far western outpost. Still she wanted to encourage the girl.

"Well, try to keep up your education by reading whatever you can," she said. "And don't be in a rush about marriage. There will be someone for you someday; I'm sure of it."

"Thank you, Mrs. Palmer." But Mary's face remained sad. She replaced Clarissa's empty cup on the tray and stood to carry it back to the kitchen. Clarissa watched her go, walking with her back straight and head held high. No doubt she was following the example that Harriett Montgomery had set for the girls here at Harmony.

The following day the Palmers were making plans to load a wagon and take supplies to Pawhuska's village. Before they could, however, the Montgomerys, along with their Osage interpreter, arrived at the mission.

William pulled their wagon into the corral and Star-That-Travels followed on his mustang. Harriett sat in the wagon bed, among supply crates and baggage. A little Osage girl sat beside her.

When Clarissa saw the girl, she immediately thought of her adopted daughter Thea. She had assumed care of Thea when her mother died in childbirth two years ago. Clarissa had left her daughter with Eliza at Union Mission while she and Marcus worked in Missouri. Now she was suddenly swamped with longing for her little girl.

Rev. Montgomery helped his wife down from the wagon, using the hub of the back wheel as a step. Then he lifted the thin and sad-faced little girl out also. She immediately wrapped herself into Harriett's skirt as if seeking to hide.

"It's alright, Lucie," Harriet said quietly to the five-year-old. She stroked her dark hair that had been pulled into tight braids.

Clarissa wanted to comfort the girl. She walked over and gave a brief hug to Harriett. "Have you brought a treasure with you?" she asked, smiling down at Lucie.

"Yes, exactly," Harriett replied. She tried to extricate the girl from her skirt, but the girl clung all the more tightly to her. "This is Lucie. She speaks French."

"Oh, *magnifique*," Clarissa said. "*Bon jour, mademoiselle* Lucie." She reached out a hand to the girl and for the first time Lucie didn't look frightened.

"Thank goodness you can speak with her," Harriett said. "My French is quite limited and she is afraid of Star-That-Travels so she won't talk to him."

"I take it her father is French?"

"Yes, a fur trapper," Harriett said as the group moved

toward the dining hall. "But he left for the mountains over a year ago and hasn't been heard from since. Most of Pawhuska's people don't think he'll return. They believe he probably met with an accident."

"And her mother?"

"Gone. Lost to the smallpox. And she has no other family. We lost so many at the village."

"I'm sorry to hear that," Clarissa said. "So you are going to take her?"

"I would gladly do so," Harriett replied. "But communication would be difficult. So I was thinking you might take her in. She'd be a dear companion for Thea." There was hope in Harriett's voice. Despite coming across as a no-nonsense disciplinarian, Harriett was quite passionate about the care of children.

Clarissa looked down at Lucie and felt her heart grow larger. "I'll have to speak with Dr. Palmer, of course, but I'm sure he'll agree." Her husband was very fond of children. He had won Thea's love just as easily as he had won Clarissa's.

The Union missionaries began the return journey to western Arkansas two days later. Clarissa and Lucie were already comfortable with one another and chatted together in French in the back of the wagon as it rolled down the rutted Texas Road. Marcus rode his horse close by. He couldn't understand a word his wife and new daughter were saying, but he wore a pleased smile on his face.

CHAPTER FOUR

Rachel Chapman stood at the front of the girls' classroom at Union Mission. In a moment of frustration, she placed her hands over her ears as if to suppress the polyglot of chatter coming from her students. A mixture of English, French and Osage brought confusion to the classroom.

"How did Miss Johnson manage?" she asked her two assistants over the noise. Phoebe Redfield and Teresa Revoir, Star-That-Travels' wife, just smiled and shook their heads. Clarissa had made teaching a group of bilingual students seem effortless.

Rachel herself was fluent in French, having studied two years in Paris. But she had never worked as a teacher and now she stood before a classroom of students in all grade levels and from different cultures. She expressed her admiration for Miss Johnson daily.

Besides her own two daughters, Abigail and Leah, the class consisted of the Vaille girls, Beth and Sarah Ann, who only spoke English. Louisa Revoir, Masina Chouteau and Marie Lombard were Osage-French and could speak both those languages. Lena Bradley, Tassie's younger sister, was also of mixed race, being Creole and Scottish. She had learned a smattering of French from her mother.

Then there were five full blood Osage girls, who knew a little French or English, but mostly spoke Osage. Teresa helped with translation for the Osage girls who had settled with their families five miles north at Hopefield Farm.

The fever had abated with the cooler temperatures and all the students were able to attend classes. It was a good thing for the girls, but Mrs. Chapman seemed overwhelmed.

"Beth, Sarah Ann, please don't fuss," Rachel admonished. The two Vaille sisters were trying to wrestle a piece of chalk away from one another. They shared a desk with a seat wide enough for two students. "Do I need to separate you two?"

"I would rather sit with Abigail," the older girl stated. Sarah Ann stuck her tongue out at her sister. Rachel hid a smile behind her hand, pretending to cough. The matter might have been more amusing had it not become a regular occurrence between the two sisters.

Beth and Sarah Ann were now two of her more unruly students which was unusual for them. Their mother had taken to her bed and paid the girls little attention. Their grief and fear caused them to act out in the classroom to get the attention they craved.

"We'll rotate chairs this afternoon," Rachel proposed. Glancing at the watch that hung at the end of a delicate chain around her neck, she sighed with relief. Amanda would soon ring the dinner bell and she could dismiss the girls for the noon meal in the dining hall.

After dinner the oldest girls would take a cooking lesson from Amanda in the kitchen. The middle girls would stay in the dining room to work on embroidery projects overseen by Sarah Requa. Phoebe would return to the school with the youngest girls and give them a time for play in the school yard. This division of teaching had helped Rachel to keep her sanity these past few weeks.

As she and Phoebe followed the girls to the dining hall, Rachel said to the housemother, "I'm going to take Mrs. Vaille's lunch to her and speak to her about her daughters. She needs to be made aware of their struggle."

"Yes," Phoebe nodded.

"Help me pray that I will say the right thing."

"I will."

After seeing that the girls were settled at the long dining

tables, Rachel went into the kitchen where Amanda was setting a bowl of stew onto a tray along with a cup of tea.

"This is for Mrs. Vaille?"

"Yes, ma'am," said Amanda. "I expect Rev. Vaille to come for it in a moment."

"I'll take it and send him to eat with his children," Rachel explained as she grasped the tray by its handles and left the kitchen.

William Vaille seemed happy to have the opportunity to take his youngest son Joseph, who would soon be turning three, and walk with him to the dining hall.

"You are an answer to prayer," he spoke softly just before stepping out of the cabin. "She needs to talk with a woman. My words don't seem to help her at all."

"Well, keep praying," Rachel replied. "I am yet unsure what I should say."

"The truth is what sets us free." Then the minister closed the cabin door.

Rachel carried the tray to the small table in the middle of the one-room cabin. Asie was in bed, though fully clothed.

"I have brought your dinner, Asie," Rachel said in a crisp tone. She seemed determined to keep any sound of pity out of her voice.

Asie turned her head to look at Rachel but made no effort to rise. "I'm not hungry."

It was clear that she had not eaten well for the past few weeks. She had grown thinner and her cheeks seemed sunken, her eyes hollow.

"You need your nourishment, Asie," Rachel countered. Then in a steely tone she added, "Get up and come eat."

Asie looked surprised at her friend's tone of voice. She shook her head slightly and started to say something, but seemed to change her mind. Slowly she struggled to rise from the rumpled bed.

Her hair was in as much disarray as the bedclothes. It looked as if she had not combed it in several days.

"Sit and eat and I'll brush out your hair," Rachel commanded.

"You shouldn't go to the trouble," Asie said as she sat down. "I'll just be going back to bed."

"No you will not." Rachel crossed the raw plank floor and grasped a hairbrush on the wash stand. "I need your help in the classroom."

"My help?" Asie picked up the spoon from the tray and stirred it listlessly in the bowl of stew. "I would be useless to you. I'm useless to everyone."

"You have made yourself useless by hiding in your bed." Rachel pulled the brush as gently as possible through Asie's tangled hair. Speaking now in an equally gentle voice she said, "You are mourning your child. I understand that. But you must not sacrifice your living children to your grief."

"They are fine. William takes good care of them."

"They are not fine at all," Rachel countered. "They grieve for Charlotte too. But they have lost more than a sister; they have lost you as well."

The spoon stilled. Standing behind her sister, Rachel could not see the tears that coursed down Asie's face. But she must have sensed them for she kept quiet and simply pulled the brush in long, soothing strokes through the blonde strands.

Finally Asie whispered in a choked voice, "I don't know how to get out of this darkness. I feel as if I am slipping away from everyone, even God. "

"Nothing separates us from God. He will not let go of you. And neither will we."

"But what can I do?"

"Don't go back to bed, Asie," Rachel advised. "That certainly is not the answer. Don't sit alone in this cabin with the walls closing in on you."

"I have become afraid even to venture out," Asie confessed. She unconsciously lifted the spoon and took a sip of the stew.

Rachel's face brightened but she did not call the woman's attention to her action. Another bite of the steaming vegetables followed and then another as if her hunger had been awakened.

Rachel plaited the blonde strands into a long braid.

Quickly pulling a pin from her own stylish coif, she fastened the end of the braid, then crossed to the wash stand for more hair pins.

"When you have finished Amanda's delicious stew, you can come with me to class," Rachel said as she wound the braid into an attractive bun.

"I can't face those bright, inquisitive faces," Asie shook her head. "I look a mess."

"No you don't." Rachel picked up the little hand mirror that rested besides Asie's hairbrush. She held it so her friend could see herself. Despite being somewhat pale and having dusky circles under her eyes, Asie still looked attractive.

She studied the image in the mirror as if seeing a new person in that reflection. "I will never be the same," she murmured almost to herself.

"None of us are after we lose someone," Rachel said. "But with the help of God and those who remain with us, we learn to accept our altered selves, our altered world, and we keep going. Someday you will find joy again."

Asie shook her head slightly but did not express her disagreement. Instead, she drew a deep breath and continued to eat with a resigned determination. This would be the day she would walk into her altered world.

From that day, Asie helped in the class each afternoon though most of the time all she could find the strength for was reading to the younger students. It was a great comfort to her family to see her make the effort to return to as much normalcy as was possible.

"Beth, get back in your chair," Rachel admonished the older Vaille girl one morning a few days later.

"I thought I heard a wagon coming," Beth defended herself as she left the window and slumped back into the seat she now shared with Abigail.

"You know you are not to leave your seat without permission," Rachel replied. Then she gave a little nod of her head at Phoebe in an unspoken request for her to check the window.

The housemother crossed the back of the room and pulled open the curtains that Rachel kept closed while class was in session. Deer bounding across the field or a line of travelers on the Texas Road proved too much of a distraction to the students otherwise.

Indeed a wagon trailed by one mustang and a second horse and rider were pulling into the mission yard and Paul was hurrying to open the corral gate for them.

"It's Dr. Palmer and Miss Johnson," Phoebe said. "With Star-That-Travels. They must have left the Montgomerys at Hopefield."

"Teacher's back!" Leah exclaimed in excitement.

If Rachel felt disappointment that her daughter was so excited to have her beloved teacher return, it did not show on the woman's face. She was smiling as broadly as the girls.

"Oh, praise be to Jesus," she breathed.

Phoebe hid her own smile. Turning back to Mrs. Chapman she said, "Perhaps the girls would like to take a break and welcome Miss Johnson home."

Hands went up to request permission and a chorus of "please" in three languages was raised. All Mrs. Chapman had to do was nod and the girls were bounding out the door to meet their teacher as Paul helped her down from the wagon.

"Miss Johnson, Miss Johnson," the girls vied to be first to greet the teacher. Clarissa was trying to smooth the wrinkles out of her dress before lifting Lucie down. She was quickly engulfed in hugs from her students.

"Miss Johnson?" Marcus said with teasing in his voice. "Now who's that?" He threw a conspiratorial smile to his wife as he stiffly dismounted from the wagon seat.

"Oh, girls it is so good to see you," Clarissa said after giving each one a hug. "But Dr. Palmer is right. My name isn't Miss Johnson anymore."

"What is it?' asked Deer-in-Water, the daughter of an Osage warrior named Bird.

"It's Mrs. Palmer now." Clarissa leaned down and added in a stage whisper, "You see, I married Dr. Palmer." Murmurs of excited approval swept through her class.

"And I have a new daughter, too," the teacher said, pulling Lucie forward. "This is Lucie. She'll be joining you in class."

The little girl seemed frightened as twelve inquisitive sets of eyes turned her way. "Lucie is a little shy so you all need to make her feel welcome," Clarissa said.

Lucie was quickly engulfed in greetings in three languages. As Mrs. Palmer's class gathered around the girl, she looked up at her new mother with wonder on her face. "Can you girls show Lucie to class?" the teacher asked. "I'll be there shortly."

Asie had stood at the back of the family gathering around the Palmers. Teresa and Star-That-Travels were speaking quietly in their own reunion after two months of separation.

"Has she no parents?" Asie asked Clarissa as the girls took Lucie by both hands and led her to the schoolhouse.

"She has lost everyone," Clarissa explained.

Asie's eyes filled with tears and she placed a hand to her mouth, clearly overcome with emotion.

Clarissa did not understand the depth of Asie's grief and gave Phoebe a questioning look. The housemother leaned in to hug Clarissa and whispered. "Asie lost Charlotte to the fever."

Marcus was standing at Clarissa's shoulder and heard the explanation as well.

"Was the fever bad?" he asked quietly.

Phoebe nodded. "Almost everyone had a bout with it. And we lost the twins to it as well."

"Moses and Miriam?" Clarissa caught her breath in sorrow. "Oh, how sad for the Chapmans and for Sarah and George."

"It's been hard," Phoebe agreed.

"I shouldn't have gone to Missouri," the doctor sighed.

"Don't blame yourself for this," Clarissa admonished her husband quietly. "You were needed in Missouri. You saved many lives there."

"You both must be very tired from your journey," the ever practical Rachel interrupted. "Instead of going to class

Miss . . . Mrs. Palmer, you should take some time to rest. I'll give you one day before I ask you to rescue me from the classroom."

"Clarissa smiled at her friend. "I'm sure you don't need rescuing."

"You have no idea," Rachel said in a sardonic tone. "I am not cut out to be a teacher."

"Coffee's hot and I'll pour you some flapjacks," Amanda then offered.

"Oh, that sounds wonderful," Clarissa agreed. Marcus and Star-That-Travels both nodded eagerly as well.

As they walked to the dining hall, Thea came running out of the Spaulding cabin where Eliza had gone to wake her from a nap. The little girl showed her delight at seeing her mother and her grin revealed two new tiny white teeth.

Clarissa dropped to her knees and threw open her arms to catch the two-year-old who hurled herself into the embrace. "Oh, Thea, I've missed you so!"

"Mes too, Mama." Then just as eagerly she raised her hands to Marcus to be picked up by the tall doctor.

"Look at you, Miss Thea," he said as they all continued to the dining hall. "Have you grown half a foot since we've been gone?"

Thea looked down at her feet and shook her head vigorously, her dark braids swishing across her back. "No new feet," she said.

Everyone laughed at her innocent reply. Clarissa smiled too, feeling a deep contentment as she looked around the mission. It was as familiar as home but it was changed as well.

A new cabin sat next to the Fullers' and foundation stones for a third one had been set nearby. Piles of pumpkins were stacked against the kitchen wall, awaiting canning. Quilts were being aired on the rope clotheslines. The trees along the riverbank were showing their fall colors.

Yes, it was good to be home.

CHAPTER FIVE

Three Forks
October 1824

Clarissa had only a week to get back into the classroom before school was dismissed for the Pumpkin Moon Rendezvous followed by the fall hunt. The Osage students would go with their families to the buffalo wallows further west and harvest the animals migrating south on the prairie.

At Union Mission, the time would be spent preparing the compound for winter. The men had made a final cut of hay for their growing number of livestock. They worked to stack it in huge piles on the south side of the barn. Several hogs would be butchered and days would be spent in making sausage and soap from the fat. The last of the corn had been ground and Stephen would take several barrels to Three Forks to sell to the fort or trade for goods available at Chouteau's or Nicks & Rogers.

Amanda supervised the harvest of the fall garden and the children helped with this chore. The potato patch hadn't produced well this year because of the heavy fall rains. But there were plenty of carrots and turnips stored on burlaps bags in the root cellar.

Sarah helped Clarissa cut her light wool cape to make coats for Lucie and Thea. The teacher planned to buy fabric for a new cape for herself at one of the mercantiles.

As Clarissa had hoped, the new cabin being raised was for the Palmer family. Their home would have two rooms downstairs – a living quarters for the family and a small office and examining room for the doctor. The girls would sleep in a loft upstairs and there would even be room for other girls who would board with them during the winter.

For the time being, the Palmers were staying in the cabin the missionaries called "the guest cabin." Most of the single missionaries who had traveled here from New England were now married and they had all used the cabin as their first home at the mission. Eliza Cleaver was the only single woman and now occupied the once crowded women's cabin alone.

Eliza had always made it clear that her desire was to return to New England. She had come to the mission at age sixteen with her sister and brother-in-law, Alice and John Spaulding. But her heart had never been in missions work, though she was proving to be a great help in caring for the younger children. Now at age twenty, she was more content here on the prairie, but still longed to go back East.

Clarissa made a point to secure a seat next to Eliza as they loaded into wagons for the trip to the Rendezvous. The morning was chilly as they set out before dawn to make the twenty-five mile trek to Three Forks.

Everyone was in high spirits as they began the one holiday away from the mission that they enjoyed each fall. From Hopefield, Star and Teresa joined them on their mustangs and the Montgomerys with Will and Susan Requa added another wagon to the group.

"We haven't had a moment to talk," Clarissa said to the beautiful young woman beside her. The teacher had once felt jealous of Eliza's natural beauty, but over the years they had become good friends.

"I've missed our talks," Eliza said with a twinkle in her eye. On more than one occasion the two had shared their hopes, fears, dreams and frustrations with many tears and laughter.

Clarissa lowered her voice so she would not be heard over the children's excited chatter. "Have you heard from Lieutenant Summers?"

"He came to call once while you were away, but hasn't

been able to get away from Cantonment Gibson more than that."

"You are not still trying to discourage his interest, are you?"

"Believe me, neither I nor Alice have been able to discourage him."

"I still don't understand why your sister is so set against him. Or you either, for that matter. He seems like a nice young man." Clarissa glanced at Alice who was talking with Asie Vaille in the wagon behind them.

"Alice is coming around, I think," Eliza said as she grabbed her bonnet to keep it from blowing away in a gust of cool wind. "And I'm not set against him. Not really. But he has three more years of duty out here. There's no hurry to form an attachment."

"I suppose." Clarissa wanted to warn her not to take his interest for granted. Some other woman might be eager for his attention. But in reality she knew there were few single American women out this far west. The only other unattached female for miles was Elizabeth Baylor, the daughter of the fort's surgeon. It might not hurt to remind Eliza of her.

"Just don't let that Miss Baylor catch his eye. She seems eager to form an attachment."

Eliza giggled. "Charles says she stops by the headquarters tent quite often on some pretense or another. He finds it amusing."

"Charles, is it?" Clarissa quirked an eyebrow at her friend.

"I mean, Lieutenant Summers." Eliza's face went red at her slip.

Clarissa smiled, but decided to hide her delight that Eliza's indifference toward the handsome officer was not as deeply held as she let on. Dropping the matter, she turned her attention to the other women in the wagon and soon joined in their conversation.

By the time they reached Three Forks, they were all tired of the bumpy wagon ride and eager to walk around the little community. It seemed like Rendezvous grew every year.

Besides Osage lodges set up around the Chouteau post, there were also Quapaws and even a few Cherokees who had come to trade their furs, as well as the honey, pecans and tobacco they had harvested through the summer.

Hucksters had set up their tents among the various trading posts and a carnival atmosphere filled the air. Gambling was a part of Rendezvous that the missionaries did not condone. The steady flow of alcohol was also a concern for it always seemed to lead to trouble. But with the fort nearby, they were hopeful the military would keep trouble tamped down and that the young soldiers wouldn't contribute to it themselves.

The missionaries parked their wagons at Nathaniel Pryor's post and then made their way along the one dirt street in town. They ran into the Bean brothers who had brought barrels of salt for trade. Captain Bean's son Jesse was unloading several barrels at Hugh Glenn's store and would take the rest across the river to Cantonment Gibson.

The mission family used the afternoon to shop at Chouteau's. Clarissa found a bolt of lightweight brown wool and bought a length for a new cape. Sarah would help her with the sewing for the mission's seamstress was far better with a needle than Clarissa was. George and Sarah had not made the trip to Rendezvous because of Sarah's delicate condition. They, along with Martha and Alexander, were keeping the smaller children at home.

Rachel Chapman had remained at the mission with her husband who was still weak from a long and difficult bout with the summer fever. The Vailles had taken charge of the four Chapman children for the outing.

Following supper over a fire at Pryor's, the missionaries walked down the Texas Road to French Point where Father Pierre Menard conducted his annual revival meeting under a brush arbor. An hour of singing gave folks in the area time to arrive for another hour of preaching.

Tassie took the ferry over with Mrs. Nicks and quickly took the seat Paul had saved for her. Several soldiers, including Colonel Arbuckle, the fort commander, also attended the church service. A number of Osages from the village nearby were there too. Clarissa looked over the audience made up of every color and thought that this was what heaven would look like.

The next morning Clarissa and Marcus joined most of their group in crossing the Neosho to pay a visit to Cantonment Gibson. Clarissa tried to hide a yawn while they stood at the foggy river bank waiting their turn for the ferry.

She hadn't slept well on the hard wagon bed last night. The horse races upriver were raucous and lasted well past midnight. Over at the fort, the faint plink of a banjo added to the noise.

"Hard to sleep last night," Marcus observed to her quietly.

"I forget how quiet it is at Union." Then leaning closer she looked up at him to whisper, "And I missed you."

Her husband smiled. "I missed you too, and our soft featherbed. The ground was hard and the boys were so restless I'm surprised I'm not black and blue this morning. Billy may be the littlest of the bunch, but he can kick with a wallop."

Clarissa laughed. "He's stout, all right. He nearly drowned me in this river last summer."

"Don't remind me," Marcus said with a shudder.

Clarissa couldn't keep the smile off her face. Her husband might not like the memory of their dramatic rescue of Billy Spaulding, but Clarissa would always associate it with one of the happiest days of her life. It was the day Marcus had finally asked her to marry him.

"Stop grinning," Marcus chided her, trying to look stern. But he didn't succeed and they were sharing a secret laugh when the ferry arrived.

The mission group crowded aboard the flatboat and their weight dropped the ferry deep into the lazily flowing Neosho River.

"What's this going to cost us, sergeant?" Marcus asked, reaching into his pocket to pull out some coins.

"Nothing today, sir," the young man responded. "Colonel Arbuckle is offering rides for free during the Rendezvous."

"We'll be sure and thank the colonel," Abraham Redfield commented. "He is here today, isn't he?"

"Yes, sir. He's receiving visitors at the headquarters tent."

They reached a sandstone ledge on the east bank of the river where a heavy metal pylon had been driven into the soft rock. Here boats arriving at Cantonment Gibson would tie up for their stay at Three Forks.

The mission family scrambled up the bank with the help of two enlisted soldiers who worked at the ferry operation. The group made their way to the garrison with its log palisade surrounding a parade ground. The fort had joined the Rendezvous holiday and several activities were underway.

The soldiers had set up a turkey shoot and a hatchet throw in a field just north of the palisade. Using huge slabs of sawn tree trunks for targets, the competition was just getting underway. Nearby, Sallie Nicks and Sophie Baylor, the doctor's wife, were supervising a refreshments table.

The missionaries scattered around the area. Richard Vaille and his best friend Thomas Chapman, the thirteen-year-olds, returned quickly from the target area.

"Can we compete in the hatchet throw, father?" Richard asked the mission pastor. "Colonel Nicks is offering a gold coin as prize."

"We've been practicing with Jean and Bearpaw," Thomas went on. "We're as good as these soldiers, I think."

William Vaille smiled at the boys' enthusiasm and confidence. "It doesn't require you to put up money yourself," does it?" he asked. "I won't have you gambling."

"No." both young men assured him quickly.

William exchanged a look with Asie who nodded though she bit her lip as if concerned.

"You must be careful," she admonished the boys.

"We will," Thomas said.

"Thank you!" Richard added as the two dashed away.

"Let's go and cheer them on," Amanda suggested and most of the missionaries made their way to the target area. The Redfields led the other children to the refreshment table and Paul joined them. Tassie was there cutting squares of gingerbread baked by her mother.

"Too bad George didn't come," Will, his older brother, observed. "He's our best marksman. He could probably win the turkey shoot."

"You should enter, Requa," Stephen said. "You're as good a shot as your brother."

Will looked at Susan, then cast an eye at the other men gathering for the shooting contest. "I will, if you will," he proposed to the farm director. Will, George and Stephen usually did the hunting at the mission for they were all good with a musket.

Stephen nodded and then turned to Star-That-Travels. "What about you, Star? You're good with a gun."

Star's face was hard as he gazed at the other competitors. "Not today," was all he said.

Will must have realized that Star-That-Travels did not want to participate because a Cherokee warrior was waiting in the line of shooters.

"Do you know him?" he asked the Osage quietly.

"That is Spring Frog. He is a good friend to Walter Webber," Star-That-Travels replied. "He led the attack on Claremont's Town a few years ago."

All the missionaries turned to look at the man wearing a muslin trade shirt and leather britches. A long length of calico wound around his head like a turban. The Cherokee had the look of an athlete.

"Teresa and I will go back to Pryor's." Star took his wife's hand.

"You shouldn't have to miss the fun," Will protested to his friend.

"I want no trouble."

With that, the Osage couple walked past the palisade and back toward the ferry landing. The missionaries watched them go, sharing looks of concern.

Will sighed. It's a shame this feud can't be settled. I don't know why Arbuckle can't do something about it."

"The Cherokees and Osages have a long history," Vaille observed. "I don't think Colonel Arbuckle has been here long enough to find a solution to such a complex problem. We will have to continue our prayers and hope the gospel will soften hearts and change minds."

"Teresa is good friends with Captain Pryor's wife," Susan Requa said in a sweet little-girl voice. "She'll enjoy a visit with her."

"Yes, and the Cherokees won't trade with Pryor because he is married to an Osage," Will added. "They won't have to worry about running into Cherokees at his post."

"Father," Richard's voice turned everyone's attention back to the competition. "I'm up next."

"Do well, son," Vaille called to the boy.

With other words of encouragement, the missionaries watched as Richard and then Thomas took their turns at tossing three hatchets at the overturned tree stumps having a bull's eye drawn with charcoal. Though neither of them hit dead center, each made a decent showing with their throws.

"Good job, boys," John Spaulding congratulated his students when they joined the group. They watched as several Osages and a few soldiers also took turns in the competition. One of the Osages was Bird, the father of Bearpaw and Deer-in-Water.

Colonel Nicks and Lieutenant Summers were judges in the sporting event. Out of the corner of her eye, Clarissa observed the exchange of smiles between Eliza and Charles. In fact, it seemed that Eliza's presence was rather distracting to the lieutenant. He twice dropped the stick he was using to measure each hatchet's distance from the center.

After all the contestants had completed their tosses, the two judges conferred. Bird was declared the winner and received the gold coin prize. Thomas and Richard placed fifth and sixth respectively and received ribbons with hand lettering. The boys seemed quite pleased and congratulated each other in good sportsmanship.

Will and Stephen decided against competing in the shooting match, but they watched it with interest. Mostly soldiers took turns aiming at various targets set up in a field near the fort. A master sergeant took the prize. The gray at his temples said he was a career enlisted man who had years of practice with a musket.

When the shooting ended, everyone drifted toward the refreshment table for some cider or coffee. Tassie was filling mugs as quickly as she could and Paul even picked up an enamel coffee pot to help out.

Colonel Arbuckle approached the missionaries who had taken seats on makeshift benches. "Dinner will be served soon in the mess tent," he said after greeting the guests. "I would like to invite you to dine with me and my officers, if you would."

"We'd be honored, Colonel," Rev. Vaille spoke for the group.

Arbuckle led the way to a large tent located up a gentle slope. Nearby a log cabin was being built with two massive fireplaces at each end. Arbuckle told them it would become officer quarters on the second floor with office space for himself on the main level.

"We're eventually going to replace all the tents with log structures," the commander explained. "We'll turn this cantonment into a real fort."

Clarissa was flattered to have the commander invite her and Marcus to his table. Also seated with them were the Vailles, Dr. and Mrs. Baylor, and John and Sallie Nicks. It was Clarissa's first time to enjoy the status of being married to a doctor. As a single female teacher, she never would have sat with the colonel.

At the next table, close enough to participate in the same conversations, Lieutenant Summers pulled out a chair for Eliza. The Spauldings and Montgomerys were at this table along with Elizabeth Baylor and two other officers. The Fullers, Redfields and Requas shared a table and the mission's children were settled on blankets just outside the mess tent.

A bevy of privates served generous slabs of meat from a side of beef that had smoked over a firepit throughout the night. Brown beans, steamed cabbage, corn pone and light bread completed the meal.

Conversation quickly turned to Arkansas politics. As a territorial legislator, Colonel Nicks was well informed about what was happening in Little Rock.

"The boundary lines for Lovely's Purchase have finally been agreed upon based on Isaac McCoy's survey," Nicks told them. "Since I represent this area of the territory, I'm going to propose that it be designated a county with a courthouse and post office."

"Will the county seat be here at Three Forks?" Vaille asked.

"Possibly," Nicks replied. "But more likely it will be somewhere along a military road between Fort Smith and Cantonment Gibson."

"Another location for John to build a mercantile," Sallie teased.

He gave her a rueful smile.

"What will the county be called?" Mrs. Baylor asked.

"Lovely County, of course," Sallie responded before John could. "Isn't that a perfect name for such a lovely area?"

"It's named for a person, dear," John said. "William Lovely, the Cherokee agent." Clarissa thought he seemed a little annoyed with his wife's saucy manner.

"I know," she responded quickly with a twinkle in her eye. She would not let her husband's humor daunt her lively spirit. "Though I think it should be named for his widow Persis. She is quite a lovely woman." Sallie was enjoying her puns.

"Then here's to the soon-to-be Lovely County." Dr. Baylor lifted his water glass and everyone else did the same.

When the toast was completed, Colonel Arbuckle resumed the conversation. "It is the hope that Lovely County will truly provide a buffer between the Osages and Cherokees."

"Will the Osages be required to move?" Marcus asked.

"Their village here at Three Forks probably will," Arbuckle said. "It's within the new boundary. But Claremont's Town is far enough west that it will not be impacted. Lovely County will be considered Cherokee land once another treaty is signed and ratified. This will pull the Arkansas border considerably eastward to the Purchase boundary. Claremont's Town will no longer be in Arkansas Territory."

"What territory will it be?" Harriett asked.

"An Indian territory, I suppose," said the commander. "It is the goal in Washington to move eastern tribes out here."

"How is this going to impact our mission?" queried Rev. Vaille.

The commander paused before responding. "That I couldn't say. But I would advise you to have a conversation with the Cherokee chief John Jolly as soon as the treaty is completed. I think he's amenable to missionary work. He'll probably allow yours to continue, provided you admit Cherokee students."

"We would certainly be open to having Cherokees attend the school," John Spaulding spoke up from the other table. He was a never-failing advocate of education for everyone.

"What about our Hopefield Farm?" Rev. Montgomery then asked.

Arbuckle looked over at Charles. "It's within the purchase area, isn't it?"

"Yes, sir."

"But we have a number of Osage families living there," Montgomery pressed. "Will they be forced to move?"

"You'll have to take that up with Chief Jolly," was all Arbuckle would say.

The conversation moved on to other topics – the harvest this year, winter predictions by the Old Farmer's Almanac, the upcoming Presidential election. As the meal concluded, Arbuckle returned to the work of Union Mission.

"I would like to make a request of you, if I might, Rev. Vaille."

"Yes, sir?"

"I believe it would do my men good to have a regular church service," the colonel said. "Could you provide a preacher? I know it's quite a journey down here but perhaps we could hold one service a month. We could meet here in the mess tent."

"We would be very happy to provide a preacher for a monthly service. We have two lay preachers among us besides myself, Rev. Chapman and Rev. Montgomery."

"Good. Shall we set it for the first Sunday of each month? Say at fourteen hundred."

Clarissa calculated in her head that this would be two o'clock in the afternoon. Whoever was to deliver the sermon would still have to travel down on Saturday. The missionaries did not travel for long distances on the Sabbath.

"We will plan on it," the minister said. "We thank you for the opportunity."

After dinner, the family walked the half mile to the Nicks Mercantile and spent a little time shopping. Then they took the ferry and walked to Pryor's to load into the wagons. It would be dark before they arrived back at Union Mission.

CHAPTER SIX

Union Mission
Winter 1824

The missionaries assigned Marcus and Abraham the duty of preaching at Cantonment Gibson. For safety, the mission had a policy of always sending at least two men when travel was undertaken. Paul volunteered to also make the trip each month to the Gibson service. No one had to ask his reason for the offer.

Clarissa and Marcus were discussing Paul and Tassie one evening after the girls had gone to bed.

"Mrs. Bradley is going to have to watch those two or they'll be getting married before Miss Tassie turns sixteen," Clarissa noted as she brushed out her hair.

Her husband looked up from a medical book he was reading. "They are both mature young people," he countered. "I don't think they'll do anything rash."

"Nothing seems rash where love is concerned."

"Like ruining a good pair of boots jumping into a river to rescue the woman you love?"

Clarissa laughed. "Yes, like that."

She set down her brush and plaited her chestnut brown hair into a long braid, tying the end with a ribbon. She went to their small table and picked up a textbook to plan lessons for school the next day.

They sat in silence for a while, each absorbed in their books. But after a time, Clarissa noticed that Marcus had stopped reading and was staring at the door to his office, a slight frown on his face.

"What's wrong?"

Marcus sighed. "I'm worried about Chapman. He isn't getting over this last bout of fever."

"He hasn't been able to preach on Sunday for several weeks," Clarissa observed. "His cough seems to be getting worse."

"Yes," Marcus agreed. "I haven't seen anyone with as chronic a cough since . . ."

"Since Sally Edwards?"

Miss Edwards had been the mission's first seamstress who had died of the fever on the journey out to the mission site. In different ways, her death had deeply burdened both Clarissa and the doctor.

"Yes, since Sally."

"Does that mean . . .?" Clarissa left her question unspoken. The thought of losing the mission director was nearly unthinkable for her; she could only imagine how devastating it would be for Rachel. Love had compelled her to leave a life of wealth and prestige in Connecticut to follow her husband to a distant mission outpost.

"I believe his best hope to recover would be to go back East. Help me pray that I can convince him of that."

"He will not want to leave. This mission is his great love."

"I know," Marcus sighed again. "I hope he will not sacrifice his life to it."

After supper on the first Monday in December, most everyone was enjoying letters from home that Abraham and Paul had brought from Three Forks. A steamboat named the *Neosho* made a fortnightly run between Arkansas Post and Dwight Mission, bringing a regular packet of mail. The mail and other supplies were then brought to Three Forks by keelboat. Ironically, the *Neosho* itself had yet to reach the Neosho River because the falls on the Arkansas made passage difficult.

Clarissa folded the letter from her sister Jerusha and returned it to its envelope. She caught sight of Asie at the next table. The woman was also reading a letter from back East and there were tears coursing down her cheeks. Catching her husband's eye, she nodded toward the woman.

"Go talk to her," he whispered over a sleepy Thea who sat in his lap.

Clarissa was hesitant because she hardly felt qualified to offer sympathy or counsel to the still grieving woman. Though the teacher had known heartache in her life, she had never lost a child.

What words could she offer that might give comfort? Phoebe or Amanda would be better suited to the task for both had experienced the loss of a baby. She almost said so to her husband, but something stopped her. Compassion tugged at her heart.

Breathing a prayer for the right words to come, she stood and walked to the next table to take the seat beside Asie.

"Not bad news from home, I hope," she said in a quiet voice.

"No, nothing like that," Asie sniffed and then folded the letter. "My sister writes that she cannot come for a visit. She expects to be engaged soon."

"Well, that is good news then."

"I suppose," Asie sighed. "You must think me terrible not to be happy for her. But I am so homesick for my family."

"Not at all," Clarissa shook her head. "I miss my family too and wish my sister could come for a visit. It's hard to be away, especially when times are difficult."

Asie's hands were trembling as she dabbed at her eyes with a delicate lace-trimmed handkerchief and nodded in agreement.

"So tell me about your sister," Clarissa encouraged, hoping a chance to talk to a friend would help.

"Ella is two years younger than me," Asie began. "As we grew older many people thought we were twins because we look so much alike. We were always very close."

"What's her young man like?"

"I don't remember Samuel well," the minister's wife

said. "He's tall, just like my William, with dark hair and eyes." She looked across the room to where her husband sat with his Bible open on a table. He seemed to be having a deep theological discussion with Mr. Redfield. Asie smiled, "I guess Ella and I are attracted to the same looks."

"Is he in a profession?"

"He works for his father, I think. They have an import business with warehouses in Fairfield and New Haven. Samuel works in the counting house, keeping the books. But my mother doesn't seem to approve of him. She thinks he is spoiled and careless with money."

"Mothers are always protective of their daughters," Clarissa observed, glad to see that the conversation had helped Asie. Her tears had stopped and her face was more animated.

"I think Mother would be happy for Ella to come out here for a long visit. She would like to separate them and give Ella a chance to meet someone else. But," Asie sighed, "we have married all the young men out here."

"But there's a whole fort of young men not far from here," Clarissa countered. "And many seem eager to make a match."

The proof of that stood across the room at the fireplace. Charles Summers had ridden up from Cantonment Gibson with Abraham and Paul this morning. He had spent the afternoon in Eliza's company and they had just come inside from a walk around the mission compound following supper. Alice insisted that the two always remain in sight of the dining hall.

Eliza's cheeks were bright from the cool evening air and she held her hands to the fireplace to warm them. The young woman stood at a distance from her suitor making it clear that she was still uncommitted to a relationship with the brown-haired lieutenant.

He was in a conversation with several of the men, including Marcus, and Clarissa was interested in what was being said. The isolation of the mission made visitors and the news they brought always welcome.

"I think I'll rejoin my husband, with your leave," Clarissa said to Asie. "Won't you come too? There's room at the table."

"No, you go ahead," Asie replied. "I think I'll retire for the evening."

"Well, good night then."

The two women stood and went their separate ways. Asie collected her children and they all left the dining hall. Clarissa took her seat again beside Marcus and eased the sleeping Thea into her lap. Lucie was playing in the corner of the room with the other girls. Their corn husk dolls were having tea in tiny acorn cups.

"So a military road is a reality?" John Spaulding was asking Charles. "I thought when Colonel Nicks mentioned it last month that it was all speculation."

"It is to some degree," the lieutenant agreed. "But Colonel Arbuckle is eager to see it become a reality. It's difficult to move men and supplies from Fort Smith. It takes far too long for dispatches to reach us out here. If war should break out with England again, we'd be the last to know!"

Everyone chuckled at his joke. It was a well-known fact the famous Battle of New Orleans was fought after the last war with England had officially ended.

"And it will be a while before you know who your new commander-in-chief will be," George Requa added.

"Exactly," Summers agreed. "Seems odd to know that an election is being held back East and we have no opportunity to vote out here."

"Who will win, do you think?" Stephen asked this question.

"Hard to say," the soldier replied. "Jackson has solid southern support, but Quincy Adams will sweep New England for sure."

"Who would you and the colonel want to have as commander?" Marcus asked.

"A soldier follows whoever is in charge." Summers gave the diplomatic answer and the missionaries did not press him on it.

"Will the military road be built soon?" John brought the conversation back around.

"The legislature hasn't appropriated funding yet. And the route will have to be surveyed. It will likely take two to three years to see it completed."

"Well, at least river traffic is improving. We get mail so regular now, we feel almost civilized," Abraham quipped. "The landing at Dwight Mission must get a great deal of traffic, I would think."

"Yes, and the town of Dardanelle is growing," Charles agreed. "But we just heard from Fort Smith that Walter Webber lost his trading post there to a fire. Colonel Nicks expects him eventually to move into Lovely County. Arkansas authorities are nudging the Cherokees this way."

Clarissa felt concern about this remark. Walter Webber was a sworn enemy of the Osage warrior Mad Buffalo and conflict had arisen between the two tribal leaders in the past. Webber was widely believed to be responsible for the death of Joseph Revoir, Teresa's first husband. Mad Buffalo had long sought to avenge his friend's death. Would Webber's presence in the neighborhood stir up old tensions?

She could tell that the thought was on everyone's mind. Frequent conflicts between the Osages and Cherokees were the primary reason Matthew Arbuckle had removed the Seventh Infantry from Fort Smith and brought these troops to Cantonment Gibson. Arbuckle would face a new challenge if the Cherokees took possession of Lovely County.

The conversation was interrupted with a sudden burst of coughing by Rev. Chapman. The concern of the missionaries immediately turned to the mission director. Marcus stood and hurried over to the man's side. He had sat through supper wrapped in a quilt and eating very little. He was losing weight and strength with each passing day. He was pale from having been abed for weeks and his light brown beard and hair needed to be trimmed.

Marcus leaned over the minister and felt his forehead to gauge the man's fever. Another spasm of coughing racked his body. He gasped for air.

"Is there any coffee left, Mrs. Fuller?" Marcus asked the cook.

Amanda nodded and hurried into the kitchen, returning a few moments later with a steaming mug.

"Drink this slowly." The doctor held the cup for Chapman. "The heat will relax your diaphragm."

The minister managed a few small sips and his breathing seemed to come easier.

"Are you ready to retire to your cabin?"

Chapman nodded. Rachel started to rise from beside him, but he held up his hand to stop her.

"Stay," he breathed in a tight whisper. "You need a break from that dark cabin."

Rachel reluctantly settled back in her chair. She sent a look to the doctor that clearly said, "Come get me if I am needed."

At the children's table, Thomas Chapman paused in a game of checkers with Bearpaw to watch the doctor's efforts to help his father. Marcus motioned for the boy to come to him. Thomas jumped up and hurried across the room.

Clarissa was struck with the noticeable changes that had come to Thomas just in the last few months. He had added two or three inches in height and his voice was deepening. He was transitioning to manhood. His father's illness seemed to have hastened his maturity.

"Help me get your father to your cabin," Marcus said in a quiet voice.

Each of them took one of Chapman's arms and helped him stand. His weakness was apparent to everyone and the minister seemed embarrassed by it.

"I'm not an invalid yet," he coughed, but his slow steps toward the door said otherwise. Thomas hurried to open it, then the three of them stepped out into the early evening darkness.

Clarissa glanced at Rachel and saw the stricken look on her face as she watched the man she dearly loved struggle with the simple task of walking across the room. Then the teacher checked on the girls at their play in the far corner of the room near the fireplace. Abigail's face, so like her mother's, wore the same look.

No one in the room spoke for a few moments as they all seemed to realize what Dr. Palmer had long known. The mission director was not likely to recover from this menacing fever and against everyone's advice he was not likely to abandon the work he loved.

The Chapmans' cabin sat in the middle of the long row of cabins that shared a common roof. Marcus helped the minister settle in bed while Thomas lit a candle in the lantern on the table nearby.

"Thank you, son," the minister wheezed. "Will you stay with your mother and help her when she's ready to retire?"

"Yes, Papa," the boy said, his voice sounding choked with tightly held tears. "If you don't need me for anything."

"No, not right now. Your mother will need you."

Thomas nodded and then left the cabin.

Marcus pulled a chair from the table and brought it close to Chapman's bed. Almost without thought he grasped the dying man's wrist to check the weak and thready pulse. What more could he do for the minister?

Sending up a prayer for wisdom, he tried again to convince Chapman to travel back East.

"You need better care than I can give you," he began. "Please reconsider returning to New England. You need to be away from this climate and whatever is causing the fever."

"I could find no better care than yours, Palmer," the minister said. "And you and I both know that I cannot leave."

He paused to gather another breath. "I wouldn't survive a journey home in this cold. If I am to die, I prefer to die here surrounded by all of you, my family."

Marcus was silent, unable to speak for a moment as he tried to bring his emotions under control.

"Perhaps you might find respite in New Orleans," he said at last.

"I will not . . . leave." Coughs racked the man's body for a time. When they subsided, he continued. "How many sermons have I preached here and at Hopefield about being willing to sacrifice all for the work of the Lord? If I am not willing to do that myself, I am a hypocrite."

"No one would think ill of you for trying to get better."

"God will either heal me here, or heal me in death," the minister said, his voice suddenly clear and strong. "I rest in his hands."

Marcus nodded, knowing there was nothing he could say to change Chapman's mind. "I will leave you to rest then," he said. Giving the minister's shoulder a squeeze, he stood and returned the chair to its place. Then he quietly shut the cabin door behind him.

Not in the mood to return to the cheery light of the dining hall, he walked in silence under a cold, starless sky to his own cabin. Once again he felt like a failure.

CHAPTER SEVEN

Fairfield, Connecticut
December 1824

Ella Selden let her suitor Samuel Douglas wrap her navy velvet cape around her shoulders as they prepared to leave her parents' home for an evening out.

"I hope you don't mind a simple carriage ride for the evening's entertainment," the young man said as he helped Ella into the smart, black phaeton that belonged to his father. "I'm a bit short of funds at the moment."

"Oh, of course not," Ella agreed as Samuel sat beside her and pulled up a thick wool lap robe to cover them. "The snow is quite pretty in the moonlight." She gave him a smile, but it seemed a bit forced.

Samuel released the carriage brake and gave a light flick of the reins to start the horse on a slow walk along the streets of the New England town. Beside the pale moon's glow, lamps set in windows cast bright squares of light onto the snow making it glisten. The two rode in silence for a time.

Samuel seemed deep in unhappy thought with a slight scowl marring his handsome features. Ella kept glancing at him as if wondering how to break the awkward quiet.

"I hope nothing is wrong," she finally said in a timid voice. "I mean . . . with your . . . finances."

He gave her such a sharp look that she bit her lip and her cheeks reddened.

"No, no, nothing of the sort," he assured her, though he now kept his eyes roaming over the scenery and would not look at her face.

She remained silent.

"It's just . . ." he began. "Well, you see, we have a client whose ship has been delayed in arriving. So we haven't been paid for his warehouse storage yet. I told father to go ahead and pay the married men their wages and I would wait for mine." The last words came all out in a rush, but then he nodded as if satisfied with his explanation. "It being nearly Christmas and all," he finished.

"That was very thoughtful of you, Samuel."

"Yes. I suppose." He still would not look at her and his words seemed angry.

Ella cast about in her mind for something else to say, but she felt a reluctance to make trivial conversation in the midst of her suitor's dark mood.

They completed a pass through the business district and had just turned around to head back when a fellow hailed them from the door of a tavern.

"Hello, Douglas," he called. "Stroke of luck seeing you just now. We need a fourth at our table." He nodded his head toward the sound of laughter coming from the building.

Samuel brought the carriage to a halt and paused for a long moment.

"Can't tonight, Rawlings," he finally said. "You know why."

"I can stake you to get you started," Rawlings offered. "Give you a chance to get it back."

Again, Samuel hesitated for a long moment as if strongly drawn to the offer.

"Sorry, Rawlings. I must see Miss Selden home. It's getting cold out." Then he turned to Ella as if he was just remembering that she rode in the carriage beside him. "Are you cold?"

"Yes," she replied. "I'm feeling very cold."

"Another time, Rawlings." Samuel nodded curtly and then flicked the reins to start the horse again.

As they moved into her parents' quiet neighborhood, Ella worked up her courage to ask, "Who was that man? I've never seen him before."

"Just an old school chum," Samuel shrugged. "No one you would ever know."

Ella didn't like his tone and almost told him so. But she didn't want to completely ruin the evening. She might be able to persuade him to come in for a cup of tea. She always kept his father's imported brand in the kitchen.

But when she made the offer as Samuel helped her down from the carriage, he declined. "Father will need me early at the office in the morning. Better not be out late."

It was hardly late, but Ella was surprised that she didn't feel terribly disappointed that Samuel wasn't going to stay. "Well, goodnight then. Thank you for the ride."

"Good night." Samuel didn't even try to steal a kiss as he had been inclined to do the last few times they had said goodbye. His lips barely grazed the knuckles of her gloved hand before he was hurrying down the brick walkway toward the carriage.

Ella closed the door behind him, sorry to have him go, yet not sorry to end the awkward evening. As she drew off her cape, she felt an odd sense of fear that she couldn't quite understand.

A few days later at Union Mission, Clarissa settled her class of girls into their chairs after they had worked all afternoon on their memorized pieces for the Christmas program. The *Arkansas Gazette* had run a new poem that was apparently quite popular back East and she thought it would be entertaining to read it to her students.

"'Twas the night before Christmas,

"And all through the house . . ." it began.

Clarissa was half way through the visit of jolly old St. Nicholas when she glanced up from the newspaper to look at the class. The girls' faces were bright with pleasure as they enjoyed the poem. All were smiling broadly except Abigail.

The eleven-year-old girl sat completely still, her hands clasped in front of her as if in prayer. She was looking at the chalkboard on the wall behind the teacher, but her eyes were not seeing the penmanship examples Clarissa had written there. A tear drifted from one eye and coursed silently down her face.

Clarissa looked back to the poem, not wanting to draw attention to her student's distress. She finished the reading to the delightful sighs of her class of girls.

Folding the newspaper, she stood and announced. "That will complete our class for today, girls. You may go to the dining hall for some of Mrs. Fuller's pecan treats. Beth and Marie, will you take charge of the class for me?"

"Yes, Mrs. Palmer."

"Abigail, will you stay and help me clean the blackboard?"

The girl looked up at her teacher, startled from her reverie. She nodded and quickly swiped away her tears. The other girls donned their coats and shawls for the walk to the dining hall. The room was quickly emptied and the girls were joined by the boys from Mr. Spaulding's class.

While Abigail slowly erased the board, Clarissa stood at the classroom door, watching to make sure all the students made it to the dining room. Then she closed the door against the cold and walked across the room to lay a hand on Abigail's shoulder.

"You seem sad today, dear." The teacher's voice was gentle. "Would you like to talk about what is making you sad?"

Abigail sighed as she set the felt eraser on the chalk tray. "Papa isn't getting better," she said with a tremor in her voice.

Clarissa had felt certain that this was what troubled the girl. "I know," she said with a sigh of her own. "The fever has made him very sick."

"He's going to die, isn't he?"

Clarissa felt her own eyes fill with tears. She wanted to offer the girl hope, to give her assurances that everything would be alright. But she knew it might be a false hope.

She sat in the chair at her desk and drew the girl to snuggle in beside her. "We are all praying very hard for your papa."

"I know. But we prayed for Moses too, and he died."

Abigail and Leah had doted on the little Osage boy adopted by the Chapmans until he had died of the fever. Clarissa herself had almost died from the mysterious disease as well. None of them was immune to its ravages.

"We don't always understand why our prayers aren't answered as we would like. Saying goodbye to someone we love is one of the hardest things we must do in this world. But your papa is very brave and he would want you to be as well."

"Yes, that is what he says. Be brave for Mother." The girl leaned her head against her teacher's shoulder. "I am trying to be. But I am afraid Mama will die too."

"Oh, Abigail," Clarissa quickly responded. "Your mother is the strongest and bravest woman I know. She loves you very much and she would fight very hard to never leave you. That's the way it is with mothers."

"She loves Papa very much too. It will break her heart if he dies."

The teacher understood the girl's fear. Rachel had loved her husband all the way to this distant outpost; had given up everything to follow his dream. How would she take his death, should it come?

"We will pray for your mother, you and I," Clarissa proposed. "And we will be strong for her together. That is the best thing we can do for her."

"Thank you, Teacher."

"You're welcome, little love."

Clarissa drew the girl into an embrace and they sat together in the companionship of sorrow and tears while the shadows gathered around them.

Christmas was a subdued celebration at Union Mission. Everyone from Hopefield came down to share a meal after a morning worship service and the students' program. The children enjoyed the gifts found in their stockings, but for the adults the day was somber with unspoken worry and uplifted prayer.

Cloud-scudded skies filled the days that followed the holiday with a dreariness that seemed to seep into everyone's spirit. Marcus spent much time with Rev. Chapman, but he reported no improvement each evening when the mission family gathered for supper. The whole Chapman family rarely left their cabin during the winter break as they kept their sorrowful vigil.

On the morning that school was to resume, Abigail helped James and Leah pull on their coats and knitted caps to walk to the dining room for breakfast before going on to school. Thomas hung back as if sensing the request that soon came from his father. The minister lay in his bed, emaciated and wan.

"Stay a moment, Thomas," Chapman said after the younger children had given him a kiss goodbye.

The young man exchanged a look with his mother as Rachel also pulled on her coat. She gave him a nod and patted his shoulder before joining the children outside.

Thomas took the seat by the minister's bedside.

"I have hung on as long as I can, son," the minister breathed softly. "It's time for me to go. I want you to know how proud of you I am. You'll be the man of the family soon and I know you will do well."

The boy could not hold back his tears. "I don't want you to go, Papa."

"I knew when I started this mission that I would give my life to it," his father said. "I had hoped to see all of you grown, but that was not what God had planned for me."

"God could heal you if he wanted to."

"Yes, and he will. I will walk through the heavenly gates totally healed and free of this fever." The man had to pause to gather his breath. "I'll be waiting for you there, Thomas. Live your life in such a way that you will join me there."

"I will, Papa." Thomas dashed away the tears on his cheeks.

"You'll go back East for your schooling this fall. Your grandparents will get you into a good school. I want you to apply yourself and continue to make us all proud of you."

"Yes, Papa."

"I love you, son."

Thomas could only nod for his throat seemed choked with tears.

"Watch out for your mother and your brother and sisters." The minister's words were halted by a coughing fit. Thomas held his hand tightly through it.

"You best go now, Thomas. Don't want you . . . late for school."

"I can stay, Papa," the boy declared.

There was a light knock at the door just then and the doctor stepped inside the cabin.

"Dr. Palmer will stay with me. You go on now, son."

Thomas nodded again and stood. "I love you, Papa," he managed to say before turning and bolting from the shrouded room.

The thirteen-year-old young man did not follow the well-worn path to the dining hall or walk past it toward the school. Instead he sought the solace of the warm barn filled with a menagerie of animals and the earthy smells of manure, corn and hay.

He made his way down the row of stalls where their oxen stood calmly chewing their cud and their two milk cows enjoyed their morning oats. Going to the stall of the big black mustang Thunder, he stepped inside.

Normally the high-spirited stallion was skittish when anyone entered his stall. But as Thomas threw his arms around the horse's neck and buried his face in the thick mane, the animal stood perfectly still. Thunder nickered softly as if trying to offer comfort.

A slat of light briefly fell upon the scene as Paul opened the barn door and stepped inside. He was returning the milk pails after having emptied them in the creamer in the kitchen.

Paul stood quietly at the door, seeming uncertain of whether he should slip back outside or try to offer his own comfort to the grieving boy. Finally, he walked toward Thunder's stall, creating enough noise with his feet to make Thomas aware of his approach.

He reached into the open stall and laid his hand, black and strong like Thunder, on the boy's shoulder.

Thomas lifted his head to look at the hired man and seemed embarrassed by his tears.

"Ain't no shame in crying about it," Paul assured him quietly. "I knows how you feel. Lost my pa when I was about your age. My ma too."

A light of sympathy came into Thomas' red-rimmed eyes. "Life isn't fair." His voice held bitterness and grief.

"No, it ain't," Paul agreed. "And sometimes you don't how you can stand it." He tightened his grip on Thomas' shoulder. "But God sees us through. He sees us through."

Later that afternoon, Dr. Palmer left the Chapman's cabin and walked with grim purpose toward the dining hall. He knew Rev. Vaille would be studying for his sermon at a table by the fire, enjoying a cup of coffee on this cold January day.

He stepped inside and paused for a moment, appreciating the warmth that radiated from the large fireplace. He noted that Mrs. Vaille was also in the room, working with Sarah Requa on a sewing project.

Marcus strode across the floor and quietly pulled out a chair to sit by the pastor. Before he could unbutton his wool coat, Amanda stepped out of the kitchen and offered him a steaming cup.

"Thank you, Mrs. Fuller," Marcus said, enjoying a sip of the strong coffee.

"How is Chapman?" William asked.

"Very low, I'm afraid." Marcus stared into his cup. "I think he and Mrs. Chapman will need you this afternoon. I don't expect him to live through the night."

The minister nodded and sighed. "We both knew the risks when we came out here. We talked about it often. But I never thought the cost would be so great."

"Nor did I. Though I understood the risk as well. We all did, and we all came anyway."

"And now Chapman will lead us in the next journey."

"Yes, without a miracle, he will."

Vaille closed his Bible and reached for his outer coat hanging on the back of his chair. He stood and pulled it on, then took his Bible and walked over to speak to his wife.

"Asie, would you join me in a visit with the Chapmans?"

The blonde glanced up from her sewing and a look of understanding and then fear passed over her face. She shook her head at first. "I don't know if I can," she whispered.

"Mrs. Chapman was there for you, Asenath," William said quietly, but with firmness in his tone. "She needs you now."

Sarah reached over and rubbed her hand on the woman's arm in a gesture of comfort and encouragement.

"Yes," Asie said, drawing in a deep breath. She passed her sewing over to the expectant mother and then also rose to join her husband in the pastoral duty.

"Will you watch Joey?" she asked Sarah.

The seamstress nodded. "And I'll be praying. Don't you worry about Joey; he'll be fine with me. Won't you, little man?" She smiled at the boy who was galloping a wooden horse across the imaginary prairie of the tabletop.

William helped Asie with her coat and the two left the dining room. Amanda and Martha joined Dr. Palmer at his table, speaking in low sympathetic tones.

In the Chapmans' cabin, Rachel sat on his bed and helped her husband take a sip of water from the enamel cup she held. Careful to prevent him from coughing, she put the cup back on the nearby table after he had taken a few sips.

"Forgive me, Rachel," he rasped.

"For what, dear?"

"For bringing you and the children out here. I should have listened to your mother."

"That is my father's job," Rachel said, trying to smile. "And he does it so well that no one else is obliged to do it." She stroked his arm tenderly.

Her attempt at humor worked for it brought a smile to the dying man's face. "Oh, Rachel, you are my treasure. I never deserved you."

"Amanda is fond of saying that none of us deserve love; it is always a gift. And I give mine to you freely."

"And you have had mine since the moment I first laid eyes on you."

The couple held hands in silence for several moments.

"I know that heaven will be wonderful, but even so I think that I shall miss you there."

"Keep an eye on the gate; I'll join you someday."

"Knowing that gives me my greatest peace." The minister's breathing was becoming labored.

"For me too." Rachel leaned down and kissed him. "Sleep now."

He nodded and closed his eyes.

A knock came at the door and Rev. Vaille opened it carefully. "May we come in?"

"Yes," Rachel said, a sob catching in her throat.

The pastors entered and came to Chapman's bedside where Rachel stood. Joining hands with her, William and Asie prayed a simple prayer for comfort. The mission director had taken his last journey. Asie gathered her friend into her arms and Rachel finally cried.

The funeral for the mission director brought the largest crowd that Union had ever witnessed. The service could not be held in the small chapel so the tables were removed from the dining hall and every available chair was set up.

Most everyone in the neighborhood came to pay their respects. Chief Claremont was even in attendance, though the venerable Osage leader did not look well himself. He leaned heavily on the arm of his son Mad Buffalo.

Several others came from Three Forks and Gibson including Colonel Arbuckle, Charles Summers, Sarah's uncle Hugh Glenn, Captain Pryor, Colonel Chouteau and John and Sallie Nicks. All of the residents at Hopefield made the five-mile trip as well.

Clarissa and Phoebe kept the younger children in the boys' classroom, allowing Mr. Spaulding to lead the hymns for the service. The sound of the songs drifted toward the school. The mournful notes made it hard for Clarissa to hold back her tears as she thought of Abigail and Leah who had joined their mother and brothers on the front row of seats in the hall.

Thea, who had just turned three, must have sensed her mother's sorrow for she climbed into the teacher's lap and patted her shoulder in sympathy. "Don't cry, Mama."

Clarissa blinked back her tears and hugged the girl close. "I'm alright, baby," she assured her daughter. "Don't fret about me."

Then looking around the room at all the children she said, "Why don't we sing the hymns too? You all know them."

With just a moment's hesitation, the children began to sing just as they often did when they "played church." Clarissa marveled at the capacity of the children to know from memory every word of the lovely songs.

After the singing ended, Clarissa had the children gather around her on the plank floor. She planned to read a story to them, but before she could begin, Marie Lombard's younger brother raised his hand.

"Yes, Antoine?"

"Can I read it to ze children?"

The boy was only seven and Clarissa thought the story she had chosen would be too difficult for him. Before she could gently deny his request, he was standing at her side, eagerly reaching for the book.

"Well, I suppose you can try," she allowed. "I'll help you with the words."

But Antoine needed little assistance. Clarissa remembered that Mr. Spaulding had called Antoine a "reading machine." Now she understood that his voracious appetite for books meant he was reading far above his grade level. His French-Osage accent on the words made the children giggle at times, but he read the story with a skill she hadn't expected.

Following the story, a knock came at the door and Amanda and Sarah stepped inside. "I've brought some cornbread and cracklin's to tide the children over," the red-haired cook said. "And we'll spell you, Mrs. Palmer, if you'd like to walk with the others to the gravesite. Everyone's gettin' their coats on now."

"Thank you, Amanda," Clarissa said, rising from her chair. "I would like to pay my respects."

She hurried to pull on her new brown cape and a pair of gloves. With a quick goodbye, she hurried to join Marcus as the funeral procession made its way to the cemetery on the hill.

The group of mourners who had chosen to gather at the grave huddled close together against the cold wind. Rev. Vaille kept his remarks brief and seemed to choke with emotion as he read from Psalm 96, one of Chapman's favorites.

Clarissa clung to her husband's arm, trying to draw enough warmth from him to keep from shivering. When the men of the mission lowered the simple pine coffin into the prairie sod, the teacher felt a small hand slip into her free one. She looked down to find Leah seeking solace from her beloved teacher. The girl's freckled face was blotched and red from too many tears shed through this difficult morning.

Clarissa squeezed her hand and gave her a sympathetic smile. After Rev. Montgomery offered a prayer, the crowd made their way back to the mission for a meal in the warm dining hall. Clarissa pulled the girl close to her and slipped her arm around her shoulder as they walked together.

Ahead of them, Thomas did the same for his mother and Clarissa noticed that the young man was almost as tall as Rachel. It was a hard role that he now took on, but Thomas had always been a mature lad, strong like both his parents. The teacher knew that Thomas would take his responsibility seriously.

At the dining hall, everyone slipped out of their wraps and gathered near the fireplace to thaw from the cold. Phoebe brought the children over and Amanda, with the help of Martha, Susan and Eliza, began the final preparations for the noon meal.

George and his brother Will, with Paul, Abraham and Mr. Woodruff, brought the tables back into the hall and set plenty of chairs around them. Most of their guests from Claremont's Town and Three Forks had already left to return home, but the Nickses, and the missionaries from Hopefield remained and would spend the night.

Clarissa helped Lucie and Thea out of their coats and settled them at the children's table. Then she stepped over to the fireplace where Rachel stood with Asie and Sallie Nicks. She gave Mrs. Chapman a hug of sympathy and the new widow seemed to cling to her for a bit.

"Thank you for helping Leah," she whispered. "And Abigail too."

"I was happy to," Clarissa responded. "If they would like to spend the night with us, we'll make room. Marie and Louisa would be happy to share a bed as would Deer-in-Water and Masina."

These girls were boarding with the Palmers during the cold months. It made their home "the giggle factory," as Marcus said. "The girls would cheer them, I think," Clarissa finished.

"I'll see if they want to," Rachel said. "But they seem reluctant to let me out of their sight right now."

"I understand. Just know that we would be glad to have them."

"Thank you."

Sallie was about to join her husband at a table, when Rachel stopped her. "Sallie, would you have some black wool at the mercantile? I'm going to have Sarah sew a few mourning pieces for us."

Yes, I think we have some," the sutler's wife said. "I'll send the full bolt up here by the next person coming this way. Use whatever you need."

"Do you also know how I might get a monument made for the grave?" Rachel asked. "I want his sacrifice remembered."

"I think there's a cutter in Fort Smith," Sallie answered. "But getting it here will be expensive."

"I don't care about the expense."

"Then write out what you want on the stone and I'll ask

John to place the order the next time he travels back that way."

"Thank you."

Amanda stepped in the room from the kitchen to announce that the food had been spread on the long work table in the kitchen. They would serve buffet style after Abraham offered a blessing over the food.

Conversations were quiet during the meal and everyone seemed reluctant to leave the dining room even after enjoying Amanda's canned peach pies. The mission seemed very different now with Chapman's indomitable presence gone. It would take some time for all of them to adjust to their altered world.

CHAPTER EIGHT

Union Mission
February 1825

A few weeks later, Clarissa and Marcus were tucking their girls into bed after they had shared their nighttime prayers. A knock sounded on the door, a sharp rapping that gave a sense of urgency.

"Someone needs you, doctor," Clarissa whispered to her husband so as not to raise concern among the sleepy girls. He clambered down the narrow stairs while Clarissa continued to tuck each girl in against the cold night air. Then she also made her way downstairs.

George stood at the door looking harried and disheveled, his shirttail crookedly hanging outside his pants. The hat he had slapped on his head also sat at an odd angle.

"Doc, we need you," the mechanic said without preamble. "Sarah says it's time."

Marcus put a steadying hand on George's shoulder. "I'll come," he assured the new father, "but have you gone for Mrs. Woodruff also?"

"Oh, I guess I should have." George rubbed his forehead as if hoping to massage his thoughts. "I'm not even thinking."

"Most women prefer another woman at a birthing," Marcus reminded him. "You go for the midwife and I will get my bag and meet you at your cabin."

George nodded and turned to sprint across the mission yard to the Woodruffs' cabin in the center of the longhouse.

"Poor, man," Clarissa said with a sympathetic smile. "I've never seen George so befuddled."

"Nor have I," Marcus agreed as he reached for his coat hanging on a peg by the door. "He's usually dead calm. That's why he's such a good shot when hunting."

Marcus reached for his medical kit and opened it to check the contents. "I think my duties for this evening will be to administer reassurance to one very nervous father."

"I'll put on some coffee." Clarissa gave him a quick kiss as he stepped out into the cold.

Marcus reached the porch of the Requas' home just as George and Martha emerged from her cabin. He waited for them to arrive. Martha carried a washtub filled with her own medical supplies.

"I'll let you assess things first," Marcus told the motherly woman. "If you feel I'm needed, let me know. Otherwise, I will wait with George in the kitchen."

"I checked her this morning," Martha said. "She was already in early labor. The baby was turned and kicking well." She also laid a reassuring hand on George's arm. "I don't expect any problems," she told him.

George blew out a relieved breath. "But you'll let me know if I need to do something?"

Martha smiled. "You'll be needed afterwards to help raise this little one."

Another deep breath came from George. "Yeah," he nodded, with a look that was a mixture of awe and fear at the responsibility he was about to undertake.

Martha stepped into the cabin and the two men each took a porch post to lean on with hands thrust deeply into their pockets to keep them warm. The midwife emerged shortly and confirmed her previous assessment. "The baby's already crowning. This isn't going to take long. You two go on and I'll come for you when your baby has arrived."

Marcus slipped an arm around his brother's shoulders and drew him toward the kitchen. Mrs. Fuller always left a few live coals banked in the massive fireplace so it was relatively warm when they stepped inside.

Marcus took a seat and unbuttoned his coat, knowing that it might be a long evening, despite the midwife's assurances. George, however, proceeded to pace between the kitchen window that faced toward his house and the fireplace. He added a few sticks of kindling and would poke at the coals each time he paused at the mantle.

The doctor watched in sympathetic amusement. He had kept vigil with most of the married men here at the mission as their wives gave birth. But now that he was married himself, he thought he understood a little better the anxiety the men felt.

Shortly, Clarissa stepped into the kitchen carrying a coffeepot. She set it on the work table on a dish towel, then pulled two mugs from the cupboard.

"How are things?" she asked quietly as she poured the coffee.

"Mrs. Woodruff seemed to feel it would be a quick and easy delivery."

Clarissa smiled at her husband's words. "I think quick and easy are words used only by those not giving birth."

George groaned a bit as he stared out the window and Clarissa immediately regretted her remark.

She crossed over to him and patted the mechanic on the shoulder. "I know they'll be fine," she assured him, "but I'll be praying just the same."

She looked back at Marcus who sipped the hot coffee. "I'd better get back to the girls."

He nodded and she stepped outside.

"Come sit down, Requa," the doctor said. "Wrap your hands around this mug and warm them up. You don't want to hold your new baby with cold hands."

George turned away from the window and suddenly grinned. The doctor had given him a useful occupation, one of hope and calm assurance. He gripped the cup of coffee with determination.

It seemed like half the night had slipped away before Martha came to the kitchen. She stepped inside with a smile on her face.

George jumped up immediately. "Is Sarah alright?" he blurted out. "Is it a Lizette or a Henry?"

A slight look of confusion passed over the midwife's face, but she quickly understood the question. "Your wife is fine, just a little tired. And you have a beautiful daughter. Miss Lizette is waiting to meet her father."

George wasted no time bolting out the door.

Marcus pushed the coffee pot toward the woman who looked tired herself. "I'll get you a cup," he offered as he stood and went to the cupboard. Many a night of birthing vigils had made him familiar with the kitchen. "You are to be congratulated yourself, Mrs. Woodruff. Another life welcomed into the world."

Martha sat down and removed her mittens. "It is satisfying work," she agreed. "Perhaps a birth of your own will be forthcoming."

A look of sadness passed over the doctor's face as he poured the coffee. "It is likely there will be no births for us," he said quietly, resuming his chair. "Clarissa suffered a bad fall as a girl. She was told she might not be able to have children."

"I'm sorry. I didn't know."

Marcus seemed to shake himself from the sorrow. "God has entrusted us with two beautiful daughters. Our home is filled . . . filled with laughter and love. I am a blessed man."

"Still," Martha countered. "Most men want a son."

The doctor shrugged. "Who knows what the future holds. God works in ways we don't always understand. I didn't expect to have two daughters within six months of our wedding." The smile of pride on his face said he truly did feel blessed.

Lizette Requa was introduced to the mission family the following Sunday and they all admired her fuzz of dark brown curls so like her mother's. The little girl didn't cry, but continually made sweet baby mews as her dark eyes surveyed all the women who passed her around to be nuzzled and kissed.

Amanda observed with a wink, "She'll be a talker like her mother."

George looked even more proud than he had after taking down a twelve-point buck while hunting last fall. It was clear he was in love with his little girl.

Though the weather had warmed considerably since the night of her birth, Lizette's parents didn't keep her out long. They returned to their cabin after Rev. Vaille offered a prayer of blessing over the new little family.

On Monday, the rattle of a heavy wagon over the hard, dry ruts on the turnoff from the Texas Road announced they had a visitor. The mulewhacker, Jose Ramirez, was guiding his animals toward the mission. Behind the wagon, three men on horseback followed.

Clarissa had just dismissed her class and she and Marie Lombard tidied the room while the other girls walked to the dining hall, ignoring the boys who romped behind them.

News of the visitors quickly circulated among the missionaries who worked at various tasks around the compound. Soon they were all gathering at the corral where Mr. Ramirez halted his mules.

In the wagon, resting within a nest of straw, was the large tombstone Mrs. Chapman had ordered from Fort Smith. She brought her black trimmed handkerchief to her mouth when she saw it as if a fresh wave of grief had poured over her.

The riders who accompanied the wagon were Colonel Arbuckle, Charles Summers and Dwight Mission's director, Cephas Washburn. Mrs. Chapman had sent a note with Colonel Nicks, asking Rev. Washburn to oversee the transport of the stone. Dwight Mission sat on the Arkansas River near the town of Dardanelle, but within a day's ride of Fort Smith.

The minister dismounted his horse and handed the reins to Paul. He walked toward Rachel and took her hands, offering his sympathy for the death of her husband.

"We were so saddened to hear of Chapman's passing," he said quietly. "He and I had many long conversations about starting the missions out here. He was the most enthusiastic and determined servant of Christ that I have ever known."

Rachel nodded her thanks. "He gave his life for what he loved."

The two officers from Cantonment Gibson had also dismounted and were greeted with handshakes by the men of the mission. Clarissa joined the women in hurrying to prepare refreshments for their visitors.

"Join us, Jose," Vaille offered. The drayman grinned behind his bushy mustache and wrapped his reins around the wagon brake. He hopped down from the seat, then brushed the trail dust off his clothes. Everyone made their way to the dining hall.

When the men had been seated with their guests, Amanda and her helpers brought out coffee and scrambled eggs, ham slices, cold cornbread and a crock of her wild strawberry preserves. The students ate at their table before being dismissed by Mr. Spaulding. They raced to the barn, a favorite spot to play during the winter months.

"What brings you our way, Colonel?" Rev. Vaille asked the fort commander.

"Mostly paying a neighborly call," the officer responded. "I want to keep an eye on conditions under the fort's purview. You've not had any troubles have you?"

"No, it's been quiet this winter. We rarely see the Osages, except for those living at Hopefield. The cold seems to be keeping everyone close to their fires."

"I'm hearing reports from trappers coming in from the mountains," the colonel said after looking around to be sure all the older children were out of the room. "They tell me the Pawnees are beating war drums. They know the Osages are to be moved. It seems they want us to know they won't tolerate them in their hunting areas."

"Do you expect us to have trouble from the Pawnees?" Mr. Spaulding asked.

"Hard to say. We don't have a treaty with the Pawnees . . . or any of the Plains tribes. They can act with impunity."

"There are some shifts in Indian policy taking place in Washington," Summers added. Though he addressed the group, he couldn't seem to resist glancing at Eliza. "Even though Jackson didn't get the Presidency, his idea about removing the Indians from the east to a location out here is quite popular. So much so that President-elect Adams will likely adopt it as well."

"That is going to impact the Osages, Pawnees, Comanches . . . ." Abraham's voice trailed off from listing any number of western tribes.

"Exactly," Arbuckle said, "The new Indian Commissioner Richard Graham has advised the Secretary of War that if the Osages are to be moved, this mission will need to move as well."

Rev. Vaille looked dismayed. "We have spent a great deal of time, effort and money building this mission. Will the government reimburse us if we are forced to move?"

"You can request reimbursement."

"And expect to see it about ten years later," Washburn joked. A murmur of uneasy laughter spread among the group.

"What are we to do, Colonel?" Marcus asked then.

"I think for the moment you will not be required to do anything. But keep in close contact with your mission board. Summers and I will keep a watch over the regular dispatches and alert you of any policy decisions. For now that's about all I can advise."

The colonel took a sip of his coffee and then went on. "I've asked the Osage leaders to come to Gibson for a powwow at the Planting Moon. Their agent will present the new treaty terms. You might want to attend the meeting."

"We will, Colonel," Vaille nodded. "Thank you for including us."

When this conversation ended, the guests were shown to the empty cabin in the longhouse where they would spend the night. Charles wasted no time storing his saddle gear and then returning to the dining hall.

He made a pretense of helping himself to another cup of coffee while waiting for Eliza to hand a sleeping Thea to Mrs. Palmer. Then he approached the two women.

"Might we take a turn around the mission grounds, Miss Eliza?" he asked the pretty blonde. "The day is nice."

Clarissa and Eliza exchanged a look and the teacher gave the girl a firm nod.

Eliza smiled her acceptance of the invitation and a light came into the officer's hazel eyes. It was clear to Clarissa that he was very smitten with her former roommate.

Charles helped Eliza into her coat and the two began a stroll around the mission yard. Clarissa threw Thea's coat around her to carry her to their cabin. In the kitchen the rattle of dishes and murmur of voices told her supper preparations were underway.

The young couple made a complete circuit around the mission compound, making small talk about the weather and their hopes for an early spring. Charles slowed his steps and finally came to a halt in the middle of the yard, out of hearing of others.

"Miss Eliza, may I ask you something?"

"Certainly."

"Am I wasting your time by calling on you? I sense a reluctance from you."

Eliza's cheeks colored in embarrassment. "No, Charles, you aren't wasting my time. I simply feel there is no hurry in this courtship. After all, you will be at Cantonment Gibson for two more years."

"I see. And you would be content for me to court you for two more years? That seems like a rather lengthy time. Have I no hope of a more . . ." he paused as if searching carefully for the right word, "a more serious commitment than occasional walks or shared meals?"

Eliza looked up at the earnest young man. "Charles, do you like it out here on the prairie?"

"Like it?" He looked puzzled and they began to walk again while he pondered his answer. "Yes, I suppose I do," he said at last. "I didn't expect to when I learned this was to be my first assignment after the academy. But I find that it has been a great learning experience. I have developed a concern for the Indians and their plight. I find their culture fascinating. I would hope that I can do some good here, just as you are."

Charles looked hopeful, as if he wanted to give the right answer and wasn't sure that he had.

Eliza sighed. They continued to walk. "You get regular leave time, don't you?"

"Yes."

"Perhaps you could visit and we could go for a ride."

Charles smiled broadly. "I would like that. Should I try to locate a carriage?"

"No, I can ride on horseback," Eliza chuckled. "I doubt that there is a carriage anywhere in Lovely County."

"I think you're right." Charles joined in her rueful laughter. "I didn't know you liked to ride."

"I enjoyed it in New England. But out here, there's little opportunity. We women rarely leave the mission. It isn't considered safe."

"No, it wouldn't be," he agreed. "We saw a black bear when we crossed the creek on our way up here. We've heard panthers at the fort."

"My sister wouldn't want us to ride alone, but I think we could find someone who would come with us. Amanda and Stephen like to ride sometimes."

"Let's plan on it then," Charles said, boldly taking Eliza's hand and tucking it into the crook of his elbow. "The first pretty day this spring."

Eliza smiled her assent but further conversation was interrupted when Amanda rang the dinner triangle.

After saying grace, the dining hall was filled with the murmur of conversation and the clink of dishes as the mashed potatoes, venison, stewed carrots and sourdough bread was passed among the tables. Amanda poured coffee for the adults and Martha brought a pitcher of milk to the children's table.

Following supper, Rev. Washburn spread out a piece of paper on the table where he sat and invited them all to take a look at it. Clarissa peeked around her husband's shoulder and saw what looked like a letter, but with strange characters on the page.

"What is it?" John asked.

"This is Cherokee in its written form," Washburn responded.

"I'd heard they had developed writing," Redfield stated. "It certainly doesn't look like the English alphabet."

"No, though the man who developed it borrowed from our alphabet, as well as others. Some symbols he simply made up. But it's easy for the Cherokees to learn. I expect the tribe to be fully literate within a generation."

"That's amazing," Clarissa and John said together. As teachers, they were both interested in anything to assist literacy.

"Missionaries in Georgia are already working on translating school primers, hymns, passages of scripture." Washburn couldn't hide his excitement. "This is a letter from back east to Edmund Webber, one of our students at Dwight Mission."

"Webber?" Rev. Vaille said in surprise. "Is he related to Chief Walter Webber?"

Washburn nodded. "His younger brother. And one of our recent converts. He is quite enthusiastic about this new development for the Cherokees. He plans to become a teacher."

"That is good to hear," the pastor said. "Perhaps he will have a positive impact on Chief Webber."

"We can pray he will," Washburn agreed. "Though for now Mr. Webber still seems quite hardened against the church."

"And still bent on revenge against the Osages?" Vaille asked.

"Yes, as far as I can tell," the Dwight director nodded. "But we are seeing a much greater interest in education among the Western Cherokees."

A murmur of approval spread among the Union missionaries and they passed the Cherokee letter around. After a time, the group dispersed, families leaving to retire for the night.

Marie led the girls to the Palmers' cabin, but Clarissa waited on Marcus. He was working by lantern light to extract some metal shards from Alexander's hand. It was a hazard of the blacksmith's trade and his scarred hands gave proof of it.

Clarissa sat quietly, enjoying watching her husband's careful work and his joking camaraderie with Mr. Woodruff. Charles came and sat beside her.

"May I speak with you for a moment?" he asked. She nodded.

"I know you are good friends with Miss Cleaver," he began. "I feel in need of some advice about her."

"I'll help if I can."

"She asked me if I liked it out here on the prairie and I assured her I did."

"Oh, Lieutenant, that probably wasn't the answer she wanted."

"It wasn't?"

"No. You see, she doesn't like it here; she wants to go home to New England."

"Oh," Charles grimaced. "I didn't know that."

"What are your plans after your tour is completed here? Do you have any say in where your next assignment will be?"

"I can certainly request a post, though there is no absolute guarantee that I would get it. A soldier goes where he is needed."

"Still, if you had a choice, what would it be?" Clarissa pressed.

"New England?"

"That's the answer Eliza would want. But Lieutenant, be sure it's the answer that's best for you, as well."

"Thank you, Mrs. Palmer. I feel I understand the situation much better." The officer sighed with regret. "Why couldn't Eliza have told me?"

"She doesn't want to manipulate a man into taking her to New England. Her sister warns her against that all the time. But if you assure her that you are planning to return to Boston, that might make a difference."

Charles nodded. "This conversation has been most enlightening. Thank you, Mrs. Palmer."

"Certainly. I hope I have helped."

He stood to go and Clarissa also rose to retrieve her cloak. Marcus was wrapping Alexander's hand so he would be ready to walk her home shortly. The quiet, starlit evening made her think that they might take the long way.

CHAPTER NINE

Hopefield Farm
March 1825

As warm days followed, the prairie soil was ready for the plow. It took several passes of the yoked oxen to get the fields ready for planting. The soil was heavy with centuries of silt deposits from regular floods along the river.

Stephen, Paul and George were busy from dawn's light breaking the sod for their corn and oats. They now had over two dozen work animals that would need feed, and they were anticipating several litters of hogs soon. Stephen was a gifted farmer and knew how to run a productive operation.

At Hopefield Farm, Will Requa was not feeling particularly hopeful about his operation. The older brother to George had yet to convince the Osage warriors who lived at the site to assist with plowing their fields. They still saw planting crops as women's work and were content to let Will and Rev. Montgomery undertake the sod busting.

At midmorning, Will halted his team of oxen borrowed from Union. Susan had carried out water for the men, along with biscuits filled with slices of ham. While he ate, Will looked across the common yard of the mission site to where the elderly clan leader Monepasha sat with his sons around a fire in front of their lodges.

The youngest, Hunts-the-Bear, was knapping new arrow points, but the others were smoking and swapping hunting stories. Star-That-Travels and his good friend Bird had gone down to the creek to fish.

Laughter from the warriors drifted to them on the spring breeze. Will's frustration was visible on his face.

Susan could read her husband's thoughts. "Centuries of tradition are hard to overcome," she reminded him.

"I know," Will sighed. "But Monepasha says he knows changes are coming soon, even out here. He says he wants his clan to learn farming. But he's not able to manage the oxen himself and he won't press his sons to try."

"I don't think they like the oxen," Susan observed. "They're not used to them. If they could plow with their mustangs, they might try."

"Those mustangs have never pulled a plow," Will said doubtfully.

"Star-That-Travels says an Osage warrior can train his horse to do anything. Maybe you should challenge them to prove it."

Susan's sweet voice always made her sound naïve, but her words had a kernel of wisdom and brought a speculative look to Will's eyes.

Montgomery had been listening to the conversation. "She's right. They're always challenging each other to demonstrate their horsemanship. Make it a warrior's challenge. Can they train their horses to plow?"

Will rubbed his bearded jaw as he gave the idea some thought. "Maybe that's the key," he finally said. "Training horses is a warrior's work. And our fields are small enough; we don't really need the oxen."

"Let's talk to Star about it this evening," Montgomery proposed as he pulled his work gloves on again.

The men returned to the plowing and Susan went to join Harriett who was working on the laundry.

The next morning, Star brought two mustangs to the mission barn, having gamely accepted the challenge to train them for plowing. Though their corral of horses was considered communal property, available for everyone's use, each warrior had his favorites. They worked with them regularly and had formed a bond of trust that was necessary in hunting or in battle.

Will waited to begin the training until all the Osage men were settled around their common fire. He hoped to stir an interest among their neighbors.

Star's horses were spirited, but he kept them well under control. A tightened rein or a low command brought them instantly in line. But when Will tried to slip a collar under the head of the larger brown stallion, he balked immediately and began to prance and kick. This caused the other mustang to shy and Star was almost pulled off his feet as he held their reins.

A rumble of laughter reached them but Star set his jaw and looked even more determined. At the fire, Bird said something that brought more laughter. But he threw out the coffee grounds in his cup and then rose and walked over to the barn.

He said something in Osage to Star who nodded. Now as Will tried again to put the collar on, Star used his forefinger and thumb to squeeze the nostrils of the horse. The discomfort stilled the mustang, except for his eyes and ears which rolled and flicked in suspicion. Bird took the reins of the other horse.

Will glanced toward the Osage men. They were watching the process with unveiled curiosity. He stepped back to allow Star and Bird to work with the animals while he simply gave directions.

It took several more tries to get collars on both horses. By that time, Hunts-the-Bear and his older brother Kickingbird had also wandered over to watch and offer suggestions. Will hid a hopeful smile by stroking his mustache.

For this first day, they decided to stop at just getting the collars and traces on to allow the horses time to adjust to the apparatus. Star and Bird walked the animals up and down the half-plowed fields. The other men trampled along, as if studying the farm equipment and how it was used to direct the horses.

Montgomery had spent the morning writing out his sermon for Sunday, but he joined Will who leaned against the barn wall, all but forgotten by the Osage men. The minister clamped a hand on Will's shoulder and gave it a squeeze.

"I honestly didn't know if these wild horses could be put to the plow," he admitted. "But the Osages are masters at horsemanship. If it can be done, they will do it."

They were joined by Monepasha. Together they stood and watched his sons and sons-in-law follow Star-That-Travels and Bird.

"Need more necklaces," the clan elder said. Though his face looked solemn, there was a twinkle in his eyes.

"We can borrow some from Union," Will assured him. "Good." The man turned and walked back to sit in front of his lodge and wait for his wife to bring him the noon meal.

Will, who understood Osage fairly well, heard Star brag that his horses were the only ones capable of plowing. The other men scoffed at the claim.

"Mine are faster than yours," Kickingbird countered. "Did my stallion not win the last race at La Saline? Did I not take the purse?"

Will interrupted as he walked toward them. Speaking in Osage he told them, "Speed is not what matters. It takes strength and fearlessness, and the discipline to go slow."

"I will show you that my horses are fearless," Kickingbird said. "They can do anything I ask of them."

"Show me," Will replied.

All the men went to get their horses.

At the Requas' cabin, Susan, Harriett and Star's wife Teresa had watched the training session from a window.

"Husbands are so easy to master," Susan said. Her voice sounded innocent, but her giggle gave away her amusement.

Harriett covered her mouth to hide her own snort of laughter. "Never let them know that," she advised her two friends. They shared a laugh as they went back to their dinner preparations.

After the noon meal, Will hitched the oxen to a wagon and drove the five miles to Union. He found Stephen working with Woodruff to repair a plow blade. They greeted him when he stepped into the blacksmith shed.

"Come to see if I can borrow another plow and gear for two horses," Will said.

"Horses?" Stephen queried. "What horses are you going to plow with?"

"Osage mustangs, if we can manage it."

"Are you serious?" Stephen straightened up from his work, a look of doubt on his face.

"We've been working with them all morning," Will explained. "I think they can do it."

"It takes endurance to pull a plow all day. You think those ponies can do that?"

"You ever see a pony chase down a stampeding buffalo? They may be smaller than draft horses, but they have endurance. Besides our fields are small; that was the whole point of starting Hopefield."

Stephen gave the idea the same consideration Will had the day before. "I suppose this also means the Osage men will be behind those plows?"

"You ever see a warrior let a woman work with his horse?"

Stephen smiled. "Good idea, Requa."

"Thanks," Will said as they started toward the equipment shed. "It was actually my wife's idea," he explained. "And she seems quite pleased with herself about it."

The farm director laughed as the men loaded the plow and gear into Will's wagon. "Well, if she's happy, you're happy, right?"

"Exactly. Right now, everybody's happy at Hopefield."

On Saturday, Marcus joined Paul at the corral as the hired man brought two of their mustangs from the barn. They were saddled and ready for the trip to Cantonment Gibson. Marcus was scheduled to preach at the Sunday service in the newly completed mess hall.

Amanda brought out a leather satchel she had packed with sandwiches for their journey. Paul had filled two metal canteens with cold, clear water at the springhouse.

Marcus tucked his Bible and sermon notes into another

saddle bag and looped the handle over the saddle horn. He waved to Clarissa and their two daughters who stood on their front porch.

The men set out at midmorning. The air was crisp but a cloudless sky promised that the day would get warmer as they traveled south. They walked their horses along the trail through the plowed fields that smelled of dirt and sunshine.

The two men took their customary break at Flat Rock Creek. As they continued south they overtook a train of covered wagons also heading south, probably going to Texas. Marcus and Paul gave a friendly wave to the settlers, but didn't slow their horses for conversation.

Within a few miles, the tree line of the Verdigris River came into view. Paul pointed toward a hill that would have a good view of the river.

"I'm thinking 'bout building a cabin for me an' Miss Tassie right there," he said. "That way she's just a few miles from the mercantile and can ride to work. I'll have the longer ride to get to Union. Star says he'll help me get some horses."

Marcus studied the site as they rode closer to it, gauging with his eye its distance from the Falls of the Verdigris. "I think it's a good choice," he told the young man who was clearly eager to get married and settle into a home of his own. "It looks to be west of the Falls. That's the starting point of the boundary line for Lovely County. You'll be outside of the area that's supposed to become Cherokee land. But you might ask Lieutenant Summers about it just to be sure."

Paul nodded. "That's what I'm thinking, too. But I'll ask the lieutenant to help me check the map."

"You could ask Spaulding also," the doctor said. "I know he copied the map Mr. McCoy made when he surveyed the area. So either one could help you make sure you'll not be in Cherokee territory."

"And it won't be Osage land either?"

"Not if they sign the new treaty that's being proposed. At that point they'll be expected to move further north because the north boundary of Lovely County will be the same as the south line for Missouri."

"That north of Hopefield?"

"Yes," Palmer nodded. "Well north of Union too. Which is why we may have to move the mission. It's all uncertain right now. I suppose it will depend upon decisions made by the Cherokees over the next few years."

Paul sighed. "That makes it hard for any of us to know what to do. If Union moves, I suppose Miss Tassie and I would have to move too."

"All we can do is wait, pray and hope for the best."

They had reached the trade community of Three Forks by this time and took the east fork of the road to cross French Point and board the ferry to Cantonment Gibson.

When the ferry reached the east bank of the Neosho, they saw a Negro man sitting on the sandstone ledge where the riverboats landed. A look of dismay passed over both faces as they observed a shackle around one ankle and a chain padlocked to the hasp driven into the stone.

"Ain't right," Paul said in a low and angry voice where only Marcus could hear him.

"No," the doctor agreed, "but be careful, Paul."

"I know."

They edged the horses off the flat ferry and up the riverbank. As they passed him, the unfortunate man looked up at them, misery on his face. Likely a captured runaway slave, he was about Paul's own age.

For just a moment their eyes met and Paul gave the briefest of nods. Then he and Palmer rode on toward the fort.

When they reached the path that turned south toward the Nicks Mercantile, Paul pulled up his horse. He was eager to pay a call on Tassie.

Marcus dug into his coat pocket and pulled out a silver coin. "Buy him some food," he said, tossing it to Paul. "Just don't let anyone see you give it to him."

Paul caught the coin and nodded, then they parted company. Dr. Palmer approached the guard at the fort palisade and Paul set out on a trot to the store.

Marcus went in search of Lieutenant Summers after an enlisted man took his horse to put up in the fort corral, promising to give it food and water. Carrying the saddle bags, he walked toward the headquarters tent.

There was no door to knock on to gain permission to enter, but the tent flap was folded open. Marcus could see Summers sitting at a camp desk so he paused to wait for an invitation to step inside. It was then that he saw another man in the tent. He was wearing civilian clothes and carried a long gun.

The officer glanced at a sheet of paper in his hand, seeming disgusted with what he read.

"See," the man said, "I got a clear right to capture that boy and take him back to Arkansas Post."

"How do you live with yourself?" Summers asked with narrowed eyes.

"I don't care what you think of me," the bounty hunter growled. "The law is on my side."

"Being legal and being right are two different things."

"You gonna sign that paper or what?" the man asked, spitting a stream of tobacco juice toward a spittoon by the desk. Then he wiped his beard with the back of his hand.

Another look of disgust passed over Summers' face. He hastily scrawled his name at the bottom of the paper he held and thrust it toward the man. "Get your dogs and get out of here."

"Gladly," the man responded, jerking at the warrant and stuffing it into a pocket. He stepped out of the tent and brushed past Marcus without a glance. His whistle brought two bloodhounds to life that had been lounging in the shade of the tent.

Charles waved Marcus inside.

"Dr. Palmer," he greeting him. "Sorry you had to witness that."

"Sorry you have to deal with that. Must be hard." Palmer set his bags on the ground and took the chair across the desk from the young officer.

"Worst part of my job," the lieutenant agreed. "Fortunately it doesn't happen often. Most runaways out this far west try to head for Texas, I think. It's outside of U.S.

jurisdiction." He paused for a moment and leaned back in his chair in contemplation.

"Do I follow orders or follow my conscience?" His words were quiet, almost as if he were addressing something inside himself, rather than Dr. Palmer.

"Do you know the decision Peter made in The Acts?" the doctor asked him.

"Yes, I know what you're referring to. He had to either obey the authorities or obey God."

"I can't advise you not to follow orders," Marcus said, but he looked Charles directly in the eye. "But following God has always worked best for me."

At the mercantile, Paul and Tassie had their heads together, speaking in low tones while Sallie Nicks waited on a young soldier buying shaving soap. Even after the customer walked out of the store, she gave the young couple their privacy.

Sallie was known to be a romantic who liked encouraging young love. She would have played matchmaker for all the lonely soldiers at the fort, but there was a distressing lack of young women available. She told her husband that she could not in good conscious encourage the men to court the Osage girls who lived at Big Tracks' village across the river. She feared the men would take advantage of their trusting nature and their lack of English skills.

But she was quite happy to encourage Paul and Tassie and so she was completely unaware that their whispered conversation pertained to helping an unfortunate slave.

"I'm going to tell Monday about him," Tassie was saying in a whisper. "Maybe he can do something."

"Tassie, you know what I told you," Paul shook his head. "Leave this alone. I'll ride over to the boatyard and tell him myself."

Tassie's eyes narrowed at Paul's tone of voice and there was a stubborn look on her face. Her fiancé met her look with a determined one of his own.

Finally, she nodded and lowered her eyes to the red

bandana she had spread out on the counter. She reached into a crock and pulled out several chaws of buffalo jerky and placed them on the cloth. Stepping to the end of the counter, she lifted the lid of a barrel and added several crackers to the meat. After that she cut a small wedge from a wheel of cheese sitting under a glass dome in the dim coolness of the back shelf.

When she had completed the collection, Tassie tied the bandana at its corners and slid it toward Paul. Then she tallied his bill and he paid with the coin Dr. Palmer had provided.

"My, you must like that buffalo jerky," Sallie drawled.

The Negro couple froze for just a second as if caught in the act of stealing the food.

Paul put a smile on his face and turned toward Mrs. Nicks. "Yes, ma'am," he agreed. "It's mighty good."

"I get that from the women at Big Tracks' Town," Sallie explained. "I'm not so fond of chewy meat myself, but I will say that I like the way the Osages prepare it. They pound berries into the meat before they dry it over a pecan wood fire. Gives it a very good flavor."

Paul kept the polite smile on his face and Tassie almost laughed. She had never heard Paul express an interest in recipes, but he would never let Sallie know that.

"Yes, ma'am," was all he said.

"And that cheese," Sallie went on, "comes from Tassie's mother. I can hardly keep it in stock. The soldiers just love it." She gave Paul a wink. "If Tassie cooks like her mother, you're going to be well-fed man."

Paul's smile widened and looked genuine as he glanced toward his future wife. "I am a blessed man," he agreed. Tassie flushed and lowered her eyes in pleased embarrassment.

Sallie took a breath and was about to launch into some other comment, but Paul interrupted.

"Well, I best get back to the fort. Dr. Palmer will be waiting on me."

"Will the doctor be our preacher for service tomorrow?"

Sallie asked as Paul took a step toward the screened front door.

"Yes, ma'am."

Oh, I am so looking forward to hearing him preach," the shopkeeper said, following Paul toward the door. Tassie trailed after them. "He has such a calm demeanor, I'm sure it will be a lovely sermon. Not like that Rev. Montgomery. He sounds like a Methodist at times." Sallie's opinion of Methodists was clearly written on her face.

Paul tried to hide his grin as he stepped out onto the porch of the store. He slipped on his hat and looked around Sallie who now stood in the door.

"Thanks, Miss Tassie," he said. "I'll see you tomorrow."

She nodded and silently mouthed the words, "Be careful."

Paul glanced between the two women and gave the briefest of nods before untying his horse at the hitching rail. He mounted slowly, keeping a firm grasp on the bandana and turned his mustang's head toward the fort.

On the way, Paul passed the bounty hunter who was walking his horse toward the store. Two dogs, with tongues lolling, bounded in and out of the brush along the trail.

Before reaching the sandstone landing, Paul nudged his mustang into the brush along the river within sight of the ferry. He dismounted slowly and stood holding his horse's head close to keep the animal quiet. Beyond the boat, two soldiers lounged in the sun and beyond them he could see the chained slave.

He waited until someone on the west bank of the river raised a small red flag on a pole, signaling a desire to cross the river. The two soldiers quickly put the flat boat into motion, poling it across the clean expanse of water.

Paul mounted his horse, but waited still until the ferry reached the opposite side. Then he rode up to the landing point close to the runaway. Without looking down at the man, he dropped the bandana beside him.

"Eat something quick," he said, barely moving his lips. "Then keep it hidden."

The man felt inside the bundle and pulled out a piece of jerky. He bit into it ravenously and chewed quickly. He tucked the bandana into the pocket of a dirty, torn coat.

"How come you ended up here? Why didn't you head to Texas?"

"Tried to," the man said also not looking at Paul and keeping his voice quiet. "Bloodhounds blocked the way. So I followed the river, hoping they'd lose the scent."

"Two blue tick hounds?"

"Yep."

Paul glanced back at the trail toward Nicks'. The man's words confirmed that he had passed those hounds and their handler. The man would likely return for the slave and take him over to Three Forks to board one of the keelboats tied up there.

Paul eased his horse away slightly as the ferry started back across the river.

"When you get to Three Forks, try to ask for a black man named Monday," he said. "I'm heading over there to let him know about you. He might can help."

The slaved nodded.

Paul directed his mount to the far side of the landing and waited for the two privates to pull the boat up onto the ledge. After their passenger disembarked and headed up the slope toward the fort, one of the ferrymen said, "Going over, Paul?"

He had used the ferry often enough that most of the soldiers who worked here knew him.

"Need to visit Chouteau's," he said. He guided his horse onto the boat, without glancing toward the slave. He dismounted and again kept a close hold on the mustang to keep it calm as the ferry slid across the river. Once on the other shore, he mounted and spurred the horse into a trot. He wouldn't have much time to try to locate Monday and explain the situation to him.

CHAPTER TEN

Three Forks
March 1825

Paul and Dr. Palmer stayed at Mrs. Bradley's home Sunday evening following the afternoon service in the fort's mess hall. Tassie's mother served a supper of fried prairie chicken, black-eyed peas and wilted dandelion greens with the always-present cornbread. When the meal was complete, Marcus returned to Cantonment Gibson where he would spend the night. Paul would camp in the Bradleys' barn.

He and Tassie sat out on the front porch in the waning light after supper, talking about the future and wondering quietly if Monday had been able to help the slave.

"I'll look around when we ride through Three Forks tomorrow on the way back to Union," Paul said. "But I don't dare try to ask around. Don't want to raise no suspicions."

Tassie nodded. "You're always warning me to be careful, but you need to keep watch too. I don't want nothing happening to you."

"I'll be careful," Paul promised as Mrs. Bradley stepped out of the house.

"Time for bed, Tassie," she said. "And you too, Paul. Work day starts early tomorrow."

"Yes, ma'am," the young folks said in unison. Giving Tassie a quick kiss on the cheek, he slid off the half-log bench and walked toward the barn to settle on the pallet Mrs. Bradley provided.

As planned, the two men from Union met at the Pryor trading post in Three Forks early the next morning to begin the ride home. Paul cast an eye over the two keelboats tied up at the Verdigris landing, but saw nothing of the bounty hunter or his unfortunate prey.

Paul was quiet as they rode north on the Texas Road but Marcus did not press him for a reason. They rode silently most of the way home, enjoying the ham sandwiches Mrs. Bradley had packed for them.

"We are fortunate, Paul," Marcus said as they paused to let their horses drink from Flat Rock Creek. The flat, shallow bank of the slow-flowing water made it an easy crossing and a good place for the horses to drink.

"Why is that?"

"We are kept supplied with traveling victuals from the two best cooks in all of western Arkansas."

Paul grinned and his pensive mood seemed to break. "Yes, sir. I know that's right."

They continued onward and within another few miles saw a wagon up ahead on the road, turning off towards Union Mission. They shortly overtook it and the two mules that pulled it slowly. The driver was the freedman, Monday.

Paul sat up a little taller in the saddle when he recognized the man. "Hey, Monday," he said as they pulled even with the freight wagon.

"Paul," Monday acknowledged with a tug at the brim of his hat. "Dr. Palmer, how are y'all today?"

"We are well, Monday," Marcus replied. The two men had a mutual respect for one another, having worked together years ago to valiantly try to save the life of Joseph Revoir. The trade partner of Colonel Chouteau had been shot by a group of Cherokees at La Saline, but had not survived the wound.

"What brings you up here?" Paul asked.

"Have some cargo for Union," Monday responded with a nod toward the back of the wagon. Paul saw some barrels and crates and a couple of trade blankets spread out in the center of the wagon bed. The two Negro men shared a look.

As they rode into the fenced yard of the mission, Paul pointed to the barn. "Pull in there and I'll help you unload."

Monday nodded and steered his mule team toward the open doors of the barn.

"I'll take your horse for you," Paul said to the doctor.

Marcus gave Paul a speculative look, but easily relinquished the reins of his mustang after he had dismounted and removed his bags. "Thanks, Paul. I'm eager to see my family."

"Yes, sir." The young man led the two horses into the corral.

A glance at the sun told Marcus he would likely find Clarissa in the dining hall for school would have just been dismissed for the day. Rubbing the stubble on his jaw that he normally kept clean-shaven, the doctor glanced at his cabin, wishing he could clean up a bit. But he knew his girls didn't mind the tickle of whiskers and he also knew Mrs. Fuller would have something good prepared to eat. So he made his way to the dining room.

Paul slipped the saddles off the two mounts and set them in the corner of the corral. After making sure there was water in the trough, he hurried to join Monday inside the cool darkness of the barn.

Monday had stepped down from his seat and was leaning against the high sides of the wagon bed.

"What cargo you got for Union?" Paul asked without preamble.

"Something of great value." Monday flicked back a corner of one of the blankets revealing the escaped slave.

"Why you bring him here?" Paul's alarm was apparent in his voice as he glanced out into the mission yard. No one was close by. Then he checked the hay mow where the boys liked to play sometimes. It was empty except for the stacks of hay stored there.

"How'd you get him away from the bounty hunter?"

"Me and Clancy was loading furs on the keelboat. We 'accidently' knocked this feller overboard and he must 'av got sucked under somehow."

The young "drowning victim" lay quietly in the wagon, as if still afraid to move or give away his presence.

"That hunter didn't send his dogs after him?"

"Tried to," Monday grinned. "But them dogs was busy chomping at a bandana full of jerky and paid him no mind."

Paul grinned too and even a hint of a smile passed over the former slave's face.

"And the hunter didn't go in after him?"

"He peered over the side of the boat like he was thinkin' on it. But I put on my spooky voice and told him there was quicksand all in that river and no one ever came out alive once they got sucked in. That seemed to change his mind. He was shorely mad at losin' his bounty." Monday nodded at the man and he finally sat up slowly.

"But why bring him here?"

"Busted his knee real bad. Won't be running for awhile. Didn't think it was safe for him to heal up at Three Forks. Too close to the fort."

"Why not take him on up to La Saline?"

Monday shook his head. "Colonel's an easy man, but he don't cotton to helpin' runaways. I thought he'd be safer here."

Paul did not look happy. "Helping with an escape is one thing; hiding a runaway is something else." He looked at the man in the wagon a little closer. His pant leg had been ripped above the knee and he could see that his leg was swollen nearly twice its normal size.

"What your name?"

"Toby," the Negro said. He was about a half foot taller than Paul and like Monday was dark-skinned and well-muscled from hard work. It was clear to see why his bounty would have been high enough for a hunter to pursue him this far up the Arkansas River.

"We get lots of visitors here at Union, so we'll have to keep you hidden," Paul explained. "Can you move at all?"

"Some."

"I thought the doctor might take a look at his knee. Might help speed up the healin'," Monday suggested.

"I don't know," Paul shook his head. It was obvious from his actions on Saturday that Dr. Palmer was sympathetic to the plight of the slave, but would he want to be involved in helping a fugitive? What had begun as a simple act of compassion had become a complicated endeavor.

Monday interrupted Paul's musings. "I thought these Yankee missionaries were against slavery."

"They is," Paul agreed. "But they're of different minds on what they should do about it. No one wants to get cross-sided with the law." After some more thought he added, "I know one of them is surefire against slavery though and he ain't afraid to say so."

"Who's that?"

"Mr. Spaulding, the schoolteacher."

"That little spectacled feller?"

Paul nodded. "I may speak to him first." Then, addressing Toby he said, "In the meantime, we need to get you hidden."

Between the three of them, they managed to help Toby out of the wagon to limp back to Paul's bunk sitting at the far wall of the barn. It was dark in this corner and the walls of the various stalls and pens kept it out of sight of most of the building. It was not an ideal hiding place, but since only a few men at the mission ever ventured into this area, it would do until Paul could come up with something better.

Monday pulled a small cask of nails and a bag of beans from the wagon. Then he took out a small tin pail from another sack. "Saw this at Chouteau's store," he explained. "Thought the folks here might like it."

"What is it?"

"Maple syrup."

Paul whistled low. "That's expensive, ain't it?"

"Yep," Monday nodded. "Paid for it from my wages. My way of thankin' y'all for helpin' me lots of times, but especially now."

Paul held the syrup bucket as if it were myrrh. "Mrs. Fuller will be right pleased to get this."

With another nod, Monday climbed onto the wagon seat

and took the reins. "I'm headin' up to La Saline with the rest of these supplies. I'll stop back by on my return trip. If there's a problem with Toby stayin' here, we'll figure somethin' else out.'"

Amanda was indeed happy to receive Monday's gift of the syrup. She added a batch of biscuits to the supper menu and everyone enjoyed the New England specialty with fresh butter melting into the flaky bread. Clarissa enjoyed watching the delight on her daughters' faces as they tasted the syrup for the first time.

After the meal, Paul approached John Spaulding's chair where he sat with his family, including Eliza.

"Could I speak with you, Mr. Spaulding?"

"Sure, Paul," the teacher replied, looking up over his glasses. "What can I help you with?"
Paul hesitated a long moment, but then a light came into his eyes as if an idea had been dropped from above. "I was wondering if I could look at that map you have of Lovely County. I'm wanting to pick out a settling spot for me and Miss Tassie."

"Certainly, Paul." John pushed back his chair and stood. "The map is in my classroom. Shall we walk over now and have a look at it."

"Thank you. That'd be good."

As they left, Alice and Eliza shared a smile. "Paul is head over heels about Miss Bradley. He'll be working on their cabin as soon as the fields are planted," Alice observed.

"No doubt," Eliza agreed with a little sigh that sounded like envy. "We ladies better start on a wedding quilt for them."

They both stood to help the other women with cleanup after supper, gathering dishes and washing children's sticky faces and fingers.

Eliza's chore for the evening was wiping down the tables and chairs in the dining room while most of the other women worked in the kitchen. The pretty blonde stepped outside to shake out the table crumbs from her cloth. She saw Paul and John leave the schoolhouse and walk quickly to the barn.

Her brow furrowed in puzzlement. Her brother-in-law rarely went into the barn. He was not good with the animals and husbandry was not one of his duties at the mission. Eliza was more comfortable among the horses than the teacher.

What could possibly have taken them to the barn? Curiosity kept her standing outside the door as the evening shadows lengthened. After a few minutes, John emerged alone and made his way to the kitchen.

That was another oddity. Few of the men ventured into the kitchen. That was Amanda's domain and she didn't like having the men underfoot. Shortly John emerged again, this time carrying a plate covered with a napkin.

"Didn't you get enough at supper?" Eliza asked, teasing in her voice. Her words startled John causing his glasses to slide to the end of his nose. He clearly had not been aware that Eliza was standing there.

With a sheepish smile he explained, "You know I like sweets. Those biscuits were quite delicious."

Eliza laughed. "They were good with that syrup, weren't they?"

"Yes, a taste of home." John seemed to reverse directions from walking toward the barn. "Well, I have some work to get ready for school tomorrow. So I'll see you in the morning."

"Good night." Eliza watched him walk to the schoolhouse and step into his classroom. She waited a few moments more, but as others left the dining room, she gave a shrug and returned to her chore inside.

CHAPTER ELEVEN

Union Mission
March 1825

A day later, the women at the mission were undertaking their spring chore of stuffing the mattresses and pillows for their beds. The mattress ticking would be opened up and the old down and feathers removed. They would boil the ticking sacks and hang them to dry in the sun. Then they would add new feathers from the harvest of fowl the men had taken last fall. The feathers had dried in the Fullers' loft through the winter and were fluffy and light. Sleep would be far more comfortable on the new, clean mattresses.

"Do we have them all?" Martha asked as they piled the mattresses and pillows outside the laundry building which sat within a few feet of the springhouse. It was a pretty day of sunshine with little breeze, perfect for working with the feathers.

"I think this is it," Asie Vaille confirmed.

"What about Paul's bedding?" Amanda asked. "Did anyone get it?"

The ladies looked at each other and all shook their heads.

"I'll get Paul's," Eliza said.

Rachel frowned. "I'm not sure that it's proper, Miss Eliza, for you to go to a man's quarters."

"But Paul is out in the fields," Eliza said, pointing to where he, Stephen and George worked behind the plows. "And I've been in the barn before."

"Well, I suppose . . ." Rachel conceded.

"I would just as soon her young legs do the fetching as myself," Martha added.

Eliza took that as her permission and turned to walk quickly to the barn. She had been looking for a reason to visit the log structure.

Not only had she seen her brother-in-law visit the stable, but just this morning Dr. Palmer had slipped inside as well. It was not entirely unusual for the good doctor to check on an injured animal, but she hadn't heard the men make mention of such a need.

She stepped inside the door that was propped open. All the horses, mules and the oxen not plowing had been turned out to their 80-acre pasture.

Eliza paused to let her eyes adjust to the dim interior and it took her a few moments to see the soft glow of a lantern at the back wall where she knew Paul had his quarters. Dr. Palmer must be working in that area.

She cautiously made her way down the center aisle between the stalls. Just as she reached the last one, Dr. Palmer stood and took a step backwards almost knocking Eliza down.

"Oh!" she exclaimed causing Marcus to whirl around in shock. He quickly grabbed her elbow to keep her from falling.

"Miss Eliza, what are you doing here?" Marcus asked as he purposely stepped into the young woman's line of vision.

Even so, Eliza was sure she had seen someone in the little room where Paul's cot and washstand stood. It wasn't Paul, so who was it?

"Who is that?" she pointed.

"Miss Eliza," the doctor said quietly as if soothing a child, still holding her elbow and trying to steer her away from Paul's quarters. "You really shouldn't be here."

His tone of voice made Eliza more determined than ever to understand what was going on.

"Who is that?" she repeated, holding her ground.

The doctor sighed. "That is Toby. He's a runaway that Monday brought here because he's been hurt. I was applying some liniment and bandages."

"A runaway? You mean, a slave? Is he going to be alright?"

"Yes, within a few days he should be able to walk and will be moving on." Marcus again tried to steer Eliza toward the entrance. "It is important that you not reveal him to anyone. Please, Miss Eliza."

"Why would I do that? I would never put him at risk," Eliza huffed. "Do you think so little of me?"

"No, of course not," Marcus said, surprise in his voice.

"We should do everything we can to help him," Eliza went on. "But why shouldn't the others – at least the adults – know about him?"

"Because if he should be discovered, they could honestly say to any authorities that they knew nothing about this. The fewer who know about him the safer we all will be."

Eliza nodded in understanding. "Is he hungry? Have you gotten him some food?"

"Spaulding brought him a couple of biscuits the other night and I slipped him a few slices of ham this morning."

"That's hardly enough for him to live on."

"It's the best we men have been able to do. You know Mrs. Fuller doesn't allow us in her kitchen except for emergencies." He smiled to himself. "Or birth vigils."

Eliza missed his remark, her mind on how she could help the poor man hiding just a few feet away. "I'll bring him a plate now," she offered. "All the women are in the laundry except for Phoebe and Alice and they're keeping the little ones in Alice's cabin."

Eliza started to leave, but then remembered her original mission. "Can you get Paul's mattress and pillows for me? I need to take them to the laundry."

"Yes, but you must make sure none of the other women bring them back here."

"I will."

Dr. Palmer retrieved the bedding and handed them to Eliza. "I'll wait here for you to bring the food," he said. "But Miss Eliza, don't visit the barn again. It will arouse too much suspicion."

"And it's not proper," Eliza rolled her eyes. "I know."

The young woman hurried to take her armload of bedding to the other women working on the feather-stuffing chore. Sarah and Rachel sat in chairs outside the building cutting the stitches on each mattress and pillow to open them up. Asie and Amanda then pulled the old matted feathers out and piled them on a stretch of burlap near the foundation of the little structure. Inside, Martha was heating water to begin the washing.

"Here's the last," Eliza said as she dropped the bedding on the dwindling pile.

"It took you awhile, Miss Eliza." Rachel's comment held a question in it.

The blonde cast about in her mind for an explanation for her delay. "It was dark in there," was all she could say. The other women chuckled at her supposed reticence.

"Miss Eliza, would you mind running to the kitchen to give that pot of beans a stir? See if you need to add more water to it," the cook asked.

"I'd be happy to," Eliza said, sounding so pleased that the women laughed again. She turned and strode quickly toward the kitchen, mouthing a silent "thank you" heavenward for the providential opportunity.

In the kitchen, she checked the beans, spooning out a little taste for herself. Though the beans were still a little underdone, they were edible so she filled a bowl, adding a little of the salt pork that flavored the pot. Then she took a couple of cold cornbread squares from the bread box. She set the bowl and a spoon on top of the bread plate and then covered all with a red-and-white checked napkin.

Eliza stepped out of the kitchen casting a furtive look toward the laundry. Sarah and Rachel had moved inside and the two other women had their heads down as they worked to remove the feathers. Hurriedly she walked to the barn and found Dr. Palmer waiting just inside the door. Handing him the food, she said, "Let me know if I can do anything else."

Marcus smiled at her determination. "You've done quite enough," he assured her.

"I want to help," she reiterated. "I believe in this."

Surprise registered on the doctor's face and the patronizing look disappeared. "I didn't know you so passionately opposed slavery."

"I don't think I knew either," she admitted. "But I do. Slavery is a moral outrage. If we have opportunity to assist someone to freedom, we must do it."

She waved a hand at the food. "I know it's not much, but I feel like I've finally done something that matters." Her eyes filled with tears and she turned quickly away to return to her original chore.

Marcus watched her go to make sure her roundabout route had not raised any suspicions. He knew he had just witnessed a metamorphosis of sorts.

He had tended to Eliza through several bouts of fever and had watched her grow from a petulant and spoiled girl to a beautiful young woman. But today, in a small way, she had plumbed a depth of her own soul, her own character, and had found a truer beauty in compassion for another person. He wished he could tell Clarissa about what he had observed, but he could only give his silent thanks to God as he carried the food back to his patient.

Over the next few days, Eliza managed to slip extra biscuits, a wedge of cheese, a turkey leg and whatever leftovers might be available each evening. She would hide the food in John's desk so that he or Paul could deliver it to Toby. Paul had retrieved his bedding from the laundry, thus preventing any of the other women from visiting his quarters.

Keeping the children out of the barn quickly became a problem. It was a favorite place to play for all the boys. To solve the issue, Marcus casually mentioned to Clarissa one evening that Paul should move to the old "bachelors' cabin" which was now unoccupied and used only for storage.

"You are right," Clarissa quickly agreed. "It would give Paul far more privacy and a better place to keep . . ." she paused for a long moment, ". . . his belongings."

Marcus looked at his wife sharply but he could read

nothing on her face in the soft lamplight. He thought it best not to question her comment.

"I'll speak to Mrs. Chapman in the morning," Clarissa went on. "I know the ladies are planning to give all the old cabins a thorough cleaning now that it's warm enough to open the shutters. They can clean out that space for Paul."

"Thank you," was all Marcus would risk saying.

So Paul was given leave to move his quarters to the end cabin in the longhouse after it was scrubbed clean by the mission sisters. He waited until after supper and three games of checkers with James Chapman before he made the move. Darkness was descending and most of the other missionaries had retired to their own quarters so no one observed the limping assistant who helped Paul carry his belongings to the cabin.

The next morning, Dr. Palmer checked the man's damaged knee.

"How does it feel, Toby?"

"Some better, sir." Toby assured him. "I be ready to leave whenever I need to."

Marcus knew the man was not as fit as he claimed, however. The knee was still swollen and ligaments were likely torn. His ankles were infected from having been rubbed raw by the shackles that had once bound him. It would take a few more days for the man to be able to travel safely.

"Don't be in a rush to stress that knee," the doctor advised. "If you injure it again, you'll be in worse shape. I know these quarters are more cramped than the barn, but try to do a little walking each day. Take it slow though."

"Yes, sir," the man nodded. "I thank you."

The women were just setting dishes out for the evening meal that day when two riders approached from the Texas Road. They fell in behind Stephen who was bringing the last yoke of oxen in from the fields.

"Looks like we have visitors, Miss Eliza," Martha noted as she watched through the dining room window. "I believe it's your lieutenant and he's brought a friend with him."

Eliza flushed slightly at Martha's words. She no longer minded when her sisters teased her about Charles, but she felt her heart begin to hammer. It wasn't just anticipation of seeing her beau that caused her heart palpitations.

She knew the soldiers at Cantonment Gibson were the law this far west. If Charles were to learn about Toby's presence at the mission, he would be obligated to put the young man back in chains. Monday might face charges if the fort learned that he had assisted with the escape. She and others at the mission were complicit in the matter as well.

The two soldiers dismounted at the corral and let Paul take the reins of their horses to lead them inside the gate. The men were arriving late, so it was likely they would spend the night at the mission. Eliza watched Charles slap dust from his uniform before coming toward the dining hall. Because he was in uniform he was on duty, paying a call to the mission and not just to visit Eliza.

Her nervousness made Eliza study the young man more closely than perhaps she ever had. He was not tall, but that suited her fine for she was quite petite herself. His wavy brown hair was cropped close and his clean shave revealed a firm jaw. He really was a good-looking man; but one she had taken for granted.

Now, as he smiled when he caught sight of her, she smiled back and wished she didn't have to keep a secret from him. She would like to share this newfound passion with the man she was coming to care for, but she didn't dare.

As everyone gathered for supper, Rev. Vaille asked Charles what had brought him to Union. "No trouble, I hope," the minister said.

"No," Charles assured him while taking a seat next to Eliza. "Colonel Arbuckle sent me out to check on things in the neighborhood. Private Waldo and I are just stopping by to make sure there's nothing going on here we need to know about."

Nothing you need *to know about*, Eliza thought, hiding a sudden twinge of fear behind a smile as she passed a platter of golden fried fish to the young officer. *And nothing you're going to find out about either.* She sent a look toward Paul who was studying his plate as if afraid to look at Summers.

"It's been quite peaceful here for the last few months," Vaille told him. "The presence of the fort seems to have quieted the old animosities between the Osages and Cherokees."

"That's what we want to hear," Charles said, helping himself to the stewed turnips.

"How are things down at Three Forks?" John asked, glancing at Eliza.

"River traffic is picking up and we're expecting a new graduating class of junior officers from the academy soon. Waldo, here will have a new crop of green cadets to haze. They have no idea what they'll be facing out here on the frontier."

The private grinned at Summers' words. He was quite a young man, looking barely eighteen, and he had pretty brown eyes framed with dark lashes. Beth and Abigail blushed and giggled every time he looked their way.

The meal passed with conversation about conditions on the prairie, the territorial legislature's efforts to get funding for the military road and the prospects of the new treaty with the Osages.

"I assume you're planning to spend the night here, Lieutenant," Rachel said as the ladies cleared the tables.

"If we would be welcome, ma'am." The two soldiers stood as the women did, prompting the other men to remember their manners and stand as well.

"Certainly, you are always welcome. We've cleaned the guest cabin thoroughly and you'll find new bedding as well."

"Thank you, Mrs. Chapman," Charles said. "The hospitality at Union is the best in western Arkansas."

Most of the missionaries lingered in the dining room for a time. Having visitors was always an opportunity to learn what was going on beyond the mission. Charles and Bill Waldo were peppered with questions which they obligingly answered.

As the women finished their cleaning chores, they drifted

back into the hall or gathered children to take them off to bed. Eliza resumed her seat beside Charles, regretful that she might not be able to secure any food for Toby this evening. She did not want to do anything that might cause suspicion on this particular day.

After a time, Charles leaned a little closer to the blonde woman and asked if she would like to take a walk. Eliza nodded, mentally calculated a route that would take them well away from Paul's cabin. It sat right next to the guest cabin which was offered for an overnight stay.

Eliza wanted to give Paul time to warn Toby to be especially quiet this evening. She hoped it would not turn out to be a mistake to have moved Paul's quarters.

The young couple strolled slowly around the schoolhouse and then over to the corral as the last rays of sunlight disappeared. The sky was a clear indigo blue and a few clouds were tinged with orange and pink. The stars were not yet visible.

They did not stay out long for Alice had always made it clear that their walks should be brief and in full view of the compound.

They stopped at the door to the dining hall. "I'll bid you goodnight, Miss Eliza," Charles said, sounding regretful. He clearly would have enjoyed more time with the beautiful woman. "Waldo and I will need to get an early start tomorrow, so I believe we will retire for the night."

"Good night, Charles," Eliza replied feeling a little sad that the evening was ending, yet also feeling some relief that the lieutenant's visit would not be a long one. "I'll see you before you leave, won't I?"

"Yes, I look forward to that."

They stepped inside and Charles waved the private over to him. "Fetch our gear from the barn," he told the young man. Waldo saluted at the order and walked to the structure to retrieve their saddlebags.

Eliza took a seat beside Sarah and Amanda who were sewing quilt pieces. She watched Charles bid goodnight to the Vailles and Mrs. Chapman, then he left the room.

She let out a breath that she didn't know she had been holding. Suddenly drained, she felt as if she could hardly move. She would rest for a bit and then retire to her own cabin at the opposite end of the longhouse from Paul's.

The lieutenant followed the path from the dining room toward the row of connected cabins. He had often spent the night at Union Mission, usually in the company of Colonel Arbuckle or other officers.

Staying at the mission, sleeping in a real bed, was far better than camping out on the prairie. Frankly it was better than sleeping on the hard, bug-ridden cots at Cantonment Gibson. Getting to visit with Eliza while at Union made the visit just about perfect.

Lost in thought, the young man went to the last cabin instead of the one next door where he usually stayed. He looked down at a faint slat of light seeping out from under the cabin door. He paused for a moment, but the light did not make him realize he was approaching the wrong cabin, for he grasped the door's handle and pushed it open.

Inside, two Negro men sat at the little table in the center of the small room. They froze when Charles came into view. Paul jumped up quickly. "Can I help you, lieutenant?"

"No, Paul," Charles replied, curious confusion on his face. "I'm sorry. I entered the wrong cabin, didn't I?"

His eyes swept over the other man in the room who remained seated with eyes cast downward as if by staying perfectly still he might become invisible. One knee was swathed in bandages. More cloth wrapped each ankle and seemed to shine against the man's dark skin. Understanding suddenly filled the officer's eyes. The air was thick with tension.

"Sir . . ." Paul began, his eyes wide with fear.

Charles held up one hand. "Don't say anything, Paul," he advised, his voice seeming cold. "I'll visit with you in the morning." Then he stepped out and closed the door.

Paul hung his head. The worst had happened.

"I best be leaving," Toby said in a whisper, struggling to stand.

Paul crossed to the door and opened it a crack. Neither Charles nor the young private were in sight and he could hear voices in the next cabin. He closed the door and went to stand close to Toby so their conversation could be quiet.

"Better wait till it's full dark," he advised. He pointed to the bed where Toby slept. "Roll up that quilt and take it with you. I'll slip over to the kitchen and rustle you a packet of food. Then you can head down to the river."

Toby nodded, his fear causing him to breathe heavily. He did as Paul said, rolling up the patchwork quilt tightly. Paul opened the door again, listening. There was silence next door and no light showed. He quietly stepped outside and walked to the end of his cabin. He would circle around on the backside of the longhouse where the shadows made it pitch black. Coming out at the other end he paused at Eliza's cabin and saw the young woman walking toward it.

Rather than risk frightening her and causing noise, he made his way up the path and met the young woman near the kitchen.

"Paul, what are you doing out? I thought you'd be . . ." Eliza let the sentence fall unfinished.

"Lieutenant Summers seen Toby," Paul said quietly. "He's lighting out tonight. I thought to get him some food to take with him."

"What? How did Charles see him?" Eliza kept her voice low, but her alarm was easy to detect.

"Came in my cabin by mistake," Paul explained. "Least he acted like it was a mistake."

A horrible dread came over Eliza. Had Charles come to Union Mission because he had somehow learned about Toby's escape and his presence here? Were they all caught in harboring a fugitive?

"What did he say?"

"Just apologized for getting the wrong cabin and that he'd talk to me in the morning."

Eliza's puzzlement showed on her face. Why hadn't he questioned Paul and Toby? Perhaps it was simply a mistake and he did not realize Toby was a runaway. Either way, they could not let Charles learn anything more about their secret guest.

Her heart began to pound more than it had all evening.

"The Fullers and Vailles are still in the dining room. I'll get the food."

Paul shook his head adamantly. "It's too risky for you, miss," he said. "Don't be involved anymore."

"It's riskier if you go in the kitchen. What reason would you give for being there? I can say I was putting away my apron."

Paul took a deep breath. "Alright," he agreed. "But please be careful, Miss Eliza. And don't come into my cabin. Just set the food around the corner right there by it."

Eliza nodded and then turned to walk quickly to the kitchen. Paul circled behind the cabins to return to his own. He slipped inside as quietly as possible, doing nothing to alert the soldiers of his movement. He was completely unaware that one of the men, hiding in those deep shadows, had seen him come around the corner of the cabin.

In the kitchen Eliza grabbed an empty sorghum can and filled it with whatever she thought would go unnoticed – some jerky, a couple of hard-boiled eggs, cornbread. Removing her apron, she used it as a pack, adding a jar of canned beans and some turnips.

At one point she heard the two couples still in the dining hall say good evening and prepare to leave the room. She grabbed the apron and shrank back into the shadow of a cupboard. She prayed that Amanda would not come to check on the kitchen.

Eliza held her breath, straining to hear. No one entered the room and soon the sound of footsteps died away. She waited several moments, giving both couples time to arrive at their homes. Then she slipped out of the kitchen and hurried down the cabin path. She kept her eyes on her goal – the darkened corner of the longhouse.

As she neared the guest cabin, she slowed her steps to be completely quiet. A feeling of guilt assailed her as she imagined what Charles would think if he knew of her actions.

Helping Toby had seemed so right when she first undertook it, but facing the law was not something she had thought would happen. She still knew her actions were right, but even so they might have awful consequences.

Carefully, she lowered the apron pack to the ground at the end of the cabins. She was just straightening up when a voice out of the darkness startled her.

"Eliza?"

She pressed a hand to her heart that threatened to jump out of her chest and stifled a cry.

"Charles! What are you doing? You frightened me to death."

"I could ask the same question of you, Eliza," Charles said, emerging from the shadows. In his dark uniform with his hat pulled low over his face, he had been nearly invisible.

"I, uh . . ." She cast about in her mind, trying to think of an innocent explanation for her actions, but nothing came. The white apron on the ground at her feet seemed almost to glow in the waning light. She could hardly deny that she had placed it there. An examination of its contents would make her mission obvious. In fact, a turnip had tumbled out and its wilted greens seemed to point accusing fingers at her.

"I really can't say, Charles." She opened her eyes wide to look appealing, hoping for leniency.

"I'm surprised at you, Miss Eliza," the officer shook his head, his eyes narrowed as he searched that beautiful face and those deep blue eyes.

"Please, Charles, don't ask me anything. I don't want to have to lie to you. I'm just trying to be a good Christian and help someone in need."

He nodded slowly. "It's dark, Miss Eliza, and getting late. You shouldn't be out right now. Let me walk you to your cabin."

Surprised, Eliza nodded, noting out of the corner of her eye that Paul was listening through the narrowest crack of his door. She turned and walked quickly to pull the officer away from the scene of her crime.

When they reached the other end of the longhouse, Eliza

paused at her door. The lieutenant stood close but with his back toward Paul's cabin. Eliza could see over his shoulder. She observed Toby coming carefully out of the cabin. He snatched up the apron and quickly disappeared around the corner, heading to the thick cane that lined the river.

Charles could see that her eyes were focused on something behind him.

"What are you going to do?" Eliza asked, keeping her voice to a whisper.

Charles hesitated for a long moment, as if wrestling with the question. "Do about what?" he finally asked.

"Oh, Charles," Eliza breathed. Did he mean he was willing to pretend he knew nothing about Toby?

He leaned in even closer to her. "I am a Christian, too, Miss Eliza, and I find slavery deplorable. But I am in a very difficult position and do not wish to face a court martial."

"Oh, no, Charles. I would never want to create trouble for you."

His eyes again roamed her face and searched the tear-brightened eyes. "We share a secret now, Miss Eliza. I will say nothing of your involvement in this if you will say nothing about mine."

She nodded and then stood on tiptoe to kiss him softly. "Thank you," she sighed, her breath like butterfly wings against his face. They stood forehead to forehead, savoring the sweetness of the moment.

Then he straightened, assuming the bearing of a soldier. "Has he left?"

Eliza could not hide her smile. "Yes, he is gone."

"Then I shall bid you goodnight. I hope you sleep well."

"I will now."

He turned and walked away and she slipped inside her room. Her sleep would be filled with dreams of a brave and dashing young officer this night.

CHAPTER TWELVE

Union Mission
April 1, 1825

Those at the mission who knew about Toby drew a great sigh of relief when Lieutenant Summers and Private Waldo rode out after breakfast the following morning. Eliza had not found a moment to speak to Charles alone before he left. Only a brief goodbye in the dining hall had given them time to communicate with their eyes their commitment to keep each other's secret.

With a reminder about the Osage meeting set for the Planting Moon at Cantonment Gibson, Charles donned his cap at the door. He threw one last meaningful look to Eliza, then the two soldiers walked to the corral to resume their tour around the neighborhood.

John spoke quietly to Eliza in the mission yard. "What did he say last night?"

Apparently Paul had shared the night's events with the schoolteacher.

"He doesn't approve of slavery any more than you do, John," Eliza said softly as she watched Charles ride northward. "He won't say or do anything about Toby."

"Praise be," John whispered, a look of new respect for the officer on his face. "I'll let Paul know. He's quite concerned that he has gotten all of us in trouble."

"It must be a secret, John," Eliza warned. "Charles could be the one in trouble if the fort finds out he looked the other way."

John nodded solemnly. "We owe him a great deal." Then

he gave Eliza a smile. "And if this young officer should wish to become a member of our family, Alice and I will give our hearty consent."

Eliza blushed but smiled also. "Do you think Alice will?"

"Oh, yes," John said firmly. "Alice will."

Two days later several of the men from Union and Hopefield made the journey to Cantonment Gibson for the Planting Moon Powwow. Rev. Vaille, Rev. Montgomery, Marcus and Will Requa represented the two missions. They were joined by Star-That-Travels, Bird, Monepasha and his sons, Kickingbird and Hunts-The-Bear.

As they rode south they overtook Mad Buffalo, Black Dog and most of the warriors from Claremont's Town. Chief Claremont still looked frail riding on his mustang and Marcus hoped he might have a moment to confer with Black Dog about the chief's condition.

At the fort, the missionaries expressed surprise upon seeing the transformation of the garrison. Dozens of Osage lodges had been put up north of the fort. To its south the soldiers had erected several tents to provide sleeping quarters for the government agents and other guests who were attending the meeting.

Among these guests were several Cherokees. Chief John Jolly was joined by Walter Webber, Blackcoat and Spring Frog standing in front of one of the tents. Marcus noted the hardened expression on Mad Buffalo's aquiline features when he saw Webber. He spat out a word in Osage that Marcus knew to be a curse.

Towards the river another set of tents had been set up but these were not a part of the fort. As with the fall rendezvous, traders and hucksters were set up to make money at the gathering. Several games of chance were among the offerings.

Most of the Osage men ignored the attempts to relieve them of any coin they might have. But Will watched Kickingbird eagerly make his way to the line of tents. The young man was highly competitive and enjoyed any opportunity to gamble.

Colonel Arbuckle had clearly worked hard to prepare Gibson for the powwow. In respect of their Indian guests, the soldiers had created a large firepit on a mowed field above the fort. Long, peeled logs were arranged in rows around the fire for seating.

Tradition dictated that many speeches would be made around the fire over the next several days. Every individual who wanted to say something would be allowed to do so. Even enemies were bound by honor to hear each other out. A powwow had a sacred element to it with dances and prayers. A truce would exist while the powwow continued and it would likely last for several days.

A private in uniform greeted the missionaries and offered to take their horses to the fort corral. Bill Waldo hurried up to welcome the men and offered to show them to the tent that would serve as their quarters. The Indian leaders rode toward the makeshift Osage camp.

The brothers had just stowed their gear beneath the canvas cots in their tent when they heard the drum from the powwow grounds. They stepped outside and with nearly a hundred other men made their way to the firepit. A place of honor was given to the principal chiefs – Pawhuska, from Missouri, Claremont and Big Tracks. On the other side of the fire chief Jolly and Blackcoat sat with their agent David Brearley and other government officials.

When everyone was seated, Colonel Arbuckle stood and gave a speech of welcome. Then he turned the meeting to the Osage agent Alexander McNair.

McNair laid out the purpose of the treaty gathering and several proposals that the government was offering to the Osages. For an agreement to relinquish all claims to land in Missouri, the Osages would be guaranteed land lying west of the state line and north of Lovely County. There would be payment for wrongs committed against them by other tribes and they would be given hunting and farming equipment, food staples and other trade goods.

For the remainder of the day, various Osage warriors stood and gave their opinion of the treaty proposed and would often list grievances they had against American settlers, the Cherokees, Pawnees, Kickapoos or other tribes.

The mission brothers watched the proceedings with interest. The Cherokees did not ask to speak on this first day, but they would occasionally confer with one another or their agent. Altogether the event seemed part county fair, part court room drama and part tent revival. The day ended with a meal provided by the fort followed by the drum and dancing.

As the week continued, nearly every man present stood to speak. Rev. Vaille addressed the gathering giving both a sermon and a plea for the mission to be able to continue its work at its present location.

Colonel Chouteau pressed his case for government reparations to cover his losses when the Cherokees attacked La Saline and killed his trade partner Joseph Revoir. He asked for land for his two older sons who ran his trading posts on the Maries de Cygnes River in Missouri. Others made claims for land as well and the representative for William Clark, the superintendent of Indian Affairs, dutifully wrote down each request.

The gathering ended after four days. Agent McNair assured the Osages that all their concerns would be taken back to Superintendent Clark and would be included in the final draft of the treaty. He asked that all return to the fort in two moons for the treaty signing.

The men from Union gathered their saddle gear and walked toward the corral to retrieve their horses for the ride home. As they crossed the former powwow grounds, Will spotted Star-That-Travels and Bird walking toward them. He waved and was about to invite them to join their group when the warriors were stopped by Mad Buffalo.

The brothers all stood watching as the Osage leader spoke with Star and Bird. They could not hear his words but it was obvious that he spoke with urgency. He gestured toward the group of Cherokees who stood near the doused firepit.

Mad Buffalo had long sworn to avenge the death of his friend Revoir at the hands of Walter Webber. This was the first time the two men had been in the same location since

Revoir's death. It would seem that he planned to act on his vow of vengeance even here at the fort.

Star shook his head and held up an open hand, the symbol of peace in the sign language among the tribes. Mad Buffalo glared at him and spat at his feet. Then he thumped Bird on his bare chest as if to challenge him to be his second in the duel he was about to initiate. Bird nodded and the two warriors strode across the fort grounds.

"What's going on?" Will wondered aloud as the missionaries watched with grim concern.

"The powwow is over," Marcus noted. "And so is the truce."

By the time Mad Buffalo and Bird reached the firepit only Webber and his friend Spring Frog remained there. Chief Jolly and Blackcoat had walked away with Brearley.

Soldiers went about their duty around the garrison, most unaware of the history between the Osage and Cherokee men who were now exchanging words.

"Someone should stop this before it gets out of hand," Vaille said, looking around to locate an officer. Before he could do more, however, Mad Buffalo had unsheathed a knife from a leather pouch at his waist and lunged with it at Webber. Soon the two men were grappling with the knife in a battle of strength and will. When Spring Frog reached for a knife of his own, Bird tackled him, knocking him to the ground. They wrestled around and through the ashes of the firepit, throwing the gray cinder everywhere.

In just a matter of seconds it seemed like the whole garrison had gathered at the powwow ground. The enlisted men gawked in boyish delight at the fracas, but none seemed inclined to interfere. Marcus thought at any moment they would begin to wager on who would win.

Webber and Mad Buffalo seemed at a stalemate as the Cherokee used both hands to keep the knife from plunging into his heart. Bird, being a slightly larger man than Spring Frog, was holding his own against the stickball player. The Cherokee had thrown off his muslin shirt and the two sweaty, bare-chested men were becoming caked with ash and dust.

Suddenly a musket blast interrupted the fight. Everyone seemed to freeze in place for a moment and the enlisted soldiers parted for a group of officers. Most carried weapons and they opened the way for Colonel Arbuckle. A sergeant called for attention and all the soldiers snapped stiff and upright. The fighting men stood still, chests heaving from their exertion.

"Sergeant," Arbuckle barked in his sternest voice. "Form an escort for these men. Take them to the brig. And separate the Cherokees from the Osages."

"Sir," the grizzled master sergeant saluted. Then choosing eight men he handed them weapons from the officers. The four Indians were relieved of their knives and marched to the log lockup. Chief Jolly protested to the fort commander. "Webber and Spring Frog were simply defending themselves," he stated.

"I'll sort it out later," Arbuckle replied, his voice still dark with anger. "For now, everyone will cool off in the brig."

Then seeing the missionaries, he turned to them. "Thank you for attending the meeting, gentlemen. Have a safe trip home."

The mission brothers shared looks but said nothing. Instead they continued to the corral to find their mounts.

"We were certainly dismissed," Montgomery observed as the men saddled their horses. "I had the impression the commander thought we should have prevented the fight."

"How could we?" Will growled as he straddled his brown mustang. "He's the authority out here. He should have arrested Walter Webber long ago."

With quieter words, Vaille seemed to agree. "I can't condone vengeance, but I certainly understand Mad Buffalo's frustration. It's been three years since Revoir was killed, but no one has been brought to justice for his murder."

"There is no court of law this far west," Marcus observed as the men directed their horses toward the ferry. "We can't be surprised when the old law of the avenger continues. It does seem like the only form of justice out here."

"The problem is," Montgomery added, "that it never really brings justice. It only perpetuates the violence."

"If we want to change that," said Vaille, "we have our work cut out for us."

The weeks that followed the powwow were filled with planting at the two mission sites. The students at Union, both the boys and girls, participated in the corn planting.

One Saturday afternoon in late April, Eliza was helping Amanda and Sarah water the big kitchen garden where spring greens and root vegetables were poking through the rich, black earth. She looked up to see a rider approaching the mission and quickly recognized that it was Charles. She set down her water bucket, tore off her bonnet and hastily refashioned her blonde hair into a bun.

Amanda and Sarah exchanged smiles. "Here," Sarah said, pulling up the tail of her apron. "You have a smudge of dirt on your face." She wiped the girl's face while Eliza scrubbed her hands on her own apron.

"You must think me silly."

"Oh, hardly," the seamstress said with a wink. "What was silly was me shrieking every time I saw a deer, just to get George's attention. But it worked, didn't it? Sometimes you have to do what you have to do. But I don't think your officer cares what your hair looks like. He's quite smitten with you."

Her fountain of words gave Eliza time to steady her breath and assume a calm demeanor, though her heart still hammered in her chest. This was Charles' first visit since the incident with Toby. Eliza had often wondered if their relationship would change now.

She certainly felt a greater interest in the young man, now that she knew they shared similar views on slavery. But she had lain awake several nights worrying that the lieutenant might have disapproved of her involvement in helping a runaway. Some men did not want women forming opinions or taking a stance on a political or moral issue. He might think it was not her place to try to make a difference in such matters.

As she walked toward the corral to meet the officer, Eliza

felt a stubborn determination replacing her nervousness. She took care to not let it show on her face, however, but gave him a smile when he immediately looked her way.

Today Charles was not wearing his uniform. This was clearly a social call. He seemed hardly to notice when Bearpaw took the reins of his horse to lead it into the corral. His eyes were solely upon Eliza.

After the usual greetings by most of the missionaries, Charles was led to the dining hall where guests were entertained. Amanda was already bringing out a pot of coffee and a batch of biscuits still warm from the big fireplace oven.

The conversation quickly turned to the fight at Cantonment Gibson after the treaty negotiations. All four men had been detained overnight but released the following day. Bird had come to the mission to reassure Bearpaw and Deer-in-Water that he was well. But it had been clear that he was still angry about the whole affair.

"This isn't going to ignite the troubles between the Osages and Cherokees, is it?" Vaille asked as the men gathered around the officer. Eliza felt annoyed that the men of the mission wanted to dominate Charles' time. She doubted he had come to see any of them. The rueful smile he sent her way told her as much.

"Well, we certainly hope not," Charles responded while nodding his thanks to Martha who poured coffee for him. "Colonel Arbuckle spoke with each man individually and reminded them of the peace treaty that was signed last year. The problem is that with a new treaty being negotiated, the Osages seem to think that the government has broken the old treaty and it's no longer in affect."

"I've heard them express that," Abraham added. "To the Indians a treaty should last forever, never be altered or updated or replaced. To the government, a treaty is a temporary contract, good only until conditions change. They have a completely different way of thinking about these matters."

"Yes, and it leads to a great deal of misunderstanding and mistrust," Charles nodded. "Perhaps Colonel Arbuckle should explain the treaty process better the next time one is negotiated."

"Will there be future treaties?" George asked.

"The colonel has been given orders to try to bring the various Plains tribes to the treaty table. He has a difficult task ahead of him."

Amanda came into the dining room then. "Will you be staying for supper with us, Lieutenant?"

"If I may, Mrs. Fuller. I have a couple days of leave time and I was hoping to spend them here."

"You're always welcome, sir." Amanda threw a sly smile toward Eliza who blushed, but also rose quickly to help with setting out the supper dishes.

Following the evening meal, Charles asked Eliza for a walk. They both were quiet as they set out to take a turn around the mission yard. Things had changed between them and it seemed as if neither knew how to proceed with their altered relationship.

"I promise not to stumble into the wrong cabin this evening," Charles said with a bit of a grin. "If that should happen to be an issue." There was a question in his voice.

"No, it shouldn't. There are no other guests here at Union." Eliza assured him. Her smile brought a light to his eyes.

He reached for her hand and she let him tuck it carefully into his own. "Good. I have been afraid since my last visit."

"Afraid?"

"For you . . . your safety," he explained. "I was very troubled that you were exposed to such a dangerous business. You should never have been asked to . . ." He let his voice trail off, unwilling to actually voice aloud their shared secret.

"But I wasn't asked," she said, her voice firm. "I volunteered. I wanted to help." She took a deep breath and plunged ahead. "And I would do it again if need be."

"Please don't say that."

"Why?"

"Because I will never get any sleep for worry of you." He stopped walking and turned toward her, taking her other hand. "You must know, Miss Eliza, how much I care about you."

Eliza lowered her eyes in the coy gesture she had often practiced with men who showed an interest in her. But as soon as she did, she realized that she no longer wanted to play the coquette with Charles. She raised her eyes to look into his.

"I do know," she confirmed softly. "I care about you too."

"You do?"

She nodded.

He swallowed hard. "Then I wonder if we might go for a ride and share a picnic after church tomorrow. I have something I would like to ask you."

"Yes," she said, thinking she knew exactly what his question would be. She sounded too eager and breathless even to herself.

"Yes to the ride and picnic?"

"Oh . . . yes." Eliza felt her face grow warm. "I'll ask Amanda to pack a basket for us. And perhaps the Palmer family would join us."

"The doctor and his girls?"

"Clarissa and I are very good friends and I think she would especially like to serve as our chaperone tomorrow."

"Then we will plan on it."

Eliza hurried to her cabin after church the next day to change into a split skirt and short jacket for riding. Amanda had promised a bountiful basket would be waiting for the picnic party. The Palmer girls, Thea and Lucie, were nearly beside themselves with anticipation. An outing was such a rare event for the women and children at the mission.

Slipping her straw hat over her blonde tresses, Eliza stepped out into the sunshine to see Charles making his way toward her from the guest quarters. They briefly let their fingers intertwine before separating to keep the proper distance between them. Charles tucked his hands into his pockets as if to make them behave.

They met the Palmers at the corral after collecting the basket and a blanket from the kitchen. With one girl behind each of their parents, they all mounted their horses and set out along the Texas Road. Charles had chosen a spot for the picnic about two miles south of the mission in a glade near a little creek. A few wild plum trees were still in bloom there and it made a lovely setting.

They spread out their blankets and enjoyed Amanda's fried chicken, fluffy biscuits, pickled beets and apple tarts, with jars of honey-sweetened tea.

"Oh, that was wonderful," Clarissa said, dabbing at the corners of her mouth with a napkin when the meal was concluded. "What is it about eating outdoors that makes food taste better?"

"The fresh air," Marcus responded to her rhetorical question. She laughed at him and he looked puzzled, but returned her smile.

Eliza envied the look of love that passed between the married couple, their eyes lingering in a kind of embrace. She hoped she and Charles would share that someday. As she looked away from the Palmers to him, she realized he was looking at her just as Marcus had looked at Clarissa. It gave her a warm feeling in the space around her heart.

"Thea!" Clarissa exclaimed as she reached for the little girl's hands to wipe them clean. "You have beet juice all over. You are pink and purple and red." The three-year-old giggled at her mother's teasing words.

Lucie held up her hands, wiggling her fingers. "Me pink too," she said. Her English was not quite perfect yet, but that simply made her all the more adorable to her doting parents.

"We need to get you two down to the creek to clean up." Clarissa picked up a couple of napkins and Marcus helped her to stand.

"This may take a while," she said to Charles and Eliza. "Come along, dear." Taking her husband's arm she steered him toward the creek.

"You need me to help?"

"Yes, dear." Clarissa threw the tiniest of winks over her

shoulder to Eliza as the little family made their way to the shallow creek.

"No diving in, Mrs. Palmer," Marcus teased. She punched him lightly on the shoulder.

Charles and Eliza watched them go. "What was that about? Diving in?"

Eliza waved her hand to try to brush away the bubbles of laughter that threatened to spill out. "Nothing," she managed to say. "It was just . . . It had to do with how he propo . . . I mean . . . it's nothing, really." Her hands fluttered in embarrassment and she knew her face was beet red too.

Charles watched the Palmers for a moment. They were still within sight, but out of hearing distance. Understanding dawned on his face. "I remember the story now. He rescued her at the river."

"Yes, that's it. He rescued her at the river."

Charles smiled, clearly remembering the entire story, including that Marcus had asked Clarissa to marry him that day.

He reached into his pocket and retrieved a small cubed box. "I'm afraid I can't offer you anything as dramatic as a dive in the river," he began. "But I hope you know that my heart is every bit as committed to you. I'm willing to dive into marriage with you. If you'll have me."

He opened the box to reveal a gold ring set with a small opal stone.

Eliza looked at the ring only for a moment, her eyes instead meeting his. "I'll have you," she whispered, "and I don't need a river . . . or even a ring."

"No ring?" he teased, grinning with happiness. He closed the box and started to put it back into his pocket.

"Oh, now." She tried to stop him by reaching for the box, but he grabbed her hand and held it. Then he flipped the box open again, lifted out the ring and carefully slid it onto her finger.

She held out her hand, admiring the pretty stone. "It's so perfect, Charles. However did you manage to get a ring out here?"

"It was my grandmother's. I had asked my mother to send it to me some time ago, hoping I might someday persuade you to say yes."

"It didn't take much persuasion."

Charles laughed ruefully. "I've been waiting for you for over a year."

"Oh, that's true," she looked down at her hand. "I was a bit of a bother, wasn't I?"

"No more than a dive in a river."

They both laughed, causing Clarissa to turn and look their way from where the Palmers walked alongside the creek.

Eliza lifted her adorned hand and wiggled her fingers as Lucie had. Clarissa clapped her hands in delight and they all rushed back to offer congratulations to the happy couple.

CHAPTER THIRTEEN

Union Mission
May 1825

Eliza was still admiring the ring a month later while she sat in the chapel for the closing school exercises. While she was certainly interested in the songs and recitations and awards of the students, it was all too easy for her to drift off into a daydream about her blissful upcoming marriage to Charles.

She sat up a little straighter as her nephew Billy took his place at the front of the room to recite a portion of Psalm 91. She noticed that Alice was mouthing the words along with her son, trying to help him along when he stumbled a bit. That was just like her sister – always needing to "help" those she cared about.

This turned Eliza's thoughts to her argument with Alice after she and Charles came home from the picnic. Charles had asked John for permission to propose, but apparently John had failed to tell Alice. She was not happy that she'd had no say in the matter. She kept a civil tone with Charles, but after he left Union, she let both John and Eliza know her feelings.

"Why do I feel as if you two have gone behind my back in this?" she stormed in the Spaulding cabin where they had gathered after Sunday supper.

"We knew where you stood, Alice," John said, looking as if he was working to remain calm. "There was no point in going over that ground again."

"Oh, no? You would just ignore my wishes, as you always do."

"Alice," Eliza interrupted in a firm tone. "I am twenty-one years old. I do not need the permission of either of you to get married. Charles asked John simply out of courtesy to the head of our family."

Alice huffed. "Well, you are not going to rush into this marriage. You will have a proper length of engagement."

And just what do you consider a proper length?"

"If we were back East, you would need a year to prepare for a wedding."

Eliza rolled her eyes. "We are not back East. There is no need to spend a year getting ready for a wedding. I'll be fortunate to find a decent length of dress goods at Nicks & Rogers. Sarah can have it sewn within a few weeks."

Alice looked as if she were about to cry and suddenly Eliza felt sorry for her sharp words. Alice had practically raised her after their parents died. It must seem like her own daughter was about to embark upon a life of her own.

"I'm sorry you feel like I went behind your back, Alice. I never meant to. But I really am very happy and I want you to be happy for me."

"I thought you weren't happy out here. I thought you were desperate to get back home. Now you're going to marry a soldier stationed out here for who knows how long?"

"I've changed," Eliza confessed. "I've grown up, as you have told me to multiple times." She cast a look toward John who seemed relieved to be out of the torrent of female emotion. "I found a reason to be happy here – just as you two have."

"All I want is for you to be happy," Alice was in tears now. "Don't rush into anything. Be sure that this is what you really want."

"I'm sure."

Eliza sighed again with happiness as she came back to the present where John was now making awards presentations to his students. Simple blue ribbons with a rosette that Sarah had sewn were inked with the special honor the students were to receive. Eliza smiled and clapped along with all the audience which included many parents of the Indian students. John and Clarissa had both managed to create an award for each student.

Billy received "the most improved reader" award while Antoine Lombard won the award for "most books read." The mission had started out with a very limited library, but churches had sent books, pamphlets and primers through the years. Antoine was a handsome child whose French-Osage heritage had given him blue eyes framed by dark lashes and bronzed skin. He was much petted by the girls and was becoming a bit vain.

Thomas Chapman received an award for "excellence in mathematics." Thomas had inherited from his mother a skill with numbers that was amazing. He could add a column of figures in his head quickly and accurately. His mother too had such an acumen which was one reason why she had always kept the accounting books for the mission. It was rare for a woman to be given such a responsibility, but Rachel had been the director's wife and was a major financial sponsor of the work.

After the awards were completed the crowd gathered in the dining hall for the most anticipated part of the day. Everyone enjoyed Amanda's fruit pies with tea and coffee while visiting and admiring the children's awards.

John made a point to congratulate his three graduates. Thomas, Richard Vaille and Jean Revoir had completed their studies at the mission's primary school.

The teacher offered his hand to Thomas. "You've done good work, Thomas. You'll be ready for any prep school in New England. Have you decided where you will go?"

"Probably Bacon Academy in Colchester," the thirteen-year-old replied. "That's where father went and my grandfather too." His voice had changed just recently but every once in a while it would slide up the scale like an instrument searching for the right note. A shadow of sadness passed over his face when he mentioned his father.

"Good school," John nodded, pressing the boy's hand a

little more firmly in silent sympathy. "I'll be happy to write you a letter of recommendation."

"Thank you, sir."

"And what about you, Richard?"

"Fairfield College," the dark-haired young man replied. "At least that's where I plan to apply."

"I'll have a letter for you as well."

"Thanks."

He turned to Teresa's son next. "And what are your plans, Jean?"

"Colonel Chouteau says I may work with him at the trading post at Three Forks. But Star-That-Travels and I will take a hunting trip first. He wants me to see the mountains of the Wichitas."

The other two boys looked envious. "Wish we were taking that trip, don't you, Rich?" Thomas nudged his friend.

"You bet!"

"Well, you two will be traveling soon enough. Will your parents accompany you back to Connecticut?" John asked.

"My mother and siblings will be going," Thomas said. "They're going to live with my grandparents. Richard is going to travel with us."

Surprise registered on the teacher's face. "I didn't realize your whole family was returning to Connecticut, Thomas."

"Mother just decided. We've been talking about it for a while." The young man did not seem enthused about leaving the mission.

"We will certainly miss you . . . all of you," John said looking each graduate in the eye. "Please keep in touch. I want to know that you are faring well."

Each boy nodded and they shook hands among themselves as if making a pact.

Word that the Chapmans would be leaving Union Mission spread quickly among the missionaries that afternoon. While the news was not a shock, it did bring sadness and served as a reminder of the loss of Rev. Chapman.

Clarissa expressed her feelings to Marcus when the

couple retired to their cabin that evening. "I can't imagine Union without Rachel and the children. They have been such an important part of the work here. Rachel was like the queen of us all."

Marcus chuckled at the characterization of the director's widow. "The queen?"

"Oh, you know what I mean. Rachel kept us all proper and civilized. All she had to do was clear her throat or raise an eyebrow and we would all sit up straight and remove our elbows from the table."

The couple shared a laugh.

"And I'll miss my two of my best students," Clarissa continued in a mournful tone. "The mission just isn't going to be the same."

Sadness hung over the mission a month later on the day set for the Chapmans to leave. In the days leading up to their departure, Rachel visited each family's cabin to offer a personal goodbye. She gave a small token of friendship to all of the women. They had survived sadness, sickness, and plenty of hard work together. They had truly become sisters.

For Clarissa's daughters, she brought a few dresses that Abigail and Leah had outgrown. "They're still good," Rachel said, as she handed them over to the teacher. "But there's no point in packing them and taking them with us. I thought your girls could get some wear from them."

"Oh, how thoughtful you are," Clarissa said. "Lucie and Thea will love them. And it's such a help. I feel as if I am constantly letting down hems; they grow so fast."

"I'm glad they can use them."

Clarissa crossed the cabin to take three small sachets from a trunk in the corner. "The girls and I collected some cedar chips and wildflowers to fill these," she explained as she handed the calico sacks to Rachel. "They'll keep away that musty smell in your trunks while you're traveling."

"How lovely," Rachel smiled. "I'll share them with Abigail and Leah. And we'll keep them long after we get home as a reminder of their favorite teacher."

Clarissa laughed to keep the tears that gathered from spilling onto her face. "Only teacher," she smiled.

"You have been a great blessing to my daughters," Rachel said as they embraced. "Thank you for everything."

All Clarissa could do was nod.

Rachel gave some books that Thomas no longer needed and clothes that James had outgrown to the Spauldings. Other small tokens she shared with Amanda, Sarah, Phoebe and Martha. The goodbyes seemed to get harder for her with each visit.

At Eliza's cabin, the two women sat at the small table. "I hate that I will miss your wedding, Eliza," the older woman said. "I want to give you a "something old" for your special day. This handkerchief was my grandmother's."

Eliza didn't want to take the beautiful linen square. "Oh, Mrs. Chapman," she said, "you should save this for Abigail or Leah."

"I have several other things that I'll be passing down to them." Rachel held out the handkerchief. "I want you to have this. I know life hasn't been easy for you here. I'm glad God has blessed you with happiness at last. Know that I will be with you in my thoughts and prayers on your special day, whenever it is."

"It will be a long time from now if Alice has any say in it. We must do what is proper." Eliza couldn't keep her annoyance out of her voice.

"Normally, I would be in favor of doing the proper thing." Rachel's smile was ironic. "But my advice to you would be to follow your heart and do what is right for you. That's what I did."

Eliza's raised eyebrows silently questioned Rachel's words.

"I have never told anyone here this," the widow confided. "Chapman and I eloped because my family didn't approve of him. But I knew it was right even when everyone else said it wasn't proper. And I never once regretted my decision."

Eliza took courage from Rachel's words. "Thank you, Mrs. Chapman."

Her last visit was to the Vailles. She brought two leather-bound books with her when she called at their cabin.

"This is the accounting book," she explained as she handed the ledger to Rev. Vaille. "It's all in order and I don't think you'll have trouble following my method. I've kept it simple and straightforward."

William leafed through the pages, looking uncertain. "It might as well be in French," he sighed. 'I've never been a good one with ciphers."

"Perhaps someone else at the mission can assist you. Mr. Spaulding?"

"He might. But he is quite busy with overseeing the school." Vaille held the book gingerly as if he would like to give it back. But Rachel didn't give him the opportunity. She turned to Asie and offered her a smaller book, bound in blue.

"I've kept a journal of the mission's work," she said. "I want you to have it."

Asie seemed as reluctant to take this book as her husband had been. "I'm not much for writing like that," she demurred. "I do good just to write letters to family back home."

"Don't feel you have to keep it up," Rachel replied. "I thought you might enjoy reading it and looking back over how the Lord provided for us as we journeyed out here."

"Well, alright. Thank you."

Rachel stepped toward the door. "I'm sure the board will appoint you as directors of Union Mission," she said. "I certainly will make that my recommendation when I meet with them in New York."

"Thank you, Mrs. Chapman. We'll be honored to follow you and your husband as directors. This mission would not have been possible without Chapman."

Rachel nodded and then left quickly, tears gathering in her eyes once again.

Several from the mission traveled down to Three Forks to see the Chapmans and Richard off. They loaded into the two mission wagons with picnic baskets and blankets. They would camp near the fort for the night and return the next day.

The travelers were set to board a keelboat at the Verdigris landing. They would transfer to the steamboat *Neosho* at Dardanelle.

"Can I sit with you?" Asie asked Rachel as they were helped to climb into the wagon. There seemed to be pleading in her eyes.

Rachel nodded. When the two had settled on a buffalo hide covering a mound of hay, Asie confided in her friend. "I'm expecting another baby," she said, keeping her voice low. "And I'm scared."

"You've given birth to five children, Asie. Why are you afraid?"

"It's not the birthing I fear," she tried to explain. "I'm afraid of taking care of a baby now. No one knows what I almost did . . . with Charlotte."

She glanced at her husband who rode on the front wagon seat with Stephen and Paul. "William says he's happy, but I see worry in his eyes too. And he and Rev. Montgomery have all these plans to travel to the villages to preach. Richard will be gone too. I don't want to be left alone with the children. I'm afraid of what I might do."

"Asie, I don't know how I can help you, except to pray. Are you asking me to stay here?"

"No, no. I wouldn't ask that." Asie gazed out over the landscape as if seeing a specter in the distant woods that lined the river bank. "I've asked my sister Ella to come to Lovely County, but she won't. I need someone from my family here. I miss them so much."

"What can I do?"

"Would you mind speaking with my sister when you take Richard to my parents? Tell her how much I need her."

Rachel slipped an arm around the fragile woman. "I'll be glad to speak to Ella. I'll do whatever I can to help. In the meantime, please confide in someone here. Mrs. Woodruff would be happy to help you in any way she can. Or Dr. Palmer."

Asie nodded, but seemed unconvinced. "I'll try," was all she would say.

The fur trade community was crowded as the wagons pulled up to Captain Pryor's trading house. There were keelboats at each bank of the Verdigris, likely the last for the season. As the weather became hot and dry, the rivers were not navigable this far inland.

They had some time before the keelboat would cast off, but Rachel wanted to be sure that their trunks were put aboard right away. Paul and Stephen each carried one to the dock and the boatmen took them below deck.

The mission family shopped for a while at Chouteau's trading post or visited with Captain Pryor and his trade partner Samuel Rutherford. They heard the boarding call from the keelboat captain and all made their way to the dock. It was hard to say a final goodbye to the Chapmans. Hugs and well wishes were exchanged all around. Asie clung tightly to Richard for a long moment. Clarissa could tell he was embarrassed by the show of emotion.

The teacher had given Abigail and Leah long hugs as well and the two girls were in tears as they whispered their goodbye.

The Chapmans and Richard stood at the boat's rail as the ropes were untied and the anchor lifted. Everyone waved as the keelboat got underway.

Clarissa slipped an arm around Eliza's waist. "A year ago you would have wanted to be taking this journey. Any regrets that you're not on that boat today?"

Eliza turned to her friend and smiled. "Not a single one."

After the keelboat had been poled around the river's bend, the missionaries all walked to the Neosho ferry to pay a visit to Cantonment Gibson and Nicks & Rogers. At the mercantile Clarissa and Eliza tried to pull Asie into their discussion about which fabric the young blonde should choose for her wedding dress. With a little coaxing, she was soon helping to pick out ribbons and lace for it as well.

The men, except for William and Paul had remained at the fort to visit with Colonel Arbuckle. After everyone had completed their purchases, they walked back to the fort and found the mission brothers sitting in the mess hall, having coffee with some of the officers. Charles immediately jumped up to greet Eliza and asked Arbuckle's permission to take a short walk with her.

The colonel waved them away, seeming somewhat annoyed and somewhat amused at the young man's eagerness to spend time with his intended.

"He's all in a dither trying to find a place for them to live," the fort commander commented about Charles. "I think I shall ask Sally Nicks if they can board with her. We're an awfully rough outfit for a young woman. That's why Dr. Baylor has built a cabin a stone's throw from here. Can't ask civilized women to live in tents."

The conversation moved on to other topics including the Osage Treaty. "About fifty of their chiefs and warriors made their mark on it last week," Arbuckle informed the group. "The boundary of Arkansas Territory has officially moved about 400 miles east. The Osages have been given a couple of years to move their villages north."

"It feels as if the whole dynamic of the territory is changing," John Spaulding commented.

"Exactly," Arbuckle agreed. "I've received a dispatch informing me that the Creeks in Georgia have been induced to sign a removal treaty, agreeing to move out here. But there's dissention among them. I don't know if it will actually happen."

"We are keeping our mission board informed of the changes." Rev Vaille said. "We certainly hope we are not forced to move."

"I hope you aren't asked to move," Arbuckle nodded. "You are good neighbors to this fort."

CHAPTER FOURTEEN

Fairfield, Connecticut
July 1825

Ella spread out a colorful quilt on the town green where folks were gathering for the Independence Day festivities. It had taken some coaxing to get Samuel to accompany her to the picnic and she was feeling out of sorts. Even now, Samuel was talking with a "school chum" near the bandstand and seemed to have totally forgotten her.

Maybe her mother was right. Maybe she had waited long enough for Samuel to make a commitment and settle down to marriage. She sat on the quilt watching him, torn by feelings of love and a growing frustration. She was determined to confront Samuel today.

When at last he returned to her, she opened the picnic basket and set out the various dishes Cook had packed for them. Samuel's mood seemed to match her own, but that was nothing new. He had been out of sorts for some time now.

They made small talk while they ate, pretending to enjoy the merchant band that was playing a selection of folk songs and hymns. When the last piece of cold custard pie had been consumed, Ella returned the dishes to her hamper. Samuel distracted himself with picking blades of grass and shredding them between his fingers.

His eyes wandered to the tavern sign down the street. "I think I'll go . . ."

"Samuel," Ella interrupted. "Please don't be so rude as to abandon me here and force me to walk myself home."

Samuel turned back to her with surprise on his face. "I wasn't going to abandon you, Ella. I wouldn't do that."

"It feels as if you already have."

"What do you mean?"

"You have been taciturn and distant for the past several weeks."

"I've had a lot on my mind."

"What, Samuel? What is going on?" Ella's frustration showed in her voice. "I thought you cared for me. Shouldn't we be able to talk about whatever is on your mind?"

"I do care, Ella," he declared, but it sounded forced. "You know I do."

She was silent, waiting.

He looked at her with uncertainty on his handsome face. Then he reached for her hand and stroked it gently. "I care very much for you, darling." This time his voice sounded false, even to her ears.

"But not enough to make a commitment," she stated.

"Darling," he began. Now his voice took on a wheedling tone. "I want to very much, honestly I do. But I can't at this time."

"Why not?"

His eyes darted around as if looking for an escape route. Apparently finding none, he looked down at her hand in his. "I'm not currently employed," he mumbled. "I can't afford to take on a . . . commitment."

"But you work for your father. At the counting house." Ella could not believe Samuel would make such a phony excuse.

"Father and I have parted ways," he said after a long pause.

"What?" This news was shocking to Ella. "But why?"

Samuel seemed to be searching for the answer. "It's just . . . well . . . Father's business had suffered a downturn and he was being forced to let someone go. So I said it should be me, rather than one of the married men."

That line of reasoning sounded very familiar to Ella. It seemed like Samuel had used it before.

"Can't you find other work?"

"Nothing so far," he said. "I am looking quite seriously and as soon as I find something, then, my dear, we can certainly begin to talk of our future."

Ella suddenly felt relieved. This explained much about Samuel's hesitancy to advance their relationship. She also felt pity for him. It must be very hard on his pride to have to admit that he was without a means of support.

"Well, I shall pray that you find something soon," she said. "And I'll ask my father if he knows of anything that might be available."

"Thank you, Ella, for being so understanding." There was a smile on his face now and he looked relieved as well.

"Certainly, Samuel."

They sat for a while longer, listening to the speeches given by various politicians and local dignitaries. When Ella raised her parasol to shade them from the sun, Samuel suggested that he walk her home.

He declined to come inside for something cool to drink when they reached her door. So Ella told him goodbye and stepped inside, trying to awkwardly manage her parasol, the quilt and the picnic basket. Her mother hurried to greet her in the entry hall.

"Oh, good, you're home, Ella," she said sounding a little breathless. "You'll not guess who is here."

"Who?" Ella dumped the quilt on the little courting bench at the bottom of the stairs.

"Your nephew Richard. He's arrived all the way from the mission."

"Richard?"

"Yes, he's come to stay with us while he attends school. I told you he was coming. You'll not believe how he has grown."

Then Mrs. Selden leaned closer to her daughter. "And Mrs. Chapman is in the parlor. She and her children accompanied Richard to Connecticut."

Ella could tell that her mother was a bit flustered by having the unexpected guest. They all knew who Mrs.

Chapman was . . . the wealthy daughter of the former governor.

"Come say hello to her, dear."

Ella hung her umbrella on the hall tree and put the basket on the bench beside the quilt. She smoothed out her skirts and then asked, "Does my hair look alright?"

"Yes, Ella, you look fine."

The two women walked into the parlor where Rachel sat visiting with Ella's father. She wore a new dress of black silk and a fashionable hat also in black. Ella remembered from one of Asie's letters that Mrs. Chapman's husband had died at the mission.

Mrs. Selden made introductions and then all were seated. They talked mostly about the mission and how the Vaille's were faring at the distant outpost.

"I know that Asenath misses all of you terribly," Rachel told the family. "It was hard for her to send Richard back for his schooling."

"We miss her as well," Mrs. Selden said, dabbing at tears. "It was hard for us to see them all go out to that wilderness. I know you all are doing an important work for the Lord there, but I fear that it may be too much for Asie. We were just devastated to learn of little Charlotte's death."

"You are right, Mrs. Selden. It has been hard on Asie. That's why she has so much wanted her sister to come for a visit. She's with child again and could use a helping hand with the children's care."

All eyes turned to Ella and she wanted to squirm with the sense of guilt that assailed her. "I feel very badly for Asie, I really do," she said. "But I couldn't leave my Samuel, you see."

"You're engaged then?" Rachel asked. She could see the look of disdain that had crossed Mrs. Selden's face at the mention of the young man's name.

"Well, not exactly. Samuel is looking for work right now so he can't really commit himself at this time."

"What's happened to the job he had at his father's warehouse?" Mr. Selden raised an eyebrow.

Ella hated to discuss Samuel's private affairs but she felt she had to justify her reason for not helping her sister. "His father's business has suffered a downturn and he had to let Samuel go. It was to spare the job of another man . . . a family man."

"But that's not what I've heard. Douglas Imports is one of the most solvent in Fairfield. Are you sure you understood Samuel correctly?"

Ella bristled inside at her father's implication that she couldn't understand business matters. But perhaps she had misunderstood. "All I know is that Samuel says he's looking for work."

"What kind of work does he do," Rachel asked politely.

"He's a bookkeeper for his father's import business. Or he was."

"Would he be interested in mission work? William might want to hire a bookkeeper."

"Well, I don't know," Ella said slowly. To be honest she couldn't picture her handsome Brit choosing to live in a log cabin on the prairie. But even so, an excitement took hold of her. This might be the very answer to her prayers. They could be married here, travel out to Arkansas Territory and then she could help Asie.

"I'll ask Samuel," she said. "As soon as possible."

"If he is interested you should write to Asie and William right away," Rachel advised. "This might be the answer to everyone's needs."

"Oh, absolutely," Ella agreed, a happy smile on her face.

The Seldens asked Rachel to stay for dinner, but she declined saying her brother would arrive shortly to escort her back to Hartford where she had left the children at her parents' home.

After she left, Ella wasted no time escaping to her bedroom to jot a note to Samuel. If there wasn't work for him in Connecticut, she'd get him a job in Lovely County.

It was a hot day at Hopefield Farm where almost everyone in the little community had been working to bring in the corn harvest. Will surveyed the wood-slatted corncrib nearly overflowing with their crop. It had been a good year.

Harriett and Susan were teaching the Osage women how to can the corn, providing them with an additional way to preserve it for winter meals. They used the large metal wash caldron to steam the jars to prevent spoilage.

When the remaining corn had dried, they would have it ground at Union's grist mill. Then they would haul the surplus to Three Forks and Cantonment Gibson. Will told Susan he was eager to trade with the fort because it would bring Hopefield and its eleven families much needed cash. Anything Gibson didn't buy could be traded for goods at the Chouteau or Nicks mercantiles.

When Rev. Vaille came to preach their Sunday service a few weeks later, he and Will planned a day in the upcoming week when they would take the corn south. School would start soon and the Union missionaries were expecting a load of supplies from churches that supported the mission. Jean Revoir had just brought word from Three Forks that a boat had docked on Saturday and left a number of crates for the mission.

On the chosen day, Will, and several of the other men had the farm's large wagon loaded with burlap sacks filled with cornmeal. Several of the Osages planned to travel to Three Forks with the missionaries to bring in a supply of pelts for trade.

The quartermaster at Cantonment Gibson offered to purchase all the cornmeal that the Hopefield farmers had brought to him. Monepasha stood with Will and Montgomery while the officer counted out payment for the ground corn.

The elder Osage watched the process with interest. It was rare for money to exchange hands on the frontier. Will accepted the stack of gold coins the quartermaster pushed across the desk. But rather than place it into the leather pouch he carried, he turned to the other men.

"We all worked together on this crop," he said to Star, Bird, Monepasha and Kickingbird. "We'll divide it evenly between the eleven families at Hopefield."

The men nodded. Kickingbird eyed the coins with clear interest.

Will counted out the agreed amount to Star and Bird and set aside the amount he and Rev. Montgomery were to receive. Then he handed the remaining money to Monepasha.

"I'll let you distribute this to your clan."

Monepasha nodded solemnly. "This is ours?" he asked.

"Yes."

"It is good." He reached for a medicine bag that he wore at his waist and opened the drawstrings. Then he carefully dropped the coins into the pouch and retied it. He wrapped the leather strings around the hilt of the knife he also wore at his waist.

The other men had gathered up their coins and stored them in similar fashion. After thanking the officer again, the men left the quartermaster's tent and crossed the fort grounds to their horses and wagon. A group of enlisted men were already unloading the sacks of grain and carrying them to a rock building used for food storage.

When the wagon was empty, Will climbed onto its seat and released the brake. "I'll take this down to the dock and help George and Paul load up our supplies. "Meet me at Chouteau's when you are ready to head back home."

The Osage men nodded and mounted their horses. They planned to visit a few of the trading posts along the Verdigris to trade their beaver and mink pelts.

Will found George at the Verdigris dock sorting through the various crates marked for Union Mission. Normally they would not get a shipment at this time of year, but good rains had made the river navigable. The boat had also brought a packet of mail with several letters for the folks at Union.

"Where's Paul?" Will asked when he jumped down from his wagon perch.

"Do you need to ask?" was his brother's grinning reply.

"Gone to see Miss Tassie, I suppose."

"He promised not to be long."

"We'll see," Will laughed. "Let's get this wagon loaded. I want to head home as soon as we can."

The two men worked together to lift the crates of books, clothing and household supplies into the wagon. They had not been working long when Paul rode up, dismounted and tied his mustang and went to work as well. By the time they had completed their tasks Star and the Osage men were waiting at the Chouteau post.

"Trade was good today," Bird said, holding up a new flintlock musket he had purchased with his pelts.

"That's a beaut," George said, admiration in his voice.

"We're ready to head home, if you are, Monepasha," Will said to the elder.

The gray-haired man nodded. "It has been a good day." He patted the medicine bag and it jangled with the coins it held. "Never have we been paid in money for our harvest. I will remember this day forever."

"I hope it is the beginning of a new prosperity for the Osages," Will replied.

Colonel Chouteau had been listening to the exchange with a frown. "You teach them to read. You teach them to farm," he grumped. "You will make them worthless Indians. They will not be accepted in their own tribe and they will never be accepted in the white man's world. How will they survive on the frontier?"

"The frontier is changing, Chouteau," Will returned with steel in his voice. "It is a wise man who can change with it." He waved his hand around the store, warming to his argument. "You're already changing; you have supplies in here for farmers . . . for the Cherokee families coming to Lovely County. You can't expect the Osages to live on the edge of poverty just because you want the furs they bring you."

The Frenchman's eyes narrowed and he opened his mouth to retort. But George clamped a hand on Will's shoulder. "The day's getting on, brother," he said. "We should be going."

Will reluctantly allowed himself to be steered out of the trading post. He was passionate about his farming project and clearly angered that the colonel would disparage it. He climbed onto the wagon seat with enough force to cause it to creak and groan. The mules shook their heads in protest when he grabbed the reins tightly.

George took his time walking to the other side of the wagon, pausing to check on their freight. By the time he climbed aboard the seat, Will had calmed down. He flicked the reins across the rumps of the mules and they began the slow pull toward home. Paul and Star-That-Travels rode their mustangs close by. The other Osage men, also on horseback, soon outdistanced the wagon.

Will caught up with them at Flat Rock Creek where the Osages had stopped to water their horses. The warriors were seated on the ground, eating cold cornbread and pemmican. The mission party also stopped here for a break. While George and Paul brought pails of water for the mules, Will sat with the other men and conversed with them in Osage.

Kickingbird sat next to his father and was quieter than usual, not joining in with the banter among his brothers. When it was time to move on, the young warrior rose quickly to retrieve his horse from the shallow creek and mounted before anyone else. He seemed anxious to complete the journey home.

Will reached Hopefield much after the other men for he stopped at Union to help unload the supplies. He was eating a late supper that Susan had kept warm for him when they heard voices coming from the Osage longhouse. It sounded like an argument.

Will stood from the table and crossed the little cabin to look out the window. Susan was wiping Susie's hands of the sticky molasses candy her daddy had brought her.

"What is it?" Susan asked.

"Can't tell for sure. Looks like Hunts-The-Bear and Kickingbird are upset about something."

The two men were standing nose to nose outside the cabin of Monepasha. Kickingbird was older by several years, but Hunts-The-Bear was as tall and well-muscled as his brother. It looked like they might come to blows.

Monepasha had been standing in the door of the cabin.

He said something in a sharp tone but Will could not make it out. A knock sounded at their door and Will opened it to find Montgomery there.

"Are you watching this?"

"Yes. Do you know what it's about?"

"I have no idea," the minister shook his head. "Should we intervene?"

Will paused for a moment, giving his answer consideration. "Unless we're asked to do something, I think we should respect their privacy."

Montgomery nodded and both missionaries stood at the window watching as more of Monepasha's family gathered in the yard. Anger seemed to build among them.

Finally Monepasha brought down his hand to silence everyone. He was the elder of the clan and as one of the Little Old Men, Monepasha was to be revered. His word was law among the people.

He said something to Hunts-The-Bear and the young man nodded. Then he went to the cabin occupied by Bird and his children, then to Star and Teresa's. He knocked at the door of the Montgomery cabin and spoke to Harriett. Then he came to the Requa cabin.

Will opened the door at his knock.

"Father has called a council," he said. "He asks that you come."

"All of us?" Will asked.

"Yes, all."

Susan pulled on her bonnet, picked up Susie and joined Will and the Montgomerys in walking toward the gathering of Osage families. It was too warm for a fire, but they all took seats on the ground in a circle around the ash pit of the Osage communal fire in the middle of the yard. The sun sat on the western horizon causing faces to seem half dark, half light.

The men sat in the inner circle and the women and children sat behind them. When everyone was seated, Monepasha addressed Will.

"You gave me the money for our harvest, did you not?" He seemed to be conducting an inquiry.

"Yes, at Cantonment Gibson."

"I placed it in my medicine bag?" Monepasha held up the leather pouch, decorated with beads. It was the bag he had put the money in but it was clearly empty, no longer bulging with the heavy coins.

"Yes," Will said. Star and Bird nodded also.

"Hunts-The-Bear says that Kickingbird took the money," Monepasha explained. "We will determine if this is true."

Kickingbird looked sullen and defensive, his eyes hooded. But he remained silent.

Monepasha nodded to his youngest son.

"I saw Kickingbird drop the medicine bag outside our father's door," the eighteen-year-old stated. "It was empty."

"I found it that way," Kickingbird protested loudly. "That is not proof that I took the coins."

"Then why not alert our father to the missing money? Why did you drop it empty on the ground?"

No response came from Kickingbird.

"I saw Kickingbird with a bag when we dismounted our horses," Bird stated. "It was full and heavy then."

"That was mine," Kickingbird said. "I sold my pelts at the trader's store."

"Colonel Love never pays us in coin," said Hunts-The-Bear. "He paid you with whiskey, a knife and two blue blankets. I saw them. We all saw you carrying them."

"Was this the bag you saw in Kickingbird's hand?" Monepasha held up his medicine pouch.

Bird studied it for a moment. "Yes. That was the bag."

"You lie!" Kickingbird slurred the words as he stood quickly.

"My words are true!" Bird responded, also standing and striking a fighter's pose. No man wants to be called a liar.

"Please, let us not resort to fighting," Rev. Montgomery interjected.

Monepasha brought down his hand in a gesture calling for silence. "Sit," he said to the two men.

They had no choice but to obey their elder. Both sat but anger remained on their faces.

"Requa and Montgomery, I ask a great thing of you," Monepasha looked both of the missionaries in the eye. "Will you assist me in finding the truth?"

Somewhat reluctantly both men nodded.

"Please search Kickingbird's lodge. We will all wait here."

Will and Montgomery stood and walked to Kickingbird's cabin, all eyes on them. In the growing shadows, Susan reached for Harriett's hand and clasped it tightly. She could see across the circle that Teresa had her head bowed in prayer. Tension was thick among the Osages while they waited.

The two missionaries stepped into the dark cabin and took a moment to let their eyes adjust. It was sparsely furnished so Montgomery crossed to a stack of buffalo robes and flipped them back. A small flat basket of woven cane was revealed. The minister lifted its lid and a stack of gold coins seemed to catch fire from the shafts of waning sunlight through the open door.

Will grimaced at the sight. Nodding to the minister, he led the way back to the council. Montgomery placed the basket before Monepasha then he and Will returned to their places in the circle.

The Old Man looked at the basket but did not touch the coins. With a mixture of anger and sadness on his face, he addressed his son.

"You do not steal from family," he began.

"I needed it," Kickingbird defended himself. "I owe Mr. Lee . . . for the horse races."

"You do not steal from family," Monepasha repeated. "Steal from the Pawnees or the Cherokees or the Kickapoos. But never from the *Wahzhazhe*."

Rev. Montgomery opened his mouth as if to protest this sentiment, but quickly closed it again.

Kickingbird hung his head. "I needed it." His voice was angry and unrepentant.

"You have lost our trust, my son. You may no longer share our fire." Then in words that clearly hurt he said quietly but firmly. "Be gone from here before sunset tomorrow."

Kickingbird rose and angrily walked to his cabin with his wife and children following after him. Without saying much everyone else left the council circle to return to their own homes. The mood was somber among them.

Montgomery and Harriett paused outside the Requa cabin to discuss what they had just witnessed. It was their first experience with such a casting out and they were frankly surprised by it.

"The Osages live communally," Will said in a low voice. "They share everything. Why did Kickingbird feel that he had to steal the money?"

"He probably knew his father wouldn't approve of how he intended to use it," Harriett suggested.

"But I think if he had asked for it, his father would have given it to him," Susan said. "They don't view gambling the way we do."

"I think the tipping point was the disrespect Kickingbird showed an elder," Montgomery said. "That just isn't tolerated."

"I hope we can mend this rift in the family," Will concluded. "We will have failed in our mission if we can't." His tone was one of discouragement.

"We won't fail," Harriett said crisply. "We have a secret weapon . . . prayer."

CHAPTER FIFTEEN

Union Mission
September 1825

Four riders approached the mission, traveling south on the Texas Road. Word spread quickly among the missionaries working at weekday chores. The men were back.

Marcus led the way along the trail through the cornfields where drying stalks rustled in a hot breeze. Following him were the ministers Vaille and Montgomery, and Will Requa. They were returning from a visit to Claremont's Town.

Paul and George met them at the corral to take their horses. The men dismounted slowly, stiff from their ride that had begun early that morning. Their mood seemed somber as well as tired.

"Come take some refreshment before heading to Hopefield," Vaille said.

Will nodded but said nothing.

Montgomery clamped a hand on his shoulder. "We tried, Requa," he said. "At least we know Kickingbird and his family have been accepted at Claremont's. I think Monepasha will be relieved about that. And in time I believe they'll be reconciled. We have to have hope."

Again Will only nodded.

The men moved toward the dining hall, but Marcus parted with them before they reached the door. "I see my girls are waiting for me," he said, nodding toward the porch of his cabin where Lucie and Thea hopped up and down. Only an order from their mother to stay on the porch would keep them from running to meet their papa.

The other men smiled as the doctor loped across the yard to be greeted with joyous hugs by the little girls. They stepped into the dining room to also be greeted by their mission family who gathered to hear the news.

Marcus picked up the girls and asked, "Where's Mama?"

They pointed to the cabin door. Still carrying them, he shouldered open the door but stopped short just inside.

Clarissa and Sarah were on their knees pinning the hem of Eliza's wedding dress. It was a pretty polished cotton in a shade of blue that matched her eyes. A froth of lace circled the rounded neckline and the straight sleeves ending at the elbows.

"Oops, I've stepped into a dress shop," he teased as he set the girls down. They dashed across the room to play with baby Lizette who lay in a basket on the floor.

Their mother whirled around in surprise, pulling straight pins out of her mouth as she did.

"Marc, you're back," she said, standing quickly to greet him with a brief hug. "We were expecting you two days ago."

"We arrived at the village to find that Chief Claremont had passed away," Marcus explained. "So we stayed for the burial ceremony."

"Oh, I'm sorry to hear that." She glanced at Thea. Chief Claremont was the little girl's natural father and Clarissa had always hoped that when she was older Thea could come to know the man. Now she wouldn't have the chance.

"He wasn't that old, was he?"

"Probably in his late fifties, I guess," Marcus said. "But a life of hunting and fighting takes its toll. The smoking too. I think he struggled with breathing the last year or so."

"How is his wife, Yellowbird?"

"Leaning heavily on Mad Buffalo. He'll be chief now."

Clarissa nodded, then looked closely at her husband. "You seem tired. Do you want something to eat?"

"Yes, but I'll go over to the dining hall. I don't want to interrupt your dressmaking session." He sent a smile to Eliza who was standing quite still while Sarah continued pinning her hem.

"You look very nice, Miss Eliza," he complimented her.

"Thank you, doctor." The smile she returned to him held a bit of irony. For several years she had pursued Dr. Palmer, but he had resisted all her flirtations. Soon he would marry her . . . to Charles. She had asked the doctor to perform the wedding ceremony on the upcoming Sunday at Cantonment Gibson.

Clarissa stepped outside with Marcus. "When you come back, I'll give you a proper hello," she whispered. He waggled his eyebrows at her causing her to blush. She was smiling so widely as he walked to the dining hall that she had to school her features before stepping back inside.

"Done," Sarah announced as she placed the last pin. "I'll have this hem stitched by this evening. I told you it would be finished in plenty of time for your wedding."

"Have you told Alice yet?" Clarissa asked her friend.

"No."

Eliza!"

"Every time I start to tell her, she makes some remark about Charles. It gets me so angry I don't want to tell her. If she misses the wedding it will be her own fault."

"You don't really want her to miss the wedding, do you?" Sarah asked. She stood to unbutton the dress and help Eliza step out of it.

"No, I don't suppose." Eliza sounded like the petulant girl she used to be.

"You would regret it if she did," Sarah said. "I know I wished very much that my family could have been at my wedding. Mrs. Palmer and I didn't have that luxury. Our families were hundreds of miles away. But your sister will only be twenty-five miles away. And how do you think she will feel if she's not there to see you get married?"

"Alright, alright," Eliza held up her hands in surrender. "I will tell her. John already knows anyway. But if she makes one remark about us rushing into it, I'll uninvited her!"

Clarissa smiled. "She just doesn't want to lose her baby sister. Try to understand her point of view. It must feel like she's losing you."

"I'll try," Eliza sighed as she slipped into her workday dress. "But I'm not going to let her ruin my special day."

When Saturday arrived, Clarissa could not tell whether Alice was happy or sad as she and Eliza joined her in the wagon that would carry them to Gibson. The Vailles and Sarah and George were traveling down with them also for the monthly church service at the fort. Phoebe would keep all their children at the mission.

George drove the wagon and Marcus rode on the bench with him. John sat beside his wife in the wagon bed with a comforting arm around her shoulders. Eliza made a point of sitting on the other side of the wagon next to Clarissa and near her trunk. The wedding dress had been packed last to prevent as many wrinkle as possible.

After a honeymoon in Fort Smith, Charles and Eliza would be living in a room that the Nickses had added on to their frame home near the fort. Ever the romantic, Sallie was happy to host the newlyweds in the "officers' quarters" as she dubbed it.

While the wagon waited for the Neosho ferry, Clarissa noticed Eliza's signs of nervousness. She repeatedly tucked strands of hair back into her bonnet or smoothed her skirt over her knees.

She leaned closer to her friend. "Getting nervous?" she asked, keeping her voice lower than the other conversations in the wagon.

Eliza nodded. "I feel both excited and scared. Is that normal?"

"Quite normal. Marriage is a serious business. It ought to scare you a little."

"My stomach is taking marriage quite seriously then."

The teacher smiled. "Has Alice reconciled herself to your wedding?"

"She's gotten over being angry. Now she just cries all the time. I almost prefer her stony silence. She will probably blubber through the entire ceremony this evening."

"She's a passionate person," Clarissa observed as she sent a smile to the teary-eyed woman. "In her own way, she's as passionate about things that matter to her as Mr. Spaulding is."

Eliza smiled at her sister too and Alice gave a trembling smile back. The older sister finally seemed determined to be happy for Eliza.

Alice was still smiling while the young couple exchanged their marriage vows standing before Dr. Palmer in the officers' mess hall. Sallie had decorated the otherwise dark and drab log building with white candles and trailing honeysuckle that put off a delicate scent. Alice dabbed at her eyes on occasion, but otherwise kept her composure.

Clarissa, who served as Eliza's matron of honor, saw no tears in Eliza's eyes, but perhaps a few in her new husband's. They spoke their vows clearly but reverently. When the couple kissed, Clarissa smiled at her husband and was sure she spotted a few tears in his eyes!

Mrs. Bradley had prepared a beautiful supper for the newlyweds with Tassie and Lena helping her to serve it. Mrs. Bradley was building quite a business among the fledgling community that was growing around the garrison.

After enjoying cake and many toasts with apple cider, the couple took their leave. Alice and Eliza shared an especially long hug of goodbye before Charles helped his bride into the covered surrey he had rented from the new livery stable nearby. From Three Forks they would travel by keelboat to Fort Smith and would spend their first night floating under the stars down the Arkansas River.

The following afternoon Clarissa realized just how much the Gibson area was growing. While Marcus preached, she noted a number of civilians among the audience. Marcus had pointed out the new livery owner, a leathery-skinned man with a bushy graying mustache. Behind him sat a family of four. The man was white but his wife was Indian, perhaps Cherokee. Their two children, a boy and girl, were school age.

After the service John weaved among the soldiers to reach the family and introduce himself. Clarissa could hear the father give his name as Tom Ballard. "I'm the new barber," he explained in a clearly southern accent. "Every fort needs a barber. This here's my wife and my young'uns, Napoleon and Nancy." Napoleon looked to be about ten years old and Nancy was probably eight.

"I'm the schoolmaster at Union Mission, about twenty-five miles north of here," John explained. "Do you plan to send your children to school?"

"We would purely love to have our children educated," the barber said. "You take Cherokee children?"

"We offer education to anyone," John assured the man.

John's passion for education was so great he was rarely concerned with potential conflicts. Clarissa sent up a prayer that the Osage students would accept these Cherokee children without the animosity their elders sometimes displayed.

The barber said something in Cherokee to his wife and she responded in her native tongue.

"We don't have the money for boarding school," Ballard said. "And it would be too far and probably not very safe for them to ride back and forth each day."

"We never charge our students to board at the school," John explained. "We have the support of many churches back East and that allows us to offer our school for free."

"It's free?"

"Absolutely."

"Well, then we would be right pleased to send our children to your school." The father did look pleased, but Napoleon and his sister exchanged a look that said they were not.

A few Sundays later, Ella sat in the Fairfield Congregational Church, her impatience with the lengthy sermon barely concealed. She had exciting news for Samuel and though he sat next to her on the pew, she dared not even attempt to whisper to him. Her mother would scold with her eyes and she would likely incur the wrath of Deacon Jones who sat facing the congregation while a visiting minister spoke.

Rev. David Greene, secretary of the American Board of Missions, brought a report to the congregation on the work around the world. Only when he spoke of the Osage missions did she pull her attention away from her daydreams to his message. "We are grateful for your continued support of Union Mission and its Hopefield Farm," the man was saying. "I know you have a family connection to the pastors at Union, Rev. and Mrs. Vaille."

Ella tapped Samuel's arm in excitement but he gave her such a look of annoyance that she stopped immediately.

"I will be traveling on an inspection tour to our Indian missions come spring," Greene went on. "And I will be happy to bring greetings from you good people. Perhaps I might take an offering from you as well."

He went on in his appeal for funds to support a proposed new mission to the Cherokees that would open somewhere between Dwight Mission and Union. "Our work among the Cherokees has been greatly aided because they have created their own written language. We hope to soon have a hymnal, and portions of scripture printed in Cherokee."

Ella's mind wandered again. In her reticule she carried the most recent letter from her brother-in-law. William had indeed offered the position of bookkeeper to Samuel if he was willing to travel to the distant post.

He implied in the letter that he hoped this would also induce Ella to come to Lovely County. She was more than willing to start married life with Samuel wherever he might choose to go. She would show her handsome suitor the letter if this Rev. Greene would ever stop talking.

After the service finally ended, she walked with Samuel to the front door and they stepped out into the fall sunshine. Taking his arm, Ella steered Samuel to the big hydrangea bush by the front door and pulled out William's letter.

"I have the most exciting news, Samuel," she said.

"Obviously," he said dryly. "You squirmed all through the service."

She ignored his tone. "My sister's husband has offered you a job, Samuel. Out at Union Mission which Asie says is quite a beautiful place. Isn't it wonderful?"

"What part of that is wonderful?"

"The job, Samuel."

"What job?" a voice behind them queried. Benjamin Douglas, Samuel's father, had approached them after leaving the church with his wife.

Ella waved William's letter. "A bookkeeping job," she explained. "At Union Mission."

"Oh that is wonderful," Samuel's mother chimed in.

"No one could possibly expect me to take a job in some uncivilized, god-forsaken territory that isn't even in the United States."

Ella's face fell. "But it isn't god-forsaken. Didn't you hear Rev. Greene? God is doing a great work there as are my sister and brother-in-law."

The younger Douglas gave Ella a look as if she had just uttered a most ridiculous statement.

"I have no interest in being a missionary," he stated flatly before striding over to the Douglas carriage and climbing into the second seat.

Ella blinked back tears.

Mrs. Douglas patted her arm. 'I'll speak to him dear," she promised. "It's just his pride, you know. He's been searching for work for such a very long time; it's left him out of sorts." She threw a reproving look toward her husband and then walked to the carriage with Mr. Douglas trailing behind her.

Ella crumpled the letter and stuffed it back into her purse. Then she joined her parents for the walk to their home.

After dinner, Mr. Douglas called Samuel into his study. He offered his son a cigar from his humidor and poured them both a glass of port. Samuel visibly relaxed. Perhaps his father was finally ready to relent and let him come back to the firm.

"You're going to take that job out west," Douglas stated as he sat down behind his desk.

Shock registered on the young man's face. "You cannot possibly expect me to take work in Arkansas Territory."

"You haven't found anything in Connecticut, have you?"

"No, and I suppose I have you to thank for that. You put the word out didn't you so no one would hire me."

I didn't need to. Your reputation at the gaming tables has preceded you with every reputable business in this state."

"Then I'll go to New York."

You will go to Union Mission or . . ." There was a threat implied in the older man's hesitation.

"Or what?" Samuel's eyes narrowed, but he looked concerned.

"Or I will tell the authorities about this." Douglas opened a green ledger sitting on his desk and turned it so that Samuel could read it. Bold black check marks dotted the page written in Samuel's hand.

"I've studied the ledgers since you've been gone," the father stated. "I found these discrepancies . . . too many to be mere mistakes. You've been embezzling funds for more than a year."

Samuel wet his lips in a nervous gesture. He was caught. "You wouldn't have your own son arrested. Think of your reputation. Think of mother's."

"It's only because of your mother that I haven't already done so. I know she's been slipping you funds from the household accounts. It's her money to give, but I doubt she would continue if she knew how you put that money to use."

Panic crossed Samuel's features. If he lost his mother's support, he would be in serious trouble.

"I have a ship sailing for New Orleans next month," Douglas said, leaning forward in his seat. "You will be on it. You can take a steamboat to Arkansas from there."

"I have no other choice?"

"None."

Douglas sat back as if suddenly tired. There was sadness in his eyes. "I know you think I am punishing you, son."

"Aren't you?"

"No, I'm throwing you a life line. I hope this experience will make you the man your mother thinks you are."

Samuel had the good grace to look ashamed for the first time during the conversation. Slowly he stood. "I suppose I shall need to pack then." He paused, as if hoping his father might change his mind. But the old man, looking older than when the interview began, sat perfectly still. Samuel walked out of the room with shoulders slumped.

Mr. Douglas covered his eyes with his hand and quietly wept.

A few weeks later at the Fairfield docks, Ella cried openly as she told Samuel goodbye. This was not how she had planned things and she was decidedly feeling sorry for herself. Not one word of commitment from Samuel. Not one suggestion that she join him out west to begin a life there together.

Now he stood looking uncomfortable as Ella sniffled into her handkerchief as if hoping her show of emotion and devotion would elicit some expression of love.

His parents had already said their goodbye and had returned to the Douglas warehouse. Their friends from church had also wished Samuel bon voyage and had left the two alone for a private farewell. Samuel looked relieved when their pastor and his wife walked down the long wooden dock to join them.

The minister extended his hand to shake Samuel's. "Son, I'm proud of you," he said. "What a great undertaking to work for a mission among the Indians. If I were a younger man, I'd be joining you."

Samuel looked embarrassed. "Thank you, sir," he mumbled.

Pastor Eldridge pulled an envelope from his pocket. "I had planned to send this offering to Union Mission with Rev. Greene," he said. "But now that you are going there yourself I'll send it with you. Your father suggested it."

"My father?" Samuel's hand stopped short of taking the envelope. He looked suspicious. The keen look in the minister's eyes seemed to confirm that this envelope held more than just an offering for a distant mission. It held a test for Samuel.

"Yes. He said you wouldn't mind."

Samuel took the check and stuffed it into his pocket.

"I'd advise you to cash it at New Orleans," Eldridge went on. "I doubt there are any banks on the frontier."

Now a speculative look came into Samuel's eyes. "I'll do that, Pastor," he said. He glanced at the ship behind him. "Looks like I'd better board. You'll escort Miss Ella home, won't you?"

"We'd be glad to."

He lifted her hand and kissed it briefly. "Goodbye, dearest," he said quietly, looking regretful for just a brief moment. Then he turned and walked up the gangplank to the ship.

Ella watched him go, a confusion of emotions and thoughts battling inside her.

"Come, dear," Mrs. Eldridge said, slipping a comforting arm around the young woman's shoulders.

Ella let herself be guided along the busy wharf. She never looked back to see Samuel standing at the ship's rail, watching her with mixed emotions on his own face.

CHAPTER SIXTEEN

New Orleans
November 1825

The waters were rough from a rainstorm as the Douglas ship *Minerva* reached the New Orleans port. Samuel had spent the morning below deck to avoid the cold rain, but he came up top to watch the ship pull into the dock. The *Minerva* made a regular run to New Orleans for raw cotton, tobacco and sugar so the sailors knew the port well and made quick work of easing the ship into its berth.

Samuel looked out over the teeming dock and nodded with satisfaction. He had traveled to the Crescent City on various occasions for his father. He was familiar with the best places to stay where a card game could be found in the men's smoking parlor.

When the anchor was lowered, he returned to his stateroom and took up his hat and overcoat. At the dock, he waited to see his trunk unloaded, then flipped a coin to a porter with a handcart.

"Deliver my trunk to the Ambassador on St. Charles Street," he said, pointing it out.

The porter easily caught the gold piece and nodded. Samuel went in search of a hack to drive him to the hotel. He had settled into his room when a velvet-coated bellhop brought the trunk up and set it at the end of the bed. Samuel pressed a smaller coin into the man's proffered hand and he bowed himself out of the room.

Douglas opened the trunk and immediately reached for the white envelope Pastor Eldridge had given him. There was a bank just up the street where he could cash this check and gain a nice wad of bills. The funds his mother had slipped him would hardly pay for the hotel and his meals for a week here in New Orleans. The funds his father gave him for the riverboat to Arkansas would pay for his passage and little more.

He was going to slip the envelope into the inside breast pocket of his coat, but his hand stilled with the envelope half in and half out. He paused for a long moment looking down at his hand as if some unseen force had gripped it and held it in a vice.

"Blasted conscience," he finally groused and tossed the envelope back into the trunk. "I'll play with father's money and have the last laugh on him anyway."

He splashed water into a basin and washed his hands, then slicked back his hair. Drying his hands on the towel hanging from the washstand, he studied his features in the wavy glass of the mirror on the wall. Then he crossed the room, skirting around his trunk and locked the door behind him.

Samuel walked down the wide, carpeted stairs and then crossed the well-appointed lobby of the hotel to its dining room. He would need to find a card game soon, or his mother's funds would not last long at this opulent resort. But for today he would enjoy the tender steak served by the white-gloved steward and live a little before he was forced to take his place at a wilderness mission. With any luck, he'd have some winnings to make this reprieve last for a while.

Two days later, he moved his trunk to the less expensive Trinity House closer to the waterfront. What a run of bad luck he was having. That made it much easier to slip the church's check into his pocket at the Trinity House and walk to a bank nearby. Just carrying two hundred dollars in crisp bills put a spring into his step. He was whistling when he returned to his room. After pulling a couple of bills from the envelope, he slipped it back into his trunk.

"I can easily replace it with my winnings," he told himself. "Why I might even add a little to it." Such a resolution seemed to ease his conscience and he left his room with a smile.

But he seemed not to trust himself or his luck entirely. That afternoon, with what remained of father's funds, he booked passage on the *Comet*, a steamboat his father had recommended that would take him to someplace called Dwight Mission. It was to leave New Orleans in four days. Surely that's all the time he would need to turn his luck around.

All smiles had left Samuel when he walked the gangplank to the main deck of the *Comet* on the appointed day. Three more "just a few dollars won't hurt" reaches into the church funds had reduced it by half. If Pastor Eldridge had written to Vaille at Union Mission, Samuel's theft would be known. Ella's brother-in-law would probably send him packing. The prospect of being stranded without funds of his own at the edge of nowhere left him looking as if he had eaten something that didn't agree with him.

Douglas stood at the rail of the deck, not bothering to try to find his quarters aboard the steamboat. He watched the busy dock, a glum look on his face. When the rivermen untied the boat from the piers, he sighed deeply.

"Might I be of some assistance, sir?" a man's voice with a decidedly Southern drawl interrupted Samuel's dark reverie.

"What?" the young man asked somewhat sharply as he turned to see the boat's steward standing nearby.

The steward was in his mid thirties and had the look of a man who had long worked on the river. He was fair haired with a full beard and friendly gray eyes.

"Might I offer assistance?"

"No, I don't need anything." Samuel's words were unfriendly and curt.

The steward nodded his head. "If you should need anything, please let me know. My name is Philip Pennywit and I would be glad to help."

Samuel didn't bother to thank him and Pennywit began to walk away.

"Wait."

Pennywit returned. Samuel dug into his pocket and pulled out his ticket. "Can you tell me where starboard B, room 6 is?"

"Certainly," the steward smiled. "I just showed your roommate the way, as a matter of fact."

"My roommate?"

"Yes. Name's Jacob Hitchcock."

"Of course," Samuel muttered under his breath. "Father wouldn't pay for a private room. I'm out here to learn a lesson."

"I'm sorry?"

"Nothing," Samuel waved a dismissive hand. "Lead the way."

The steward led him to a set of stairs as the giant paddlewheel slowly turned, sending a thrum of noise throughout the boat. Pennywit showed him to the small cabin and introduced him to the other man who would share the room. Then with a tug at his cap, he left the two passengers to get acquainted.

"Where are you headed, Douglas?" the man named Hitchcock asked from where he sat on one of the narrow bunks. He was older than Samuel by several years and looked to be a laborer with frayed cuffs on his woolen jacket and calloused hands.

"A place you've probably never heard of," Samuel supplied. "Union Mission."

"Oh, I certainly know of Union."

You do?" Surprise registered in Samuel's voice. "I thought it was miles from anywhere."

"Well, that does about describe it," Hitchcock laughed. "Union's further west than any mission I know of. Right in the middle of the Osages."

"Have you been there?"

"Not myself, no. But my boss, the director of Dwight Mission, has traveled there a few times. So I know quite a bit about it."

"Your boss? You're a missionary?"

"I work at Dwight Mission, but I'm no preacher. I'm sort of the jack of all trades there. I take care of the farm, the stock, the buildings. Keeps me busy and out of trouble. I'm returning there with a load of supplies."

"Dwight is where this boat will dock?"

"Yes, we're end of the line for the steamboats. Big waterfall further up the Arkansas keeps them from making it all the way to Three Forks."

"Yes, I was told I would have to take a keelboat to get there."

"And then hire a teamster to haul you and your trunk on to Union." Hitchcock pointed to Samuel's trunk that had been delivered before either man had reached their quarters.

"There isn't even a stage line?"

"Not so far," Hitchcock said cheerfully. His happy countenance seemed to irritate the young Englishman.

Samuel flopped onto the bunk not occupied by Hitchcock. There were no chairs in the room. The mattress was thin though it looked clean. He was definitely not in one of the "luxury" suites he had seen advertised by the steamboat line.

"How can you stand it out here so far from civilization?"

"I like it out here," the man said and from the satisfied look on his face, he seemed to be speaking the truth. "It's quiet, peaceable, for the most part. And like I said, it keeps me out of trouble."

Samuel's eyes narrowed as if wondering what kind of trouble Hitchcock was referring to.

He cast out a speculative query. "I don't suppose you would know about a card game aboard. I've heard that gambling is common on the riverboats."

"Too true, that," the older man shook his head. "And that's the very kind of trouble I try to avoid. Learned my lesson the hard way on that."

"You were a gambler?"

"Ain't proud to say that I was." Hitchcock seemed genuinely regretful about this part of his past.

"I'm surprised you were welcomed to work at a

mission?" Samuel looked uneasy. "Those missionaries frown at that sort of thing, don't they?"

Hitchcock nodded slowly. "They rightly do," he agreed. "And if I hadn't turned away from it, I'd likely not be welcomed. But Rev. Washburn knows of my past. It was he who helped me see what it was doing to me. Helped me get free, he did."

"Free?" There was sarcasm in Samuel's question.

The mission worker looked closely at his young roommate. "It can take hold of you, if you let it," he explained. "Maybe you haven't experienced that yet, but you likely will. Then when you want to quit, you can't."

Samuel's eyes roamed around the small cabin as if he were searching for the exit. "I could easily quit," he said, diffidence in his voice. "It's just a harmless diversion."

"Harmless for some, perhaps. But not so for me. I had to face up to what it was doing to me."

Samuel looked at the man for a long moment and Hitchcock waited quietly. Finally, as if the question was being dragged out of him against his will, he asked, "What was it doing to you?"

"First it made me a liar. Then it made me a cheat. And finally it made me a thief."

Douglas flinched as if he had been slapped in the face. He glanced at his trunk as if expecting the half-empty church envelope to be visible. Then he looked back at Hitchcock now with a knowing expression on his face.

"My father arranged for you to be on this boat, didn't he? Or perhaps Pastor Eldridge?"

"I know neither man," Hitchcock assured him. "Why would you think so?"

"An amazing coincidence to be sharing a cabin with a gambler turned missionary, I think. My father must have arranged it somehow."

"Perhaps," the older man said with what seemed to be a twinkle in his eye. "But it may not have been your earthly father who did the arranging."

"What?"

Hitchcock simply smiled. "I think I hear the dinner bell," he said, instead of answering Samuel's question. "Shall we make our way to the dining room? The *Comet* has a fine chef in its galley."

"I'm not feeling hungry right now." Samuel's faced seemed pale as if he weren't feeling well.

Hitchcock stood and walked the few steps to the cabin door. "Suit yourself," he said before stepping into the passageway. "I'll leave you to your thoughts."

The man walked with bowed head toward the dining room on the upper deck. "Heaven help him," he whispered in a prayer. "I know you can, Father God."

Samuel eased back on the bunk, an unhappy frown on his face. "A liar . . . a cheat . . . a thief," he muttered. "Heaven help me. What have I become?"

For the next two days of the journey, Samuel tried to avoid Mr. Hitchcock as much as possible. H would leave the cabin early and spent most of the day in the men's smoking room. It was one place that Hitchcock didn't seem inclined to visit.

As he had heard, finding a card game was easy aboard the steamboat. In fact, some of the players seemed to be professional gamblers who lived aboard the boat and made their living off the travelers along the river.

Samuel seemed determined to prove to Hitchcock and to himself that he didn't have to gamble. For the first few days, he managed to avoid the card tables, but only through the sheerest of willpower.

When the *Comet* made a stop at the new town of Vicksburg, however, many of the travelers went ashore since the boat would be in port for several hours. Already Vicksburg had a reputation as a gambling town and a card game could be had at any hour of the day. Samuel was soon sitting at a green-felt table at one of the waterfront hotels with a stack of chips in front of him.

He declined the complimentary drinks designed to make him forget time and become reckless with his bets. He pretended to be a novice at poker and found that the other players believed it for they had never seen him in town before. They were willing to let him win a few hands while patiently waiting for the pot to grow and the bets to increase.

But he showed none of his usual euphoria at these wins and played without his normal enthusiasm. The game had lost its luster since he'd met a missionary named Hitchcock. It was all this man's fault that while he toyed with his chips, letting them click one at a time that they seemed to accuse him. Liar . . . cheat . . . thief!

"You in or not?" the player with the blue brocade vest asked, interrupting Samuel's reverie of guilt.

Samuel glanced again at his cards and then tossed his wager into the center of the table. "I'm in." He had a good hand, but there was no smile on his face, no widening of his eyes or flaring of his nostrils that would have alerted the other players. His mind seemed elsewhere and that made him hard to read.

Samuel watched the cards carefully and when the bet came around to him, he hesitated for a long time. He could bet everything in front of him and double his money -- if he had the winning hand. Or he could lose all of the church's money. He licked his lips as if tasting the victory. But just as he was about to push all his tokens forward, another player clicked his chips slowly.

Liar . . . cheat . . . thief, those slow clicks whispered.

Young Douglas pulled his hand back and took a steadying breath. He tossed only one stack of chips to the center of the table. Then he laid down his cards revealing a full house. The other players sighed with disgust and threw their cards on the table. He had won, but there was no sense of victory as he pulled the pot towards him.

Samuel stacked his chips in a tray to cash them out.

"You aren't quitting, are you?" Blue Brocade asked.

"You have to give us a chance to win some of that back," Chips Clicker added.

"Sorry, gents," Samuel said. "I need to be going. I'll stop in on my return trip."

"We'll expect it then," the dealer said and the other players nodded.

Samuel walked away without letting on that he had no idea when he might pass through Vicksburg again.

His hands were shaking when he slipped a new set of crisp bills into the white church envelope. He had not won back everything he had "borrowed," but at least the envelope was no longer empty.

When the *Comet* reached Dwight Mission near the little town of Dardanelle, the few travelers who had continued this far disembarked along with Samuel and Jacob Hitchcock. Another man from the mission was at the dock to meet Hitchcock and help him load the boxes of supplies in a wagon.

At Samuel's query, he pointed out a keelboat tied up to the dock nearby. He informed the young bookkeeper that it would be leaving for Three Forks later in the day.

Samuel thanked the man, shook hands with Hitchcock and then walked down the wooden wharf to inquire about passage on the boat. Assured that there was room for another passenger, he returned to the *Comet* and asked that his trunk be delivered to the keelboat.

Before it was put aboard, he pulled out the guilt-inducing church envelope, took the cost of the ticket out, and then tucked it into his pocket.

"What a mess I have made of things," he sighed that evening as he struggled to climb into his hammock aboard the boat. The dark, airless room had a fetid smell from so many men being crammed into the space. He slept little that night, for persistent scratching noises told him that men weren't the only occupants of the room.

The two days to Fort Smith were soggy with a constant cold drizzle falling. Still the air was better outside on the upper deck so Samuel, along with most of the other passengers, simply donned their rain gear and spent the days watching the mules pull the boat upstream on a well-worn path along the river banks.

The boat stopped at Phillips Landing to take on a load of

firewood and then again at Fort Smith to unload supplies. They passed the landmarks of Sallisaw Creek and Mulehead Bottom and saw a group of military surveyors marking the route for a road between Cantonment Gibson and Little Rock.

The captain warned the passengers of upcoming rough water at the Arkansas Falls after they passed the Illinois River. But because water levels were high from a wet winter of rains, the rocky shoals were hardly felt.

Samuel was waiting eagerly at the rail when the keelboat docked at Three Forks. He was one of the first passengers to disembark and he made his way to the Osage Agency that one of the rivermen had pointed out.

The next morning he found a freighter named Jose who was on his way north and would pass Union Mission. Samuel loaded his trunk and climbed into the wagon bed to find a seat between the crates that filled the space. He spent the bumpy ride listening to the teamster sing one Spanish song after another in between the curses and cajoles aimed at his mules.

Though it was late afternoon when they arrived, the lamps had already been lit at the mission for the day was dreary and overcast. When Jose pulled his wagon to a stop by the corral gate, most of the mission workers made their way to greet the freighter.

"Welcome, Jose," George greeted him. "What brings you to Union?"

"Got you a visitor." Jose nodded to the passenger. Samuel struggled to rise from his cramped seat, obviously stiff from the long, uncomfortable ride.

All eyes turned to him as he clambered down from the wagon bed. He brushed himself down, trying to look presentable at his new place of employment.

"Hello," he said. "I'm Samuel Douglas, your new bookkeeper. I'm to report to Rev. William Vaille."

"I'm Vaille," the minister said stepping forward to offer Samuel his hand.

Also moving forward eagerly was Asie Vaille. "But where is Ella?" she asked.

"Ella?"

"Yes, my sister. Ella Selden."

Samuel looked confused. "She's in Fairfield, of course."

"But we were expecting her to come with you."

"With me? But it would hardly be appropriate for us to travel together unchaperoned."

Asie looked about to cry.

Vaille quickly stepped toward Samuel and placed a hand on his shoulder. "Let's talk inside," he suggested, gesturing toward the dining hall. "No need to stand out here in the damp."

George helped Jose lift Samuel's trunk out of the wagon and then carried it to the guest cabin. Jose gratefully accepted an invitation to coffee and everyone walked to the dining room. In the kitchen most of the women were working on the evening meal.

Vaille led Samuel to a table to sit with him and Asie and the men gathered around Jose to hear of any news from Three Forks.

"Mr. Douglas, we were under the impression from Ella's letters that you two had an understanding," Vaille said quietly, trying to state the matter delicately.

"We expected you to come here as a married couple," Asie interrupted.

Samuel's face registered his surprise.

"Did we misunderstand your relationship?" Vaille asked.

"I'm afraid you did," Samuel stated. "I highly regard your sister, Mrs. Vaille, but I did not feel I was in a position to take on the responsibility of marriage while I was unemployed."

"But you have a job," Asie pointed out.

Samuel paused for a long moment as if trying to arrange his words carefully.

"When I received your kind offer of a job, my father just happened to have a ship leaving very soon for New Orleans. It was to be the last ship out before winter. There was hardly time for Miss Selden and I to prepare for a wedding. To have rushed into something and then leave immediately would have tainted your sister's reputation."

Asie sat back in her chair and crossed her arms in a gesture that signaled her unhappiness.

William sighed. "Well, there is nothing can be done about it. You are here now and we will simply have to find a way to enable Ella to join you."

Samuel's smile seemed forced. "Yes, of course." He took a sip of the coffee Amanda had poured for him. "I must express my gratitude for extending this opportunity to me without knowing anything about me. Pastor Eldridge didn't by chance send a letter of reference . . . or anything, did he?"

"No, we haven't received any communication from Eldridge."

Samuel let out a heavy breath. "Good," he said. "I mean, it's just as well."

CHAPTER SEVENTEEN

Fort Gibson
March 1826

Will Requa stood with all the other men who had gathered at the fort for a meeting between the Osages and their new agent Major John Hamtramck. Not much had been accomplished at this council, but at least the Osage chiefs in Arkansas Territory had been able to meet the new man in charge of their affairs on behalf of the government.

"I can't believe Hamtramck has been their agent for nearly a year, but this is the first time he's even visited the Osage lands," Will noted quietly to Rev. Montgomery as they mingled with some of the officers of the fort.

"I can see why Rev. Pixley at the Neosho Mission filed a complaint against him with the Indian Superintendent," Montgomery agreed, but he kept his voice low also.

"I was proud of Monepasha, though. He let Hamtramck know that the Osages aren't here just to provide him with furs for his trading post in St. Louis. They want to learn farming and he's supposed to be supplying them with the tools to do it."

The two men eased toward the exit of the log mess hall at Gibson. No longer a garrison of tents; the fort was now a fully completed military installation. There had been pride in Colonel Arbuckle's voice when he announced that Cantonment Gibson was now Fort Gibson. He expected they would soon have their own post office as well.

The men from Hopefield were soon on their horses and riding northward. A light drizzle had turned into a full rain by the time they neared Union Mission. Will and Montgomery stopped for the night there, but Monepasha, Bird and Star-That-Travels continued on to Hopefield. Rev. Vaille had asked the two Hopefield missionaries to attend the council and report back to him about it.

They rode their horses into the barn, quickly dismounted and shook the rain from their hats and coats. Paul met them in the log structure and offered to care for the animals while they got coffee. Gratefully, the Hopefield men thanked him and ran across the yard to the welcoming shelter of the dining hall.

Inside they found Rev. Vaille sitting across a table from the new bookkeeper Mr. Douglas. The two men greeted them as Amanda bustled out from the kitchen with coffeepot and mugs in her hands.

"Have a set-to," she invited in her cheerful Irish brogue.

"Mrs. Fuller, you are a lifesaver," Montgomery said as he took the cup she poured for him.

"Got us a raw day today, do we not?"

"Indeed," Will said as he took a seat near the fireplace and sipped the welcome drink. "If this rain doesn't stop, it's going to wash all our seed out of the fields."

"My husband says the same," Amanda nodded. "Nothing more frustratin' to a farmer than that. Would you care for some cornbread to tide you over before supper?"

"No, this is fine," Montgomery replied and Will nodded.

While they enjoyed the warmth of the fire and the coffee, Will's brother George entered the dining hall. He was also wet from the rain and his boots were caked in mud. He tried to wipe them on the horsehair rug at the door.

Martha Woodruff poked her head into the room from the kitchen so see who had entered. "Coffee?" she asked.

"Thanks, Mrs. Woodruff," George said. He hung his coat and hat on a peg by the door and crossed the room to sit at the same table as Will.

"River's up," he said after Martha had poured coffee for him.

"Out of its banks?" Will asked.

"If the rain doesn't stop soon, it will be. I've been

keeping an eye on it. The water is over our fishing rock and has nearly covered the cane."

The thick cane that lined the banks of the river rose over six feet tall. For the Neosho to have reached such heights was alarming.

His words caught the attention of Rev. Vaille who rose from his seat and approached George's table. They also brought the women from the kitchen.

"Should we consider moving our possessions?"

"We may want to," George said. "At least from the longhouse cabins and the tool sheds. They're closest to the river. The water may get inside them. I think lifting everything we can into the lofts would be wise."

"We'll alert everyone at supper," Vaille said. "How long until you'll be serving, Mrs. Fuller?"

"Half an hour."

"That's enough time to help Woodruff move his tools from the blacksmith shed," George said. "He was already starting when I came in."

"I'll help as well," his brother said. They stood to get their coats and step outside. The two ministers joined them. Samuel kept his seat in the dining hall. Amanda and Martha exchanged a look that said what they thought of the new man. They returned to the kitchen to finalize supper preparations.

By the time supper ended, the rain had stopped, but the river continued to rise toward the mission compound. The evening was spent in packing clothes, linens and personal items and lifting them along with small furniture into the cabin lofts. All the while, the ominous sound of the rushing river could be heard in the distance.

Samuel had declined help in putting his cabin's contents in his loft. He occupied the cabin that had been Eliza's but he had not been at Union long enough to have accumulated much to furnish the small room. He packed his clothes and shaving kit, nervously checked the church envelope twice and then shoved the trunk up into the loft. It was followed by his washstand and two chairs.

"Probably a complete waste of time," he mumbled to himself.

Samuel awoke in the morning to hear voices outside. He put his bare feet on the floor, but drew them back quickly in surprise. About an inch of water covered the pine planks. He reached for his britches at the foot of the bed and stood on his mattress to pull them on. Then he rolled up the cuffs and stepped out again into the muddy water.

He crossed to his door and opened it to an even greater surprise. About half of the mission yard was underwater. In the distance he could see Will Requa and Rev. Montgomery on their horses, quickly making their way to Hopefield.

Samuel sloshed back to his bed to strip the sheets and quilt off it and hastily stuff them up into the loft. Then he pushed his feather mattress and pillows up as well. He grabbed his socks and boots which were already wet and while sitting on the ropes strung across his bed frame, he pulled them on.

When he stepped outside, he almost lost his footing. He'd had no sense of the fast movement of the water while still inside. The water rushed and swirled around the longhouse and lapped at the dining hall. The small blacksmith shed had already been moved off its rock foundation.

Soon it was lifted by the river and knocked into the corner of the dining hall. It quickly broke free and continued across the compound. It next bumped the Fuller's cabin, damaging one of the porch posts. Then it floated on downstream.

Soon the river water - normally clean but now quite muddy - seeped between the planks of the kitchen and dining room. Everyone worked at clearing the building. Even the mission children were involved with relaying pots and pans to the school house.

All of the other buildings held against the river current. The longhouse cabins took in the most water and each one would have to be repaired. By afternoon the waters had receded and the cleanup began.

Stephen and Paul loaded barrels into the wagon and

drove to a creek west of the mission to get clean water. They would need to clean their rock springhouse before they could use its water.

When they unloaded the barrels into the laundry, Marcus called for everyone's attention. "Please be sure to use only the clean water from the creek for the next week, maybe two," he said. "Dirty water can carry diseases such as cholera."

The mission family nodded solemnly and then went to work to heat the water and begin the cleanup. It would take a week or more to get the mission back to normal. But as Amanda stated, all were grateful that no one had been injured or lost in the flood.

Two days later, Bird stopped at the mission on his way to Three Forks. He told them that the structures at Hopefield had been spared any damage. But much of the seed in the fields had been washed away by the heavy rain. They would have to plant again.

In mid-April, the missionaries at Union were surprised by a visit from Rev. David Greene. He was accompanied by Cephas Washburn from Dwight. Abraham stepped out of the boys' classroom to meet their visitors at the corral and take their horses.

Stephen, Paul and George were out in the fields. Most of the other men did not hear the visitors arrive for they were cutting pine logs in the noisy sawmill. They were cutting boards to construct a house for the growing Vaille family.

Abraham invited the visitors to the dining hall. Samuel had been writing out a supply order for Nicks & Rogers when the visiting ministers entered the dining hall. There was immediate recognition of David Greene on his face following by a look of panic. Pastor Eldridge had originally planned for Rev. Greene to bring out the Fairfield offering. Did he know that Samuel was to have brought it instead?

Samuel nodded a greeting to the men, but said nothing while Sarah met them with coffeepot in hand and chatted amicably with them about the weather and their journey.

Abraham alerted the men at the sawmill who dusted off the wood chips and also made their way to the dining room.

In his office, Dr. Palmer finished bandaging the scraped knee of Francis Chouteau, sent the boy back to class and also joined everyone in sitting down to coffee with their guests.

"It's a pleasant surprise to have you visit, Rev. Greene," Vaille said after everyone had exchanged greetings and introductions. "We were unaware that you planned to come out here."

"Yes, my apologies for that," the mission leader said. "I'm touring all the missions among the Indians and I wasn't sure of my arrival time. Since the American Board is now in charge of this mission I thought I should familiarize myself with your operations."

"What is your impression so far?" Marcus asked with a smile.

Greene smiled as well. "You have a very hospitable place here and your reputation for that is widespread. Looks like your buildings are a bit rough though."

"We were inundated with floodwaters last month," Vaille explained. "It did take a toll on the lower logs of the buildings. We've been working on repairs."

"That reminds me," Greene said, as he reached into his inside coat pocket to pull out an envelope.

At the sight of it, Samuel gulped his coffee and almost choked.

"On my journey out here, I collected offerings at several churches for our various missions," Greene explained as he set the envelope on the table. "I know you will find good use for these funds."

"We are certainly grateful for this," Vaille said. "We will use it for the repairs."

"I was sure you could use it," Greene nodded. "From looking over your year-end financial report, I noticed a drop in funds."

"Yes, I suppose that is due to the fact that we are no longer so generously supported by Mrs. Chapman." Vaille sent a look toward Samuel. The young bookkeeper had helped him with the financial report just after he arrived at Union. Samuel studied his coffee cup.

"I hope the downward trend doesn't continue," the director stated. "I am finding that the zeal for missions once so common in our churches has waned somewhat. It's becoming harder to raise the support we need."

"Well, as you noted, we are known for our hospitality here. Until now we have offered meals and medical service and blacksmithing repairs for free. We may have to charge for these things."

"That may be your best option," Greene said.

At this time Clarissa and John came to the dining room with the students, having dismissed school for the day. The two teachers found chairs by their spouses while the children took their seats at the table reserved for them. Martha brought out a tray of molasses cookies and poured them all mugs of milk.

"You have only a few Osage students?" Greene asked while the children helped themselves to their afternoon repast.

"Most of our Osage students are of mixed blood," John explained. "And attendance can be sporadic especially at this time of year."

"Rev. Dodge at Harmony reports the same thing," Greene added. "Dwight Mission seems to have a better record. The Cherokees are very interested in educating their children."

"We're even serving Cherokee students here," John informed the visitors.

"That brings me to another purpose of my visit," Greene went on. "Rev. Washburn wants to open a substation for Dwight. There is enough interest that he believes they could offer a day school among the Cherokee settlements between Dardanelle and Fort Smith. I brought him with me to help scout out a location. We found a spot on the Mulberry River and Chief Jolly has given permission for a school to be built there. The Cherokees will assist with construction."

"That's excellent," Vaille stated, but his words seemed a little flat. There had been a worried look on his face ever since he had sat down across from the board secretary.

Rev. Greene took a slow sip of his coffee as if considering his next words carefully. "I know the American Board has just taken responsibility for the Osage and Cherokee missions and I don't want to make any hasty decisions. But I see changes coming to Union and we need to consider all options for this work."

"Options?" Vaille asked.

"I know the Osages have signed a treaty moving them out of Missouri and Arkansas Territory. This is going to impact both Harmony and Union, maybe not right away, but eventually. This mission may have to move if you end up in Cherokee land."

"But we can serve the Cherokees just as well as we can the Osages," John protested.

"We've spent a great deal of money building this mission," Vaille added.

"I appreciate that," Greene nodded to both men. "Just hear me out on what I am thinking. I would propose that someone from Union take the leadership of the Mulberry Mission. I know from your reports that Dr. Palmer helps pastor a congregation at Fort Gibson. I came here to ask Dr. and Mrs. Palmer if they would consider heading up this new mission effort."

A murmur of surprise ran through the group. Clarissa herself suppressed a gasp at the unexpected question. Marcus looked at her, trying to read her thoughts on this opportunity being presented to them.

"When would you need an answer on that Rev. Greene," the doctor asked.

"The new station won't be built for several months. It is not a prairie location and will require the land to be cleared of many trees. You have plenty of time to prayerfully consider this. I don't require an answer right now."

"But we need a doctor here," Asie Vaille spoke up while glancing over at her baby sleeping in his cradle. She looked very distressed at the thought of losing their beloved physician.

"Dr. and Mrs. Palmer are valuable members of this

mission family," Vaille quickly added. "There isn't a day goes by that Palmer isn't attending to some medical need. And Mrs. Palmer does an excellent job as the girls' teacher."

"I don't intend to deprive you of a doctor," Greene assured them. "I've spoken with Dr. Weeks at Dwight. He has no interest in pastoring a church but would be willing to transfer here. His wife also is a teacher. It would be a trade of sorts between your two stations."

Everyone was quiet as they absorbed this proposal. They understood that beneath it was the unspoken suggestion that Union would eventually be moved or closed.

Greene looked around at the Union family. "I did not want my visit to be upsetting to you. I just want you to be aware of some of the decisions we are facing as a mission board. We want to do what is best for you and the important work that you are engaged in here. I know you have all sacrificed a great deal for this mission and I for one am very grateful for it."

"We thank you for your honesty, Rev. Greene," Vaille said.

"On a brighter note, I would like to now make it official," Greene smiled. "Rev. Vaille we would like to appoint you as director of Union Mission in place of Rev. Chapman. We will appoint Rev. Montgomery as pastor of Union and Hopefield. And for the time being, Dr. Palmer and Mr. Redfield will be co-pastors at Fort Gibson."

This information seemed to put everyone more at ease. Even Samuel breathed a sigh of relief as the women rose from the meeting to finish supper preparations.

Later that evening, Marcus and Clarissa discussed Rev. Greene's proposal after putting Lucie, Thea and their border Deer-in-Water to bed. Clarissa brushed out her hair while her husband banked the embers in the fireplace.

"Tell me honestly what you think about this?" Marcus prodded as he came to their bed.

"Honestly, it took me by surprise. My first reaction was that I didn't want to leave all my friends here. But I know you've always wanted to pastor a church and I want that for you too. I will go wherever you go."

"I'm torn too," Marcus confessed. "I've spent six years trying to learn the Osage language. I think I finally have their trust so that they will come to me whenever they have a medical need. We would have to start all over at Dwight. It won't be easy."

"Nothing worth doing is easy."

Marcus smiled. "No it isn't. And Rev. Greene is right. Things are changing out here. We will be working with the Cherokees even if we stay at Union. Let's give it some more thought and prayer. We don't have to decide now."

He turned down the lantern wick and then blew out the flame, plunging the room into darkness.

"Don't forget I'm riding up to Hopefield tomorrow to check on Susan Requa," he whispered.

Um, uh," Clarissa nodded sleepily. "I'll be starting on final exercises. Hard to believe the end of school is just a month away."

"We have a good life here, don't we?" Marcus reached for her hand and pulled it close.

"Yes," she sighed in contentment. "We do. But anyplace will be good as long as we are together."

The boys' classroom was packed for the final exercises of the school year. Charles and Eliza rented a surrey and drove up from Fort Gibson to hear her nephew Billy recite the multiplication table and a brief bit of Plato. Most of Monepasha's clan came for the event also.

Clarissa was nervous, as usual, for her girls but they did well with only a minor mistake here and there. Two of her students were graduating this year – Beth Vaille and Louisa Revoir.

They would now pursue very different paths in their young lives. Louisa would help her mother Teresa with the work of the household at Hopefield until she married, probably within the next few years. Beth would travel back east to attend a finishing school. She had confided to Clarissa that she planned to take her teaching exam and return to Union Mission to help her parents with the work here.

After the bestowing of ribbons and certificates, everyone walked to the dining hall for refreshments. It was a fine day with a bright blue sky, scudded with white clouds. The soft air had the rich smell of spring growth. The corn was already to the horse's belly and would be tasseling soon.

Clarissa greeted all the parents of her students and made sure to congratulate Beth and Louisa once again. Then she edged through the crowd toward Eliza. They hadn't had an opportunity to visit since Christmas.

"So how is married life?" she asked in greeting the young woman with a hug.

"Oh, it's hard work," Eliza replied with a wink.

"And you're enjoying it?"

"Every minute of it. And I'm learning how to be a storekeeper since Sallie Nicks is now in the family way. She lets me and Tassie just about run the store."

"I'm sure she's glad to have you there."

Charles and Marcus joined them then, each with a bowl of blackberry cobbler in their hands.

"Charles has some interesting news from Washington," the doctor said before taking a bite of the warm dessert.

"Oh?" Clarissa queried. Others standing nearby also looked interested in the news.

"We just received a dispatch from the Secretary of War," the lieutenant said to everyone gathered around him. "He informed us that the Creeks in Georgia and Alabama have signed a removal treaty. They're trading land back east for something out here. We're to expect a surveying party to arrive at Fort Gibson within the next few months."

"I thought the Cherokees were to be given Lovely County," John Spaulding remarked.

"Yes, that is still the plan, I believe. The Creeks will be given land south and west of the Verdigris River. The actual boundary lines are yet to be worked out."

"Are the Cherokees and Creeks on friendly terms?" Abraham asked.

"Colonel Arbuckle has had dealing with both tribes. Though they've taken different sides in various conflicts, they are neighbors back east and generally get along well. But the fort will be expected to ensure that their peaceful relations continue out here."

"Who are the Creeks?" Star-That-Travels asked.

"Descendants of the Mound Builders, I'm told. Many have married Scottish settlers so they have surnames like McGillvary, McIntosh or McQueen."

Everyone smiled at this bit of information.

"They're farmers; some own large plantations," Charles continued.

"And slaves?" Vaille frowned.

"Yes, some do." The officer's voice was solemn and he and Eliza exchanged a look.

Then Charles changed the subject. "Mrs. Fuller, this cobbler is wonderful. My compliments."

"I thank you," Amanda smiled, "but most of the credit must go to Sarah and Martha. They hardly let me into me own kitchen these days." Amanda was seated at Martha's insistence. Her baby was due soon but that was not something discussed in mixed company.

Looking a little uncomfortable, Charles turned to John. "I have received a letter from my parents in Boston. My mother works with a mission organization that has started a school for Indian students. The school is in search of a headmaster and I thought of you."

"The school is in Boston?" John asked.

"Actually in Holyoke. You have the kind of experience they are looking for. Eliza and I thought since we'll be settling in Boston when I'm out of the military that you and Alice might want to be settled near there as well. Just a thought."

John and Alice exchanged a look. "If you will, write to your parents and let them know I'd like more information about the position."

"I will do that."

Clarissa felt a sudden sadness at the thought of the

Spauldings leaving Union. She supposed nothing stayed the same, but she couldn't help but wonder if Union Mission itself would soon be no more. The federal government seemed bent on bringing new tribes to this prairie location. They couldn't be sure that those new tribes, the government or the American Board of Missions would want Union to remain here.

Shortly the gathering broke up as the Osage parents gathered their children for the long ride home. Clarissa made sure to hug all her girls and wish them a good summer. As she helped the other women clear the dishes and clean the dining hall, it felt to her as if nothing would ever be the same.

CHAPTER EIGHTEEN

Fairfield, Connecticut
July 1826

Ella sat on a quilt at the village green for the annual Independence Day picnic. She was trying to seem interested in the conversation between her parents and the stodgy Mr. and Mrs. Stewart who had joined them for the day's festivities. Mr. Stodgy, as Ella called him in her mind, was senior law partner at the firm where her father worked.

Instead of feeling any interest in the conversation about the upcoming mayoral election, however, she was inwardly fuming. One year had passed since she had confronted Samuel at this very time and place about his intentions. He had confessed to being without employment and she thought they had reached an understanding. Once he found a job, they would wed.

Six months since he arrived at Union Mission and she had only received two letters from him. Neither provided her with concrete plans for their marriage. She was feeling desperate. She was another year older and now considered a spinster. All her friends from school were married and had started families. Yet here she sat with her parents for another Fourth of July picnic.

Ella twirled her parasol in an unconscious gesture of her frustration. She had tried everything she could think of to get an escort out to Arkansas Territory. Apparently not a soul in all of Fairfield had any interest in traveling further west than Pittsburgh.

"Ella, dear," her mother interrupted her angry reverie. "You're twirling your parasol like a top. It's liable to spin off into the clouds."

"Sorry, mother," Ella said with contrition that she didn't feel. She stilled the umbrella and took a deep breath. At least there was some hope for the future.

Just this week, they had received a letter from Asie to say the Vaille family would be coming home for a visit soon. They would bring Beth for school and stay through Christmas. Asie was eager for her family to meet her two sons, Joseph and Scott, who had been born out on the prairie. It was the first letter in quite a while in which Asie had sounded happy. Ella, she wrote, could then travel back with them to Union Mission early next year.

At least another six months before she could be married. But now she had something she could tell her friends who politely inquired about Samuel. Now she wouldn't seem quite like an "unclaimed treasure," as her mother sympathetically called those unmarried women in their acquaintance.

Ella was twirling her parasol again, but this time in anxious anticipation. She was packing her trunk in her mind and planning what new items she should purchase for the trip. Her mother had to ask her twice to help gather up the picnic supplies for the walk home.

Quite a number of folks were gathered at the boat dock on the Verdigris River to see the Vailles on their way back east. Joining them was the Spaulding family also. John had accepted the position as headmaster at the Holyoke school. Abraham Redfield would take his place as the boys' teacher at Union.

Several of the missionaries had come to Three Forks for the sendoff. Amanda, Susan and Sarah who all had nursing babies had stayed home, but insisted that Phoebe make the trip south. Because of her little ones – Jane and the twins, Jacob and Esau – she had not left the mission in well over a year. She was obviously enjoying the day, despite the heat and the whine of mosquitoes in the cane along the river.

The departing families exchanged hugs and handshakes all around while their luggage was put on board the large keelboat tied up at the dock. Samuel seemed embarrassed by the show of emotion among the women as they said goodbye to Alice for a final time. After shaking hands with Rev. Vaille and receiving a stiff hug from Asie, he left the dock and wandered over to the Pryor trading post.

A group of men had gathered on the front porch to watch the doings on the dock. Samuel peeked into the shadowy interior of the shed where Captain Pryor did business. But the smell of the hides stacked inside kept him from entering.

One of the traders lounging on the porch looked Samuel up and down as he leaned against a post. "You one of them missionaries?" he asked before launching a spit of tobacco.

"No," Samuel said, "I'm not a missionary. I just work at Union."

"Same thing, ain't it?" The man wiped his mouth with the back of his hand.

"Not in the least." Samuel's face said what he thought of the man whose dirty beard testified that his tobacco didn't always launch very far.

The man shrugged and turned to another of the loungers. "You going up to the races tomorry?"

"Probably," the second man said. "Hear tell that Chouteau's brought in some Kentucky horses. Gonna put them up against them Osage ponies. Bet there'll be a big crowd to see it."

"Big purse, too," the first man said with a glint in his eye.

"Purse," Samuel straightened up. "Do you wager on the races?"

"Sure," several of the men responded. "What's the point otherwise?"

"And where are these races held," Samuel asked, trying to sound nonchalant, but barely hiding his interest.

"At La Saline, up north from the mission," one of the men provided. "You just follow the Texas Road; it fords the Neosho right at La Saline."

Samuel nodded thoughtfully. "And anyone can wager?"

"Yep," he was told. "Even missionaries." There were snickers all around, but Samuel ignored them.

He stepped off the porch and made his way around back of the shed where the mission wagon was parked in the shade of tall cottonwoods. Their horses were hobbled nearby, cropping the tall grasses and rapidly flicking their tails to fight the flies. Paul had ridden Thunder on over to see Tassie at the sutler's store.

The other missionaries left the dock when the Vailles and Spauldings boarded, and gathered at the wagon to open the baskets of food Amanda had packed for them. After dinner they planned to cross the Neosho and visit the folks at Nicks & Rogers. Then Marcus would preach in an evening service at the fort. They would leave at daybreak the next morning to return home.

Marcus and Clarissa shared a cottonwood tree to lean against while enjoying ham sandwiches with pickled eggs and jars of honey-sweetened tea. The heat and food seemed to make everyone drowsy so the little campsite was quiet.

"I've had a thought," Marcus said quietly to his wife while they sipped the warm tea.

"Yes?" Clarissa drew out the word in a question, teasing in her voice.

"I do occasionally have them, you know."

"I know. Sometimes they're even good ones."

"Thank you." Marcus pretended to be insulted.

"So what was your thought?"

"If we take the Mulberry Mission, we'll need to hire some help. Rev. Greene told me the Board would allow us two positions. I'm thinking we should hire Paul and Tassie."

"Oh, that would be perfect," Clarissa said. "Tassie could do the cooking and housekeeping while I teach and Paul would manage the farm and stock."

"Exactly. We know them and know they're good people; good workers. I'd feel better about taking on the mission if we had someone with us we knew we could rely on."

"That is a good thought," Clarissa smiled.

"Yes, well, I do have them occasionally."

Clarissa laughed. "So does this mean you've made a decision about the new mission?"

"I'm leaning toward saying yes to it," Marcus replied. "I spoke with John about his decision and we both agreed that Rev. Greene signaled that Union Mission may not have as much support in the future. The fact that they chose not to hire a new teacher says as much."

"I think Abraham will make a good teacher. He's always helped John with his class."

"He will be good I'm sure. But now we don't have a mission superintendent. Abraham can't do both jobs."

"So make George superintendent."

"That was my other thought."

"Ooh, two good ones in a single day." She leaned in towards him, crinkling her nose with a smile to assure him that she was simply teasing.

"Just for that I'm taking a nap," Marcus said. "I've done enough thinking for today."

"You do that," she said. "I'll help Martha and Phoebe clean the dishes."

She gathered their tea jars, plates and napkins and joined the other women at the wagon. Marcus pulled his hat down over his eyes, settled back against the tree and was soon asleep.

The following afternoon, Samuel made his way to the barn. From the moment he had heard about the horse races, he had been restless. Now he saddled a horse and told Paul that he was riding up to La Saline.

"You know how to get there?" Paul asked.

"Take the Texas Road north to the ford, right?"

"Yes, that's right. But we usually don't travel alone. Is someone riding with you?"

"I'm perfectly capable of taking care of myself." Samuel's voice held disdain.

Paul had a questioning look on his face, but Samuel ignored it and provided no information on why he wanted to visit the Chouteau trading post. He swung up into the saddle and started out across the cornfield path where the tall stalks waited for harvest.

If his father had meant for this job to provide a cure for his gambling, the isolation of Union Mission might well have served that purpose. The young man had asked about opportunities to "have a little fun out here" but the folks at Union had been unable to suggest anything more stimulating than fishing at the river or picnicking by the creek.

Now that he had received his first pay, brought by Rev. Greene, he'd counted the money repeatedly as if dreaming of a chance to double it. He had avoided the church envelope still tucked away at the bottom of his trunk. No one at the mission knew anything about it.

He had started to leave half of his pay in his cabin, but at the last moment had placed all of it into his leather wallet and slipped it into the pocket of his jacket. Now he whistled a bawdy tavern song as his horse loped northward on the road.

Once at Chouteau's place, he easily found the race track east of the trader's two-story home. A group of fellow gamblers were mingling among the horses and riders in a completely casual atmosphere. It was clear that rules were only loosely observed at this track.

Most of the men were Osages, recognizable by their shaved heads with only a tufted scalp lock. Most were heavily tattooed as well. But several other men, dressed as farmers or trappers, were also sizing up the horses and laying bets with a talkative Frenchman the gamblers called Antoine.

"You betting or just here to take up space?" the garrulous little man asked.

"I'll watch a few runs," Samuel said cautiously. "I don't know the horses."

A sly look crossed Antoine's face and he spoke in French to an Osage warrior standing by. "Here's a cock ready to be plucked."

That warrior was Kickingbird and he grinned in response. What both men didn't realize was that Samuel understood French having spent a year of his schooling on the Continent.

He slipped both hands into his pockets, wrapping his

fingers around his wallet, and walked away toward the dirt track. Soon most of the bettors were lining up along the circle to watch the first race. It was a wild melee with neither riders nor horses being numbered. The audience seemed to know each horse by name or the man who was riding it. Samuel watched closely, familiarizing himself with the various players. There didn't seem to be any Kentucky horses; only the rangy Osage mustangs.

As the night progressed and more races took place, Samuel seemed comfortable with placing small wagers. A few he won; others he lost. But the intensity on his face and the delight when Antoine counted out his winnings said his father's wish would not be fulfilled this night.

Samuel made his way to his own horse after several races had been run.

"Leaving so soon?" Antoine challenged.

"I need to get back. Don't want my friends to have to come looking for me."

As he prepared to mount, he found the warrior named Kickingbird by his side. Kickingbird had raced a few times, but spent most of the evening gambling and passing around a flask of whisky.

"You ride back to the mission tonight?" Kickingbird asked.

Samuel's eyes narrowed. "I'm riding home," he said vaguely.

Kickingbird nodded. "I'll ride with you." With an easy leap he mounted his mustang and pulled another along behind him.

There was nothing Samuel could do but mount his own horse. "Should have listened to Paul," he muttered under his breath.

The men walked their horses south in uneasy silence.

"Why you gamble?' Kickingbird finally asked. "Preacher men don't gamble."

"I'm not a preacher," Samuel explained in annoyance. "I just work at the mission."

"Preacher men try to change the Osage," Kickingbird

went on as if he made no distinction between the workers at the missions. "Everybody gambles, everybody lies, everybody steals. Always have. Now my own father says it is wrong. All because of preacher men."

Samuel looked at Kickingbird sharply when he spoke of his father. Then he sighed, "Fathers always expect too much of their sons. Sometimes we just can't be what they want."

Kickingbird looked as if he did not understand what Samuel meant. "You have plenty big money?"

"No," Samuel said sharply. "I lost most of it."

Kickingbird nodded. "Don't owe the big trapper, Mr. Lee. He make you sorry."

"I'll remember that," Samuel said.

Kickingbird nodded and then turned his horse toward Claremont's Town. Without another word, he moved westward toward the setting sun. Samuel continued south, a glum look on his face. Some sons seemed destined to disappoint their fathers.

At the end of the week, Stephen announced at breakfast that the corn was ready to harvest. The weather had been sweltering for the whole month of July and the missionaries had joked that the corn would pop out of the husks in the heat. Now it would be hot, dirty work to bring in the harvest.

After their morning devotions, the men went to the barn to haul out the bushel baskets they would collect the corn in. Paul hitched two oxen to their wagon to carry the golden grain from the fields to the corn crib. They would be short two men and all the older boys this summer. Everyone who was able needed to be in the fields.

Samuel, however, sat in the dining hall by one of the open windows. He had found that his job as bookkeeper was not particularly demanding. If the mission had not been so deadly dull, it might have been the ideal job. The most work he had to do was write out receipts for payment on the services offered at Union and record the transaction in the ledger. He also completed a quarterly report of the mission's finances to send to the board.

The blacksmith was called upon nearly every day to shoe a horse or repair a wagon for travelers on the road. The sawmill brought a few customers as well. Once the corn was harvested throughout the region, the gristmill would also be busy, but most folks paid in meal rather than cash. In fact, cash was always scarce on the prairie.

It was just as well that Rev. Vaille had left the money box with Redfield before his family departed from Union. There was probably little in it to tempt Samuel anyway. When Dr. Palmer and Rev. Montgomery conferred and then asked George to take over as mission superintendent, Redfield had passed the box on to him.

Samuel was looking at his coffee cup as if pondering whether he wanted another one on such a hot day. George opened the door with more force than necessary and stepped into the room.

"Are you coming, Douglas?"

Samuel looked up at the stocky man who was quickly standing over him. "Coming where?"

"We need everyone to help with the harvest. That includes you."

"I wasn't hired to harvest corn."

"Neither was I. We all share the work that needs to be done. Our survival out here depends on it."

Samuel looked as if he were going to refuse. There was a stubborn set to his jaw and his eyes narrowed. But George looked just as determined. He squared his shoulders and thrust his chin forward. The two men sized each other up for a few seconds. Would this missionary actually enforce his demand with his fists?

Douglas was a few inches taller than George, but the mechanic was solidly built and clearly much stronger. The bookkeeper blinked.

He stood slowly, all his reluctance and resentment visible on his face. "I know nothing about picking corn."

"It's simple. You pull the ear off the stalk and toss into a basket. Then you do it again."

Martha poked her head in from the kitchen at that

moment to see the two men standing nearly nose to nose. She started to say something, but then wisely chose to silently retreat to help Amanda prepare the jars for canning corn.

Slowly Samuel removed his light linen jacket and rolled up his sleeves as George had already done. Then he followed the new superintendent out into the sunshine and to the cornfields.

By the midday break, Samuel moved as if he had discovered muscles he didn't know he had. Pulling the ears of corn wasn't strenuous, but once he had filled a bushel basket he had to carry it to the wagon, heft it up to dump the corn into the bed and then return to his row to start all over again.

He had quickly followed the example of the other men and had wet his handkerchief in the bucket hanging at the wagon. Then he tied it around his neck to protect it from the sun. He had failed to bring a hat and his face was red from the sun's blistering rays.

While the other men washed their hands, arms and faces at the dining room door, he went to his cabin and found the widest brimmed hat he owned. Even though the cabin was hot, he paused for a long moment looking at his bed. The sheets looked cool, the pillows soft and beckoning. He crossed the room and sat on the feather mattress.

"I've done all I'm going to do, Requa," he muttered to the open door. But he did not stretch out on the bed as he clearly wanted to. Moments passed while an inner battle played across his features. Finally with a growl of determination, he fought his aching muscles and stood, slapped his hat on his head and walked toward the dining hall. He was not going to quit.

After dinner, which included fresh corn on the cob slathered with butter, the men returned to the fields. Samuel groaned through gritted teeth as he took one of the baskets and chose a row to work in. Soon he fell into the rhythm of the harvest chore.

The afternoon continued quietly with only the occasional sound of Paul hupping the oxen and the rattle of the wagon as he took a load of corn to the crib. But as the day wore on, Samuel looked up in surprise at the sound of singing. Woodruff was belting out a hymn in a rich baritone voice. Paul added a tenor harmony. A few rows over Palmer and Redfield were laughing about a joke and further over George and Stephen were calculating the number of bushels they would get per acre.

The bookkeeper paused to lift his hat and use his shirt sleeve to wipe the sweat that threatened to sting his eyes. He shook his head at the sound of . . . what was it? Happiness? Satisfaction? It seemed to puzzle him for he had never been asked to do something as difficult as this task and had never known the satisfaction of plain hard work.

When the dinner bell sounded, the other men tossed a last ear of corn in their baskets and took them to the wagon. Samuel joined them in walking to the dining room and standing in line at the wash basin.

It had been a hard day of work for everyone and so no one lingered long after supper though the sun still hung above the horizon. Samuel walked to his cabin, the sound of goodnight calls following him. He stepped inside and with some difficulty slipped his suspenders off his tired shoulders. He eased off his boots and socks and stretched out on the feather bed, looking grateful for the first time for its softness. He was quickly asleep, but there was a smile on his face that looked like satisfaction.

CHAPTER NINETEEN

Fort Gibson
August 1826

The corn harvest took several days and everyone was
weary when it was completed. Dr. Palmer was kept busy
dispensing salve for sunburned faces and wrapping blistered
hands.

But the corn crib was full and the root cellar shelves were
lined with jars of corn. There was no fear of winter when the
larder was full. The crop was abundant enough that they
would be able to sell cornmeal at the fort and trade jars of
corn for goods at the mercantile.

Paul and Tassie had set their wedding date for after the
harvest. The first preaching Sunday at Fort Gibson would fall
in early August so they would be married the day before.
Most everyone was planning to attend the wedding for Paul
was a well-liked and respected member of the mission family.
But when the Saturday of the wedding arrived, several at the
mission had taken ill with the summer fever.

Only the Palmers and the Woodruffs were able to attend.
Paul had begun his work at Union as the blacksmith's
apprentice and having no other family he had asked
Alexander to stand with him at the wedding.

Before the group left for Fort Gibson, Marcus made a
quick round to all the cabins where the sick were in bed. All
three of the Redfield children had the fever and Sarah and her
little girl Lizette were sick as well. Amanda and Stephen
promised to keep a close watch on everyone.

Martha and Clarissa rode in the wagon bed with their

parasols raised against the hot sun while their husbands rode on the wagon bench. Paul was mounted on a new mustang that Star had brought him in the spring. He had worked with the horse in the early morning hours through the summer and now it stepped lively as they traveled south.

"Are you getting nervous, Paul?" Marcus couldn't help but ask the young man as they neared Three Forks.

"No, sir," the young man replied. "I'm too happy to be nervous."

The women shared a smile. It was nice to see a young person embarking on a new endeavor in life with such a positive attitude.

They drove the wagon to the fort's ferry and rode across, then headed to Nick's & Rogers to meet Tassie there. The wedding would take place at the Bradley home in a few hours, but Tassie was working even on such an important day.

Paul dismounted quickly, tied his horse to the hitching rail out front and bounded into the dim interior of the store. More slowly, Marcus and Alexander helped their wives down from the wagon and they too entered the mercantile.

Eliza was there working alongside Tassie. She came around the counter immediately to hug Clarissa and Martha. Tassie greeted them with a shy smile. Paul was leaning on the counter beside her studying his bride.

"You act like you never seen me before," Tassie laughed at him.

"Ain't never seen you as my bride."

"Some would say it's bad luck to see her now," Sallie Nicks interrupted as she entered from the back storeroom. "But I don't hold to such nonsense myself."

"Nor do we," Marcus agreed. "The only thing wrong with this day is the heat." There were murmurs of assent from everyone.

"You should see how miserable the soldiers are in their wool uniforms," Eliza added. "Charles says he has given the road crew permission to be out of uniform while they're on the work detail. We received a shipment of cotton pants for them to wear instead."

"Is Charles still out on the project?"

"Yes, he and Captain Bonneville left two days ago. They've reached someplace called Greenleaf Prairie with the surveying."

"My husband says the crew working near Fort Smith is making good progress despite the heat," Sallie said. "But he thinks it will take another year to actually get the land cleared and leveled all the way to Little Rock."

"Have you moved all your things to our cabin?" Paul asked Tassie, unconcerned about a road to Little Rock.

"My papa moved everything out earlier this week."

"So he made it back from the mountains?"

"Mama woulda killed him if he hadn't," Tassie laughed again. It was clear that she was as happy as Paul on this day.

Paul had taken the advice of Charles Summers and had built a cabin near the mercantile rather than up on the Verdigris River as he had planned. While there were a few cabins in that area, it still would have been isolated and too far for Tassie to ride safely to work each day. The fort was receiving word from scouts and trappers that some of the Plains tribes were threatening war against the Osages. The prairie could still be a dangerous place.

With the help of Monday and his boat crew and the men from Union Mission, Paul had raised a small dog trot house between Fort Gibson and Nicks and Rogers. He and Woodruff had spent several days chopping pine logs in the spavinaw and dragging them by oxen down to the cabin site. More logs had been sawn for flooring and rafters. The house had a shake roof and a single chimney in the kitchen side.

To build a home with a dog trot between the two rooms was the southern way of dealing with the heat of summer. The family could sleep in the kitchen side with the fireplace in the winter and in the parlor side during hot weather. The open area between the two rooms – the dog trot – was roofed and also could serve as a sleeping area if needed.

Tassie would stay at the cabin but Paul would continue to spend much of his time at Union Mission. It wasn't an ideal situation, but Tassie's parents had made such an arrangement work for many years. Ian Bradley was a trapper who was away often on long hunting forays. Mrs. Bradley kept the cabin, a large garden and a menagerie of livestock, and she made her own living with her wonderful cooking.

The mission folks looked around the store for a bit and made a few purchases. Then Marcus pulled out his pocket watch to note the time.

"Well, Tassie, will you ride with us to your mother's house?" he asked.

"If I'm free to go." Tassie looked to her employer for permission.

"Of course," Sallie said, making a shooing motion with her hands."You, too, Eliza. I'll find my husband and we'll be over shortly."

The Bradley cabin was quite crowded when everyone gathered later that day for the simple ceremony. In fact, Lilla Bradley suggested that they move the wedding outdoors where a bit of a breeze and the shade of a large oak tree made it cooler.

The guests all stood in a semi-circle around Marcus and the young couple. Lena, Tassie's thirteen-year-old sister stood with her, a marked contrast to Mr. Woodruff who was nearing sixty.

Mrs. Bradley beamed proudly through the short recitation of vows, but her husband was a different story. The big, red-headed Scotsman wiped his eyes several times as his daughter was wed.

After Marcus pronounced the couple husband and wife, the guests swarmed them to give hugs of congratulations.

"Now just wait a minute; we ain't done," Mrs. Bradley announced loudly over the murmur of voices. Silence fell over the group and everyone turned to the mother of the bride.

She walked over to the porch of the house and took a broom that had been leaning by the door.

Stepping back out into the yard, she laid the broom in the grass. Then she gestured to Paul and Tassie.

The couple stepped up to the broom and then together

jumped over it. "Now you're married," Lilla announced.

The New Englanders had never witnessed the old tradition and Clarissa was quite curious about it. After everyone had been served plates of fried prairie chicken, buffalo tongue, steamed greens, black-eyed peas and cornbread, she found a place to sit next to Lilla on the edge of the porch.

"Tell me about jumping over the broom," she requested.

"You never seen that?" Mrs. Bradley asked.

"No."

"It's an old tradition in our families," the woman explained. "I thought it came from Africa, but Ian says they do it in Scotland and Wales too. It means the couple is starting a new household together. Least that's what I was always told."

"It's a nice tradition," Clarissa said. "I'm happy for Paul and Tassie. They are good people."

Mrs. Bradley's eyes filled with tears. "It means a lot to me for you to say that. There was folks who weren't too happy when Ian and me got married. That's why we moved way out here."

Clarissa nodded solemnly. "The frontier is a place for new beginnings."

She looked across the yard where Monday was visiting with Paul and Tassie. Tensions certainly existed out here, but when folks made the choice, there could be harmony and peace as well.

Mrs. Bradley rose to help Lena dish up her buttermilk pecan pie. The guests were all paying compliments to the cook, when she looked around the yard.

"Now where did Tassie and Paul get off too?"

"They slipped away a while ago," Ian told her.

Lilla looked off into the growing shadows in the direction of her daughter's new home. It was the only time during the day that she had looked sad.

"I don't care how happy you are for your children," she said more to herself than anyone else. "It's still hard to let them go."

When the missionaries arrived back at Union on Monday afternoon, they were struck with how quiet the compound was. No one came to greet them at the corral as was their custom.

"Something's not right," Martha said, worry in her voice.

"No it's not," Marcus agreed and he jumped down from the wagon seat before Alexander had halted the mules. Striding across the dusty yard, he hurried to the kitchen. He stepped inside and found the room empty. The kitchen was never empty during the day. He felt a tremor of fear run up his spine.

He stepped back out into the afternoon sun. Alexander was helping the two women down from the wagon. Across the yard, he saw Stephen coming out of the springhouse carrying two buckets of water. The doctor hurried over to greet him.

"Fuller, where is everyone?" he asked without preamble. "There was no one in the kitchen."

"Amanda took the baby to our house to change her diaper so I came to get more water," Stephen explained. "Nearly everyone else has the fever."

"Everyone?"

"Nearly all. The Redfields are all abed and Douglas is too. Your girls are fine; they're at our house." Stephen paused as Clarissa and the Woodruffs reached them. "The Requas little girl passed away just a while ago. Mrs. Requa is so sick I doubt she is even aware."

"Oh, Lizette," Clarissa murmured and the two women reached out to one another for comfort.

Marcus looked grim. "I shouldn't have gone."

Clarissa took his arm. "Don't do that. Don't always blame yourself."

"We've been dosing them with the quinine every four hours just as you instructed," Stephen said. "I doubt that there was anything more to be done. We've all dealt with this often enough; we know what to do. It just isn't enough sometimes."

Quiet Mr. Woodruff nodded sadly. "I'll start on a coffin." He gave Martha's shoulders a squeeze and then walked slowly to his work shed.

"I'll check on the Redfields," Martha said. She went to the kitchen to retrieve her apron. Stephen followed and dipped out a basin of the cool spring water for her. She carried it to the Redfield cabin.

Marcus and Clarissa walked to the Requas' home. The doctor tapped lightly on the door, but didn't wait for a response to enter. They found George sitting in a chair beside the bed, applying a cloth to Sarah's forehead. He looked weary and grim with two days' growth of beard and red-rimmed eyes.

Clarissa looked over to the cold fireplace where a cradle sat. A sheet had been pulled over it. She felt tears sting her eyes and a surge of compassion for her friend filled her heart. George had adored his baby girl.

Marcus moved to the bed and reached for Sarah's hand to check her pulse. Clarissa knelt beside George and reached for his hand. "I'm so sorry, George," she said softly.

He worked to keep his composure and nodded but said nothing for a moment.

"At least she won't have to know this sadness," he finally spoke, nodding toward his wife.

Did he not expect Sarah to recover? Clarissa glanced up at her husband and saw the stricken look on his face and it answered her unspoken question.

How would George bear this? How could God ask that of him? She wanted to run from the room, find her girls, and race away from this prairie and its awful disease. Instead she slipped an arm around George's shoulders. Marcus laid a hand on his arm and they gave what comfort they could to their friend.

Sarah lingered a few more days, but her racking cough told that the illness had invaded her lungs. Her grave was dug beside Lizette's and just a little ways from the Redfield's youngest twin, Esau. At Hopefield another child also died, one of Monepasha's young grandsons. Everyone else at Union and Hopefield recovered, but the sadness lingered.

The fever raged among all the settlements and villages along the rivers. Besides worry about illness, there were also rumors that the Pawnees were in the area. This small Plains tribe had no treaty of peace with the United States or any other tribe. No parent in the neighborhood wanted to send their children to school, so it was postponed indefinitely.

A few days after Sarah's funeral, Paul brought a pail of milk from the barn and poured it into the creamer. "Is Mr. Fuller around?" he asked the cook who was slicing the cornmeal mush for breakfast.

"He's in the dining room," she said with a nod of her head in that direction.

Paul stepped into the room where Fuller sat with Redfield and Woodruff enjoying their first cup of coffee.

"Somebody's been in our hog pen," the hired man said while he poured himself a cup at the sideboard by the fireplace. "Best I can tell, we're missing about forty hogs."

"Forty?" Stephen repeated in shock. "Was it a bear?"

"Naw; there were moccasin prints in the mud. And no blood. They just opened the pen and herded them out."

"Moccasins." Now Redfield seemed shocked. "But the Osages have never stolen from us."

"I don't think it was the Osages," Paul said, taking a seat. "He pulled a small knife from his pocket. "I found this." He handed the weapon to the blacksmith who was their expert on such things.

"No, this doesn't look like an Osage knife," Alexander said after examining it. "They have taken to using trade knives almost exclusively. This is homemade. Maybe Pawnee."

"They're getting closer," Redfield observed. "And bolder."

"Forty hogs," Stephen shook his head. "That's more than half our stock. And we were just a few weeks away from butchering. Our smokehouse won't be full this winter."

As the rest of the mission family gathered for breakfast, the men shared this news. Everyone was reminded to keep a close watch around the compound and no one was to travel or hunt alone.

Within the next few days more reports of theft came to

the mission. Farms in the area were targeted. Horses or other livestock were stolen, haystacks were set on fire, menacing sightings of the Pawnees occurred. An outright attack had not happened, but the harassment of the folks in the region was just as frightening.

Soon families living on neighboring homesteads began to arrive at Union Mission seeking protection. Even the women, children and Old Men from Claremont's Town moved their lodges to the fields nearby while the men of the village, led by Mad Buffalo, chased after their enemies.

The missionaries conferred in the dining hall one morning in late August.

"Can we afford to feed these folks indefinitely?" Marcus asked, looking to Samuel.

"Certainly not indefinitely," the bookkeeper said.

"We haven't enough food for everyone in the neighborhood," Amanda huffed.

"Then we'll need to charge them so we'll have funds to resupply our larder," George stated.

Marcus went with George to discuss the charges with the families. All but one expressed understanding and even offered to barter some of their own food supplies for board. One family left, the father saying they would go to Fort Gibson instead.

It was only a few days later when Colonel Arbuckle himself rode up from the fort with ten soldiers. He met with all the men gathered at Union and did indeed offer to provide protection to anyone who wanted to travel down to the fort.

Most of their guests left with the group of soldiers as escort. But several parents allowed their school age children to stay for school under the protection of the mission. School began with the largest classes they had ever seen.

Arbuckle assured them that a regular patrol from the fort would pass Union and Hopefield every day. The increased presence of the Seventh Infantry had a calming effect on the prairie. The Pawnees slipped back to the western buffalo trails anticipating the return of the migrating beasts to the southern plains. For the moment, quiet returned to the neighborhood.

CHAPTER TWENTY

Union Mission
September 1826

It raised concern among the missionaries when from the Texas Road they saw a group of riders approach on a warm day in September. Two of the riders were in uniform, clearly soldiers from Fort Gibson, but there were civilians in the group as well. Clarissa saw them from the classroom window and immediately worried that some problem with the Pawnees had arisen.

She glanced at the watch she wore pinned to her dress. It was not quite time to dismiss school for the day, but she was very anxious to learn the reason for this visit. She could see Marcus and George walking to the corral and waiting for the riders to arrive. Mr. Douglas and the blacksmith soon joined them. She noticed that George seemed to deliberately put some distance between himself and the bookkeeper.

"Who is that?" asked Eva Lombard, one of the new students.

Clarissa realized she had been staring out the window, something she never allowed her students to do. "I don't know, girls," she said. "but we all, myself included, need to bring our eyes back into the classroom."

Obediently the students turned to look at their teacher.

She glanced at her watch again and saw out of the corner of her eye that the visitors were dismounting and Paul and Stephen had come to take their horses. She recognized Colonel David Brearley, the Cherokee agent, Charles Summers, and the young private Bill Waldo. But there were three other men with them, dressed in similar fashion to the Cherokees but with many beads, tassels and ribbons adorning their clothes. Curiosity was taking over her thoughts.

"It's almost dismissal time, girls," she said. "Shall we call it a day?"

She certainly didn't have to ask twice. The girls were out of their chairs quickly. She walked with the students toward the dining hall, noticing that Mr. Redfield had also dismissed the boys. They reached the dining room before their visitors so Clarissa asked Phoebe to feed the children outside. If these visitors were bringing news that might cause fear among the students, she didn't want them to hear it.

"Oh, certainly," Phoebe said. "It's a beautiful afternoon, isn't it girls?" The students nodded as they made their way to the kitchen for their apples. They gathered in the shade of the Redfield cabin to eat before enjoying one of Phoebe's fun games. The boys soon joined them.

Clarissa helped Amanda and Martha gather coffee mugs and slice sourdough bread to serve their guests. The men entered the dining hall, removed their hats and took seats at the long tables.

Clarissa poured coffee while Colonel Brearley explained the visit.

"I know the lieutenant has informed you that the Creeks have signed a treaty to trade lands in Georgia and Alabama for land in Arkansas Territory," he said. "They've sent a delegation out to look at the area and make plans for the removal. I'll let these men introduce themselves."

The men stood each in turn to give their names.

"I am Roley McIntosh, Koweta Town."

"David Winslett, Hitchitee Town."

"Benjamin Perryman, Tullasi Town."

Clarissa closed her mouth for she realized she had been

staring again. How curious, indeed. These men had English names, but their town names were obviously of the Creek language. They spoke English, but it was heavily accented showing that it was not their first language.

Their clothing was of bright calico and tasseled bands circled their pants legs and sleeves above the knee and elbow. They wore necklaces of beads and brightly polished metal and turbans wound their heads. These Creeks were an amazing contrast to the bare-chested and tattooed Osages.

And they were apparently going to be their new neighbors.

Brearley went on to say that he had been appointed by the government as a liaison between the Cherokees and Creeks and was to assist the Creeks in any way possible with the move.

"When do you expect the Creeks to begin arriving here?" Marcus asked.

"A small party may come as early as next spring," the agent said. "But the main body won't arrive for another year or more. Some are reluctant to move and it has created tension. Mr. McIntosh's brother was killed for signing the treaty. But eventually you will have several thousand new neighbors."

Clarissa and the others absorbed this information. She wondered if more tribal troubles lay ahead for them. Not to mention the addition of a new language and different traditions and beliefs. It felt as if the clouds of a prairie thunderstorm were looming on the horizon.

The visitors spent the night at Union before leaving early the next morning to travel back to Fort Gibson. Later that Saturday, the Montgomerys, Will and Susan, and Teresa and Star-That-Travels arrived at the mission. They had come down from Hopefield for Sunday services the next day.

After supper, the Montgomerys told the mission family about their recent trip to Harmony Mission in Missouri. As the men discussed conditions further north, Harriett moved to a seat next to Clarissa.

"I had a long visit with Mary Austin while I was at Harmony," she said quietly.

"How is she?" Clarissa asked. "Not still pining for George, I hope."

"I do believe she is. She seemed quite concerned when I told her that he had lost his wife and daughter to the fever."

"George is having a hard time dealing with his loss." Clarissa looked over at the mechanic where he sat among the men, not saying much. "He's angry at God, I think, and at the mission."

"I thought that too, the last time we were here," Harriett nodded. "I hope I didn't overstep my boundaries for I certainly don't want to interfere in someone's life, but I encouraged Mary to write to him."

Clarissa turned back to look at Harriett. "Playing matchmaker?"

"No," Harriett said emphatically. "I did not want to imply to Mary that George might take an interest in her in a romantic way. After all she is only fifteen and I'm sure he still thinks of her as a little girl."

"He probably does since he hasn't seen her since Will and Susan were married." Clarissa was thoughtful for a moment. "Mary might be able to reach him in a way that none of us can."

"That is what I was hoping when I made the suggestion," Harriett said. "But I also was hoping you would help me keep a watch out for the two of them. I don't want either of them to be hurt. Mary is too young and George is too hurt already."

"I'll do what I can."

The two women turned their attention back to the men's conversation.

Rev. Montgomery was saying, "I wish I had been here to meet the Creek delegation. If they do indeed move out here, we'll need to start a mission among them."

"We may find that Union Mission has a much expanded work in the near future," Marcus said. Everyone nodded in agreement and in their closing prayer Montgomery made sure to pray for the Creeks as well as the Osages and Cherokees."

Several days later, Will stood at the glass-paned window in his cabin at Hopefield watching the rain fall in sheets. Jagged streaks of lightning lit the sky and the rumbles of thunder rattled the window. This was the third day of rain, making everyone at the missions glad that most of their gardens had been harvested.

He sipped coffee left from breakfast while Susan finished feeding the baby. A sigh escaped his lips prompting Susan to set Peter into his cradle. Then she helped their three-year-old daughter out of her chair, gave her a toy to play with and crossed the room to stand beside Will.

"We've never had such rain," she said. "This is worse than what we had in March."

"It's the worst I've seen since we've been here."

Susan could hear the concern in her husband's voice. "Is the creek going to flood?"

"It's already bank high," he said. "It's a greater threat to us than the river, but it will bring the river up as well. What seems odd about this storm is that it's moving west instead of east as usual. So it will continue to feed the creek upstream of us."

They stood at the window in silence for awhile, the barn in the distance barely visible through the rain. Across the yard, the Osage lodges were being flailed from the wind. Their Osage neighbors had all taken shelter in the cabins of their log longhouse.

Will drained his coffee cup and set it on the table. "Let's move what we can into the loft."

They worked through the morning to fold all their clothes and linens into the trunks they had traveled with from New England. Between the two of them they managed to lift them up the ladder into their loft. All the while, the rain steadily drummed against the roof and the sound of water rushing through Pryor's Creek seemed ominous.

To keep from hearing it Susan chattered to Will and Susie while they worked. Peter slept in blissful peace.

Susan glanced again out the window."Will!"

The fear in her voice brought the mission director down the ladder quickly.

"What is it?"

"The creek. You can't even see where the banks used to be."

Will peered out the window, shock registering on his face. The water had risen quickly and it now rushed with fury down toward the Neosho and was spreading across their fields.

"It's almost to Monepasha's cabins." He reached for a heavy canvas coat and his hat and crossed the room to the front door.

"I'll see what help I can give them. Get the children ready. We'll need to leave as soon as I can get the wagon hitched."

"You help the Osages. I'll ask Montgomery to see to the wagon."

Will nodded and after a quick kiss to his capable wife he stepped out into the deluge.

Susan set the sleeping baby into one of her pretty cane baskets and then placed it on the bed. Covering her head with a shawl, she dashed out the back door to the Montgomery home.

She could see that Star-That-Travels had brought two of their horses and he and Teresa were preparing to leave. Little Turtle had outgrown his cradle board, so he sat on one of the mustangs.

Bird and Hunts-the-Bear rode into the settlement on their mustangs trailing enough horses behind them for their family members. Quickly the Indians worked to load their household goods onto the horses.

Susan spoke to William and Harriett and then rushed back to her own cabin. She took the oilcloth from their table and wrapped it around the basket where Peter slept. Then she helped Susie into her coat and little bonnet. With one last look around her beloved cabin, she closed the door and made her way through the slick mud to the barn.

She met Will there and he held the door for her to step

inside the dry building. Then he ran to the hog pen and opened the gate to enable the animals to escape. Susan handed the baby's basket to Harriett and then went herself to the chicken coop and opened its gate also. They might never be able to round up the animals again, but at least they would be able to flee the rising waters.

While they worked, a sharp crack made them all jump. It sounded like a gunshot, but was actually the breaking of a tree growing along the creek. The water was so forceful it had toppled the tree at its roots and now the tree became a battering ram against other trees and brush.

All four of the missionaries stood in the barn door and watched as the water swirled around the Osages longhouse. It looked unlikely that it could withstand the force of the water. If it could be swept away, their cabins likely would also.

"We'll lose everything," Susan cried. "We shouldn't have left it in our cabins."

The water continued to rise and spread across the Hopefield land. A canoe that the Osages kept at the creek floated into the yard. Hunts-the-Bear snagged it before it could be hurtled down to the river.

"You women stay here," Montgomery directed. Then he and Will waded through the water back to their cabins. They brought out what items they could carry to the wagon. Beside their trunks, they added butter churns, chairs, lanterns, tools, cookware and anything else that could fit.

The horses were growing skittish so when they had a load, they helped their wives and the children up into the wagon also. Montgomery leapt into the wagon seat and slapped the reins to get the balking mustangs to move out from the barn.

He directed the horses toward the Texas Road which ran along higher ground. Once the wagon had cleared the muddy water, he stopped the horses. He handed the reins to Harriett and then jumped down.

"Get on the other side of the road," he told her. "I'll help Requa."

Harriett nodded and struggled to keep control of the still

skittish horses while Susan held Susie and Peter in the wagon bed. The little boy, now awake and frightened by the jostling wagon was wailing in protest.

Montgomery waded back into the water toward the barn. Their two milk cows were still inside.

By this time, the water had pressed the Osage longhouse off its stone foundation and was eating away at the mud mortar between the logs. Most of the Osages had abandoned the cabins already and were carefully walking their mustangs through the rising water toward the road. The rain had slowed to a steady drizzle, but everyone from the Hopefield community was sopping wet.

Montgomery tugged hard at the halter ropes he had slipped over the heads of their cows. The animals were frightened and fought him as he tried to pull them out of the barn and through the creek's flow.

One cow shook her head belligerently causing the minister to lose his hold on the rope. Before he could grasp it again, the water lifted the cow and swept her away. Her frightened bellows sent shivers down Susan's spine as they watched her fight for footing and ultimately fail. She was carried down to the river and they lost sight of the cow around its bend. Montgomery struggled on to pull the remaining animal toward the wagon.

Teresa and Louisa held their two mustangs at the edge of the water while Little Turtle sat quietly astride the roan stallion. Star brought blankets loaded with pottery, baskets and cookware from their cabin. Will and Hunts-the-Bear were carefully helping Monepasha's elderly mother into the canoe. Then each man walked beside it keeping the canoe steady in the water while fighting the current.

Suddenly Louisa thrust the reins she held into her mother's hand. "I forgot my dance shawl," she cried. She waded into the current toward their cabin.

"No, Louisa," her mother called after her. "It will be wet and ruined by now. We can make another one."

"I left it in the loft," the thirteen-year-old called over her shoulder. "There won't be time to make another one."

Louisa and her mother had worked all summer on the dance shawl. They had taken a standard blue trade blanket, cut it down and then added an intricate pattern of beads, shells, quills and stones to the shawl.

The fall powwow would be the first one since Louisa had turned thirteen. She would participate in the dances as a woman now and her shawl needed to be special to reflect this important rite of passage. It would announce that she was of courting age.

Star was at the back of the cabin retrieving a new bow he had hung on a peg. The bois d'arc wood found down near Fort Gibson was best for shaping a sturdy bow and he clearly didn't want to lose his handiwork. He didn't realize Louisa had entered their cabin until he reached Teresa and Little Turtle.

"Where is the girl?" he asked.

"She went back for her shawl."

Star was just stepping back into the current when the logs of the longhouse collapsed with a mighty crash. Teresa was nearly pulled off her feet as the horses she held bucked up in fear. The mustang carrying Little Turtle was able to jerk free of the woman and he whirled away from the frightening sound. With Little Turtle hanging on with two fists full of mane, the horse raced toward the mission wagon.

Teresa cried out and Star immediately turned back, grabbed the reins of the other horse and jumped onto its back even as it began to run. Teresa fell to the ground. Star was gaining on the runaway horse but Little Turtle was being thrown about and would likely take a tumble before his father could reach him.

Harriett checked the brake of the wagon to be sure it held, then quickly hiked up her sodden skirts and climbed down from the wagon seat.

"What are you doing?" Susan called to her friend.

Harriett stepped into the mustang's path and lifted her hands in a gesture meant to slow the horse. The stallion shied and bucked again and Little Turtle went sliding backwards. Harriett was able to reach out and grab his shirttail and pulled the boy off the horse as it went by. They both landed in a heap by the wagon.

Star slowed his horse and called out, "Is the boy good?"

"He's fine," Harriett confirmed. Little Turtle had not once cried out, but he blinked his eyes as if astonished by his wild ride.

Star looked back to see Teresa standing and Louisa cautiously stepping out of their cabin door. "You help Teresa?" he asked of Montgomery. The minister nodded while he tied their cow to the wagon.

Star then continued to try and retrieve the runaway horse.

Will and Hunts-the-Bear had barely avoided the avalanche of logs from the longhouse but the canoe fishtailed in the splash they made. Will glanced with concern at the elderly passenger in the canoe. Grandmother simply grinned a toothless grin and patted his hand. Will couldn't help but smile back. She seemed to be enjoying the excitement.

They were almost to the water's edge when Louisa screamed in fright. She clutched a deer hide in which she had wrapped her shawl and was trying to push through the water toward Teresa. But the pine logs were floating by her in a mad rush. She could not keep a secure footing and was driven back toward her home. She managed to catch the open door and clung to it, still keeping her precious shawl above water.

Teresa was about to wade into the creek but Hunts-the-Bear held up a hand to stop her. To Will he said, "Keep care of Grandmother. I will go for the girl." Will nodded and pushed the canoe onward.

Hunts-the-Bear splashed back into the main current of the creek that now cut right through the Hopefield yard. Pushing the logs away from him, the young warrior struggled to maintain his own footing. He could see that the water was crumbling the mortar of the cabin and it would not stand much longer. If it fell, Louisa would be crushed. Teresa stood knee deep in the water, terrified for her daughter.

"Please, my Jesus, help him save her, please," she prayed.

Will pulled the boat out of the water and helped

Grandmother into the waiting arms of her daughter. Most of the Osage men were tending to their frightened horses, unaware of the drama at Teresa's home.

Hunts-the-Bear reached Louisa as the cabin leaned precariously. "Hold on to me," he told her and Louisa nodded. She let go of the door and grabbed the warrior's arm. He pulled her close to him just moments before the cabin collapsed with a sucking sound and the logs tumbled into the swirling current.

The force of it jerked Hunts-the-Bear off his feet and the two young Osages were caught in the current, floating helplessly for several yards. The warrior caught hold of a scrubby bush that had not been uprooted. But the strain of their weight on it would not allow it to hold for much longer.

Though only eighteen, Hunts-the-Bear was tall like all the Osage men. He managed to get his footing again but could not turn back into the current. Logs and debris rushed by them while he caught his breath. Louisa held fast to him, her dark hair clinging to her face.

"Get on my back," the young man said.

Louisa nodded then put the leather cord that bound the deer hide in her teeth to free her hands. Indian children grew up being carried around on their mothers' backs so Louisa was experienced in holding on with arms and legs.

By this time, Will and Montgomery were wading carefully into the current. "Let's form a chain," Will suggested and the minister nodded.

Being the taller of the two, Will led the way, cautiously feeling the ground with his feet. Seeing what they were planning, Hunts-the-Bear heaved himself forward using the bush as leverage. Soon he was able to reach Will who helped Louisa into the water and held one hand while she reached for Montgomery with the other. From there she could reach out to her mother who had joined the chain.

Then Will grasped the hand of the warrior and helped the tired young man continue walking to the water's edge.

Teresa and Louisa collapsed on the ground clinging to one another. Grandmother held out her arms to Hunts-the-

Bear and he went to her. The missionaries walked slowly toward their wagon where their wives waited anxiously.

After a few moments, Louisa pulled back the deer hide to check on her precious shawl. It was wet and while not completely ruined it would not be as beautiful as she had hoped.

"Was it worth risking your life?" Teresa chided, her fear still visible. "It is only a shawl; not as valuable as you are to me."

"I wanted it to say that I was of value; worth courting."

"Oh, Louisa," her mother said, pushing the wet strands of hair from the girl's face. She glanced over at Hunts-the-Bear with his family gathered around him. "Someone already thinks you are worth courting."

Louisa smiled shyly and looked down at the soggy shawl. "Then the shawl has done what it was supposed to," she said. "For it has told me who I want to marry."

Teresa hugged her daughter close and then helped her to stand. Star-That-Travels had returned with the runaway mustang. Little Turtle rode in front of his father. Star helped the two women to mount the other horse and they joined Bird and his children and other Osage families. They would travel to Three Forks for the Pumpkin Moon Rendezvous which was only a few days away. Then they would join the larger Osage villages in the fall hunt.

The Indians passed the mission wagon still sitting on the Texas Road. Star spoke with Will, telling him their plans.

"We'll go to Union," Will replied. Star nodded solemnly and passed on with the others.

The missionaries remained for a time, watching as one by one their cabins and then the barn were all carried away by the flood. Their harvest of pumpkins floated and bobbed on the current. The full corncrib had easily toppled with the barn. Nothing was left of Hopefield.

They climbed into the wagon and Montgomery turned the horses south to Union Mission. All of them were still wet from the rain. Even so, Will could see that tears were coursing down his wife's face. She had silently watched as their pretty little cabin had been mauled by the torrent of muddy water and carried down to the river and out of sight.

He pulled her close and she rested her head against his shoulder. The children were asleep, exhausted from the excitement of the day.

"We'll build again," Will whispered.

"Yes," Susan nodded. "We are all safe and that is what matters. We will build again."

CHAPTER TWENTY-ONE

Union Mission
Winter 1826

"I don't know if the board even wants Hopefield to be rebuilt," Will said several weeks later as the mission family sat together in the dining hall after supper. The Montgomerys and Requas were now living at Union and would likely remain for several more months. Union had suffered far less damage from the flood and the men had been hard at work making repairs.

Will was studying a letter he had received from Rev. Greene in reply to his notification of the flood. "Greene is very vague about what he wants us to do."

Marcus had read the letter as well and had to agree with the stonemason. The mission board seemed to leave the decision totally to the Union staff. But there was no offer of additional funds to help with rebuilding.

"We started with nothing before," Montgomery noted. "We'll simply have to do that again. I believe Monepasha and the other families truly want Hopefield to continue."

"Yes," Will agreed. "At least their agent was more responsive. With the money he authorized, the Osages will finally be able to buy tools and food supplies."

Major Hamtramck had secured $50 in funds for the Osages at Hopefield in response to their losses in the flood. The Secretary of War authorized Colonel Arbuckle at Fort Gibson to dispense these funds. He had ridden up to Union, bringing the money to the missionaries since the Osages were still away on their hunt and would not be back for some time.

Samuel Douglas had eyed the money hungrily as the fort commander passed it to Dr. Palmer who in turn had handed it to George. Samuel's visits to La Saline each full moon for the races had left him truly without funds of his own. He had resisted taking the remaining money from the Fairfield church, but that might soon change.

Being paid only twice a year was hard on a man who liked the thrill of the win and the feel of coins counted into his hand. Altering the mission's ledger would be pointless if he couldn't access the funds.

George kept the money box in his cabin most of the time and conscientiously accounted for every coin going in or out of it. He had almost caught Samuel in the till one day. The bookkeeper had to pretend that he was getting change for the blacksmith who was shoeing a horse for a traveler on the Texas Road. After that, George had never left the box sitting out in the dining hall.

Samuel had questioned Dr. Palmer about why George had been named the superintendent of the mission. The man was certainly a skilled mechanic and an excellent hunter. He and Fuller had brought in two large elks just last week but Stephen had given George full credit for their success. The bookkeeper didn't care much for the gamey meat, but the mission needed it to replace the hogs that had been stolen.

Samuel had heard George readily admit that he had little formal education. So the bookkeeper had taken it upon himself to write to William Vaille who was staying with the Seldens in Fairfield.

Samuel suggested that he be named superintendent of the mission, never mentioning that Palmer and Redfield had already given the job to George. Samuel implied that the mission was badly in need of a steward.

Now he had received Vaille's reply and the pleased smile on his face told that he was unconcerned about the need to rebuild Hopefield. As soon as the group dispersed for the evening, he approached Marcus.

"I've received a letter from Rev. Vaille," he began while offering the missive to the doctor.

Marcus was surprised that Douglas would want him to read a letter from the director. He took it and quickly scanned its contents.

"Vaille wants you to be the superintendent of the mission?"

"Yes," Douglas nodded, trying to seem nonchalant, even humbled at the assignment. "As you can tell from his letter, he realized that he hadn't addressed the matter before he left."

"I see," Marcus said, but the careful look he gave the younger man suggested he saw more than Samuel wanted. "I think George is doing a fine job. It was my failure to write to Vaille and let him know that."

"Yes, well," Samuel replied with seeming indifference. "Do you what you think is best. I simply want to serve where Vaille would have me to. He is, after all, the director of Union Mission."

Marcus nodded, but his jaw was tight. "I'll speak to George in the morning. May I show him this letter?"

"Yes, certainly," Samuel smiled. "We can discuss my new duties tomorrow."

He was still smiling as he walked to his cabin.

Marcus was not smiling when he showed the letter from Vaille to Abraham the next morning. He had asked the schoolmaster to visit him in his office before breakfast. Behind closed doors they discussed the dilemma they found themselves in.

"I suppose we did overstep our bounds when we asked George to be superintendent," the sandy-haired teacher said. "But I don't think Douglas is qualified for the job. He has no idea what it entails."

"I agree," Marcus said from behind the table that served as his desk. "But it would only be for three months or so. The Vailles are set to return after Christmas. When they arrive, we can explain the situation to Vaille. By then we'll know whether Douglas can do the job."

Abraham sighed while shaking his head. "It seems as if everything has gone wrong since Chapman died. I never realized how well he and Mrs. Chapman held everything together."

"Our situation has certainly changed out here," Marcus agreed. "Which is all the more reason why we need an experienced man like George Requa."

"Do you need me here when you speak to him?"

"No, I'll ask Clarissa to be here. Mrs. Montgomery or your wife can watch her class."

Abraham nodded and stood to leave. "Thanks for handling this. I don't envy you. I don't think George is going to take it well." Then he left the office to walk to the dining hall.

When Marcus told Clarissa about the situation, she was furious.

"I don't believe this!" she said, waving the letter Marcus had handed her to read. "Mr. Douglas doesn't know anything about managing this mission. Why on earth would Rev. Vaille ask him to be superintendent?"

"I can't say, Clarissa," Marcus said, trying to keep his voice calm. "I think George is the right person for this job."

"George is perfect for the job," she agreed vehemently. "No one else could do better. I don't think Mr. Douglas even likes being here. He certainly doesn't want to work very hard. George had to insist that he help repair his own cabin."

Marcus took Clarissa's hand to keep her from waving the letter in his face and to still her torrent of words. He'd never seen his wife so upset.

"Dear, you aren't telling me anything I don't already know. I feel terrible that Redfield and I put him in the position and now must take it away from him."

"Why do you have to? Can't it wait? Can't you write to Rev. Vaille and explain things?"

"I doubt that a letter would reach him before they leave Connecticut. We'll just have to follow his directive, which is very clear, and hope that we can straighten things out when he gets back."

"This is unfair," Clarissa said, now sounding close to tears. "George is going to be so hurt by this. He hasn't healed from losing Lizette and Sarah. I don't know if he can bear losing something more. This job gives him purpose and he needs that right now."

"I know," Marcus looked as distressed as Clarissa. "That's why I need you here when I tell him. Can you hide your anger and assure him that he still has purpose here?"

Clarissa set her mouth in a grim line and drew a deep breath. "I'll try."

When George entered their cabin following breakfast, he looked puzzled, especially when seeing Clarissa there and not in class.

"Am I in trouble with the teacher?" he asked as he removed his hat and took the seat across the table from Marcus. Clarissa stood at the door and tried to smile at his words.

"I owe you an apology, George," Marcus began.

"Oh, I doubt that," George responded.

"No, I have made a mistake and I am deeply sorry for it."

"I can't think what you mean," George said, but he now looked concerned. "You aren't blaming yourself about Sarah, are you?"

"No, George, it's not that." Marcus fingered the letter on his desk. "We have received a letter from Rev. Vaille. He has appointed Mr. Douglas superintendent of the mission. My mistake was in putting you in a difficult situation. I should never have offered you the job without consulting Rev. Vaille."

"Douglas?" There was disbelief in George's voice. "Why would he appoint Mr. Douglas? The man knows nothing about running this mission."

"I know," Marcus acknowledged. "I don't agree with Rev. Vaille's decision but I feel that I must abide by it for now. I will try to straighten everything out when he returns."

"You know he gambles, don't you?" George asked with

anger in his voice. "He's up at La Saline every full moon for the races."

"I suspect you're right, but we have no proof of it. And Rev. Vaille certainly knows nothing of the possibility. When he returns, we'll discuss it."

"Don't bother," George said, standing. "If the mission board would have a man like Douglas in charge, then they don't need me. I quit being a missionary; maybe I never really was one." He turned abruptly and strode to the door. "I'll be packed and out of here by the end of the day."

"No, George," Clarissa pleaded, but the mechanic was out the door before she could say more. The Palmers looked at each other, their anguish visible. Marcus ran his fingers through his hair in frustration.

"Oh, I have made such a mess of this," he groaned.

"You can blame me." Clarissa paced across the small room. "I pushed you to give George the job."

"You didn't push me. I wanted to do it. I still think it was the right decision."

"Yet here we are about to lose George," Clarissa cried. "We can't let him go. He is too important to our survival out here. He can do any task at this mission; he keeps us in food as much as the Fullers. He keeps us safe." She had never forgotten how he had rescued her from a copperhead in the garden.

"We'll give him a while to cool off, then we'll talk to him. Maybe take Stephen and Amanda with us. They have taken him under their wing since he lost Sarah."

"We have to convince him to stay. He absolutely is a missionary." Clarissa dashed away a tear from her face. "He may not preach or teach, but aside from you, he is the man most respected by the Osages. He is a hunter like them. They understand him. It is likely because of George that they have tolerated this mission for as long as they have."

"You need to tell him that. I don't think he realizes it."

"Oh, Marc, we have to pray that he doesn't leave. We certainly need him, but right now he needs us too."

George walked with purpose from the Palmers' cabin to his own. He cast a glance toward the dining hall and could see Douglas standing at one of the windows sipping another cup of coffee. He opened his door with far more force than necessary and closed it in the same fashion. He pulled his trunk away from the wall, removing the crocheted cover Sarah had made to cover the scarred wood.

He opened the trunk to find it full of Lizette's things. Someone, probably Mrs. Woodruff, had packed them away for him when he was in a fog of grief. Now as he saw the turtle shell rattle he had made for her and the patchwork quilt of bright calicos that Sarah had stitched, the grief washed over him again. He crumpled to the floor and clutched the little quilt in his work-roughened hands.

"Why, God?" he moaned like an animal in pain. "Why are you punishing me?"

He sat in silence too hurt and too tired to move for a long time. When he heard the cook's triangle calling everyone to the noon meal, he stirred himself. He carefully folded the quilt and gently placed it back into the trunk.

He stood and crossed the room to the wash stand. He splashed water onto his face then scrubbed it dry with a towel. Going to the bed, he knelt and pulled out the satchel that had been Sarah's. He folded his clothes and packed them tightly inside. All the anger had burned out of him and now he seemed simply resigned.

He was sitting on the bed, staring at the dying fireplace embers when the Palmers and Fullers came to him. Marcus knocked but didn't wait for a response before entering.

Amanda carried a plate of food covered with a napkin. She set it on the little table in the room that had grown cold as the fire died.

"I brought you some food, George," she said softly. "I made elk stew. You need to eat something." She had said that to him often in the days after Sarah died.

"I'm not hungry . . . . but thanks."

Stephen went to the fireplace and stacked pieces of wood on the embers, stirring them up to flames again.

Clarissa sat by George on the bed. It wasn't proper, but she didn't care right now. She was determined to get through to her friend and convince him not to leave.

She slipped an arm around his shoulders and tried to pull him close but he resisted.

"Come to gang up on me, have you?" he asked.

"Absolutely," Clarissa responded. "We can't let you leave, George. You're too important to this mission. Who will protect us? My husband is a terrible shot." She glanced up at Marcus, hoping he wouldn't be offended by her words.

"She's right," he said, following her lead and offering a rueful smile. "I'm terrible with a gun."

"You're not; I've seen you shoot." George's words were curt, but there was a hint of humor in them as well.

"The truth is we need you, George," Stephen said. "Our numbers are down, but the work load isn't. I can't imagine Paul and me being able to keep up the farm without you."

George shook his head. "I won't work as a missionary. I can't work for Rev. Vaille."

"Then work for me," Stephen said. "I have the authority to hire as much farm assistance as I need. I'm offering you a job working with the stock and also managing our meat supply."

"I'd be a hired man? Like Paul?"

"Yes."

They all understood the distinction George was making. Missionaries were appointed by the board. The missionaries could then hire additional workers as needed and as funds allowed.

The mechanic paused for a long time, giving the offer consideration. Clarissa held her breath, praying he would agree to it.

"Alright," he said at last.

Clarissa heard all of them let out a release of breath. "Good," she said before George could reconsider.

"I'll move to the barn," George offered. "Douglas can have this place."

"No," Stephen said firmly. "If the new mission

superintendent wants a cabin of his own, he can oversee its construction."

Marcus tried to hide his smile, but he didn't succeed. Neither did anyone else in the room. Was it unchristian to be amused at the thought of Mr. Douglas building a log cabin? Yes, it probably was, but they would all simply have to ask for forgiveness.

"Come eat this stew before it gets cold," Amanda directed the new farm assistant. She lifted the napkin and let the aroma drift into the room.

George licked his lips at the sight of the food. "Yes, ma'am," he said.

When the Palmers and Amanda left a few minutes later, Stephen and George were busily making plans to turn the cornfields once more before the first snow.

Later George brought the money box to the doctor. "Count it before you give it to him," he advised. "Let him know that you know exactly how much is in there." Then without another word he walked back to his cabin.

Several nights later, a bright starry night seemed especially cold on the prairie. Charles and Eliza were asleep in their room at the back of the Nicks' house. The sound of baying dogs woke them.

"What is that?" Eliza murmured sleepily as Charles sat up and reached for his wool uniform pants.

"Don't know," her husband responded as he pulled his suspenders up over his undershirt. "I'll step outside to see."

"Oh, don't, Charles. It's so cold," Eliza protested trying to wipe her tousled blonde tresses out of her eyes.

"Something's wrong." Charles looked through the shutters at the window but could see nothing in the darkness. The dogs continued their noise and were coming closer. It sounded like they were chasing a prey. Now they could also hear voices urging the dogs onward and the splashing of riders entering the river.

Charles pulled on his coat and grabbed his army rifle. He checked the powder and then opened the door cautiously.

"Be careful," Eliza called after him.

Charles nodded, stepped outside and made sure the door was closed tightly against the cold and whatever was happening down near the river.

Eliza rose also and pulled a shawl around her shoulders while slipping her feet into her kid leather boots. She went to the door and opened it just a crack to see what was taking place outside.

Charles proceeded carefully through the dark. The stars were bright, but there was no moon so it was hard to see into the shadows of the tree line along the Neosho. To his left, the outline of the Nicks' smokehouse was barely visible. He could just make out movement near it and heard a low murmur of voices.

At the smokehouse, two Negroes, a man and a woman, were hiding in its shadow. The object of the dogs' search, they had paused there to catch their breath after wading through the cold water.

"Get in here, Precious," the man said into her ear. He carefully pulled open the door and pushed her into the small space where several hams and sides of bacon hung from its low rafters.

She grabbed his hand. "You get in here too," she pleaded, trying to pull him inside.

"No," he said, pulling back from her. "I'll draw the dogs away then circle back around here. Just keep quiet."

"No, please, Ned," Precious whispered desperately. "Don't leave me. You won't come back. They won't let you."

"I will come back," Ned promised, but he threw a fearful look over his shoulder. "Take care of our baby." He briefly placed both his hands around her face, looked at her as if memorizing her features, and gave her a quick but passionate kiss. Then he closed the door and ran.

The moment had given Charles and Eliza enough time for their eyes to adjust to the darkness. As the realization of what they had witnessed at the smokehouse hit them, they shared a look of horror.

Charles ran toward the sound of the dogs, hoping they

would catch his scent and it would cause enough confusion to give the runaway time.

Eliza remained at the door, praying for her husband and for the two people who were running for their lives. She looked out at the smokehouse only a few yards from her room. Thank God, the Nickses were not at home. They had traveled to Little Rock for the holiday social season.

"What should I do? What should I do?" Eliza desperately sought direction from above. Soon a light came into her eyes, as if the direction had come. "Tassie," Eliza said.

Cautiously the young blonde opened her door, shut it quietly and hurried to the smokehouse. She opened its door to find the Negro woman, about Tassie's age, hunkered back into the corner. Tears were streaming down her face and she wrapped her arms protectively around her mounded abdomen where her unborn baby was sheltered.

Eliza motioned for her. "Come," she whispered. "Quick! I'm here to help you."

Precious shook her head. "He won't know where to find me."

"I'll watch for him," Eliza promised. "I'll bring him to you. But you have to come now."

Precious continued to hesitate as if uncertain about trusting this blonde woman in her nightdress.

"I'll take you to a friend," Eliza said. "A Negro friend."

The sound of the dogs grew louder. "You have to come now!"

Finally Precious moved from around the hams and let Eliza draw her out of the smokehouse. Eliza closed the door and then slipped an arm around the woman's shoulders. Nearly at a run, she led her past the sutler's store and up the road to Tassie's cabin.

They stepped onto the porch and Eliza rapped softly on the door. Tassie opened it almost immediately. She too had been awakened by the dogs.

"What you doing, Miss Eliza?" she asked. But as soon as she saw the other woman, she knew.

"Come inside," Tassie invited.

Eliza pushed Precious in the door but said, "I have to get back. Hide her, Tassie. And don't go outside yourself."

Tassie nodded in understanding and Eliza turned to dash back toward her home.

Charles continued his race toward the river, unaware of his wife's actions. As he had hoped, the three bloodhounds reached him and circled around him whining and sniffing his shoes and pants. But they quickly recognized that this was not their target so they searched again for the scent they wanted. Soon they were running toward the smokehouse. He had only delayed them for a few seconds.

Two men on horseback followed the dogs out of the woods to the clearing around the Nicks' home. Charles called for them to halt, but they did not hear him above the baying dogs and the clattering horses' hooves. He followed them, trying to get their attention without having to fire his rifle. They might fire back before realizing he was an officer from the fort.

Out of the corner of his eye, Charles saw lantern lights bobbing through the woods. The sentries at Fort Gibson had no doubt come out to investigate the commotion.

The dogs were circling around the smokehouse, noses pulsing against the ground, an exultant pitch in their voices. They scratched at the door, trying to gain entrance, showing their certainty that they had cornered their prey.

Charles was about to call out again, when the Negro man raced out from the woods about fifty yards away. He threw his arms open wide, his tattered white shirt nearly glowing in the darkness.

"Haw!" he yelled to get the attention of the dogs.

In his shock and fear, the moment seemed to move in slow motion for Charles. The man standing with arms open wide, willing to sacrifice himself for his wife made the lieutenant immediately think of the Savior on the cross.

The dogs lifted their heads and whirled toward him, saliva dripping from lolling tongues. They were quickly upon him, savagely tearing at him with their teeth. He managed to break free and tried to run for the woods, but the dogs brought him down. The bounty hunters were exultant. The man fell to the ground and one dog gnawed at his ear.

"Call off your dogs," Charles ordered, putting as much force as possible into his words.

The men whirled on their horses in surprise. Behind Charles, they could see the lanterns bobbing along the road.

"Call off the dogs," Charles repeated.

Reluctantly one yelled, "Hey, now, Brutus! Heel now!" The dogs, with equal reluctance, left their prey and came to sit at their handlers' feet.

Charles rushed to the downed man and rolled him over. Blood poured from a dozen bite marks. "He's dead! You've killed him."

Now the hunters looked disappointed. "Ain't no bounty for a dead slave," one of them groused.

"His woman's still somewhere here," the other man said. They looked around where the dogs had been.

"Bet she's in the smokehouse," the man with the dirty red beard said. He started to dismount his horse.

"This is my property," Charles bluffed. He stood and hurried back, trying to head the man off. "I want you off it."

"You hiding a fugitive, Lieutenant?" the man still on his horse sneered. "Now that's a crime, ain't it? There's somebody in that smokehouse. Get her, Red!"

Red jerked the door open to reveal Eliza standing inside. She jumped in fear and then looked around in pretended sleepiness.

"This isn't the outhouse," she said, hiding a yawn.

The bounty hunters snickered at the pretty woman's daft-headed mistake.

Eliza kept the confused, wide-eyed look on her face. Let these fools think her a fool if it would protect the woman and her baby.

"Now who are you, Missy?" Red asked, starting to reach out and touch her tousled hair.

Charles cocked his rifle. "She's my wife."

Red raised both hands and took a step back. "Don't get all riled," he said. "I didn't know."

Eliza stepped out of the smokehouse and went to Charles. She deliberately left the door open so it was obvious to all that no one else was in the shed.

"Private Waldo," Charles ordered as the soldiers reached the Nicks' yard. "Give these men an escort to the fort."

"Yes, sir," Waldo saluted.

"You can't arrest us," Red protested.

"You're not under arrest," Charles replied. "You're being offered accommodations for the night. You'll want to get an early start for your ride back home in the morning."

The two hunters looked at one another as if trying to decide whether to protest further. Then Red shrugged and mounted his horse. The men and their dogs followed two soldiers, while another two followed them.

"What did you do, Eliza?" Charles asked when the hunters were out of sight.

"Do about what?" Eliza responded with her perfected wide-eyed look of innocence still on her face. She would protect her husband just as capably as she hid the runaway slave.

Charles shook his head but couldn't help smiling. He'd seen that look before and refrained from asking any more questions.

They walked toward the house but Charles remembered the poor dead man. He stopped and reluctantly looked back toward the trees.

"I'll need to take care of the body," he said, "or it will draw the wolves. I'll send a litter down from Gibson. We'll have to take him to the fort and try to determine something about him."

Eliza nodded solemnly. She could only imagine the poor woman's sorrow when she learned of her husband's death. She would have to tell her after Charles left for work in the morning.

"Be careful," she said. He nodded and walked her to their door. He set his rifle across the table, then turned and walked past the smokehouse to the spot where the dogs had done their deadly work.

But the man wasn't there.

Charles shook his head as if trying to clear it of confusion. This was the place where the man had finally fallen. He was sure of it. But it was too dark to tell what might have happened here after they had all turned their attention to the smokehouse.

The officer retraced his steps back to the house. He entered their room to find Eliza removing her boots. She looked up at him in surprise. "I thought you were going to the fort."

"He was gone," Charles explained.

"Gone? You mean he wasn't killed?"

"I don't know," Charles shook his head again as he took off his jacket. I checked for a pulse, but I was in a hurry. Maybe he wasn't killed. I don't think an animal would have pulled him away that quickly.

Eliza pondered the mystery for a while. Finally she said, "Monday has a cabin further down river. Maybe he heard the dogs and came up here to see what was going on."

Charles nodded. "That's possible." He stood at their window for a while peering out into the silent darkness. "I'll check the area again in the morning. But I won't pursue it any further unless Bonneville or Arbuckle order it."

The couple returned to bed and lay close and quiet for a time, sleep seeming to elude them.

When Eliza resettled on her pillow, Charles whispered, "He was willing to die for her."

"There is no greater love than that," Eliza said softly.

CHAPTER TWENTY-TWO

Fort Gibson
Winter 1827

The following morning neither Charles nor Eliza made any mention of the night's excitement while they shared breakfast. The officer kissed his wife goodbye and walked up to Fort Gibson. Eliza went to the store to make sure everything was ready for opening up in an hour. Then she grabbed a Tontitown apple and put a penny by the cash register to pay for it.

She walked slowly to Tassie's house, watching the road to the fort to be sure no one was out this way. When she stepped onto the Gillards' porch, Tassie opened the door before she could even knock.

"Come in quick," Tassie said, urgency in her voice.

"What is it?"

"She's having pains," her friend explained. "We think the baby is coming, but we're not sure. It's too early for it!"

"Running may have started her labor." Eliza stepped into the room to see the Negro woman sitting in a rocking chair looking awkward and uncomfortable.

"Can you get your mother to come check her?"

Tassie shook her head. "Papa took her and Lena down to Natchitoches to see her folks."

Precious grimaced as a pain hit her. "Did he get away?" she asked after the pain subsided.

"We think he did," Eliza said, coming to kneel by the

chair. "But the dogs hurt him. We don't know where he is now."

"He got away?"

"As far as we know he did."

"Oh, praise you, Jesus," Precious closed her eyes and prayed. Then she looked at Eliza in fear.

"Who's we?"

"My husband and I." Eliza saw the alarm on the young woman's face. "Don't worry. He won't say anything."

Then she looked up at Tassie. "We could send for Mrs. Woodruff." Then she thought better of that. "But that might arouse suspicion. Neither you nor I have need of a midwife."

"Maybe we could sneak her up to Union. I don't like that we're so close to the fort."

"Traveling might make things worse for her though."

Precious looked back and forth between her two rescuers. "I can travel," she said.

"If we could get a wagon . . ." Eliza let her words trail off as she thought how to get Precious to the mission. "When will Paul be down here?"

"Next preaching service. Not for two weeks."

"What about Monday? He has a wagon."

"Yes, and he'd be willing to help." Tassie was already reaching for her shawl. "I'll run to his house and catch him before he goes to the boatyard."

Monday was willing to haul a load of "cargo" to Union Mission. He arrived shortly with his wagon, but when asked said he knew nothing about the woman's husband. Eliza wasn't sure if he was speaking the truth.

Tassie wanted to ride with them, but Eliza said that would not be appropriate and might raise questions. So Monday alone drove the wagon into the Union barn after a slow and careful journey to the mission.

Paul didn't even ask why Monday was putting the wagon in the barn. But his face registered shock when he pulled back the tarp from the bed of the vehicle and saw that it was a young woman hiding there.

"She needs a midwife," Monday explained in low tones.

"Help me get her to the cot in back," Paul said.

They helped Precious walk carefully back to the quarters in the corner. Then Monday unloaded a barrel of apples that Eliza had sent and took his leave, needing to return to his job as quickly as possible.

Paul asked the woman if she needed anything, looking uncomfortable and uncertain of how to handle this new situation.

"I'll be alright," she said, but she winced when another birth pang hit.

Paul backed out of the little room. "I'll get the doctor." Then he hurried to find Marcus.

He reached the doctor's office but could see through the window that Dr. Palmer was examining a man named Murphy who had a homestead down near the Arkansas falls. So Paul turned and walked to the kitchen where he knew Mrs. Woodruff would likely be found.

"No, she's in the laundry," Amanda told him when he didn't find her there.

He hurried across the yard and found Mrs. Woodruff folding sheets.

"Mrs. Woodruff," Paul said, then he hesitated.

"Yes?"

"I could use your help."

"Certainly," Martha smiled. She was fond of Paul and had often said so. "What can I help you with?"

"Well, actually, um . . .it's someone else who needs your help."

"Oh, who?"

"Um, Monday brought a . . . neighbor . . . who is having a baby."

"He brought her here?"

"Yes, she's in the barn."

"Why did you leave her in the barn? You should have taken her to a cabin."

"We wasn't thinking, I guess. Just wanted to help her to a bed real quick."

Martha smiled. It was obvious that Paul was not

comfortable around a woman having a baby. Pity him when it was Tassie in labor.

"I'll get my basket and meet you in the barn. If she can be moved, we'll get her someplace more comfortable."

Paul nodded and then hurried to check on the woman. He found her curled up on the cot, looking miserable.

Martha arrived shortly and after a quick assessment declared that they would not be able to move her. "Run to the kitchen and get the teakettle. It should be hot; I was planning to have a cup after I finished the laundry."

"Yes, ma'am," Paul looked relieved to be given an assignment that took him away from the barn.

Amanda seemed puzzled at first when Paul told her Mrs. Woodruff wanted the teakettle, but she sent him on his way with the kettle, a mug and some tea leaves. She assumed the older woman had decided to take her tea in her own cabin.

Paul set the teakettle on the towel at the little washstand as Mrs. Woodruff directed. Then he took his leave.

Martha worked quietly, helping the woman through the ever-stronger contractions.

"What's your name, dear?" she asked during a lull.

"Precious."

Martha waited for a last name, but when one was not forthcoming, she gave an understanding nod. "What a lovely name. You're having this baby early, aren't you?"

"Yes, ma'am," Precious nodded. "He weren't due for two more months, I think."

The two women passed through the vale together and in about an hour welcomed a tiny boy child. Mrs. Woodruff cleaned him, wrapped him snugly and placed him at the woman's breast.

"Hold him close; he needs your warmth."

"He gonna make it?"

"I don't know," Martha answered honestly. "It will be a struggle for him. But I think he has a very strong mother so he has a fighting chance."

Precious nodded and studied her baby with the awe and love that mothers feel. Soon she began to cry and she spoke to her child. "You are free," she whispered but with a fierceness in her voice. "You was born free just like your daddy and me wanted. You won't never know no chains."

By this time Martha had joined her in tears. When the little boy died about an hour later, the two women held each and truly cried.

"He's free forever now," Precious said when the tears subsided.

"Yes," Martha agreed.

"Will you give him a proper burial?"

"My husband and I will see to it. Did you have a name chosen for him?"

"No," Precious shook her head sadly. "Don't need no name on a marker. People don't need to know about him. All I cares about is that he is free."

Martha waited until Precious had drifted off to sleep then she took the child and carried him under her shawl to her cabin. Alexander made a little coffin for him and the Woodruffs went the following evening to bury him in the cemetery apart from all the other graves. Only Paul was present when Alexander set a small stone over the grave.

"I'll carve his name later," the blacksmith said.

"He doesn't have a name," Martha sadly told him.

"He has a name," Woodruff countered. "It is known to God."

A few days later, Monday came by with a wagon load of supplies for La Saline. He stopped in for coffee and stayed late enough that he was invited to spend the night in the guest cabin. When Martha went to check on Precious the following day, she was gone. Martha breathed a prayer for the brave young woman and trusted that she would find a safe place where she would know no chains ever again.

At the Pittsburgh waterfront, Ella stood with Asie and her family impatiently waiting to board a steamboat bound for her new world. The journey to get here had tried her patience in every way for William seemed in no hurry to return to Union Mission. At least it seemed that way to her.

First they had taken the stage from Fairfield to Colchester so Asie could say goodbye one more time to Richard who was attending school there. She had blubbered like a baby in bidding Beth goodbye that morning. Then they had traveled to New York where William met with Rev. Greene and the mission board.

Ella had been introduced to the men who made up the board and with a recommendation from her brother-in-law she had been hired to work at Union as a seamstress. The Vailles had learned by letter from Dr. Palmer that Sarah Requa had died of the fever and the mission was once again in need of someone to do the sewing.

So now Ella was employed for the first time in her life and it gave her a great sense of accomplishment though she hadn't taken a stitch yet. She was a decent seamstress and had made most of her own clothes. She had never considered working as a seamstress before, but now it seemed perfect for when she would join Samuel out on the frontier.

After leaving New York, they had traveled by stage to Washington City. The mission board had asked William to visit with the Secretary of War and give him a first-hand report of the work among the Osages. While Ella, Asie and the children had strolled along the Potomac, William had met with Secretary James Barbour. He came away from the meeting less than satisfied however. Barbour was more interested in the removal of Indians from the east than in the work of missionaries.

Now finally they were boarding a steamboat at Pittsburgh and would reach Dwight Mission in two weeks with good weather. Even Asie seemed happy to have the river voyage begin and she shared stories with her sister of the months-long journey it had taken seven years ago when the Vailles had first traveled to Arkansas Territory.

Ella barely heard her sister. She was too busy planning her wedding and imagining the cozy cabin she would share with Samuel. Everything would just be perfect once she finally arrived.

At Union Mission, Samuel seemed only to be thinking about hurrying through supper. It was the first full moon since October that the weather was fine enough for racing at La Saline. With the money box in his possession, he would now have real funds once again to take to Chouteau's post.

He had studied the horses and knew the riders now. One good win and he could replace the Fairfield money and it would then stop eating at his conscience. Samuel exhibited his own impatience at sitting through evening devotions before he could slip away from the mission and ride north.

George watched Samuel out of the corner of his eye. He well knew that tonight would have a full moon for he had invited Paul to go hunting with him this evening. The wood ducks and geese were beginning their migration north and it would be a good night to find the birds on the river sand bars. It would be a good night for the races as La Saline too.

While Abraham read from scripture, George pulled the letter from Mary Austin out of his pocket and looked at the envelope. He didn't open it to read the amusing letter again though it looked like he wanted to. He was content to hold the note. It seemed to give some comfort to him.

He had told Clarissa when she asked about it, that he thought it very sweet of the girl to write to him. The teacher had reminded him that Mary was a young woman now, but to George she was still a freckle-faced ten-year-old declaring to everyone's amusement that she was going to marry him someday. It was flattering – nothing more – that she would look up to him like that.

George rolled his neck to work out some of the muscle strain. He had been helping his brother Will build a new cabin at Hopefield for the past few weeks. It made him tired, but that was good for it enabled him to sleep at night. He hadn't slept well since Sarah died.

After Rev. Montgomery closed the devotion time with prayer, everyone stood to retire to their cabins. Samuel wasted no time in stepping out of the dining hall and walking to his room. He pulled the strongbox from under his bed and opened it.

The leather pouch holding the Osages' government stipend lay to one side. This money had never been recorded in the mission's ledger and though everyone knew about it, no one had ever asked to check it. He knew it would be handed over to the Osage elder named Monepasha when he and his clan returned from the hunt. That might be any day now. Could he risk taking it to La Saline?

His hand hovered over it for a long moment, but then moved on. He'd heard plenty of stories at La Saline about the Osages. While some thought nothing of stealing themselves, they apparently didn't appreciate anyone stealing from them. Samuel didn't want to stir up anger for himself or for anyone here.

Taking up the few bills that belonged to the mission, he stuffed them into the inside pocket of his coat. Then he went to the barn for a horse.

At La Saline there were fewer Osages than usual as most were not back from their hunt. Samuel placed a few small bets with the loquacious Frenchman Antoine. His picks won or placed in each race so he grew confident, bolder with each bet.

After one race he was claiming his winnings when the trapper everyone called Mr. Lee sidled up to him. The mountain man matched all the stories told about the hunters and trappers of the west. He was big and menacing with dark eyes and a perpetual frown. A scar ran from his left eyebrow down into his beard that was sprinkled with a little grey.

Samuel had asked once what Lee's first name was, but no one seemed to know. "Don't call him Lee," he was advised. "It's Mr. Lee."

Mr. Lee asked in a graveled voice, "You're one of them missionaries, ain't you?"

"I'm not a missionary," Samuel replied for what seemed like the hundredth time. "I just work at Union Mission."

It seemed to make no difference to Lee. "You know an Osage warrior named Bird? He never comes here for the races. I've never seen him. But I hear he has a tattoo of an eagle on his chest." Lee had a cabin on a creek close to

Cherokee land and while he was familiar with the Osages, he apparently did not know this particular warrior.

"I may have seen him," Samuel replied, squinting in thought as if trying to remember when or where. "Why do you want to know?"

"I don't," Mr. Lee said. "But I know some men from down near Wild Horse Prairie that are looking for him. Will pay money to the man who tells where he is."

Samuel's eyes narrowed. "Why are they looking for him?"

"You ask a lot of questions."

Samuel shrugged and took a step back from the man. "I might know him. How much are they willing to pay?"

"Plenty."

"I'll have to verify his whereabouts," Samuel hedged. "Can I let you know next month?"

Lee nodded. "But you better be sure of your facts. These men I know don't like being crossed. That's why they want Bird. They say he shot their father a couple years back while hunting down near the Red River. They've been itching for revenge ever since."

Samuel swallowed hard, visibly disturbed by this information. "Well, like I said, I'm not sure. I'll have to do some checking."

"You do that," Lee said. "I can't find an Osage willing to tell. But if you are, it might make you some good money." Then with a jerk of his thumb, he pointed to the track. "Looks like you're gonna need it."

Samuel's pick had placed last in the final race. Just like that his winnings had all evaporated.

When he reached his cabin well after dark, Samuel pulled open his trunk and took out the envelope from the Fairfield church. All these months at Union he had avoided reaching into that envelope. But now he had to cover the loss of the mission money.

He pulled out the last of the bills in the envelope, counted out the correct amount and placed them in the money box. There were two dollars left.

"I will not go back to La Saline," he said aloud, in a desperate promise to himself. "I can't keep doing this."

It was only a week later when Will Requa rode down from Hopefield with a group of Osage warriors. Monepasha's clan had returned to the farm and had put up their lodges, this time much further away from Pryor's Creek.

They were riding down to Three Forks to buy farm implements and seed for their fields. The group included Star-That-Travels, Hunts-the-Bear, Bird and Monepasha. They rode their horses into the corral, dismounted and walked to the dining hall where several missionaries met them.

"We came to get the Osage money," Will explained after greetings were exchanged and coffee was poured.

"I'll get it for you," Samuel volunteered. He stood to walk to his cabin. He passed one table where Amanda held up her coffeepot.

"More coffee, Bird?" she asked.

Samuel looked sharply at the man. Yes, the tattoo on his chest looked like an eagle. Bird must live at Hopefield. He swallowed hard and went on to his cabin. When he returned he handed the money pouch to Will and let out a breath of relief. It would no longer be a temptation. But his information about Bird, that was different.

The Hopefield residents didn't linger long at Union, wanting to reach Three Forks before late afternoon. They arrived to find the community bustling with activity. Three keelboats were tied at the Verdigris Landing. Besides several Osages visiting the trading posts with their furs, there seemed to be a rather large group of Cherokees as well.

At the Chouteau Trading Post, Will asked Colonel Chouteau the reason for so many Cherokees being in town.

"A delegation has been meeting with Colonel Arbuckle at the fort," the trader explained. "They will leave for Washington soon. New treaty in the works."

"We've been hearing about this treaty for months, years even. Is it finally going to happen?"

Chouteau shrugged. "Who can say with the Cherokees."

Like all the Chouteaus, who had close ties with the Osages, the trader had little liking for the other tribes.

"Who's in the delegation?"

"I know Blackcoat, their second chief, will be going. Walter Webber too, I think, and their great elder Sequoyah. There's a white man with them who I'm told is their legal counsel."

"A lawyer, eh? This must be serious then."

"Yes," Chouteau agreed flatly. It was widely acknowledged that if Lovely County became Cherokee the Chouteaus might be pressured to leave. They had always traded with the Osages, intermarried with them and often acted as the government's agent to them.

Will shared Chouteau's concern. Hopefield would depend upon the good graces of the Cherokees should Lovely County be given to them in exchange for their lands around Dardanelle and Dwight Mission.

The uncertainly was being felt by the Osages at Hopefield as well. Monepasha had declared that they would not build new homes with logs. They would reside in their lodges until these questions were settled.

Will stepped outside the Chouteau Trading Post to see Star mounting his mustang. "Where are you headed, Star?"

"Going to Nicks'. Get beads for Louisa. Teresa send two pairs rabbit gloves to trade."

"Is Louisa still working on a new shawl?" Will asked. "Susan was helping her with a design."

Star nodded. "It will have so many beads it will be too heavy for dance." He smiled indulgently. No matter the culture, young women all seemed to like beautiful things.

Will stroked his beard as if considering whether to join his friend. But he made no move toward his own horse. "See you back here in about an hour?"

Star glanced at the sun, his timepiece. "An hour," he agreed, then nudged his horse into a trot.

The Osage interpreter crossed French Point quickly and waited at the ferry crossing for the flat boat to pull across the river to him.

When it reached the western bank, he dismounted and led his horse onto the ferry. He was the only passenger crossing at that moment so the soldiers manning the boat pushed off immediately. Once across, Star-That-Travels rode south to the mercantile.

After completing his transaction with Sallie Nicks, he returned to the ferry. He had just walked his horse onto the boat when he heard another man coming from the fort hail the ferrymen.

Star turned to look at the man who approached. He frowned slightly when he saw that it was Walter Webber.

The Cherokee chief was easily recognizable for he always wore a mixture of clothing that reflected both his Scottish and Cherokee heritage. A business suit, a wide-brimmed hat trimmed with a feather stuck in its band, moccasins and two long black braids were his trademark attire. Webber did not recognize Star-That-Travels until the ferrymen had pushed off. When he did, his features went dark. The chief had never hidden his malice toward the Osages. He must have known that Star-That-Travels had married the widow of Joseph Revoir, the man so many Osages wanted to avenge. But not this one. Curiosity, then a look of derision crossed Webber's face.

Star seemed determined to keep silent. He stood close to his horse's head and held the reins tightly, keeping his eyes on the bank. Webber stood alert on the other side of the ferry a hand at his back where he no doubt kept a knife sheathed. Between them the two soldiers manning the ferry pulled hand over hand on the rope strung between the banks inching the boat to the western shore. Star could see that one of the soldiers kept glancing back and forth between the two passengers as if he sensed the tension between them.

When the boat bumped the rock landing, Webber was quick to step off and follow the path meandering up the shallow bank. Star took his time to walk his mustang off the ferry and follow Webber.

He was taken aback when he crested the bank to find Webber waiting for him.

"You are afraid to fight?" the Cherokee asked, his eyes narrowed, his voice holding a challenge.

"Not afraid," Star said, seeming surprised that Webber spoke English. He had only heard the man speak Cherokee. "I will fight when it is right to do so. But I have chosen the path of the Jesus-God and I do not seek revenge. My God says I must forgive."

Webber looked as if he didn't understand the word. But after some thought the meaning must have come to him for he said, "To forgive is the way of the weak."

"I see that you have never tried to forgive," Star returned. "If you had you would know that it takes great strength to forgive. More strength than pulling a bow or throwing a tomahawk."

Then the Osage warrior sprang onto his horse and kicked the mustang into a cantor. He left Webber watching him, his eyes still narrowed, but this time holding a begrudging respect.

There was a feeling of spring in the air a few days later at Union Mission. The redbuds along the river were putting on their showy blooms and the prairie grasses were greening up. The children were enjoying their noon recess playing outside the school house when a wagon approached from the south.

Clarissa could see it through her open classroom door from the desk where she sat looking over the slates of her students. She paused from reviewing their arithmetic problems to watch the wagon turn onto the lane through the cornfields. It jostled past Stephen, Paul and George who were each following a yoke of oxen and a plow. Recognizing the travelers, the plowmen turned their teams for home.

"It's the Vailles," she said to no one in particular. Then she rose, stepped outside and admonished her students to behave while she joined the other missionaries to greet their returning director. She saw Mr. Douglas approach from the dining hall, seeming almost reluctant to reach the corral.

The wagon, driven by an unfamiliar freighter, halted at the corral fence. Clarissa saw a young woman sitting by Asie and assumed it must be her younger sister. She looked very much like Asie with the same blonde hair and flawless complexion. She was holding baby Scott on her knees. My how the little boy, nearly one year old now, had grown since they had been gone.

Rev. Vaille quickly climbed out of the wagon and then helped the women and children down. The mission sisters all offered hugs to Asie and she introduced her sister to each in turn. Samuel stood back outside the circle of female sentimentality and Ella impatiently endured the introductions.

When she had been told everyone's name and had made some appropriate exchange of greetings, she then stood waiting for Samuel to come to her and greet her himself. But he didn't.

She waited as William answered questions about their journey. She waited while the schoolteachers took their leave to return to their classes. She waited while the red-haired cook with a baby girl in her arms offered to fix something for them to eat. She waited while the blacksmith asked about moving their trunks to their house.

Samuel just stood there awkwardly. It annoyed her at first and then frightened her. Was something wrong? Had he found some new love out here?

Finally she went to him and extended both hands in greeting. "It's so good to see you, Samuel," she said.

The handsome bookkeeper seemed to shake himself and appeared relieved that she would speak to him. "It is good to see you as well, Miss Ella. I trust the journey was not too strenuous for you."

"Not beyond expectation," she assured him. "How have you fared out here?"

"Well enough."

Ella took his arm and they walked together to the dining room. She looked around the mission compound in curiosity. How rustic it seemed to her. She supposed it had required some adjustment for Samuel to make this his new home.

He pulled out a chair for her at one of the tables and then sat beside her. Ella removed her shawl and bonnet and tried to smooth down the wayward strands of hair that had been teased by the constant prairie wind.

While the cook and another of the women bustled about pouring coffee, William shared news from back east and talked about his visits with the Secretary of War and the mission board. He then told the group that Ella had been hired as the new seamstress for the mission.

This news did not seem to set well with one of the farm workers, Ella could tell. A look came over his face, not so much of anger but almost of hurt. He finished his coffee in a gulp, said something to the Negro man sitting beside him and then took up his work gloves and stepped outside.

His movement seemed to bring the gathering to a close. Others rose to go back to their chores. The doctor stepped over to William as he stood.

"After you've had a chance to rest, I'd like to speak with you," he said.

Vaille nodded. "Yes, I need to catch up on what's been happening here," he agreed. "I'll stop by your office later today."

Dr. Palmer shook William's hand and said, "It's good to have you back." Then he also left the dining hall.

"Come, children, Ella," Asie was saying. "We need to get unpacked and see to any cleaning the cabin might need."

Ella felt she had no choice but to join her sister in a walk to the Vaille home. She sent a smile to Samuel who sat and watched her go.

"I'll want to speak to you later as well," William said to the bookkeeper.

Samuel turned his eyes away from Ella to look up at the director. The frown on the man's face told him this talk would not be one he wanted to have.

CHAPTER TWENTY-THREE

Union Mission
Spring 1827

The meeting between Samuel and Rev. Vaille took place just after the director had spent an hour at the doctor's office. What those two men had discussed, Samuel couldn't know, but it did not seem to have improved Vaille's mood.

He found Samuel in the dining hall at the little desk in the corner that the bookkeeper used as his work space. Now that the mission charged for most of its services, Samuel was kept relatively busy each day writing out bills or receipts and recording the transactions.

William picked up a chair and sat it across from Samuel. "I had a long visit with Pastor Eldridge of the Fairfield Church," he began.

Samuel did not look surprised. He kept his eyes on the ledger sitting in front of him.

William waited a moment for the bookkeeper to speak but when he didn't he proceeded. "He told me he gave you a check from the church to bring to the mission. I don't recall you mentioning this money and never saw it recorded in the ledger."

Samuel sighed. "I lost it," he mumbled.

"Lost it? How?"

Samuel drew a deep breath, glanced up at the minister then looked down again. "The truth is . . ." he began. "I mean, I lost the money. Somewhere along the journey. I had a roommate you see on the steamboat and the money was in my trunk. But I'm not accusing anyone, you understand. It's just that . . . well . . . you see we docked at Vicksburg for a time."

William looked as if he were growing impatient with the rambling confessional. "Are you saying it was stolen?"

"It perhaps was."

"Perhaps? But you don't know for sure?"

"I don't wish to accuse anyone," Samuel said more firmly as if he had finally hit upon the explanation he wanted to convey. "That wouldn't be very Christian would it? I only know that I didn't arrive here with the funds and I was embarrassed and ashamed to tell you. I know I should have said something . . . ." His words trailed off.

Vaille's mouth was still set in a firm line, but compassion filled his eyes. "There is a great deal of thievery along the rivers."

"Yes," Samuel seized upon the man's words. "I should have realized that and taken better care of the funds. I truly am sorry." The final words sounded sincere.

William leaned back in his chair. "Dr. Palmer explained to me that there was some confusion as to your appointment as mission superintendent."

"I would understand if you gave it back to Requa."

"I offered it to him, but he declined it." William seemed disturbed by that turn of events. "For the moment we will continue as is."

Samuel smiled. "I will give the job my best effort."

"I expect you to if you are going to marry Asie's sister."

"Well that really isn't settled."

"It is settled as far as Ella is concerned. I trust you have not led her on." There was a warning tone in the minister's words.

"No, sir. We simply haven't settled on the time."

William nodded slowly. "In the meantime, I think it would be best if I keep the money box and you keep the books. This way there will be no question about the accounts."

Now Samuel looked grim. "If you think that would be best."

"I do." William rose then and left Samuel to stare at the window for a long time.

"You brought this on yourself, old chap," he said under his breath.

All around him the missionaries went about their work with a dedication he seemed not to understand. In the kitchen the comforting clink of crockery told of supper preparations. From the fields he could hear the "gee" and "haw" directing the oxen in pulling the plows. The ring of a hammer sounded from the blacksmith shed. It wasn't an unpleasant place, this mission on the prairie. But Samuel had always held himself aloof from it -- not out of a sense of superiority, but out of feelings of guilt. Now as the shadows of the small square window frames fell across his desk, they looked like bars of a prison.

"You deserve nothing better, old chap."

Ella noticed Samuel's morose mood at supper that evening. Though he agreed to walk with her around the compound, he spoke little while they strolled along the well-worn paths between the buildings.

Ella's attempts to draw him out seemed futile and when he suggested that it was growing late and he should escort her to the Vailles' house she readily agreed. He took his leave of her and she watched him go with mixed emotions.

All the dreams she had held of their happy reunion; all the expectations of declarations of love had been a fantasy she now realized. Samuel had not been changed by his life at a prairie mission as everyone in Fairfield had hoped. She was no closer to marriage now than when she was still back East.

But she loved Samuel and she would continue to hold out hope. What else could she do at this isolated outpost where she was needed by her sister but apparently not wanted by the man she loved? Ella dashed away a tear from her cheek before stepping inside the little house that was now her home.

The planting was completed a few weeks later. Stephen had decided to grow less corn this year since the mission had fewer workers. He increased the acreage they fenced for pasture for their livestock and added to their potato and oat fields. By the Planting Moon of April, the fields were a carpet of green and it looked like they would have good crops this year.

After school one day, Clarissa walked with Thea and Lucie up to the little cemetery. The girls had gathered wildflowers from the prairie and they were taking them to the grave of Thea's birth mother, Whitestar.

Clarissa knew that the six-year-old was still a little young to understand that she was adopted, but the teacher wanted the girl to be familiar with the grave. They might have few chances to visit it in the future. Marcus and Clarissa had decided to accept the mission board's appointment to the new satellite post near Dwight Mission.

Marcus planned to visit Dwight to look over the site for the new work. Jacob Hitchcock was building a house, barn and school for Mulberry. The Palmers and Gillards would move there when everything was completed.

As she topped the hill with the girls, Clarissa was surprised to find George there. He had brought up a small scythe and had cut back the grass around the graves. He now sat near the marker at Sarah's grave staring at the name he had carved in the soft stone last year.

Clarissa stopped, thinking she should turn back and not disturb his reverie. But the girls were chasing a butterfly and caught his attention. He looked over to where she stood and smiled.

"I didn't mean to intrude," she said softly.

"You're not," he replied. "I'm just thinking, remembering."

She came closer and took a seat near him, keeping an eye on the girls as they played.

"They are good memories, I hope."

"Yes," George smiled.

Clarissa was glad to see the smile. Her friend had rarely smiled since his wife's death. She had noticed, however, that a letter from Mary Austin would bring a look of amusement to his face. She had also seen him laboring to pen letters of his own to send back to the girl at Harmony Mission.

"Sarah loved it out here on the prairie," George said as he

absently brushed some dirt from the carved letters of her name.

"She certainly did. I think she was almost as enthused about it as you were when we arrived. She was a good match for you."

Clarissa questioned her words when she saw George's smile disappear.

"Do you think Sarah would . . . would she mind if I were to . . ?"

"She would want you to be happy, George," Clarissa assured him. "I'm sure she would not wish you to live alone for the rest of your life."

He nodded, looking grateful that she had understood his meaning.

"I think I might ride up to Harmony." He left his intentions unspoken, but Clarissa could guess them. He wanted to see this girl who wrote him such warm letters, stirring his heart back to life. He wanted to test the possibility of courting her.

"I think that would be a very good idea," the teacher said.

When Clarissa and the girls arrived back home, she found Ella waiting for her in one of their cane chairs on the porch.

"I'm sorry, Miss Selden," Clarissa said after sending the girls inside. "Have you been waiting long?"

"No, not long," the new seamstress said. "Your husband told me you'd be back soon so I decided to wait. I've finished letting out the hems for your girls' dresses." She held up the two dresses for Clarissa's inspection.

"Oh, wonderful. Can you come inside for a cup of tea? We haven't had a chance to get to know one another."

"I'd like that. And please call me Ella."

"Alright, Ella."

They settled at the little table in the Palmers' cabin and while the girls busied themselves with their dolls they chatted about life at Union Mission.

"Do you think you'll enjoy your time here?" Clarissa asked after she'd poured the hot water for their tea to steep.

"I hope so."

Clarissa looked closely at the young woman. She clearly wanted to talk with someone and perhaps didn't feel she could share her thoughts with Asie.

"I know Asie is very glad to have you here."

"I'm glad about being able to help her. She says she feels better with me around. I hope that's true."

"And Mr. Douglas must surely be glad to have you here as well. I mean, we understood from Asie that you and he are to be wed."

"Well, I suppose I let everyone believe that," Ella sighed. "But in truth, we really aren't. Samuel has never actually asked me to marry him. I had hoped with this job, this mission would give him a sense of purpose and make him more inclined to settle down and get married. But I fear I was wrong."

"I'm afraid I haven't had an opportunity to get to know Mr. Douglas very well. I don't wish to speak out of turn, but I've never felt he was totally comfortable here."

Clarissa checked the tea and then poured it through a strainer into their cups. She twirled a bit of honey into her cup and then offered it to Ella who took some as well.

"Samuel seems to only be comfortable or happy when he's with his chums playing cards. William has told me that he thinks Samuel gambles. I haven't wanted to admit it, but I think he's right. But there are no card games to be had at this mission. We were all so sure it would give Samuel a chance to make a change."

Clarissa hesitated for a moment. "I believe there is gambling at the horse races at La Saline, a trading post north of us."

"Oh," Ella said, nodding with understanding. "That explains a lot."

They sipped their tea in silence.

"Do you think a man would change for someone if she asked him to?"

"Perhaps," Clarissa said carefully. "But I don't know about gambling. It can take hold of a man, I think."

"I suppose. But love can change someone, can't it?"

Clarissa shook her head. "I've never faced this myself, Ella, so I'm hesitant to give advice. But I don't know that we women can change our men, no matter how much we love them. It is God who changes men's hearts and only if they are willing to be changed. None of us, not even God, can force a change upon others without their consent and cooperation."

"Should I confront him about this? About us? About his gambling?"

"You should certainly have an honest conversation with him. Let him know how you feel. But you must also be prepared to walk away if he doesn't value you enough to want to change. My mother gave me a bit of advice years ago. She said, 'If a man won't fight to get you, he won't fight to keep you.'"

Ella thought over the teacher's words. Then she set her mouth in a firm line, squared back her shoulders and nodded. "I see what you're saying. I should have enough self respect not to allow him to continue to string me along without a commitment, without a willingness to change."

She finished her tea and stood to go. "Thank you, Mrs. Palmer."

"Call me Clarissa."

"Thank you, Clarissa. You've given me much to think about. Would you say a prayer for me to do the right thing?"

"Yes, I will." Clarissa walked the young woman to the door and then watched her take the path back to her sister's home. Then she crossed the cabin to open the door to her husband's office. He was sitting as his desk, labeling bottles of medicine.

"Marc," she said.

"Yes?" he looked up from his work.

"I love you."

He seemed surprised at her unexpected words. "I love you too, dear."

Then she closed the door and left him looking at it with a puzzled expression on his face. He shook his head, smiled to himself and went back to his work.

George had asked at Hopefield if anyone there would be making a trip to Missouri in the next few days. Will sent word that Bird planned to take Bearpaw up to visit Pawhuska's village as soon as school dismissed for summer.

So at the Strawberry Moon, George joined the two Osages for the journey north. Now thirteen years old, Bearpaw had graduated from school and this journey was to be a time of preparation for manhood.

While a student at Union, Bearpaw had been given chores to perform so he knew George well. Between his understanding of English and George's grasp of the Osage language, they were able to communicate easily. They chatted amiably on the journey while Bird, who spoke French but only a little English, smiled indulgently at his son.

When they reached the Neosho Mission west of the Missouri state line, George parted company with them and traveled the remaining miles to Harmony on a well-marked buffalo trail.

He had not visited Harmony since Will and Susan were married four years ago. As he approached the mission, he tried to beat off some of the trail dust from his coat. He seemed nervous when he pulled his horse to a halt at the corral.

Daniel Austin, Harmony's millwright, came from the barn to meet him.

"Why it's Brother Requa, isn't it?" he greeted George and held out his hand to shake.

"Yes, sir." In his nervousness, George mistook Austin's gesture and handed him his horse's reins.

"Up for a visit, are you?" Austin took the reins and pulled open the corral gate to let the horse enter. There was a twinkle of amusement in his eyes.

"Yes, sir."

"Well, you'll find Mary in the dining hall. She's looking after the little ones and they're probably having a bite to eat about now."

George glanced in the direction the millwright pointed. "I don't want to interrupt anything."

"She'll not see it that way," Daniel assured him. "And she would flay my hide if I didn't send you right in to her."

George looked surprised that Mr. Austin seemed to know that he had come to call on his daughter. But he shouldn't have been. Mary had never been shy about expressing herself and had never hidden her interest in a certain mechanic at Union Mission.

Requa nodded and again swatted at the dust on his clothes. Then he walked to the dining hall while Mr. Austin watched from the corral with a satisfied smile on his face.

Opening the door cautiously, George stuck his head inside before entering. He saw two women and four young children in the room, but did not see Mary. Her father must have been mistaken about her whereabouts. He was starting to close the door when one of the young women turned at the squeak of its hinges. The pretty auburn-haired lady jumped up from her chair quickly.

"Brother Requa!" she exclaimed and hurried to the door. "Come in."

George stepped inside the room and removed his hat. "I didn't mean to bother you ladies. I was looking for Mary Austin."

"I'm Mary Austin. Don't you know me? Has it been so long that you've forgotten what I look like?"

George's mouth dropped open. Gone were the long red braids and spray of freckles across the face of a girl. An attractive young woman stood before him. But the saucy smile and deep green eyes were the same.

He slowly stepped inside and removed his hat.

"Miss Mary," he said, but couldn't seem to think of anything else.

"Oh, it's so good to see you," Mary enthused. "Come in and I'll fetch you some coffee."

She took his hand and pulled him further into the room. "Unless you'd like some cider . . . or tea. We have milk too."

"Coffee will be fine."

Mary indicated a chair for George to take while she went to get a cup of coffee. The other housemother wiped the children's hands and faces and shortly took the little ones outside for play.

Mary came back, bringing coffee and a slice of raisin pie. She sat the food in front of George and then took a seat opposite him at the table.

It took a moment for George to relax, but Mary's smile and cheerful chatter soon put him at ease. Before he realized it, they had spent the afternoon in conversation and the folks from Harmony gathered for supper.

Mr. Austin came in with his wife Martha and the two of them greeted George again and made introductions to the other missionaries.

"How long will you be with us, Brother Requa?" Martha asked.

"Only a couple of days," George replied. "Can't be away from Union too long; there's too much work to do."

"Oh, yes," Daniel nodded. "There's always work."

"We have an extra bed in the boy's dormitory if that will do for you," Martha offered.

"That will be fine, ma'am."

George spent the two days almost constantly in Mary's company. The other women had taken over her chores, giving her free time with the man they all had heard about. There could be no doubt by anyone how Mary felt about this suitor.

It was clear that George had quickly made up his mind to be a suitor. He spent the last half hour before his departure with Mr. Austin.

"I'd like your permission to pursue Mary's hand in marriage," George said.

"She's still rather young," Daniel said, but he was smiling. "I'd like her to wait until she's sixteen to marry."

"I understand," the mechanic agreed. "When will she be sixteen?"

"October 25th."

"I'll be back to celebrate her birthday, then. If that's agreeable with you?"

"Yes. She's never had a mind towards anyone but you, George. And I heartily agree with her choice. You have the respect of the Osages . . . you and your brother . . . and that's no small thing out here. I couldn't hope better for her than to marry a godly man doing a work for the Lord."

"I'm no preacher, sir."

"Neither am I." Austin looked down at his work-roughened hands. "But there's more than preaching needed in the Lord's work. You and I have our place."

"Yes, sir." George looked pleased at the man's words. "I'll see you in October then."

He shook hands with the millwright and then walked to where his saddled horse waited at the corral. Mary waited there too.

"When will I see you again?"

"How about October 25th?"

Mary's smile rivaled the sun in its brightness. "That's perfect! I'll be counting down the days."

He untied his mustang, but before he could mount the horse, Mary stood on tiptoe and pressed a quick kiss on his cheek.

Grinning, George climbed into the saddle. Looking down at her he said, "I'll write you. I have something I want to ask you."

It was hardly possible but Mary's smile widened. "I'm thinking my answer will be yes." Her green eyes snapped with pleasure.

George was whistling when he caught up to a line of wagons heading south on the Texas Road. He stayed with them all the way to Hopefield where he stopped and asked his brother to plan a trip with him to Harmony come fall.

Clarissa noticed at dinner a few days later that Ella and Mr. Douglas did not sit together for the noon meal. She wondered if Ella had finally gotten the courage to confront the bookkeeper about his life choices. She looked sad and he looked, well, he looked furious. She caught Ella's eye and raised an eyebrow in a question. Ella simply shook her head.

After most everyone had departed the dining room for afternoon chores, Clarissa and Ella worked together to clean the tables. Clarissa asked in a low voice. "Are you going to be alright?" Standing closer to the young woman she could tell that Ella had been crying.

"Yes," Ella said, wiping with vigor at an imagined spot on the table. "Samuel and I are through. I asked for a wedding date and he flailed around like a fish on the bank. I asked him to give up gambling and he denied that he ever placed a wager."

"I'm sorry, Ella. I was afraid it might come to that."

"Oh, he tried to sweet talk around it. He always could sweet talk me into hanging on a little longer. But I told him I wasn't going to wait anymore."

"He seemed upset at supper."

"He's angry . . . at me! As if this were my fault." Ella tried to keep her emotions under control, but she could not hold back more tears. She sat down in a chair and buried her face in the cleaning rag.

Clarissa sat beside her, waiting for the storm to pass. Martha looked in from the kitchen, assessed the situation and gave an understanding nod to the teacher. "I'll pray," she mouthed and then went back to the kitchen chores.

"What am I going to do?" Ella asked, as she wiped away the tears.

"My sister Jerusha once answered that question for me. She said, 'You will get on with your life.' So that's what I did and that's what you must do."

"I don't know if I can. I have made Samuel my life for the past three years."

"He wasn't your life. He was your dream of life. You can dream again. Samuel needs our prayers. This might be the very thing that will help him see his need."

Ella nodded but didn't look convinced. Clarissa gave her a hug and they returned to their work. Neither woman glanced out a window to see Samuel walk from his cabin to the barn. He strode inside with angry purpose and saddled a horse.

Paul looked up from where he was mucking out one of the stalls. He watched the bookkeeper cinch up the saddle and lead the horse toward the door.

"You traveling?"

"None of your business," Samuel ground the words out. Then he mounted the horse and soon had turned it north on the Texas Road.

Paul stood in the barn door watching him. "Lawd, help that man," he prayed. "Cause he shorely do need it."

Samuel knew he was wrong. He knew it. But he just kept riding toward La Saline as if pulled by a string. He had little money to take to the races, just two dollars from the Fairfield offering. He'd probably lose it in the first race. But he could not seem to control the urge to take the risk and hope for riches. He could not control the urge, the need, to gamble despite his denials to Ella and William, despite the promises he had made to himself.

He arrived at La Saline earlier than he usually did and this gave him more time to study the horses and listen to the talk among the men who had come to watch them run. There was a crowd at La Saline today. The summer solstice was almost here and the day would have many hours of sunlight. The Green Corn Moon would provide light well into the night. There would be several races so there was a large number of horses running.

Across the crowd he observed the warrior Kickingbird talking with Mr. Lee. It reminded him of Lee's query about the Osage named Bird. He fingered the money in his pocket, watching the two men talk. The thought of turning a man over to folks wanting revenge was distasteful. A man would have to be desperate to stoop to such a level. But Samuel was almost there. When the trapper parted with Kickingbird and came Samuel's way, he hailed him.

"Are you still seeking information on the warrior named Bird?"

"I was, but not anymore," Lee replied. "That fellow Kickingbird just told me he keeps his lodge at the mission farm down on Pryor's Creek. He's upriver for the summer though."

"Well," Samuel said, looking disappointed, "I suppose Kickingbird will get the bounty then."

"Yep. He has some kind of grudge against Bird, says the man betrayed him to his father and got him kicked out of the clan or some such thing. Now he's got his revenge. But he'll see little of the money for he owes most of it to me." Lee chuckled with a sadistic satisfaction.

Samuel nodded, not following the explanation and not really caring. He'd just bet with his two dollars and be done with it.

Samuel's luck ran hot and cold that evening, but he ended the night with winnings of twelve dollars. Not a great sum, but the first time since leaving Fairfield that he had come out ahead.

He rode back to Union feeling much better than when he had left. Winning had a way of assuaging one's conscience. Winning convinced you that your luck had finally turned. Winning told you that you weren't such an awful person, that God must surely approve or at least understand why you had to gamble. Winning made you want to try your luck again.

When Samuel reached his cabin that evening, his step was light and he was smiling. He went to his trunk, pulled out the soiled church envelope and put the two dollars back in. Then he thought for a moment and added four more bills. He closed the trunk and sat on his bed.

"I'll pay it all back," he said aloud as a sort of prayer and a promise. "And I'll win back Ella too. If you'll help me, God."

He sat for a long time in the darkness, staring into the silence. It was the first time in years that he had actually prayed. It made him feel both hopeful and ashamed.

CHAPTER TWENTY-FOUR

Fort Gibson
October 1827

It was a hot and dry summer in Lovely County. With little rain, the river level dropped and the rocky base of the Neosho was easily visible. Traffic along the road slowed to a crawl and there were no races at Chouteau's post. Samuel might have gone to the races at the Persimmon Moon, but William asked for his help in completing the quarterly report for the mission board and so that opportunity slipped away as well.

Nothing much moved for several weeks in the oppressive heat. The horse flies were so bad, the animals were in torment. Stephen and George turned their horses, mules and cows out into the canebrake where the flies tended not to be so thick.

River travel ground to a halt until rains in late August brought the water levels up some. Marcus took a keelboat down to Dwight Mission to visit with Rev. Washburn about setting up Mulberry Mission. The cabin Hitchcock had built was complete, but the school was not. The two men agreed to wait to open the mission until next spring. Clarissa would finish one more school year at Union.

Most everyone at Union and Hopefield traveled down to Three Forks for the Pumpkin Moon Rendezvous in early October. They welcomed the cooler weather that stirred the yellowing leaves of the cottonwoods, sycamores and pecan trees that lined the creeks and rivers.

When they arrived at the fur trade community, changes

immediately caught their eye. As Stephen directed their mules along the road through the town, they passed one of the older trading posts.

It had stood empty for awhile though Colonel Chouteau owned it and had used it as an office of sorts for a time. He had recently sold the log building to Colonel David Brearley and he was making improvements to it. The building would serve as the agency now that Brearley had been named government agent to the Creeks.

In fact, as the missionaries passed, workers were raising a canvas sign to hang across the front above the door. It read: CREEK AGENCY. It was the first building at Three Forks to actually have a sign.

"Makes the place look civilized," George laughed as they watched the men nail the canvas in place.

"Colonel Brearley told me he expects the first group of Creeks to arrive early next year," Marcus told everyone as they pulled into their usual camping spot near the Pryor Trading Post.

"We'll need to make our plans for a work among the Creeks," Montgomery noted as he helped Harriett and his daughter Mary out of one of the wagons. She shook the hay out of her skirts and pulled bits of it out of the braids of the eight-year-old.

Their custom was to visit the various trading posts and tent vendors for a time, then have supper at their campsite. This was usually followed by Father Menard's brush arbor service, but the priest had retired to St. Louis and no longer trapped in the area or lived in his cabin on the bayou that bore his name.

Instead, there would be a social at Fort Gibson this evening, with music and dancing. Rumor had it that there would be iced cream served as well. Colonel Nicks had managed to bring several large blocks of ice packed in hay on a keelboat. The New England missionaries had all tasted iced cream, but for their southern neighbors, this would be an unknown treat.

Paul wasted no time turning his horse to cross French

Point and the Neosho to find Tassie at the Nicks' mercantile. Most of their group went to Chouteau's to shop. Having been paid by the mission in July, they had funds with which to make purchases in preparation for winter and Christmas.

Among the hucksters who always showed up for rendezvous was the usual assortment of games of chance. Samuel had spotted a card dealer standing just outside one tent, displaying his dexterity with fancy shuffles of his cards clearly hoping to draw in a crowd.

Samuel needed to purchase some shaving supplies, but after that he exited the Chouteau mercantile and turned to walk up toward the card shark's tent. Stephen stopped him on the porch of the store.

"Samuel, George and I are going over to Gibson to get some target practice in before the turkey shoot tomorrow. Why don't you join us."

Samuel's eyes narrowed in suspicion. He had never been included in the working men's group before. He was considered in the professional class and even on the prairie, these distinctions divided men. But now he was surrounded by Fuller, Requa and Woodruff. It was as if they had decided to keep him away from the gaming tents. Did Ella have something to do with that? Or perhaps Vaille?

"I'm really not much for shooting matches," he said, glancing up the trail toward the tents.

"You've handled a gun though, haven't you?" Stephen asked.

"Well, yes."

"Come along," the normally quiet Woodruff said, clamping a hand on his shoulder. What a grip of strength came through Samuel's shirt. "Let's see what you've got." A none-too-subtle nudge directed the bookkeeper off the porch and before he could protest more he was walking across the Point toward the Fort Gibson ferry.

Despite himself, Samuel enjoyed the banter the men engaged in during the two-mile trek. He had never made any effort to become a part of this mission family, pointedly rebuffing friendship and camaraderie.

While everyone had thought him Ella's beau and nearly a member of the Vaille family, they had believed he had the fellowship he needed and had respected his desire for privacy. But now it was obvious even to the men that he and Ella were no longer together. Perhaps this extension of friendship was merely pity. Samuel worried his lip as they rode the ferry across the Neosho.

They walked up to the fort and found the competition area set up in a field north of the fort. Various targets had been set up at different heights and distances. The fort provided the rifles that would be used in the shooting match and George wanted to test them out. He was a dead shot with his own musket, but he wanted to get a feel for these newer weapons.

They spent some time at the target practice and eventually even Samuel gave it a go. With a few pointers from the others, he even proved to be a decent marksman. Woodruff spent most of the time studying the craftsmanship of the guns.

After an hour or so of shooting, the men decided to walk down to Nicks & Rogers and spend a penny on some bottled sarsaparilla. Then they walked back to Pryor's post to enjoy Amanda's cold fried chicken, pickled squash and baked beans.

The women cleaned the dishes and then brushed out their clothes and tidied their hair for the evening's social event. Ella pulled a little mirror from her reticule and studied her face. She pinched her cheeks to give them some color and then smoothed back her blonde hair. She felt nervous at the thought of facing a fort full of soldiers.

Samuel watched her out of the corner of his eye, pretending not to notice her efforts to look her best. He'd seen her check her hair like that when standing before the mirror in her parents' home in Fairfield before they went out for an evening event. He'd never truly appreciated how beautiful she was . . . until now . . . now that it might be too late.

They all walked to the ferry, crossed quickly and were drawn up from the riverbank to the fort lit with lanterns all around. A band of sorts made up of banjos and fiddles was tuning up in one corner of the palisade. The soldiers were in their dress uniforms with shined shoes and spit-polished buttons.

Neighbors from far and wide were at the social. Osages and Cherokees, farm families and lone trappers, tradesmen and missionaries were all present. Clarissa remembered the first rendezvous she attended when there were barely more than fifty people at the event. There were around two hundred gathered at the fort this year.

She walked with Marcus to the refreshment table where Tassie and her mother were pouring cider and coffee. At one end of the table stood the fort commander surrounded by a number of officers including Charles with Eliza and Colonel Nicks with Sallie. Like several others, the Palmers sipped their cider and listened to the conversation that flowed around the military men.

"So you convinced the legislature to establish a county seat for Lovely County?" Arbuckle asked the sutler.

"Yes, finally," Nicks said, looking quite satisfied with himself. "I've also secured a post office for it and I've picked out the site."

"Where will it be located?" Charles asked.

"On the new road about half way between Fort Gibson and Fort Smith, near the river. Steamboats will soon be reaching the falls, mark my words. My thinking is that new settlers will want to be close to this road and will want easy access for trade and for their mail."

"So there will be a third Nicks mercantile there?" asked Elizabeth Baylor, daughter of the fort's doctor.

"Of, course," Sallie confirmed with a merry look on her face. "John will have a chain of stores from Fort Smith to the mountains."

"Don't exaggerate, dear," Nicks chided his wife. But he didn't contradict her.

Clarissa could never tell if the sutler was actually annoyed with his wife for her comments or if it was simply an act, a sort of game that the two played. She could tell that the other men around her enjoyed Sallie's humor and admired her charming personality.

"What will be the name of the county seat?" An officer with the rank of captain asked this question. Clarissa surmised he was newly assigned to this post for she had never seen him before.

"Why, Nicksville, of course!" Sallie exclaimed with a flirtatious snap of her fan.

There was a smattering of laughter among the group. Nicks looked slightly embarrassed, but mostly pleased.

"What can I say? My wife insists on that name."

"Of course she does," Marcus whispered for Clarissa's ears only. They joined the good-humored laughter.

Soon the post band began to play in earnest and the party-goers drifted toward the center of the palisade where the hardened parade ground provided a smooth dance floor. The men present far outnumbered the women so Clarissa found herself frequently asked to dance. She declined, however, not feeling it appropriate for a missionary teacher.

She and Marcus took seats on split logs supported by sandstone rocks set around the perimeter of the grounds. They enjoyed their cider and tapped their toes to the lively music.

Clarissa saw that Ella did not share her scruples about dancing. She and Miss Baylor hardly missed a dance as a line of young soldiers kept them busy. Sallie and Eliza were often on the dance floor as well.

Even Samuel asked the dark-haired Miss Baylor to accompany him on the dance ground while Ella danced with the new officer.

"Do you know who that captain is?" Clarissa asked her husband.

"That's James Dawson. He's been here a few months. From Baltimore originally, I think."

"Not married, I assume?"

"No. Are you planning some matchmaking?"

"I don't think I'll need to." She nodded toward Ella and the captain as they were clapping at the end of the song. She quickly noticed though that Ella was not looking up at

Dawson. She was looking across the yard to where Samuel stood with Miss Baylor. And Samuel was furtively glancing at Ella as well.

"Oh, dear," she sighed.

The following day even more people were at the fort for the competitions. Besides aiming at targets with guns, there was also the bow and arrow competition and tomahawk toss. Burlap bags over hay and sawn rings of massive tree trunks were painted with charcoal for the targets. There were several men participating so the heats would last most of the morning.

Samuel quickly recognized that he could not match the skills of the various hunters and soldiers signing up for the shoot so instead he walked around the crowd's perimeter searching for someone who was taking bets on the competition. But he found none. Colonel Arbuckle had outlawed gambling at the post. Samuel would have to be content to merely watch.

George and Stephen planned to compete in the gun shoot, while Bird, Bearpaw and Hunts-the-Bear were among the bow and tomahawk competitors. Captains Dawson and Bonneville joined Nicks and Charles Summers as judges this year.

Clarissa eased her way through the crowd to reach Eliza. The two friends shared a hug and bemoaned the fact that they saw so little of each other these days.

"I don't imagine you've heard that Charles has received his next assignment," Eliza said.

"No. Where will you be going next?"

"Jefferson Barracks, in Missouri," the petite young woman replied. "We'll have thirty days' leave first and we plan a visit to Boston."

"That will be so good for you. You'll get to see family."

"Yes, we can share our news," Eliza's eyes sparkled as she laid a hand on her stomach.

"A baby?"

"Yes, due early next summer."

"Oh, I'm so happy for you, Eliza." Clarissa gave her friend another hug, partly to hide the bit of pain this news brought her. She was never destined to share such news for herself and sometimes the sorrow hit hard.

"Marcus and I will be moving about that time," she said when the hug ended. "Write to me at Dwight Mission; we'll get our mail there. I want to know all about this baby and your life in Missouri."

"I will."

The women turned back to watch the competition then and clap for their mission brothers. Stephen made it through three rounds of the competition before being eliminated. George continued to move through the various targets with remarkable skill.

Clarissa watched along with everyone else as the mission's hired man displayed his prowess with the gun. He would take his pose, sight down the gun barrel, then let out a long, slow breath. Standing so still he seemed to be a statue, he would wait while everyone watching seemed to hold their breath and silence fell. Then with no movement except for his pull on the trigger, he would fire. Clarissa never failed to jump even though she was expecting the blast.

Soon all the competitors were eliminated except George and the master sergeant who had won the last few years. A private set up a row of glass bottles on a narrow table. Both men hit every bottle in their turn.

The table was carried back five more feet and following another perfect round of shots it was moved five more feet. At this distance the soldier hit every bottle except the last one.

George stepped forward for his turn. Again he displayed the certainty and calm that marked his shooting. One by one he took up a single-shot rifle, sighted along the barrel and fired, shattering the bottles in turn. One bottle remained.

Clarissa found herself praying that George would win then chided herself for doing so. She doubted that God tipped shooting competitions in anyone's favor. But she couldn't help it. She wanted George to win!

Everyone was literally holding their breath as George lifted a rifle once more. He seemed to take even more time getting the barrel of the gun exactly in place. Glancing around, George could see the breathless anticipation on everyone's face. Grinning a little he held his pose, released his breath, pulled the trigger. The final bottle exploded and the crowd erupted with applause. George had won.

"Thank you, Lord!" Clarissa breathed and then laughed at herself.

Stephen was the first to reach George and offer congratulations but a crowd was quickly surrounding him with thumps on the back and handshakes. The master sergeant offered his hand in good sportsmanship. Colonel Nicks presented George with a gold coin and the mechanic held it up for everyone to see.

Samuel had a look of jealousy on his face. But it wasn't the coin he seemed to long for. It was the jovial camaraderie surrounding his fellow mission laborer. "Good show, old chap," he said under his breath. But he didn't try to press through the crowd to congratulate George.

While George was enjoying the adulation from admirers, the soldiers were setting up the targets for the bow and arrow competition. Soon the crowd had moved back to the perimeter of the field to watch as mostly Osages, but a few Quapaws and Cherokees, took their places in front of the targets.

As Samuel watched the first match with interest, he noticed across the circle of onlookers were two men dressed as farmers with wide brimmed hats and bandana neckerchiefs. They seemed very interested in Bird, pointing to him and scowling his way.

Samuel wondered if they were the men Mr. Lee said were looking for Bird. Surely not, for they would have notified Colonel Arbuckle to have the warrior arrested. What better time than now while surrounded by soldiers. Wasn't the military the law out here?

Bird won the bow competition while Bearpaw and Hunts-the-Bear were in the top five at the tomahawk toss. After receiving their coins and ribbon trophies, the mission family gathered around their Osage friends to congratulate them. Hunts-the-Bear promptly gave Louisa Revoir his ribbon and told her to add it to her new shawl.

The competitions were followed by a barbecue dinner served by the solders for their guests. After everyone had enjoyed the smoked beef, fried potatoes and boiled cabbage, they purchased gingerbread from Mrs. Bradley and lemonade from the Nicks' mercantile.

The missionaries returned to Three Forks, loaded into the wagons and began the journey home. It had been a very enjoyable holiday and welcome time away from the mission.

The following week, George along with Will, Susan and their children made the journey to Harmony Mission for Mary's birthday. Since she had given George a yes to his question, they would be married on the following Sunday.

While traveling north, they stopped at a creek some ten miles north of Hopefield. It was to this location that Will thought they might have to move the farm. It was north of Lovely County and therefore not a part of Arkansas or any other organized territory. It would likely not become Cherokee land should a treaty be signed.

George displayed none of the nervousness that Will had felt when he had made the journey to Harmony to marry Susan. Perhaps because the mechanic had already been married, he was not nervous, but full of happy anticipation.

With his prize money from the turkey shoot, he was planning to take Mary to Jefferson City for their honeymoon. The sweet girl had rarely traveled away from Harmony Mission so he thought she would enjoy the adventure.

The wedding ceremony was simple and Martha Austin cried all through it. Mary, with her auburn curls piled atop her head and wearing a new green dress, never shed a tear. With a mature certainty she repeated the age-old vows and welcomed George's tender kiss when prompted by Rev. Dodge. At long last her dream of being Mrs. George Requa was fulfilled.

Will and Susan waited at Harmony while the newlyweds were away, giving Susan a chance to visit with her friends and former co-workers. When the younger Requas returned, they loaded Mary's trunk and a rocking chair her father had made for her, plus piles of quilts and linens lovingly stitched for her by the women at Harmony.

CHAPTER TWENTY-FIVE

Fort Gibson
Early Spring 1828

The quilts were quite welcome during the months that followed. It was an unusually cold winter with several snowfalls that drifted into wet piles along the fence line but blew across the freeze-hardened bed of the road.

Stephen was grateful for the many snows for they would replenish the moisture in the fields and raise the river levels. Everyone in the neighborhood stayed close to their fires, staying busy with what hand chores could be done by lantern light for the days were often dreary.

Then suddenly in mid February it was spring . . . or at least the first foray of spring onto the prairie. More snow might come, but within a day of the first warm breeze, it had melted off the roofs and formed long icicles that the children liked to break off and lick like candy. The snowman that Mary and George had built for the children was soon a misshapen lump in the schoolyard.

Marcus and Paul rode to Fort Gibson for the February preaching Sunday. When they reached Three Forks they were surprised to see a great many people filling the road that wound through the little town.

"Somethin's going on," Paul observed, while trying to sit higher in his saddle to see what might be the reason for such a gathering.

"I wonder what it could be," Marcus said, also curious.

They came around a gentle curve in the road and an amazing sight met them. Anchored at the Verdigris Landing was a large side-wheeled steamboat, the first one ever to reach Three Forks. On the side of its bow, in fancy script, its name had been painted: *Facility*.

"Well, look at that!" Marcus exclaimed. "A steamboat finally made it over the falls."

"Brought a whole passel of folks too."

They nudged their horses toward the waterfront to get a better view of the boat and its passengers. Besides these newcomers, it seemed like everyone who lived within the sound of the boat's whistle also crowded the landing. It made for a chaotic scene.

The men from Union decided to tie their horses at Hugh Glenn's trading post and walk the rest of the way to the landing. They wanted to view this marvel right along with everyone else.

Easing their way through the crowd, they were able to get close enough to see the boat's captain assisting a number of women and children down the gangplank from the boat to the shore. They were also now able to see that two keelboats had been tied to the steamboat and hauled upriver behind it. Such an undertaking was truly remarkable and Marcus wondered what captain had managed it.

He studied the man in the navy uniform, certain he had seen the captain before.

"Why, it's Mr. Pennywit," he said.

"You know him?"

"He was the steward on the boat that brought us from Pittsburgh" Marcus explained. "A skilled riverman, if I ever knew one."

"Looks like he's a captain now."

"Yes, that was always his goal."

They edged in closer and saw that Colonel Brearley was also at the gangplank, helping the passengers come ashore. Looking closer, Marcus realized these women must be some of the Creek emigrants Brearley had been preparing for. They wore bright calico dresses embellished with many ribbons. Their skirts fell in gathered tiers just above beaded moccasins.

Already on shore, having scrambled up from the first

keelboat, were many Creek men, each searching for their family members. Apparently the women and children had traveled in the steamboat, while the men had ridden aboard the less comfortable keelboat. The second keelboat looked to be fully loaded with boxes, crates and barrels, no doubt the household goods and personal items the Indians had brought with them from Georgia.

One older woman came slowly down the gangplank, helped by a girl who was perhaps her granddaughter. The woman clutched a little pot holding what looked like a stick. As she got closer Marcus could tell the item was a cutting from a rose bush, its thorns visible. The woman had brought a cherished bit of home with her and obviously wanted it handled with care.

Brearley was directing the Creeks toward the agency building though there was no way the small log structure would be able to accommodate these several hundred people.

"That's Mr. McIntosh, ain't it?" Paul pointed to one of the men who seemed to be in charge of getting his people ashore. "He visited us last year."

"Yes, I think you're right," Marcus agreed.

As the crowd shifted toward the agency, Paul took his leave of the doctor. "I'd better get home to Tassie," he said. "You know she'll expect you for supper."

"I'll be there," Marcus replied. "I think I'll try to talk with the captain."

Paul nodded and returned to his horse then eased it through the crowd and pointed it toward home. Marcus edged up to the landing area and waited.

"Pennywit," he called when the man had helped the last person off his boat.

The captain turned, searching for who had hailed him. Finally he spotted Dr. Palmer and walked toward him.

"Don't know if you'll remember me," Marcus began, extending his hand to captain. "I was with a group of missionaries who came out in 1820."

"Oh, yes," the captain said. He shook the doctor's hand but seemed to be searching his memory for the name.

"I'm Dr. Palmer."

"Of course, Dr. Palmer. I remember you. You saved a young woman from drowning in the Mississippi as I recall."

Marcus smiled. "Yes, and now I'm married to her."

"Well, that seems about right," Pennywit grinned.

"How did you manage to get here with that large a boat?"

"A lot of prayer and little bit of luck," the man said. "I honestly wasn't sure we could get the *Facility* this far. But I hired a pilot who knows the river. We had the boilers burning hot and just rammed through them. The water levels were high enough that we made it."

"Must have been a challenging journey all the way."

"Aye," Pennywit agreed. "Would you like to come aboard and look around?"

"I'd love to."

The two men walked up the gangplank and stepped onto the middle deck. The wood was polished to a sheen and the brass fixtures looked new.

"It's not very old, is it?"

"No, just completed last year. This is only my second trip as captain."

"Well, you know you are the first captain to reach Three Forks by steam, don't you."

"I thought that was the case." Pennywit tried not to seem proud, but he was clearly pleased with the accomplishment.

"It's certainly different than when we came out."

"But we had some of the same challenges. You lost two women on your journey, didn't you?"

"Yes," Marcus nodded sadly.

"We lost twelve folks on this trip. Had to stop for burials all along the way between here and Paducah."

Marcus looked back to the shore where Brearley and McIntosh were getting the emigrants organized by family around the agency.

"They've left everything behind, haven't they . . . to start over here."

"Yes. Some say it's a tragedy; some say it's an opportunity. I suppose it's a little of both."

"Well, it's a good land. We've built a good life out here. I hope they can as well."

"They seem determined to do so. They brought seed, peach tree cuttings, and most important to them, the sacred fire from their towns."

Marcus quirked an eyebrow.

"I don't know their traditions all that well," Pennywit tried to explain. "But the fire represents life to them, their way of life, I think. Anyway it's sacred."

Marcus nodded. Then they made their way back off the steamboat. As they parted, the doctor invited Pennywit to come for preaching at Fort Gibson the next day.

"I'll be there," the riverman promised. "I want to look over the area; talk to some of the traders. I hope to make Creek Agency a destination for the *Facility* for years to come."

Marcus went for his horse and started toward Fort Gibson. While he rode he thought about the name Pennywit had chosen for his boat. From the Latin, the word meant easy and opportunity. Marcus smiled. Philip Pennywit had certainly made it look easy for a steamboat to reach Three Forks and no doubt other riverboat captains would follow him to this new land of opportunity.

Through the spring, Clarissa found herself growing nostalgic over soon leaving this prairie home to the more wooded hills northwest of Dwight Mission. She had come here seven years ago with a great deal of fear and uncertainty but had found love and a family. She grew teary-eyed when thinking about leaving her mission sisters and her dear little students.

She was also finding it difficult to pack. She had already put their winter clothing into their trunks and there was now hardly any space for the rest of their clothes.

"How did I acquire so much to pack while living here?" she mused aloud one evening in May while she stared down into the two nearly full trunks.

Marcus looked up from the book he was reading. "My

dear, you acquired a husband and two growing girls. We came with a lot of stuff."

Clarissa laughed. "Yes, it's all your fault. Do you think we could purchase another trunk from Nicks & Rogers?"

"I'll check or have Redfield ask. He preaches next week at Fort Gibson. Perhaps we could borrow a trunk or two from someone here and then return them later."

"That might work." Clarissa looked around at their neat little house. Only two rooms and a loft, but it was home and she was suddenly feeling quite sad to leave it.

"We won't be that far away," Marcus reminded her, understanding the look that crossed her face. "We'll see everyone here for our annual mission conference. Union will host it this summer."

"I know. That helps it not seem so final. This move makes me sympathetic for the Creeks that have come out here. Picking up and leaving everything you've known behind . . . it's not easy."

"No, but we did it. We started with nothing out here. Every pioneer does exactly that. I see a resiliency in the Creeks so I think they'll do well out here. Some are coming to Gibson for the services."

"So they are believers?" Clarissa gave up on packing and came to sit opposite Marcus at their table.

"Some are. Others, like Roley McIntosh, are vowing to avenge his brother's murder. He carries a lot of anger and bitterness."

"The law of the avenger," Clarissa said. "We can't seem to get past that, can we?"

"It takes changing people's hearts . . . and that is the work of God."

On the last day of school, Clarissa watched her students during the final exercises, silently cheering when they remembered their lines, quietly agonizing when they forgot, trying not to laugh at funny mistakes. Oh, how she loved her girls.

And they loved her too. When everyone went to the

dining hall for refreshments, all the girls, even Thea and Lucie gave her hugs. Several of the students also gave her little gifts . . . an embroidered handkerchief from Sarah Ann, a fistful of slightly wilted wildflowers from Nancy, and a pretty beaded necklace from Deer-in-Water. Bird's daughter had graduated this year.

Clarissa smiled at the Osage girl who clung to her neck. Having lost her mother at a young age, Deer-in-Water had been shy and uncertain when she started school. She had blossomed into a sweet and confident young woman who clearly loved her teacher. She clung to Clarissa with tears flowing.

"I won't be so far away," the teacher reminded her student. "We'll see each other at Rendezvous . . . and other times too perhaps."

Deer-in-Water shook her head. "My father says we will move to Pawhuska's village. We have no people here and he doesn't like the changes coming to this land. But I don't want to go; I don't know anyone at Pawhuska's town."

Clarissa slipped an arm around the girl's shoulders. "You'll do fine there, Deer-in-Water. And we can always write to each other. You'll be near Neosho Mission and can get mail there."

"If I don't like it there, can I come and live with you?"

Clarissa was surprised by the request. "You must respect your father, Deer-in-Water. But if he gives his permission, then I suppose you can live wherever you choose."

Seeming relieved, the girl hugged her teacher again and then moved away so other students could visit with Mrs. Palmer.

After everyone had left the mission, Clarissa and Marcus walked to their cabin. He had parked one of the mission wagons by their door and they had been loading personal belongings over the last week. They would pack it in earnest now, hoping to begin the journey to their new home within a few days. Marcus would preach for the last time at Fort Gibson the following Sunday. From Gibson, they would take the new military road to Dwight.

The Palmers were invited to spend Sunday night in the room once occupied by Charles and Eliza behind Colonel Nicks' home. The next day, they rose early, settled the girls on a pile of quilts in the wagon bed and drove to the Gillards' house.

Paul and Tassie were adding a few last items from their home, including a couple of chickens in cages given to them by Mrs. Bradley. The Ballard family had bought Paul's cabin so the younger couple were starting this new venture with a nest egg of their own. Clarissa guessed that they would need it later in the year when they welcomed a new baby.

It was a slow journey east with their heavily loaded wagons, but the road was good and the weather mild. They stopped at Colonel Nicks' new store in Nicksville. The town consisted of the store, a building for county government and a little log home that was occupied by the clerk who kept the store and post office for the colonel.

The travelers waited out a brief shower inside the store, but saw little that interested them to buy. Of course, the girls each received a peppermint candy from their father.

Covering about fifteen miles a day, they reached Dwight Mission on Saturday, tired from the journey. After resting a couple of days, Mr. Hitchcock and Rev. Washburn accompanied them to the Mulberry Mission site.

When they pulled into a little glen where the buildings had been constructed, Clarissa smiled at Marcus. He took her hand and squeezed it, hoping her smile meant she liked the house, built in the dogtrot style. They had passed a number of little homesteads in getting here, so there would be plenty of neighbors for them to live and work among.

The two couples looked over the spacious rooms of the house. Paul and Tassie would occupy the side where a kitchen was planned and the Palmers would have the other side with three rooms, one intended as the doctor's office.

Clarissa walked through each room, enjoying the fragrance of freshly cut lumber.

"Well, what do you think?" Marcus asked.

"She glanced out a glass window to the outbuildings and

the many trees that surrounded them. It was so very different from their prairie home. But it felt just right.

"It's perfect," she said.

They could not realize that only a few days earlier in Washington City, the Cherokee chiefs Blackcoat, Sequoyah, Walter Webber, and their attorney John Flowers, were signing a new treaty. It stipulated that the boundary line for Arkansas Territory now would run from the southwest corner of Missouri to Fort Smith and then due south. Their Cherokee neighbors were given one year to move west of this line and come to Lovely County. The future of Mulberry Mission was already uncertain.

CHAPTER TWENTY-SIX

Union Mission, Indian Territory
June 15, 1828

Three weeks later following breakfast, Stephen and George were in the west cornfield, inspecting the crop to see how it was developing. If they received just a little more rain this year, it should do well. George looked up to see five men riding horses along the road. They did not look familiar to him and their horses were not mustangs but the heavier work horses used by farmers in Arkansas Territory.

The men paused when they saw the mission brothers.

"Is this Hopefield Mission?" asked one, wearing a blue plaid flannel shirt.

"No, it's Union Mission," George replied. "Hopefield is five miles further north."

"Can we help you with something?" Stephen added.

"No," another of the farmers responded. "Then La Saline is on further from that?"

"Yes that's right."

"Much obliged," the first man nodded and without saying more they continued on northward.

"Must not be from around here," George observed as he and Stephen walked back to the mission yard.

"Guess not."

The five men rode with singular purpose toward the mission farm. After a half hour, they smelled the smoke of a cooking fire and slowed their pace. Up ahead they could see several Osage lodges and a scattering of log buildings.

Cornfields surrounded the settlement but there was little else to provide cover where they would not be seen.

They eased off their horses and left one man holding them while the other four advanced, crouching low below the green cornstalks. Easing through the fields they came to a place where they could observe the mission.

The men could see Osage warriors sitting in front of their lodges, while the women worked at cooking or hand chores. A white farmer was splitting wood near one of the log cabins. At a nearby creek an Osage and his young son were fishing.

From a rudimentary corral closer to the trees along the river, an Osage emerged leading two mustangs. One of the men observing the mission, pointed to this warrior, making a motion toward his own chest.

The others nodded. This man, the one with an eagle tattoo, was who they were seeking.

"I seen that tattoo when them Osages attacked us down on Red River," one whispered.

"You certain sure, Liam, that he's the one who killed Pa?"

"You saw how good he was with a bow and arrow at that Rendezvous," Liam hoarsely whispered. "Even if he weren't the exact one who did the deed, he's the one I remember. Just as well to get our revenge on him as on any of them others."

All the men nodded, then turned back to watch the warrior with the eagle on his chest. The man approached a lodge where a girl and young man waited. The boy took one set of reins and quickly mounted while his father said something to the girl. She nodded and then watched as Bird took up a quiver of arrows and his bow and also mounted. The two men rode their horses at a walk toward the river.

"Come on," Liam waved his companions back to their horses. "Don't let them get too far ahead."

Crouching low, they hurried back to the road and quickly mounted. Then skirting well south of the farm, they entered the tree line along the Neosho and worked their way north again.

Ahead of them they could hear a splash of water telling

them the two Osage riders were fording the river somewhere just beyond their location.

Easing their mounts closer to the river, they could see Bird and Bearpaw emerge from the water and climb the opposite bank. They waited until the men were lost from their sight among the trees then as quietly as possible took their horses through the shallow river as well.

Climbing the low bank, Liam and his brothers quickly spotted the two Osages ahead. The men were traveling slow, watching for game among the trees.

"Let's wait here," one of the men suggested. "We can't get closer without them spotting us. We can wait for them to head back this way."

The others nodded then dismounted, easing out of their saddles to prevent any noise. Then one of their number took the reins of all the horses and led them further back into the trees.

They waited for only about twenty minutes and then saw Bird and his son returning, each with a buck straddled across the back of their horses. They were returning to Hopefield.

"Hank, you're our best shooter," Liam instructed. "You take him."

Hank nodded and lifted his musket to draw a bead on the eagle tattoo. He waited while the two hunters approached. They were talking, looking at each other, rather than watching the trees.

The report of the gun broke the tranquil silence of the morning.

Bird clutched his chest and fell low on his horse's mane.

"Get down, son," he said in a gasp of pain.

Bearpaw also threw himself down on his horse to make a more difficult target.

"Who is it, father?" he whispered, trying to see into the trees.

Bird did not respond.

Bearpaw reached for his father's reins and guided the horses into the trees, still crouched low, expecting another shot. But all was silent.

"I will find who did this, father," Bearpaw said.

But again Bird was silent. Then slowly the man's weight pulled him off his horse and he fell to the ground. Bearpaw flung himself off his horse and went to his father. Instantly the massive wound in the man's chest told him what he did not want to know. His father was dead.

Bearpaw took his bow and slung the quiver over his shoulder. Then he crept slowly from tree to tree in the direction of the gunfire. In time, he saw the men peering in the direction where the two warriors had entered the trees. There were five men, dressed like farmers, all with guns. Rather than attempt a response by himself, the young man went back to his horse. He pulled the dead buck to the ground then holding the horse's mouth closed, he led it down to the river. Once in the water, he spurred it and raced back home.

At Hopefield everyone had heard the gun blast. Instantly the Osages were alert, the warriors coming to a stand, ears tuned for any other sound, eyes scanning the trees along the river. The wild splashing of a horse informed them that a rider was approaching from across the river. Men reached for their weapons. Will stepped inside his cabin and took down his own musket and grabbed his powder horn.

"What is it?" Susan asked, looking up from the bread she was kneading.

"Don't know," Will answered, his concern obvious. "Stay inside."

As he stepped back out, he saw Bearpaw riding into the yard. The young man had ridden with fear and fury to get help.

"They have shot my father," he called as he ground his lathered horse to a halt in the center of the little settlement. Then looking down at his sister who was gathering with the rest around his horse, he said with a steely tone of anger, "Our father is dead."

Deer-in-Water covered her mouth with both hands. Teresa hurried to her and gathered the girl into her arms.

With terse words, Bearpaw explained that five men, likely Arkansas farmers, had ambushed them and shot his father. Bearpaw's words brought an immediate reaction from the Osage men. They raced to their own horses, carrying their weapons and preparing to ride.

Will hurried to stop Star-That-Travels who was also preparing to leave. Taking the man's arm he said urgently, "We don't need any more killing. If you find them, capture them. Let the fort prosecute them."

Rev. Montgomery joined them. "I'll ride to the fort right now," he said.

Star nodded but looked both men in the eye before saying, "I will do what I can. But I don't know if I can stop them."

Then he took the reins of a horse that Hunts-the-Bear had brought him and joined the race across the river.

Montgomery pressed his own mustang into a fast lope to cover the five miles to Union as quickly as possible. He turned in toward the corral and quickly dismounted. It was nearly dinner time, so he hurried to the dining hall, expecting to find most of the men there.

"I need someone to ride with me to Gibson," he said without preamble as he stepped into the building.

He was met with startled looks of concern.

"What is it, Montgomery?" Vaille asked.

"Bird has been shot . . . killed. I need to get word to the fort or there is liable to be more killing."

"Who would do such a thing?" George asked as he stood from his chair. "Can we do anything for Bird?"

"Bearpaw says he's dead, but I didn't see the body."

"George, why don't you ride with Montgomery and Stephen and I will go to Hopefield," Rev. Vaille suggested.

George nodded and then hurried to the barn to saddle a horse. Mary followed him out. She caught up with him at the barn door. "Do you want me to get your gun?" she asked while he pulled tack from the wall.

George hesitated a moment and then nodded. "Bring the powder too."

Mary hiked up her skirts to run to their cabin. George

couldn't help but smile at her even as he worked with his horse.

Amanda stepped into the kitchen and quickly wrapped some slices of ham and cornbread in a napkin and filled a canteen from the barrel of spring water. She thrust these items in the minister's hands before he left to meet George at the corral.

Mary brought the musket and powder horn and George secured them to his saddle. Then he gave his young wife a kiss before mounting his horse and heading south with Montgomery. A few minutes later, Fuller and Vaille were also riding, this time north on the Texas Road.

Everyone remaining at Union was quiet as they sat down to dinner, no one seeming to have an appetite any longer. Abraham led in prayer, asking for comfort for Bearpaw and Deer-in-Water and for peace and safety in the neighborhood. Then they all ate almost in silence. Such a shocking and unexpected event left them feeling vulnerable.

Samuel ate little, in part to hide the shaking of his hands. Bird was dead and he knew who was responsible. How close he had come to selling out the Osage warrior to Mr. Lee's friends. If he had done so, there would now be blood on his hands. He had truly, desperately, wanted the money offered for information on Bird's whereabouts.

He must look as sick as he felt for he was aware that Ella watched him with concern in her eyes. But when he glanced at her, she looked away.

When the noon meal was concluded, Samuel walked to his cabin. He was shaking as he sat on his bed. "My God," he breathed as he ran his fingers through his dark hair. "What a wretched bloke I am. I almost became an accessory to murder!"

Word of the murder spread quickly through the neighborhood. Colonel Arbuckle had sent a contingent of soldiers to Hopefield, but they arrived several hours after the tragic event and could do nothing to stop the retribution exacted by Bird's friends.

When the warriors had reached Bird's body they found he had been scalped. A trail of the five horses was easily followed toward La Saline. A crowd would be gathering there for the races and the men clearly had hoped to blend in. But the Hopefield warriors, joined by others when they learned the news, caught up with the men too quickly for them to escape.

Bird was buried the following day and mourned in traditional fashion. Bells were tied into the manes of the men's horses and a bier was pulled by Bird's mustang. He was wrapped in his blanket with his prized possessions and taken to a beautiful bluff overlooking the creek where Bird always ran his trap lines. He was buried with five scalps, taken from the men who had laid in ambush and killed him in cold blood.

Will and Rev. Montgomery had traveled with the Osages to the burial place along Bird's Creek. Both were visibly upset not just about the tragedy of Bird's killing but in the quick fury that had taken other lives. It felt as if all their teaching, all their efforts to demonstrate a forgiving and peaceful life had failed.

Samuel did not go to the races, too shaken and afraid to venture away from the mission. In fact the entire neighborhood seemed on edge over the incident. Colonel Arbuckle stepped up patrols along the Texas Road again. The viciousness of the attack on Bird and the reprisal that followed caused everyone in the region to keep a close watch over their homes and families.

As the missionaries prepared for the regional mission conference they would host in a week, Samuel willingly worked alongside them without being asked or told he must. He helped George cut the grass around the corral and the paths between buildings. He carried aired-out bedding to the guest cabins for Martha. He seemed to be offering penance, and while the others noticed this change, they were not sure about the reason behind it.

He tried to start a conversation with Ella as he helped

with cleaning the windows of the dining hall, but while she was polite to him, her words were cool. He retired early that evening, feeling tired though he hadn't really worked that hard. Failure was a debilitating emotion. For years, his failure had left him angry and led to excuses for his behavior. Now he felt so weary and uncertain. How had he reached such a low point and how could he ever rise above it?

Within a few days, the other missionaries with the American Board of Missions arrived for the conference. Rev. Dodge came from Harmony as well as Dr. Belcher and the Austins. They came, of course, for a visit with Mary to see how their daughter was faring as a married woman.

Marcus and Clarissa joined the group from Dwight Mission, leaving Thea and Lucie in Tassie's care. Traveling up by steamboat, the trip had only taken two days. Their group included the Washburns and Jacob Hitchcock with his wife and grown son.

With them were Dr. Gage Weeks and his wife Eleanor. They would stay after the conference concluded and take up the work vacated by the Palmers. They were a young New England couple with no children, both quiet but enthusiastic about missions work.

Clarissa noticed immediately that there was an air of solemnity at Union. When she joined her sisters in the kitchen to help with supper, she found Deer-in-Water working with Amanda. The young woman immediately went to her teacher for a hug.

Clarissa knew something was wrong. She sent a questioning look to the cook.

Amanda crossed the kitchen to give Clarissa a hug as well. She whispered in the teacher's ear. "Bird was killed last week; ambushed and scalped. Deer-in-Water has been staying with us."

The women parted and Clarissa reached for the Osage girl again. "I'm so sorry, dear," she said. She stroked the girl's dark, straight hair. "You may come live with me and my family if you want."

"I may?" the girl's face brightened a little.

"Yes."

Deer-in-Water slipped her arms around the teacher's waist, buried her face against Clarissa's shoulder and for the first time allowed the tears to flow. Clarissa stood still for a time, holding the girl and letting her cry out her sorrow. The other women quietly went about their work, wiping away a few tears of their own and praying for the bereft young woman.

At the corral, Samuel helped George feed the several extra horses that had brought their visitors. Working alongside them was a young man Stephen had hired to take Paul's place. His name was John Davis, one of their new Creek neighbors. Davis was about eighteen, but had expressed an interest in attending their school when it started in the fall. The young man had become a convert at a Baptist mission in Georgia and had plans to become a minister someday.

When he had finished forking hay into the corral from its stack by the barn, Samuel paused to take a drink from a water pail hanging on the corral fence. He saw the superintendent from Dwight approaching him and he stiffened. He remembered the conversations with the man in their shared cabin aboard the *Comet*.

Mr. Hitchcock was the one individual among the missionaries who knew for certain about his gambling. Would this man tell everyone what they had discussed? Though Hitchcock wouldn't know it, Samuel had practically accused him of stealing the Fairfield money. The bookkeeper's sense of guilt made him wary of the man.

Hitchcock extended a hand of greeting, at first unaware of the young man's discomfort.

"Mr. Douglas, isn't it?" he asked, as Samuel half-heartedly shook his hand.

"Yes, how are you, Mr. Hitchcock?"

"Fine, just fine. Enjoyed a steamboat ride from Dwight all the way to Three Forks." Hitchcock smiled, but then looked more closely at Samuel. "So how are you faring out here on the prairie, son?"

"Fine," Samuel lied, but then caught himself. If he was

going to reform, he must do so completely. That meant no more lies.

"Well, that isn't really true. I haven't done well out here . . . and you of all people will understand why."

"Ah," Hitchcock nodded in understanding. In a low voice he asked, "Has it caught up to you then?"

Samuel nodded, but seeing George nearby he asked, "May we talk privately?"

Hitchcock waved a hand and the two men walked along the fence toward the cornfields.

"How do you quit?" Samuel asked when they were out of earshot of anyone at the mission. He didn't say what he needed to quit, guessing that Hitchcock would understand. "I've tried repeatedly. I keep making promises to myself, to God, but I just go back to it."

"I couldn't do it in my own power," the older man said. "I had to do more than make a promise. I had to repent and then surrender my will to God. Only with his help was I able to defeat the thing. It had too strong a grip for me to win on my own."

"Win?"

"Perhaps a poor choice of words," Hitchcock smiled ruefully. "But maybe not. It is a win when you can get set free from gambling. It's a type of bondage, isn't it?"

"Yes, that describes it right. A taskmaster I finally owed too much. I was exactly what you said . . . a liar, a cheat and a thief," Samuel looked down at his shoes, "and I almost became something worse." The distraught faces of Bearpaw and Deer-in-Water following Bird's funeral had clearly been upsetting to the bookkeeper.

Jacob did not ask what Samuel meant. Instead he laid a hand on the young man's shoulder.

"We have a forgiving Father who helps us in our weakness," he assured Samuel. "And you have friends here who will help as well. You must be willing to ask for help to walk the straight and narrow path. You have to swallow pride, just as I did, confess your wrongs and try to make amends."

"But how do I start? I lied to Ella and William, I cheated

Requa out of a job, I stole from the mission. I'm sure I'm a great disappointment to God."

"I have found the best way to start over is with two simple words," Hitchcock advised. "They have a great power in them. Start with 'I'm sorry.'"

The supper bell sounded just then so the two men joined the other missionaries making their way to the dining hall. The room was crowded with their extra guests. Deer-in-Water sat in a chair between Marcus and Clarissa. She was comfortable with both the Palmers because she had boarded with them while a student. Marcus draped an arm across the back of the girl's chair in a simple unspoken gesture of comfort and support.

Samuel ate his supper quietly, not entering into the conversation around the table. Clarissa watched Ella as she watched Samuel and knew that the young woman was still in love with the dark-haired man.

Following supper, the group moved to the chapel and again the space was crowded. As senior minister, Rev. Washburn preached the first sermon of the conference. Mindful of the recent tragedy, he spoke of the need to live one's life as if each day might be the last one on earth.

"Let us bear no grudges, withhold no forgiveness or owe no one anything other than love," he said as he concluded the sermon. "Let us take a moment now to examine our lives and make sure that all is right between us and our Lord and our fellow man."

The little congregation stood then for prayer. Out of the corner of her eye, she observed Mr. Hitchcock laying a hand on Samuel's shoulder. The bookkeeper was bent low as if he had a heavy burden on his back and his hands tightly gripped the back of the chair in front of him.

She added her prayers for the young man to those of Mr. Hitchcock.

When the minister prayed a final benediction, Samuel surreptitiously swiped tears from his face. Then he gave a nod and a handshake to Hitchcock. The missionary grinned in approval and slapped the new man on the back.

CHAPTER TWENTY-SEVEN

Union Mission
Late Summer 1828

The mission family all noticed a change in Samuel after the conference concluded. He cheerfully worked in the corn harvest and helped the women shuck the ears they would cut and can. At the next full moon, he stayed at Union, going over the accounts with Rev. Vaille. He even volunteered to offer a higher level of math classes for the older boys and so spent one afternoon a week diagramming and explaining algebra formulas to Mr. Redfield's students.

But despite a much more positive approach to life at Union, Samuel still seemed a little discouraged. Ella remained aloof and refused his offers to take a walk or sit with him at supper. She was not unkind, simply not interested. He would always nod in understanding when she said no, but he was not content to let their relationship completely die.

He was also determined to pay back the money he had taken from the Fairfield church offering. With the semi-annual pay he received during the conference, he had returned $150 to the worn-out envelope. He started to take it to William, explaining that it was all he had, but decided against it. He had used the full $200 to gamble with and now there was only $172. He would find a way to raise the remaining money, through some means other than gambling.

Another matter Samuel had determined to set right was his theft from his father's business. He wrote a letter to his father, confessing his wrongs and pledging to repay not only the church, but his parents as well. He asked their forgiveness and hoped that they would believe he had truly changed.

The day after he had finished the letter, he placed it in an envelope, affixed a half penny stamp and slipped it into his pocket. He'd find out at breakfast if anyone from the mission would be traveling to the fort soon and could post his letter.

Another matter needed to be dealt with and Samuel was finding it difficult to address it. He owed George Requa an apology and that would require confessing that he had written to Rev. Vaille, requesting the job of mission superintendent. He knew he wasn't as qualified for the job as George was; he had just wanted access to the mission's money. His pride was making it hard to approach the man who had clearly been angered by the loss of the job.

Stephen announced at breakfast that they would start grinding corn today and any of the men who were free to help would be needed. Samuel had no experience at such work, but neither did Dr. Weeks and he quickly volunteered to help. Samuel sucked in a deep breath and raised his hand to say he would assist as well.

He found himself working alongside George in lifting a yoke to place over the thick necks of the oxen that would turn the millstone. George gave quiet directions to the bookkeeper, but said nothing else.

Samuel closed his eyes for a moment, saying a silent prayer. Then he plunged into his apology before he could lose his nerve.

"I owe you an apology, Requa," he began.

George looked surprised for a brief moment, then a look of understanding crossed his face. But he said nothing, only waited for Samuel to continue.

"I had no business asking for the superintendent's job. It was wrong of me; selfish of me. I want you to know that I see that now and I'm truly sorry I did it."

"Well, I didn't exactly handle it well myself," George said after a long pause. "I let my anger get the better of me. I'm willing to put that behind us if you are."

"Yes, I want to do that."

The two men shook hands, at first a bit awkwardly but in a moment both were smiling.

"You would be doing me a tremendous favor if you took the job back," Samuel went on as they moved to yoke another pair of oxen. "You are far more knowledgeable than me about caring for the mission. I really haven't even been doing the job. You and Stephen and Redfield have covered for me all these months. I've been in over my head."

"You could learn it."

"I think you should have it."

"You're sure?"

"Yes. We can talk with William this afternoon, if you'd like."

"Let me pray about it. And talk to Mary, if that's alright with you."

"Fine," Samuel agreed. "Whatever you want."

They continued on with the work of getting the mill ready for another year of operation. Woodruff was slopping bear grease into the gears and axles and Stephen was working on the hopper that fed the grain into the mill.

Weeks was watching the whole procedure as if fascinated by it, and grinned with the other men as the oxen turned the big stone.

That afternoon, Richard Bean and his nephew Jesse arrived, bringing a wagon load of burlap sacks filled with shelled corn. While the oxen worked to grind their meal, the mission brothers gathered around the visitors beside their wagon to hear the news from their neck of the woods.

"How's the salt business?" Stephen asked Richard while his nephew Jesse helped George lift their bags of corn out of the wagon.

"It'll be our best year," Richard responded. "And it will be our last." He face was grim.

"Last? Why?"

"Got a letter from the government," the miner explained. "We're being evicted. Our land . . . our farm . . . the spring . . . all our improvements now belong to the Cherokees. We got no say in any of it." The man was clearly bitter about the treaty giving Lovely County to the Cherokees.

"You have no recourse?" Gage Weeks asked. "Perhaps the Cherokees will let you stay. A salt business is of great value to a community."

"Already asked Chief Jolly," Richard said. "We got ninety days to vacate."

"Will you be compensated?" Samuel asked.

"Supposedly, but I don't think we'll see it any time soon," Richard shook his head. "Not from the government. The only thing good in any of this is we'll be given land in Arkansas. My brother Mark's gone to Little Rock to talk to the governor and check on land."

"Dad's even angrier than Uncle Rich," Jesse commented quietly to George. "He's fit to be tied and plans on giving the governor a piece of his mind."

"It doesn't seem quite fair, does it?" George commiserated with him. He knew how it felt.

Jesse shook his head. "The chiefs who went to Washington just got back. They're already marking the corners of the land they want. Walter Webber's chosen a swath of bottom land across the Illinois River from us. Chief Jolly will be south of him. We've heard that their lawyer John Flowers has his eye on our land."

"I thought Flowers was white, not Cherokee."

"He's married to a Cherokee woman so I guess that gives him Cherokee land." They finished lifting out all of the Beans' corn and walked around to the front of the wagon where the other men stood.

Jesse went on, "I just wish I was going to be here to help my folks with the move. But I've been accepted to the military academy. I leave for New York in about a fortnight."

"Congratulations," George offered him a handshake. The other men did as well.

The young man accepted their well wishes, looking

pleased that he would follow his father's footsteps in a military career.

"Jesse's good news is 'bout the only thing keeping Mark from going to Texas," Richard remarked and they all laughed.

The men took a break from the mill for supper, asking the Beans to join them in the dining hall. The discussion around the tables was mostly about the changes the Cherokee treaty was bringing to Lovely County.

"You know, I just had a thought," Redfield said while everyone lingered after their devotions to enjoy a last cup of coffee with Amanda's grape dumplings, a dish that Nancy Ballard had shown her during a cooking lesson.

"What's that, Redfield?" Vaille asked.

"We no longer live in Arkansas Territory. Where are we now?"

There was a smattering of laughter across the room. "According to the surveyor Isaac McCoy, we're in the Indian Territory," Vaille said. "In a way that's where we've always been. The government in Little Rock hasn't had much to do with us way out here."

"Yes, but that was a good thing," Weeks joked. Everyone nodded as they laughed some more.

But they all sobered with Vaille's next words. "We'd better have a meeting with Chief Jolly soon," he said. "We haven't received an eviction notice of our own, but who knows what the future will hold."

"You've worked with Mr. Jolly, haven't you?" Asie asked their new doctor.

"Yes, Ooluntuskee, as he is called," Weeks confirmed as he adjusted the wire-rimmed glasses he wore. "He's a progressive man, I think. While not necessarily interested in the church, he does want education for the children."

"Education is what we will offer him then," Redfield concluded.

The group all stood to clear the dining hall and retire to their own cabins. Ella left her shawl at her seat to assist the other women with washing the dishes. When she returned for it, she found a single yellow wildflower on her chair.

Ella paused before picking up the pretty offering. Who had put it there? She thought she knew, but was afraid to hope that Samuel would make such a thoughtful gesture. He had never done so before. She lifted the flower to catch its light musky scent.

It would be wilted and dead in a day or two, but this simple gift had stirred life back into the dying embers of her dreams. She told herself not to let it, but she couldn't help but feel hopeful as she walked to the Vaille cabin. A brilliant red sunset behind the little house seemed like a promise and she was ready to receive it.

The following Sunday, at Mulberry Mission, the Palmers were hurrying through breakfast to get ready for church. It would be their first service in the little chapel built across the glen from their house.

Cherokee neighbors had helped Mr. Hitchcock build the little log church, donating materials and labor. It was of a simple design, but looked pretty before a backdrop of hardwood trees just beginning to show their fall colors.

"Girls, finish up and then wash your hands and faces," Clarissa told her three daughters. She had tried to keep them eating quietly all during the meal, giving Marcus peace to go over his sermon notes one more time. He seemed a little anxious.

"Hurry, Deerie," Thea said using the name she had given Deer-in-Water years ago. She hopped up from her seat and went to wait at the wash stand. Deer-in-Water always helped pour the water and assisted the younger two girls to clean up after a meal.

Clarissa went for her bonnet in the bedroom and emerged to see all three girls staring at a wet stain down the front of Thea's pinafore.

"Oh, Thea," she sighed.

"I'm sowwy," the little girl said in such a sincere apology that her mother couldn't be angry.

Marcus hid a smile behind his cup of coffee. Clarissa threw him a warning look.

"Deerie, can you help her into her other pinafore?"

The girl nodded. "Come on, Thea." She took the hand of the seven-year-old and with Lucie trailing behind climbed to the girls' bedroom to make the change.

"Don't you dare laugh," Clarissa said to Marcus in a low voice as he stood and pulled on his black coat.

"I wouldn't think of it," Marcus responded with a look as innocent as Thea's on his face.

Then he gave her a quick kiss and said, "I'm going to go ahead and walk on over to make sure everything's ready."

"You're going to do fine," Clarissa encouraged him as he took his Bible and stepped out the door. Through the window she could see Tassie and Paul emerging from their room.

"Come on, girls," she said. "Let's not be late."

"Who would know if we were late?" Deerie asked. "No one but us has a clock."

Clarissa smiled at the girl's logic. While it wasn't exactly true, she understood that to Deer-in-Water letting a clock be your taskmaster was an odd way to live.

"Well, Doc will know if we are not there when he expects us."

Deerie was not yet comfortable with calling Marcus her father so they had settled on the names Doc and Teacher for her new guardians. Perhaps someday, like Thea and Lucie, she would call them papa and mama.

The Palmer women joined the Gillards for the short walk to the church. Clarissa felt herself growing nervous as they stepped inside the new building. They had no way of knowing who might make up their congregation on this first day of services. She hoped for her husband's sake that at least a few of their neighbors would come.

During the past few weeks, Marcus and Clarissa had paid calls at most of the farms in the area. Their purpose was to get to know their neighbors and issue invitations for the start of school and the first Sunday service. Edmund Webber who had just returned from school back East had accompanied them to act as a translator. He would be translating the sermon this morning as well.

Most of their Cherokee neighbors knew some English, but not all were proficient speakers of the language. That would make Clarissa's job as teacher of the one-room school a challenge. Thankfully Edmund, Walter Webber's younger brother, had offered to assist at the school also.

Clarissa helped the girls get settled on one of the benches at the front of the small sanctuary. They did not have the funds for nice pews or even a pulpit, but perhaps if the church grew they could secure those furnishings later.

Marcus stood at the front door and Clarissa joined him, waiting to greet anyone who might come.

They stood for about thirty minutes watching an occasional leaf drift downward from the trees and listening to the faint movement of water from a tiny little creek that flowed toward the Mulberry River.

Marcus pulled out his pocket watch one more time. He was about to ask Paul and Tassie to start with a song, when they heard the clop of horses' hooves. Shortly a carriage came into view with Edmund driving. He had a woman and two boys with him and Clarissa wondered who they were for she knew Edmund was not married.

The young Cherokee alighted from the carriage and tied the horse's reins to a tree limb at the edge of the yard. Then he helped his companions down and walked with them to the church door.

Marcus greeted Edmund with a handshake. "Welcome, Mr. Webber," he greeted him.

Edmund nodded to acknowledge the greeting then made introductions.

"This is my sister-in-law, Elizabeth Waite Webber and her sons Walter, Jr. and Charles."

Immediately Clarissa and Marcus understood that this was Mrs. Walter Webber.

Clarissa hoped her face did not register her surprise. Even Edmund had acknowledged to them that his older brother had no interest in the missions and wasn't likely to support their efforts here. She wondered if Mrs. Webber had come to church against his wishes.

"Liz and I both want to help this church get started among our people," Edmund explained.

"Wonderful," Marcus said. "Your support means very much to us."

The Webbers stepped into the church and found seats close to the front. While they had talked with the Palmers, others had begun to arrive. One family came in a farm wagon and others had walked. Within a few minutes they had nearly twenty congregants seated in the small chapel.

Paul and Tassie sang one song together, an old hymn that some of the Cherokees seemed to know. They joined in when they could or just hummed a beautiful harmony, providing the music that they lacked with instruments.

Marcus preached a short sermon with Edmund translating. Then he asked how many present would like to be charter members of this new church. Most all of the adults raised their hands.

Clarissa smiled at Marc. She knew such an interest in founding a church here in the Ozarks would be a great encouragement to him.

Marcus closed the service by reminding everyone that school would begin the following day. As he left, Edmund promised to be present for school to help with introductions and assessment of the need of a translator. He was about to step out of the church, when he paused and searched the pockets of his coat.

"I almost forgot," he stated, as he pulled out an envelope. "Rev. Washburn wanted me to give you this letter. It's from the governor." Then he stepped out into the early afternoon sunshine to drive Liz and her sons home.

Clarissa and the girls joined Marcus while Tassie and Paul went on ahead to get Sunday dinner on the table. When they were seated and had said a blessing over the food, Clarissa said to Marcus, "Go ahead and read it. I know you want to."

He smiled at her. "I can wait."

"Well, I can't, so go ahead."

He laughed at her eagerness and reached over to the

washstand where he had placed the letter. Breaking the wax seal and pulling out the official stationery, he quickly scanned the lines. The smile left his face.

"What is it?" Clarissa asked for all of them. Marcus raised his eyes to see concerned faces looking at him.

"It's what we anticipated. Mulberry Mission will be required to move with the Cherokees out of Arkansas Territory."

"When they expect us to leave?" Paul asked.

"The Cherokees have a year, but it doesn't sound as if the governor wants us to take that long. He says we should be prepared to move as soon as possible."

"But we're just starting the new school year," Clarissa said, her frustration showing.

Marcus met her gaze across the table. He understood her feelings. Even though their Cherokee neighbors and students would likely be moving they had hoped they would at least have the school year before they had to make their own move.

"How come Chief Jolly let us build this church and school if we were going to have to turn right around and move again?" Tassie asked.

"I believe Jolly hoped the Cherokees would be given all of Lovely County. But the treaty only gives them what lies west of Fort Smith. I suppose the government in Little Rock thought Fort Smith was too important to lose."

"Should we even start school?" Clarissa wanted to know.

"Yes, there's no reason not to be doing the work we were hired to do. But I'll go down to Dwight tomorrow and speak with Rev. Washburn. He may already have a plan for moving the missions."

They completed their meal mostly in quiet thought, the adults all pondering the prospect of moving once again. Even Deerie and Lucie understood that something was amiss for they ate quietly as well. Only Thea was too young to grasp the worrisome situation and so she happily ate Tassie's potatoes and gravy and managed to spill several drops on her clean pinafore.

When Clarissa realized it, she tried to dab the spots clean

with her napkin. "Oh, Thea," she laughed, "what am I going to do with you?"

"I'm sowwy."

Tassie winked at Deerie across the table from her. "Good thing tomorrow is wash day."

When Marcus arrived at Dwight the following afternoon, he found the mission director was already making plans for a move. Washburn had requested a meeting with Jolly and the other chiefs at Nicksville for the following month. He hoped they could settle upon a location for all their missions in the new Cherokee Nation, including Union and Hopefield.

At the appointed meeting date, Rev. Vaille, Will Requa, Dr. Palmer and Rev. Washburn were all present. Colonel Nicks was acting as host along with Chief Jolly. Walter Webber, Spring Frog and Blackcoat represented the Cherokees as well.

They gathered in a large room in the county building Nicks had constructed. He had planned for the space to serve as the county courthouse but it had seen little use. When Marcus stepped inside with Washburn, he saw a table at the front of the room with a rolled up parchment sitting on it. Shortly Nicks and Arbuckle arrived and the sutler proceeded to unroll the map and use small stones to hold it open at the corners.

There was an awkward moment among the men, as if no one was sure who should start the meeting. Finally Chief Jolly motioned to Colonel Arbuckle, "Please begin," he said.

Marcus studied John Jolly as Arbuckle walked to the front of the room. Everyone had taken seats in the straight-backed wooden chairs.

The chief was a man in his fifties of mixed race and like Webber he dressed in a combination of Cherokee and American styles. His long, bushy sideburns seemed out of place with the turban he wore on his head. Jolly seemed to fit his name for he had an affable smile on his face unlike Webber who seemed to wear a perpetual scowl.

While Arbuckle made introductions, Jolly offered quiet

translation to his fellow Cherokee leaders. Soon the discussion moved to the Arkansas missions. The men gathered around the map which Nicks had provided. It was based on the survey Isaac McCoy had completed in 1822. Nicks informed everyone that the legislature was set to abolish both Lovely and Miller counties west of the new boundary established for Arkansas Territory.

"What will happen to Nicksville?" Vaille asked.

"I'm not sure," the colonel responded. "I still have the post office contract, but it obviously will no longer be a county seat. I might be open to selling the buildings to one of your missions."

Rev. Washburn looked surprised but quickly assessed the building. It would do well as a school and church. "This might serve our needs perfectly."

"We'll talk money later then," Nicks nodded, seeming satisfied. He was a keen businessman and had found a solution that met a need but also would likely make a profit for him.

Rev. Vaille spoke up then. "We at Union Mission are hopeful that the Cherokee Nation will allow us to continue in our present location. We have invested considerable funds in building the mission."

"You have a school, don't you?" Jolly asked.

"Yes, and we have Cherokee students already attending our school."

"I see no reason then that you can't continue where you are."

"What about Hopefield," Will added. "We're about five miles north of Union upriver on the Neosho."

"On the Grand River," Jolly corrected. These Cherokees seemed not inclined to use an Osage word to name a river running through their nation. "But you have no school, is that right?"

"No, not a grammar school. But we teach farming."

Jolly conferred with the other Indian delegates in their language. Whatever Webber and Spring Frog said, their words seemed adamant.

"The Cherokees already know how to farm," Jolly said. "I don't think Hopefield is needed in our nation." The chief's words were not unkind, but there was a sense that they wanted the Osages out and Hopefield would have to go as well.

Will seemed set to argue for Hopefield, but a slight shake of Vaille's head kept him silent.

Now Marcus took up the discussion. "Do you want to see Mulberry Mission moved from Arkansas?"

"Our land is large here and the people will be spread out," Jolly said. "I think three schools are needed."

The men all turned their attention to the map. Nicks placed a pebble where Nicksville and Union were located. They agreed that the third school should be located somewhere between and settled on a point almost due east of Fort Gibson. Using his mercantile string to measure with, Nicks marked a spot roughly 30 miles from Union, Fort Gibson and Dwight in the eastern section of the Cherokee Nation.

"Is that agreeable to everyone?" Colonel Arbuckle asked. There were nods all around, but there was little to be said otherwise. None of them had visited this location to know what the terrain was like.

"I will be happy to visit the area with you," Jolly offered, "to select a specific site."

"We would appreciate that," Washburn stated and Marcus added his thanks.

"Our government will be located here," Jolly pointed to a spot just above where the Illinois River emptied into the Arkansas. This location was very near the infamous falls of the Arkansas. "I will build my home there as well."

"We hope to be able to continue school at Mulberry until winter break," Marcus stated then. "I trust it will be agreeable to you that we not move until then. It will take a certain amount of time to raise the funds and then build a new school and homes for those of us who will work there."

"What do you expect the cost to be for your buildings?" Jolly asked.

Marcus deferred to Rev. Washburn on this question. It

had been Dwight Mission funds that had paid for building Mulberry.

"The church and school will each cost about one hundred dollars," he said. "The homes will be another fifty."

"The Cherokees might be able to contribute funds to the building of this mission," Jolly said.

"I will give fifty dollars," Webber offered, speaking first in Cherokee, then English. Absolutely everyone in the room looked surprised.

"We are very grateful for that," Marcus managed to say after he had recovered from the shock.

Webber nodded. "Elizabeth, my beloved woman, has spoken," he said as his only explanation for the offer. The other Cherokee men chuckled at his comment. He still looked stern, but Marcus thought there was something else in his eyes.

CHAPTER TWENTY-EIGHT

Union Mission
Fall 1828

Ella stepped out the door of the Vaille cabin with an armload of clothes destined for the mission's laundry. She had just helped Asie get Scott fed, bathed and down for a nap. She'd join the other women in the laundry for Monday's chore and then had promised Mrs. Weeks that she'd help with a needlework lesson for the girls.

She automatically glanced at the cane chair that sat outside the door. This was where she sat on most pretty days, stitching new clothes or mending old ones in the sunlight. She always checked the chair for this was where Samuel often left a small gift or note for her.

Today it was a polished apple sitting on a gold leaf from a cottonwood tree. It made her smile, as all his gifts did. She had even consented to walk with him the other evening after supper and he had made a most sincere apology to her for all his many transgressions. She had offered him forgiveness. When they had parted at this door, his face bore the same look of hope that she felt in her heart.

She took up the apple and bit into it, enjoying the tart crispness. As she walked across the yard, she saw Samuel helping Stephen and the hired man John Davis load a wagon with barrels of cornmeal. They were heading to Fort Gibson to sell the corn to the quartermaster.

Ella raised the apple and called a thank you to the man

who could still make her heart skip a beat. He tugged at his hat brim and grinned. "I'll bring you something back from Three Forks," he called.

"No need," she shook her head. She knew that he was trying to pay back the Fairfield offering and was carefully watching the few pennies he allowed himself. He had even let his beard grow out in order to avoid the expense of shaving every day.

"Have a safe trip," she called and then walked on to join Amanda, Phoebe and Martha in the laundry.

After they concluded their business at the fort, the men rode down to Nicks & Rogers to pick up a few supplies. They found Sallie Nicks working with a new clerk in the store. She was a young Cherokee woman who wore her hair in a single long braid and had a black shawl over her shoulders.

"Hello, gentlemen," Sallie greeted them when they entered the mercantile. Each man removed his hat and returned the greeting.

"Let Diana or me know how we can help you," the shopkeeper said. "But take your time in looking around. We received a shipment of new goods just this week."

Stephen and John drifted toward the farm implements at the back of the store, but Samuel walked directly to the counter where the two women stood.

Sallie looked up from the ledger she had been working in. "The bookkeeping is never done, is it Mr. Douglas?"

Samuel smiled, pleased that she remembered him and his job at the mission. "No it isn't," he agreed.

"You haven't met my new clerk have you?"

"No, I don't believe I have."

"This is Diana Gentry," Sallie said. "Her name is actually . . ." she turned to the woman for help.

"It's Tsiana," the clerk said, her voice husky but pleasant. "But Diana is fine."

"She lets me call her that because I just can't quite get the Cherokee pronunciation."

"Hello, ma'am," Samuel said politely. He assumed she was married for she wore a gold band on her left hand.

"Diana is the daughter of my husband's partner John Rogers. Sadly she's been recently widowed. She lost her husband to the fever this summer so she has returned to her parents' home."

"My sympathies, ma'am." Samuel nodded toward the attractive woman. He had the impression that Sallie was hoping to stir an interest in him for the new widow. But his interest, his love, waited for him back at Union.

"I was wondering," he said, as he pulled out a watch from his pocket, "If you purchase items like this?" He extended the gold piece for the merchant to look at.

"What a fine watch," Sallie said as she took it and opened it. "Surely you don't want to part with it." She looked curious, but Samuel did not care to share his reasons for selling the watch.

"I find I rarely even look at it out here," he said.

"Oh, I see." Sallie turned the watch over and examined it closely. "Well, I can understand that for I don't have much demand for watches here either."

Samuel looked disappointed.

"I could offer you four dollars for it," she said, "but I'm afraid not more than that."

Four dollars would still leave him twenty-four dollars short in paying back the church. But it was better than nothing. "I'll take it," he said.

"Very good, then." Sallie reached down for the till below the counter and counted out the money into Samuel's hand. He put the coins into his pocket, thanked her and then wandered around the store while Stephen paid for some purchases of his own.

Samuel wanted to get a gift for Ella, but wasn't sure what she would like or what he could afford. He entered an area of the store clearly intended for women shoppers. There were gloves and boots and buttons and ribbons, fabric and lace and other items he couldn't even identify.

His eyes fell on a pair of combs decorated with light blue beads and seed pearls. He definitely knew Ella would like these for she was always smoothing back her hair and sighing over the way the constant wind teased the blonde strands around her face. But they cost a whole dollar.

He was torn. He so wanted to give Ella those combs for her birthday which was coming up in a few weeks. But should he take money he knew was needed to pay his debt?

He did something that he was just learning how to do. He prayed for guidance then he waited. Soon he felt a sense that buying the combs would be right. So he picked them up and carried them to the front counter where Mrs. Gentry took his coin and then wrapped them in brown paper.

"*Wado*," she said then blushed. "I mean, thank you."

"You're welcome." Samuel smiled at her.

The men were just leaving the store when Sallie called to them. "Oh, Mr. Douglas," she said. "I have something for the children." She pulled out a little brown paper sack and filled it with lemon drops. After folding the top down a few times, she handed the sack to the bookkeeper.

"Thanks," he said. "They will love these."

"And share one with whoever will be getting those combs." Sallie winked at him.

"I will."

Even though Samuel was pleased with his purchase, he still felt discouraged. Now he lacked twenty-five dollars in paying his debt. *Where can I get the money?* His thought was like a prayer. *I want to do what's right, Lord, but I need your help.*

As they rode northward, Stephen pulled a stack of mail out of his pocket. "I think there's a letter in there for you," he said to Samuel and handed the whole stack to him where he rode in the back of the wagon.

Samuel sorted through the envelopes until he found one addressed to him. He saw that it was from his father and he immediately felt nervous. What was his father's response to the confessional he had sent to his parents? Was he forgiven or cut off permanently? Would his father demand immediate repayment of not only the church debt, but the debt to his business as well?

Carefully he broke the wax seal and pulled out the folded

sheet of paper. When he opened the letter, he was shocked to find money inside. Quickly he scanned the lines. His father offered not only forgiveness, but assistance in paying the church debt also. He had sent cash knowing there were no banks nearby.

Samuel counted the crisp bills. His eyes filled with tears. His father had sent exactly twenty-five dollars. Some would say this was a coincidence, but Samuel knew it was a miracle.

That evening after supper, Samuel went to his cabin, picked up the offering envelope now holding $200. He walked to the Vaille cabin and knocked on the door.

William answered it. "Oh, Samuel, come in. If you're calling on Ella I'm afraid she's over at Mrs. Redfield's house right now."

"No, it is you I wished to speak with."

"Alright. Come in." William stepped back and waved the younger man inside. They took seats at the table. Samuel could hear the low murmur of Asie's voice in the other room. It sounded like she was reading a story to the children.

"What can I help you with?" William asked. He must have sensed that this was not simply a social call.

The bookkeeper pulled the tattered envelope from his pocket and pushed it across the table to the mission director. "It's all there. Everything the Fairfield Church sent. I've repaid it all, with my father's help."

William opened the envelope and thumbed through the bills. His faced showed his emotion.

"I know this wasn't easy for you, Samuel," he said. "I'm proud of you for doing this."

Samuel shrugged at the compliment. "I don't know exactly what Pastor Eldridge thought the money should be used for, but I was thinking maybe the Palmers could use it. You said they needed funds to build the new mission."

"Yes and this amount is exactly what they needed. I think that would be the best way to use these funds. It seems as if God's timing is perfect."

"Yes," Samuel shook his head in amazement. "You don't know how perfect."

"I'll see Palmer at Rendezvous," William stated. "I'll give him this."

"Good." Samuel stood to go. "Will you tell Ella I'm sorry I missed her? I'll speak with her tomorrow."

"Yes, Good night, Samuel. I hope you sleep well."

"I believe I will . . . for the first time in a long time."

The fall months were busy for the missionaries. Will, Montgomery and Star-That-Travels were working steadily on a new mission cabin at the creek located north of La Saline and outside of the Cherokee Nation. They were making it an extra large dogtrot style home big enough for the Requas on one side and the Montgomerys on the other.

This cabin was being built with planks rather than logs. The memory of the flood destroying their mud-daubed cabins made Susan and Harriett determined to have a "real" house for a change.

Star and Teresa and most of Monepasha's clan had moved their lodges to this new location. The Osages called the home the "planche cabin," in French because of the sawed lumber. Everyone else just called it the big cabin. They had dubbed the mission New Hopefield.

To the southeast, Marcus and Jacob Hitchcock were working with a group of Cherokee volunteers to build the church and school for the new Cherokee mission. Two small cabins had been completed already. Since their mission would no longer be on the Mulberry River, the Palmers felt a new name was needed. Fairfield Mission seemed the appropriate name. Dwight Mission had just been moved to the Nicksville site. Now all their missions were in the Indian Territory.

Marcus and Clarissa hoped the Fairfield buildings could be completed by Christmas. They were planning to host a celebration of the sacred day at their home with their Cherokee neighbors.

To the doctor's surprise, Walter Webber rode out to the Fairfield site about once a week.

Webber was involved with building his own new home near the Arkansas falls. But the Cherokee leader would spend an hour or two at Fairfield, talking with Marcus and asking questions about Christian doctrine. The teaching about forgiveness and redemption seemed to be one he felt a need to understand.

Marcus knew Mrs. Webber was praying for her husband to come to faith just as she had. He seemed to be searching for a way to do so without losing face with the other Cherokee leaders who had not yet shown an interest in such matters.

"Perhaps you will lead the way for them," Marcus suggested during one of their discussions. It seemed to him that Webber was burdened with the violent feud that had long existed between his people and the Osages. He was looking for a change and recognized that forgiveness was too difficult a task without help from a higher power than his own.

One day in late November, Webber came to the site when the men were working on the roof of the church. Marcus recognized his horse from a distance and made his way down the ladder to greet the man.

After Webber dismounted and tied his horse he walked with Marcus around the church to inspect the work nearing completion. Marcus asked if the chief would like a cup of coffee in his cabin.

Webber consented and the two of them stepped inside. Marcus had a little fire going in the fireplace making the cabin warm and hospitable despite a lack of many furnishings or any of the nicer touches that Clarissa would bring to it when she and the girls moved here next week.

Webber sipped his coffee and the two talked about the mission, especially the school. They planned for it to be a day school with few boarders. Several of the Cherokee families who had lived around Mulberry had moved to this area. Clarissa had only a few students remaining at the Arkansas mission.

"My home is complete," Webber informed the doctor. "It is large as Elizabeth wanted. Would you allow us to host the holiday gathering you plan?"

"That would be very gracious of you, Chief Webber."

"Do not worry about bringing anything. We will provide

all the food. Our gatherings usually last at least three days so come prepared for that. Come and preach too."

"Thank you, Chief Webber. It will be an honor for me."

The man nodded, drained his coffee cup and then stood to go. They shook hands and Marcus stood in the cabin door watching as he mounted his horse and rode west. Chief Webber had just offered a gift that would likely assure the success of Fairfield Mission. He couldn't have given them anything better for Christmas.

At Union a few days later, Ella was opening a birthday gift from Samuel. He had waited until they were alone on the porch of the Vaille home to offer it to her after the noon meal. Ella's fingers trembled a little as she pulled on the string securing the brown paper package.

It had struck her when Samuel pulled the package from his pocket that in all the four years that she and Samuel had courted, this was the first real purchased gift he had ever given her. He was finally thinking about her instead of when the next card game would be.

She pulled back the paper to reveal the pretty combs. "Oh, Samuel, how lovely." She picked up one and admired its tiny beads and pearls.

"I wish it were more."

"I don't need anything more."

"You deserve more and I know that, Ella." Samuel sighed. "I am sorry I took you for granted for so long. I hope I can spend the rest of our lives making that up to you."

"The rest of our lives?"

"Yes," Samuel smiled ruefully. "I guess I did just ask you to marry me . . . finally. Can you find it in your heart to make me the happiest man in the world?"

"Well, that would only be right," Ella said as she slipped her hand around his arm and drew closer to him. "Since I'll be the happiest woman in the world."

Clarissa was still trying to get unpacked and settled even on the day they were to leave Fairfield and travel to the

Webber plantation for the Christmas gathering. She was unwrapping a pair of candlesticks from old *Gazette* newspapers when Marcus stepped into the door of the new cabin.

"I've brought the wagon round," he said. "Are you ready?"

Without waiting for his wife's answer, he picked up their two valises and took them out to the wagon.

"Deerie, can you take Lucie and Thea over to Aunt Tassie?"

"Yes, ma'am," Deer-in-Water replied as she tied her bonnet strings under her chin. The two youngest girls would stay with Tassie while the Palmers were away. Clarissa gave them a kiss and reminded them to be good. They stopped to receive a good-bye kiss from their father as well. After she saw the girls to the door of Paul and Tassie's cabin, Deerie hurried back and quickly climbed the wagon wheel to burrow down among the hay and blankets spread in the back.

With a last check that all was well in the cabin, Marcus closed the door and then helped Clarissa onto the wagon bench. He directed their horses out of the Fairfield yard to follow a narrow wagon path south to the military road. Webber's home was on the road between Fort Gibson and the Illinois River.

It was a cold, sunny day and they made good time, slowed only by having to ford the clear but fast running Illinois. When they arrived at Mr. Webber's home, they found several other guests had already arrived. Among them were the Washburns from Dwight and the Cherokee leader Sequoyah who was building a new cabin of his own down near the Nicksville site.

One of Webber's people met their wagon as they pulled up in front of the two story house. The slave took the reins of their horse and held it steady while Marcus helped Clarissa and Deerie out of the wagon. Then Marcus pressed a coin in the man's hand before he led the horse away.

Another man met them at the steps of the wide front porch. He offered to carry their bags and then showed them to a guest room in the house. The Palmers removed their coats and hats and were looking around the room when Deerie spotted a friend from Mulberry out in the yard.

"There is Esther Chisholm, Teacher," she said as she looked out the window. "May I go speak to her?"

"Yes, Deerie," Clarissa said. "Mind your manners."

"I will." The girl grabbed her cape and was pulling it back on as she left the room.

Shortly another servant came to their room and invited them to the parlor to visit with Mrs. Webber. The doctor and teacher took tea with their hostess while the servant named Etta acted as her translator.

Over the next three days, many of their neighbors arrived for the Christmas gathering. By the final day, when a great feast had been prepared, there were nearly a hundred and fifty Cherokees sitting at the meal on makeshift tables in the Webbers' yard. Later in the afternoon they gathered under a brush arbor for singing and a sermon.

The Palmers had learned that the Cherokees in their congregation enjoyed music and would sing for an hour or more if given the chance. Edmund Webber led the singing and while Clarissa could understand only a few words, she often recognized the melody of familiar hymns.

Marcus chose to offer a simple telling of the Nativity story as his sermon. Storytelling was much appreciated by their neighbors and Clarissa could tell the audience was captivated with the story of God's gift of love to the world offered through a baby.

"This child showed us how to walk a new path of forgiveness and brotherhood," the minister explained.

As he concluded, Marcus asked who wanted to receive this gift of love and forgiveness from the risen Savior. He invited any such individual walk forward to pray with him. Then he waited.

Marcus had learned the gift of silence while sitting at the bedside of his patients. He didn't fill this moment with pleas or extra words of explanation. He simply waited.

The quiet made Clarissa nervous so she bowed her head

and prayed fervently. Still Marcus waited as if he knew it was important for him to do so.

Clarissa could sense that some were getting restless. She peeked up at Marcus and saw her husband smiling as he looked toward the back of the arbor. So she closed her eyes again. Then she heard a stirring and she knew someone was coming forward.

She peeked again and felt a shock run through her. Walter Webber was walking forward from where he had stood at the back of the crowd. As he passed each row of benches a few others worked their way past family and neighbors to walk with him. Nearly forty individuals joined the chief at the front of the arbor and prayed. Tears were streaming down many faces including Clarissa's. What a moment of grace.

The Palmers returned to Fairfield the following day. They did not see Chief Webber emerge from the barn on his horse shortly after they left. He turned his horse toward Fort Gibson but did not stop at the military post. He continued northward on the Texas Road, a solitary figure riding with purpose toward Claremontown.

When he rode into the Osage village, word spread quickly from lodge to lodge that the Cherokee leader was present. Soon Mad Buffalo emerged from his home. Other warriors stood in their doorways watching as the Cherokee approached their chief.

Webber held up his hand with his empty palm forward, a sign of peace. He had painted white stripes across his face also in the color of peace.

The two men spoke briefly in the basic English they both knew and using native sign language as well. Then Webber turned his horse slowly and walked it out of the Osage camp. Mad Buffalo watched him go, shaking his head as if he could not believe what had just happened.

Then he turned and said loudly for those around him to hear, "We fight no more."

The next morning, Will and Susan were finishing breakfast in the big cabin when they heard a horse approach at a trot. Will stood from the table and crossed the room to look out a window. Susan joined him.

"Who is that?" she asked.

"It's Walter Webber."

"The chief? The one who killed Joseph Revoir?"

"Yes."

"What is he doing here?"

"I'm not sure. I hope this doesn't mean trouble." Will glanced at his musket hanging above the fireplace. Will had once taken a Cherokee bullet and he didn't want to again.

They watched as Webber spoke to Hunts-the-Bear who was sitting in front of one of the lodges. The young warrior pointed to Teresa's home. Webber nodded and made his way toward it. Star-That-Travels stepped out of the lodge to meet the Cherokee.

The Requas saw Star and Webber exchange words, quietly with no shouting. Star called for Teresa to come outside. She joined her husband, the stalwart Christian man she had married after Joseph died.

Time and again Star and Teresa had refused to seek revenge against Webber and he knew it. More than anything else, their steadfast choice to walk the path of peace and forgiveness had been a hammer that struck at the hate around his heart.

Now Webber dismounted and sat cross-legged on the grass. Star and Teresa joined him and their conversation continued for a time.

"We ought to get to the dishes," Susan said.

"Yes," Will agreed. But neither moved from the window.

Shortly Webber and the two Osages stood. The men shook hands. Then Webber remounted his horse and left Hopefield.

Will and Susan looked at each other in amazement at what they had just witnessed.

"Does this mean the feud is over?" Susan asked.

"Yes," Will grinned. "I think it does."

Peace and goodwill had come at last to this once untamed land.

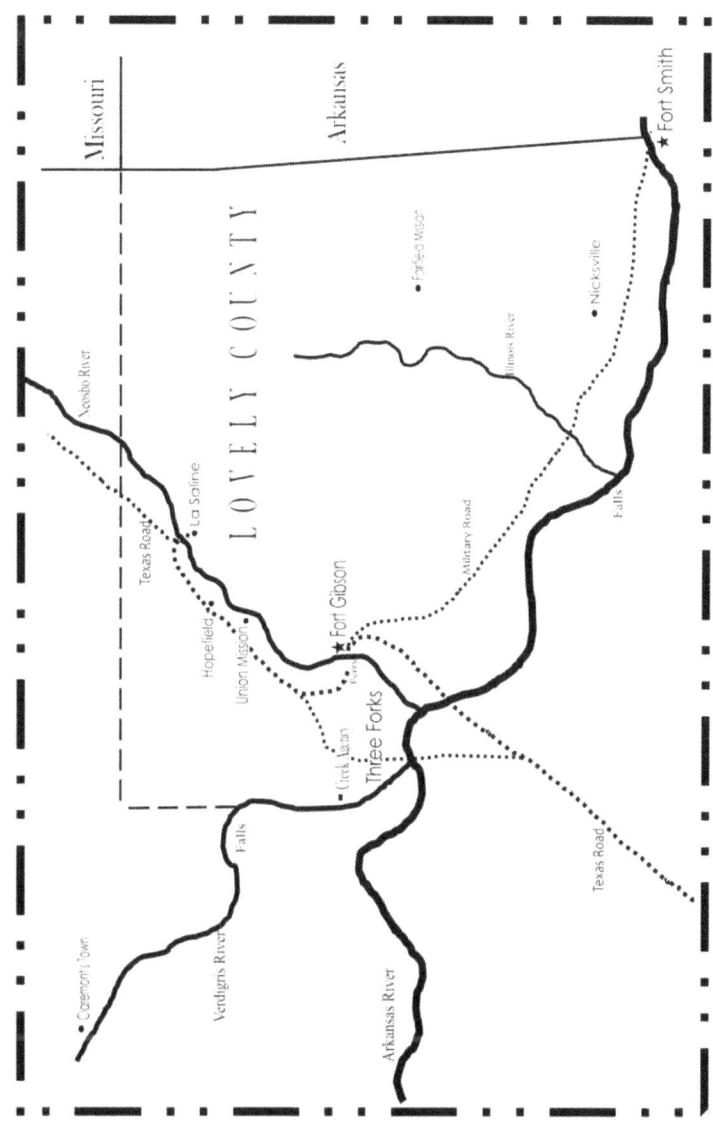

BOOKS BY JONITA MULLINS

The Missions of Indian Territory
1. Journey to an Untamed Land
2. Look Unto the Fields
3. Come to Lovely County

Glimpses of Our Past
1. A Look Back at Three Forks History
2. Life Along the Rivers

Haskell: A Centennial Celebration

A Kitchen on the Frontier

The Jefferson Highway in Oklahoma

Jonita Mullins is a popular speaker on topics of history and inspiration. She also offers history tours in and around her home community of Muskogee, Oklahoma. More information is available on her books, gifts, tours and preservation projects at her website: okieheritage.com